ALSO BY SUSAN FROMBERG SCHAEFFER

The
Golden
Rope

The Golden Rope

SUSAN FROMBERG
SCHAEFFER

ALFRED A. KNOPF   *New York*   1996

THIS IS A BORZOI BOOK
PUBLISHED BY ALFRED A. KNOPF, INC.

http://www.randomhouse.com/

Library of Congress Cataloging-in-Publication Data

Schaeffer, Susan Fromberg.
The golden rope / Susan Fromberg Schaeffer. — 1st ed.
p. cm.
ISBN 0-394-58821-5
1. Sisters—Psychology—Fiction.   2. Twins—Psychology—Fiction.
3. Missing persons—Fiction.   I. Title.
PS3569.C35G65 1996
813'.54—dc20   96-7431
CIP

Manufactured in the United States of America
First Edition

For Ruth Fried
and
For Neil

And with special thanks to
the Gang of Three:
Abner Stein, Sonny Mehta,
and the invaluable Jenny Minton

CONTENTS

PART
ONE

And So I Left

CHAPTER

ONE

AND SO I LEFT, and I began to walk, and it was the last of the gray hours, when there are no colors left in the world, when his face on the sheets would be gray and set, like stone, when the wrinkled sheets on the bed would look like a frozen slate-gray sea, or like plowed land dead beneath the first killing frost, those gray, grainy hours when everything resembles funerary sculpture. And it was a full moon, I remember it was a full moon, it is odd what you remember, and of course I thought the sun would never rise. I thought I would walk through that grayness forever.

Even after the sun rose, I didn't see colors around me—not for a long time. But by noon, when the sun was so hot, I did see them, I saw geraniums splashed like blood against sun-baked whitewashed walls. They were the first brilliant things I saw, and then I knew I was tired and I wanted a dark place, a soft place.

And later I came to a huge white brick house whose windows were boarded up and it might still have been noon, it seemed to have been noon for hours, because I cast no shadows, nothing cast a shadow, everything was stark, and I thought, Possibly time has stopped, for me time has stopped, possibly I am dead, for so long I have wanted to be dead, and I wondered, Did you know? When you were dead? When you did die, how did you know? If your consciousness survived death, what told you you had died?

The trees in the distance were black and sharp, and I thought, This is where I belong, in a place without shadows. I've always hated and dreaded my shadow, like a dirty cloak, slipping and sliding over the ground behind me, tasting the dirt and the stones ahead, that filthy thing, its appetite for earth and dirt, my shadow.

And I thought of the geraniums again, small, smashed, red.

The boarded-up white brick house had blue shutters. It was enormous and baronial, two-storied, two great chimneys in the center section. There was an alley of cone-shaped pines leading up to it. I went behind the house. Someone had taken down a board meant to be nailed over a back-wall window. The window was open. I thought, Is it a trap? Here, guns are rigged to fire at burglars, at tramps. I hoped for a flash, a searing pain, the smell of gunpowder. It would take the matter out of my hands. I climbed in. The house was empty and quiet. I leaned back against the wall under the window and fell asleep.

CHAPTER

TWO

I AM the other sister, the twin, the other Meek, the one no one knew existed, born five minutes after her sister, the second child, the unwanted one: Doris, shadow of Florence, the famous one, whom everyone thinks he loves. I am the one who led a sheltered life, was married at nineteen to a man who loved her, a man who said he would never love anyone else, a man who kept his word. My mother said how lucky I was. She said my husband adored me, he was one of those men who fall in love and never look at another woman again, and he didn't, it didn't matter to him that I was childless, nothing I did could turn him against me. Do you think you deserve him? my mother asked me, and I didn't, I never thought I loved him well enough, I never thought I deserved him, and I still don't. In my life I have loved only one person well enough, and she is gone.

I was hidden, submerged in my own ordinary life, in my husband, in running the household, in designing my strange jewelry, which I turned over to an agent who placed the pieces at exclusive stores, in writing my books, my odd fables, which I published under my married name. After my sister's disappearance, I was not happy, not . . . stable. I was not really in this world. "If you drift any farther," my husband said, "there'll be no coming back." I wouldn't have minded—drifting off and not coming back. It would have been the easiest thing. But of course life is sticky. We do not free ourselves so easily from the web.

Often I believe I don't deserve to live.

Money can be the glue that holds us, can't it? We had too much money, all of us, although we began quite poor, my mother, my sister, my sister's husband, my brother, who died young, and I. My sister's paintings earned her a fortune by the time she was twenty-one. I could have supported myself on my own income—a jeweled lizard of mine costs many thousands of dollars—but of course I never had to do it. My mother, who began poor, inherited a small fortune when her foster mother died, and so it was not necessary to worry about her. My husband, a psychoanalyst in private practice, came from a family so wealthy he would not have needed to work a day in his life. Even the reporter who found me had too much money. He had written a book about Vietnam and now he never needed to work again. We had too much money and too much time, or so I think now.

If we had remained poor, our lives might have been different. We would have had quite a different perspective. We would have gotten up each morning worrying about where our next meal was coming from. My husband says this is all nonsense and that only someone leading a privileged life would come to see poverty as a form of salvation. It is the sign of an unsettled mind, he says, such thinking.

I'm not certain he's right—although usually he is right.

I can still see the newspaper articles that came out when she disappeared, as if I were holding them in my hand. Everything about them is vivid: the thick black newsprint letters, the white, pulpy paper. They still act like acid on my eyes.

FLORENCE MEEK VANISHES
REVERED PAINTER OF THE WHITE PAINTINGS SOUGHT

Florence Meek was reported missing by her husband, the playwright Jack Pine, when he returned to his home in Goult, France, from a brief vacation in Scandinavia. He reported her absence to the local police. Neighbors saw nothing unusual at the Meek house before her disappearance. "She went to the market to buy some beets and potatoes as usual," said the owner of the local café.

A week later came the following article:

FLORENCE MEEK DISAPPEARANCE DEEMED SUSPICIOUS
FAMOUS ARTIST VANISHES WITHOUT A TRACE

Police are investigating the unexplained disappearance of Florence Meek, who was reported missing from her home in Goult, France, on March 25, 1967. Miss Meek was twenty-six.

Police are questioning Miss Meek's husband, the internationally famous playwright Jack Pine, as well as her neighbors. New evidence continues to appear, but the results will not be divulged until the investigation is complete.

I reacted badly. First I was hysterical. Then I was depressed and motionless and cold, almost catatonic. My husband tried to call the authorities in France, but her disappearance and possible—some said probable—death was followed by an incredible outburst of public mourning. One paper said it was as if a president or a queen had died, not a young painter. When my husband called and said he was Florence Meek's brother-in-law, no one believed him. He would have gone to France himself, but I was in no state to be left alone. Search parties were sent out for her and found nothing. There were false leads. Someone thought he had seen her in Marignane, near the airport, but when he was questioned and shown her picture, he said no, he had seen someone else. He was one of many who raised our hopes to no purpose. Eventually, the search was given up, as it had to be. And then articles began to appear which made it clear that Florence had told everyone who knew her that she had no family at all. She claimed to be an orphan.

You might have thought that *I* would have gone immediately to Goult and the sight of me would have convinced everyone that Florence did in fact have a sister, who was, moreover, her identical twin, and I suppose I would have gone—I would have interrogated her husband far more mercilessly than the police—had I not been weeping in a locked cell in one of the most luxurious mental hospitals in the country. I was in utter despair—not only was my sister gone, but it was clear to me that she had wanted to annihilate me, to murder me. What else had she done when she declared herself an orphan without family? She had erased me. She had looked straight at me and said I wasn't there.

At that time, I was afraid to sleep, because when I slept, I saw my sister coming toward me, her hands out, ready to close over my throat. Or she began stroking my cheeks, and I cried with relief because she was back, and she sat up to see me better and then rested her long fingernails on my cheekbones, and smiled, and I knew she intended to gouge out my eyes.

Gradually, I stopped having these dreams, and when I did, they were replaced by dreams in which I walked through a field toward my old house in Peru and tripped over something. It was my sister's body, and while I stood over it, my hand sealing my lips, a huge crow flew down and settled on her shoulder and sank its beak into the skin over her clavicle. As it ate, the bird watched me out of the corner of its eye. Then the dreams became less dramatic and more frightening, and my sister and I would be lying in bed, and something would wake me, and I would lean over to whisper to her, and when she didn't answer, I somehow knew she was dead, and I would awaken, sobbing instead of screaming. The first dreams—the dreams in which my sister blamed me and then tried to kill me—had made me scream. The doctors said it was progress. "Sobbing means acceptance," one of them said.

Of course, I hadn't accepted anything at all.

Even while I was in the hospital, I scoured the papers for mention of her. Of all her maniacal admirers who waited for news of her, I was one of the worst. I watched the way the world appropriated Florence. I saw how it created the image of her that it wanted. Soon after she disappeared, while I was still dreaming of her attacks upon me, an excerpt from my sister's journals appeared in a glossy magazine. It was written when she was eighteen and when we were both undergraduates.

No one knew who had found the journal or how it got into the hands of reporters. Like everything else about my sister's disappearance, even this was inexplicable.

⟋ᴏᴄᴏ⟍

I ʟᴏᴠᴇᴅ him. I fell in love with him in the terrible way one might fall in love with a killer, knowing full well that he might take anything I had, including my life, hoping that, if he was a killer, he would take my life, because what larger thing could I give him? And my soul. It is barely worth speaking of my soul, because that flew out of my mouth the moment I saw him, and when he opened his mouth to speak to me, that small, insignificant, incomplete thing had its chance and flew in and found his soul and twined itself about it so that no one, not even God, could disentangle them again. . . . All of this in a fraction of a second. In the rest of that enormous second, I thought, White paintings! I will paint more white paintings, canvases full of snow. They will be his paintings. . . .

And I had no misgivings. None. No warnings, no hints, no intimations, no premonitions, no omens, no shiverings, no swiftings, no quiverings of flesh, no harbingers of danger.

THIS JOURNAL ENTRY set my hair on end—but no one knew about me—and its contents made headlines everywhere. So did her comments on it, published at the same time, which she must have made three or four years later. On the flyleaf of her first journal, she wrote, "As everyone knows, the walker who loses his way in the woods tends to walk in circles. I am keeping this journal because I hope—in defiance of what I already suspect to be the truth, that I am one of those walkers in the woods already destined, like the donkey fastened to a long stick which is in its turn fastened to a pile of stones, to wear out the grass beneath my feet as I walk in the one circle allowed me—I hope to take a few steps in a straight line, to see something a little grander than the circular world to which I already seem condemned."

Directly beneath the last line of this entry, she wrote in her tiny handwriting, in brilliant green ink, "What a self-pitying, self-important ass I have always been! What flowery, adolescent maunderings! But reader (I am the reader, an inconstant reader, always changing), it is nevertheless amazing, isn't it? I had no forewarning. That passage about premonitions, inklings, glimmers, hints—what was that but precocious posturing? I thought I ought to have such mature thoughts. Some corner of my mind thought this. Much of my mind was otherwise engaged, with this man, this vision, this annunciation which had fallen on me like a rain of white stones. The truth is I was as innocent as the shining day. There was no warning. Why should there have been? And if there had been, I would not have listened."

Florence used to reread what she'd written and make cruel and sardonic comments about her younger self. I did the same thing. We both felt free to be self-pitying and self-dramatizing in our journals, but both of us must have felt we had a reader looking over our shoulders, and so we would reread what we had written, and comment on our emotional excesses. *See! We are sensible, well-balanced, sensible girls after all!* But Florence was never sensible. She was never less than extravagant. Believe me, I know.

Still, as it turned out, this strategy worked wonders on Florence's admirers. Now there were two Florences: the passionate, madly raving young girl, and the more sober, rational Florence, the young married woman. Most seductive of all was the sensation produced by reading these two versions of events. It was as if they were watching Florence grow in front of their very eyes. They assumed they knew her thoughts.

As everyone now knows, less than six months passed before Florence married Jack Pine and went with him to Provence, where she continued painting and he continued to write his plays. And then, after seven years of marriage, she vanished.

And I watched as she became inhuman, a figure of ever deepening mystery, a creature of greater and greater fascination, a woman in white who seemed to beckon as she disappeared into a mist. Pale suicides began to pile up at her feet. She was the woman in the boat crossing the River of Oblivion. I saw how her meaning underwent a change. She had become someone dangerous, a creature who lived on, lonely in her dark world, tempting others to join her.

I watched as new passages from her journals appeared. I read their brief and disconnected accounts of her courtship and married life and her increasing disillusionment with both her husband and her work. For some time, these passages from the journals arrived at newspaper offices. No one knew who had sent them, but there was no doubt they were written in Florence's own hand. I read Jack Pine's frequently repeated assertion that there were no journals. He had never seen them, and if they existed, he would have known. Certainly there were no journals in his possession now.

No one believed him.

And now my sister's followers became more bitter and more vengeful, and they began to ask the questions I had asked from the first. They turned their attention to Florence's husband. Why had he gone to Sweden just before she disappeared? What was his role in her disappearance? Was it true that anonymous letters accused him of having murdered her? *A full investigation is necessary.* Oh, I thought so too. But Jack Pine produced his passport and conclusively proved that he had been out of the country when my sister disappeared.

This satisfied the police. I couldn't forgive him.

There was a time when I awakened every morning with a new plan for ridding the world of that man, the creature my sister had married. The doctors in the hospital paid close attention to my murderous thoughts about Jack Pine.

I watched as a few clear-eyed people attempted to look for my sister. And there *was* one woman, author of the first article commenting upon the passages from the journals, who I thought might point the way. This woman, writing in the *Times,* saw one of their more curious aspects. Although my sister minutely recorded the doings of each day, she never made any reference to her childhood or her family.

"The parents of the painter who kept these journals," she said, "are almost conspicuously absent. As we try to form an opinion of Florence Meek's life, we must keep in mind our lack of knowledge of her early years. We have no information whatever of the family or the community that helped form her. We are thus in the position of evaluating Florence Meek as if she were really born as her journals tell us she was, at the instant she caught her first glimpse of her future husband, Jack Pine. Can this belief currently gaining ground really be true? Was she entirely formed by her husband and then entirely destroyed by him?

"If this were true, we would have to lay Florence Meek's White Paintings as well as her body at his feet. The lunacy of such an approach should spur us to learn more of Florence Meek's early life. Otherwise, even though we walk through the night holding our white candles, we are really in the dark."

This was one of the earliest and best articles written about my sister. It was sensible and intelligent and so of course it was ignored. No one wanted to listen to the voice of reason. The poor woman was vilified and accused of having gone over to the husband's camp, because by this time there *were* camps. She was dismissed by another woman, who wrote, "Far too many women who read Florence Meek's journals will end by falling in love with Jack Pine. Florence Meek could paint as seductively with words as she could with pigment." The author whom I so admired was not, in the end, a true "Florentine," which is what my sister's worshipers had begun calling themselves.

Before I left the hospital, I thought I wanted to write to the author, to tell her that she was on the right track, to invite her to come and talk to me, but by the time I came home, I had all I could do to stay awake, to walk in a straight line, to impersonate a human being.

Much later, people wanted to hear what Jack Pine had to say about her, but my sister's husband would not speak.

Everyone believed, or appeared to believe, the account my sister had given of herself. I think people felt it would have been wrong to doubt Florence. Her journals had become sacred things. What she'd said had become gospel.

It is frightening, even now, to think how desperately she wanted to erase me. And of course I cooperated in this. I let myself be erased. At that time, I wanted to be erased. Completely.

In the hospital, one of the doctors asked me, "What purpose would it serve, making yourself known? Are you envious of the attention people pay her?"

I was not going to buy myself a place in the world at Florence's expense. I was not going to be taken up as a poor substitute for my vanished sister. I was not going to offer myself up to those who would think I was better than nothing.

You might have expected that someone would have recognized me, someone would have stopped at my table in a restaurant and said, "Aren't you the famous painter? Aren't you Florence Meek?" But even before my sister disappeared, I had cut my hair short, I had dyed it blond, and on the few occasions when people did come up to me and say, "Excuse me, but aren't you . . . ," I would stare at them, then smile, and ask them who they thought I was. And then I would say, "Famous? I look like someone famous? Isn't that wonderful! Who is she, exactly?" And their faces would fall and they would retreat, shaking their heads. How could they have made such a mistake?

Later, after she had been gone for some time, after age had changed my face, I let my hair grow. I stopped dyeing it blond. I wore it long and black and wild with curls, and no one came up to me and said, "Aren't you Florence Meek?"

It is a horror, really, to look back over those years.

I think about my sister, and I think about the myth she's become, and I ask myself, What are people, really? I think of people as clouds, seemingly clear in outline but always moving through other clouds, reconstituting themselves perpetually, as clouds do. Everything is fluid. Nothing is fixed. Most people are lucky and don't think of themselves in this way. They don't think of themselves as debtors to crowds of people they no longer remember. They like to say they owe their beauty to their mother or their strength to their father, but they would be appalled if anyone believed them. In their hearts, they believe they belong only to themselves. They believe that at a given moment, they became themselves, unique, independent, autonomous, precious in their singularity. That we are none of us singular or unique—they will not hear such nonsense. They know better. It takes so little to make a human being happy and confident in his destiny, his deserved, well-earned place on the face of the earth.

This is what it means to be young, isn't it? To believe yourself unique? If so, most people stay young forever.

People in love believe they are unique and radiant. It may be that only people who believe themselves to be unique are capable of love.

My husband has had a hard time with me. He is a patient man, but no one should have the need for such patience. It is over twenty years since Florence walked out of her house in Provence and disappeared. For a while, I did quite well without her. For a time, I went on as if nothing had happened. I wrote my books, I got up in the morning, I smiled at the light in the windows. We lived in London for a year while my husband worked at the Tavistock, and I adored the very stones of that city. And then we went home and the tenth anniversary of her disappearance approached and I began to fall asleep—in the middle of movies, of TV programs, in the middle of dinner parties: my own dinner parties. Finally, I gave up going out. I awakened late and slept again in the afternoon and at night I was in bed early.

At first I was frightened by this endless somnolence. I thought of it as a relapse. I was afraid I would once more find myself in the hospital. Then I began to welcome sleep, because when I was asleep I dreamed, and in my dreams, I always saw my sister. To dream of myself is to dream of my sister, my twin, the one who exactly resembles me, the one who once threatened to take a knife to her cheek and scar it—simply so people could tell us apart.

I had a friend who said she had been cheated twice by life. First the people closest to her died and left her, and then her dreams bereaved her a second time. No one who died would come back to her, not even in her dreams. My dreams did not cheat me. At least I didn't think they did. I would close my eyes, and there she would be. Florence. Of course, I might only have been seeing myself. I might not have seen Florence at all. But I believed I saw her, and in my dreams, Florence was always very busy, always traveling here to there through unknown landscapes. She was always alive and she was always moving toward me. And so I had no reason to stay awake.

I often thought that if I could go back to London, I would once more be happy. It was the last place I had been content—cheerful and awake. I said this to my husband often enough. He said, "It would take more than a change of scene, don't you know that?"

And I thought I did.

I've always had trouble believing in the reality of other people. For so long, the world was small and complete and consisted only of the two of us, my sister and I. We always had trouble taking other people seriously— until Florence met her husband, Jack Pine. Then she changed. Before she left for college, she had already taken a new name. Once she met Jack Pine, she created a new history for herself, one in which I had no place—as if I had never lived, as if none of us had. She obliterated all traces of us so that no one could trace her to her origins. She was very convincing and very thorough. She was devious. She would have made an excellent criminal. She had that kind of mind.

Once she met Jack, it was as if she placed the palm of her hand against my chest and pushed me back into the shadows, the misty places, and with her other hand, she drew Jack Pine to her. He replaced me. Or so, in her ecstasy, she thought, and so, in my despair, I thought.

She was very happy in the early days of her marriage, and I was very unhappy. She must have thought she'd succeeded. She must have believed she was free of me forever.

When the twentieth anniversary of her death came and went, and the biographies published to coincide with that anniversary came and went, and the articles about Florence and the exhibits of her paintings were written about everywhere and still no one found me, I thought they never would. In spite of everything, I believed in the principle of inertia, the tendency of the world to resist any change, to stay as it is. Even if they had found me, I would have turned them away.

My mother used to call and ask my husband, "How is Sleeping Beauty?" But I was not the Sleeping Beauty of the fairy tale. I was a Sleeping Beauty who would have pushed away or bitten the hands of the prince. I was in my enclosure of thorns and I intended to stay there. And yet someone did come.

But before he did, I was asleep and my husband was the last one who could have awakened me. Anyone who has been married for many years will understand why. A long marriage requires patience more than passion, endless and daily adjustments of the one to the other, a capacity for acceptance that none of us possesses when we are young but which develops daily, year after year, until it is the single striking thing about us: how much we can accept, how much we are willing to accept. As if we had begun as selfish, impatient humans but had ended by possessing the transforming acceptance of saints. Love does this to us.

It is not what we expect from love, not in the beginning, not when we are young. Jealousy, rage, passions like forest fires, all this is expected, not this endless patience, this almost infinite, almost inhuman acceptance. People who know how to love have this patience, but not everyone knows how to love. In the end, it is a talent, like everything else. Almost everyone thinks he has it, but almost everyone is wrong. My husband was and is a genius at love. He has to be, to remain in love with me.

My husband, John, was the one who suggested that if he accepted an invitation to teach for a year at the Institute in Prague, I ought to spend a year in London. "We'll call each other every week," he said. And I said, "No; if I'm going to be on my own, let me be on my own. Let me decide when I want to call."

And then I said, "What will I do in London? For a year on my own?"

But of course it had already been decided. He wouldn't have suggested I go unless he knew I wanted to go. I wouldn't have said, "Let me decide when I want to call," unless I had already decided to go. This was the audible end of a long, silent conversation.

"That's the point," he said. "You'll find out what you'll do. You'll be all right," he said gently.

And so the decision was made.

And of course there was a long story behind this decision to separate for a year, because that was what we were resolving to do. We had disappointed each other so many times, exhausted each other, blamed each other for our difficulties. There were times when I believed we were no longer people to one another, but constructs. Yet we loved one another and could not love anyone else. I knew my husband thought that if I was on my own, the scales would drop from my eyes and I would learn to see and value what was there. We would once more be what we were before my sister disappeared. He never doubted that would happen.

And because I knew what he thought, I was unworried about going off on my own. I was like a child who bravely swims out into deep water when all the time one end of a rope is tied about the child's waist and the other end is fastened to the wrist of her mother or father. I am not very brave and have never been particularly courageous, much less reckless. Florence was the brave one, the courageous one.

But I must tell you how I came to meet Dennis Cage, the reporter, because if I had never spoken to Dennis Cage, I would never have left for London. And if I had never agreed to speak to Dennis, I would never have picked up the telephone and heard the voice of the Impostor, who at first seemed so amazingly cruel.

All stories have their true beginnings in the past, in the mists, in those first, blacked-out years. First things are truer, more important, than second ones or third ones. Everything that comes later is an accident. The true drama of our lives lies in those first, forgotten, blacked-out years. We spend the rest of our lives searching for those first, lost selves, and if we are lucky, we become, as we grow older, more and more what we then were. It is because I believe this that I am going back there, to what I believe is the beginning.

WHEN WE were children, especially during the afternoons, when my mother slept the sleep of the dead, my grandmother told us stories. She was a wonderful storyteller, but I don't believe she ever told us a story she made up. She loved true stories, and she kept a scrapbook of clippings, which she called her Book of Remarkable Events, and when we were young, she often read to us of earthquakes in Chile, tornadoes in Illinois, the people of Pompeii preserved lifelike by lava when the erupting volcano caught them, and we loved to hear these stories and would beg her to read them again and again.

I listened to them and was frightened and thought how dramatic a place the world was, dramatic and dangerous and terrifying and unpredictable, and so it was best to cling to those you knew and trusted.

Florence, I think, heard something else, the wild and dangerous music of the world, and because she was not afraid—she was never afraid—she wanted to rush forward, to see for herself, to have everything happen to her. She immediately understood how fragile human life was and how dangerous it was to put off living. If she was afraid of anything, it was that—having life flutter past her, like a beautiful butterfly you reach out for too late.

Florence asked for one story again and again. My grandmother called it "Over the Falls." And while my grandmother read aloud from her clippings, or from a booklet once published about this particular incident, I sat behind Florence, pressing my cheek into the flowered muslin of her back, and when the story became truly frightening, I turned my head slightly and pressed my face flat against her back, through the fabric of her dress, into her spine. It was difficult to breathe with my nose squashed into her and my lips pressed against her, and I remember how dusty her dress always smelled and the wonderful fragrance that rose from her, that biscuity odor, part vanilla, part yeast, part flour, that perfume that was, to me, the essence of Florence, that perfume that even today stops me in front of bakeries, where I stand still, smiling, feeling her small, hot hand in mine.

And all the time I sat there, my face pressed into her, I knew she was completely oblivious, utterly unaware of my presence.

"A long time ago," my grandmother began, "near the turn of the century, there was a disaster at Niagara Falls, and all the newspapers in the United States and Canada carried articles about it, and people all over the country were affected by it, and we all believed no one would ever forget it, but now almost no one remembers—isn't that strange?—except people who live near the falls.

"They may remember, the way we remember how Aaron Hinckle hung from the bridge showing off, until his fingers froze to the railing he dangled from, and he didn't expect this, did he, he hadn't counted on his fingers freezing to the railing, he only wanted to impress that girl from

Duffington, and everyone who saw him said he panicked, and that's what did him in, that's why he let go and fell into the water under the bridge, and you know how deep it is there and how fast the current moves. But that's another story.

"In those days, Niagara Falls was a popular spot for honeymoons, and so there was always a crowd standing on the American side of the river, or the Canadian side, gazing away at the falls, its thundering rush of foaming water, the rainbows dancing in its mist, and on this particular day, a group of people decided to cross from one shore to the other over an immense bridge of ice that always forms above the falls. It still forms there, you can still see it, that bridge of ice joining the American side to the Canadian side. I went there once, just to see it, on my honeymoon.

"But on this particular day, the ice bridge was disturbed by a strong current and so began to crack and drift. A riverman saw this, and he well knew the ways of the river, didn't he? And so he shouted to those on the ice, warning them to make for the Canadian side, because that way they would have a better chance of reaching safety. Soon they were all safe on Canadian soil. Except for two of them, a young couple—a young man and a young woman.

"This couple, a woman in her late twenties and her husband, a man in his early thirties, didn't pay attention to the riverman. Instead they ran toward the American shore, where they found themselves facing open water. Then they turned around and ran back toward the Canadian shore, but before they got there, the woman, evidently exhausted, sank down on the ice and shouted to her husband, 'I can't go on! Let us die here!' "

" 'Let us die here,' " Florence whispered. " 'I can't go on!' " She was entranced. I was beginning to cry.

"The riverman came to help the husband, and the two of them attempted to drag the woman to safety. They were only three yards from the shore, three yards! How far is that? Not very far! Three yards of ice spanned the water separating them from solid ground. This ice was soft, but it was strong enough to hold up the woman and her husband, and the riverman pleaded with them to trust it, and he even ran back and forth over the ice to show how easily it might be done. They were in no danger at all.

"But the woman appeared terrified of the soft ice and she wouldn't set foot on it, and her husband wouldn't abandon her to the river."

"Wouldn't abandon her to the river," Florence whispered.

"Then the ice on which the couple rested broke loose and began drifting down the river, breaking into ever smaller pieces, drifting toward the deadly rapids that lead into the great Niagara whirlpool. For an hour, they drifted in this way, until they floated under a railway bridge that crossed the ravine sixty feet above their heads. They were now not far from the deadly rapids. Someone on the bridge lowered a great rope with a harpoon attached to one end, and it was clear to all who watched that if they did not seize hold of it, they would lose their last hope."

"They drifted and drifted," murmured my sister, becoming the chorus.

"The ice on which they rested was now moving very fast, but the husband made a great effort and he caught hold of the rope. The woman, however, would not trust the rope unless her husband could fasten it about her. People on both sides of the river now witnessed the man's futile attempt to fasten the rope around his wife's waist. His hands were too numb and stiff with the cold to do it. When he saw that his wife could not be rescued in this way, he threw the rope from him, knelt down beneath his wife, embraced her, and held her. Their death was waiting for them, only a few seconds away. In this position, kneeling on the ice, clasped to one another, they were swept into the rapids and the whirlpool and so died together."

"Their death was waiting for them," Florence whispered.

"Later investigation revealed that the couple had been married seven years, had no children, and had always been devoted to one another. It was felt that the husband's behavior explained itself. No one believed a husband could abandon his wife in order to save himself, especially under such dreadful circumstances."

"Dreadful circumstances," Florence said softly.

"His wife's conduct continued to cause discussion, not only then but for years after. Why had she shown so little courage in the face of impending tragedy? Why had she not taken advantage of the many opportunities to save herself? It is well known that people are often paralyzed by fear, yet her behavior seemed purposeful, if not perverse. Her actions— running toward the American shore rather than the Canadian, refusing to walk across the soft ice or allow herself to be dragged across it, fatally refusing to take hold of the rope or to grab hold of her husband, who had secured it—had guaranteed her own death by drowning as well as her husband's.

"According to the many spectators, she seemed—once she had grasped her situation—determined to die. *I can't go on! Let us die here!* That cry removed any doubt that she had failed to grasp the significance of what she was doing, dooming herself and her husband to certain death."

"Dooming herself," breathed Florence.

"Speculation about this young woman was inevitable. Investigations into her background continued, but nothing was ever found to suggest why she was so thoroughly prepared to seize death when it presented itself. Still, everyone seemed to agree that she *was* prepared. She had time and again rejected salvation. Perhaps hidden deep in her nature was a hopelessness, a despondency. Perhaps she feared that, because he was older, he would die before her. If this was so, dying with her husband might have seemed better than living on alone. In any case, the spectacle of this young woman and her husband going needlessly to their death in a maelstrom of ice and water disturbed and moved those who saw the tragedy (many of whom had come to the falls as honeymooners) and those who read of it later.

"I can see them when I shut my eyes," my grandmother said, "in their dark clothes, on the white ice, the woman wearing the long black skirts we all wore then, the white blouse with its high collar, the thick black fur cape—it would have been so heavy when the water soaked it—the black hat she pinned to her hair with long hairpins . . . oh, I can see them when I shut my eyes. I can hear the water, the way it roars, I can hear that whenever I want to."

"I see them now," Florence said.

"Do you?" asked my grandmother. "Of course you do. And you, Doris?"

I had nothing to say. I was, as usual, white and silent and trembling with fear.

"Well, the truth will never hurt you," my grandmother said, although she didn't sound absolutely convinced. "No, the truth will never hurt you," she said again.

When I think of our childhoods, this is the story I remember best. And it is because of this story that I agreed to meet Dennis Cage.

CHAPTER

THREE

ENNIS CAGE HAD BEEN a prominent war correspondent who had written a much admired book about his experiences in Vietnam during the 1960s and '70s, and a year ago he went to see Jack Pine, my sister's husband. When Jack Pine told him that my sister said she came from Peru, Dennis, who grew up in Vermont, in a town called Athens, put two and two together and on a hunch went back to the United States, found Peru, Vermont, spoke to the doctor who knew our family well, and went to see my mother in Florida, where she now lives. He didn't succeed in speaking to her, but he had little trouble prying my address out of the woman who looked after her. He then wrote me, saying that he would give almost anything to speak to me. I was about to drop his letter into the wastepaper basket, when my eye skipped to the bottom of the page and I found myself reading about the couple who had been swept over Niagara Falls.

He wrote that he'd always intended to look up the original accounts of that incident, but he never did, and would have forgotten about it altogether had he not seen my sister's painting *The Golden Rope*.

I know this painting as well as I know anything in the world.

When you first see it, all you see is the ground, sketched in, differentiated from the falling snow only by its solidity and gray color. But then you begin to make out the golden rope, and once you see it, it seems to become clearer and brighter. Then you see the small figure who's scaled the rope until she's climbed almost one third of the way up the painting. She's tiny and almost obliterated by the snow. Her gloveless hands are reddened by the cold and glow like embers and they hold tightly to the golden rope, suspended, evidently, from the sky itself. And then you see that immediately above the head of this small being is a gap in the rope, as if someone cut a section from it, and then you see that the climbing girl is looking up at this empty place, her face wet with falling snow, her eyes half closed and empty. And then you see the second figure, climbing *down,* and her face, although far less distinct than the first one's, is more hopeless and less determined. You see then that the two girls are identical in face and figure, and in that instant you understand that until they both saw the gap in the rope, they expected to be reunited.

People still study *The Golden Rope.* They have yet to discover how Florence managed to create its textures and levels, the images that swim up and then submerge again.

The painting of the golden rope—how I hate it.

Dennis said he thought this was the most terrible of my sister's White Paintings, perhaps the only terrible one, and when he saw it, the couple kneeling on the ice merged with the two children on the rope, and after that happened, it seemed inevitable that he would begin searching for her. There were other reasons, of course, and he would tell me about these later—if I would agree to see him. He went on to say that he wasn't a particularly impressive person and he had trouble expressing himself in writing, so it was probably foolish of him to try writing a book about my sister, but if I would give him the chance, he would tell me everything he knew about my sister. "I know," he said, "how reluctant you are to discuss your sister."

Reluctant? I was absolutely unwilling.

But when I sat down, I was holding on to his letter and I read it again. There it was, the story of the woman swept over the falls. How likely was it that someone else would not only know this story but connect it to my sister's painting, and then write me about it? I knew what my husband would say—coincidence. But it seemed to me that I was meant to meet Dennis Cage. As children, the same story had haunted us both. Now, when I thought of us listening to our grandmother as she read to us about the couple going over the falls, it was as if Dennis were sitting there with us: indistinct—I couldn't yet see his face—but somehow he was there. And I felt, irrationally enough, as if he belonged to us. And he'd said he'd tell me what he knew about Florence, and this was catnip to the cat, and I suppose I, who am so tentative in my dealings with the world, was touched by his insecurity. And so I wrote to him and told him he could come and see me whenever he liked.

My husband was stunned and happy. He thought this change in me meant progress, although when I asked him to what he thought I was progressing, he couldn't say. I suppose he thought any change was a change for the better.

Dennis Cage came to see me where I live in Manhattan, and when I opened the door and he found himself confronted by my face, he was so unnerved that I thought there was no harm in him.

I felt, I suppose, protective of him. And I was relieved to find someone who thought the spectacle of a weeping woman nothing out of the ordinary. When I cried, he simply waited for me to catch my breath.

It was a relief to talk to him, and at first I was pleased with myself for having invited him to see me.

I sat on the little love seat in front of our window and he sat on the couch across from me and began to question me about Florence, and of course I dissolved in tears. But he was not put off. He took a handkerchief from his pocket, got up and handed it to me, sat back down, and continued asking questions. He had been a war correspondent, after all. He wasn't alarmed by the sight of weeping women.

Eventually, even though I was still crying, I began answering questions and finally I stopped crying altogether and began speaking to him—as my husband would say—like a normal person. In fact, I think it was Dennis Cage's insistence on treating me like a normal person that led me to trust him. And, at least in the beginning, he told me far more about my sister and her husband than I told him.

Most of all I wanted to know about Jack. Had he remarried? What did he look like? What did he have to say for himself now? What I really wanted to know was how unhappy he was. Was he miserable enough to satisfy me?

"Tell me about Jack," I said. "Tell me what he's like now."

From the way I sat forward on the edge of my seat, motionless, my hands folded in my lap, my eyes on him, he must have known how important it was for me to hear what he had to say. As I listened, I had to remind myself to blink. I didn't want to frighten him. Intense people are frightening to others. Florence was very intense.

CHAPTER

FOUR

ENNIS TOLD ME that when he first began his search for my sister, he read all the clippings and articles about her, and then he started to look for Jack Pine. After all, who else knew anything about Florence? But how was he to find him? Everyone said Jack Pine traveled. No one knew where.

Florence had never attended her own openings, nor did she appear on television or radio, saying it was the business of the artist to create art, not to perform for the public. No one knew what she thought when critics described her paintings as "exquisite visual hallucinations." No one knew how she felt about the collectors who bought her paintings before her shows opened to the general public. But her husband was present when his plays were first performed, had a say in the casting, sat in an old Windsor chair in the back of the hall during rehearsals, and was in the audience for the first few weeks of performances. When the actors came out for curtain calls, audiences knew that the cry of "Author! Author!" would quickly produce him. He frequently spoke on the radio, was interviewed on television, and was sought out for quiz shows. He had bit parts on popular BBC programs and liked to describe himself as the uninvited guest in other people's works of genius.

After Florence's disappearance, he walked to the edge of the earth and stepped off. People said he had kept his house in Goult, but for years after Florence's disappearance, no one saw him there. And even after he reappeared in Goult, he refused to talk to anyone about my sister, and of course he disappeared altogether when the twentieth anniversary of his wife's disappearance would have brought a flood of reporters to his doorstep.

At first Dennis thought Jack Pine was wise to stay out of sight. The intense public preoccupation with my sister had grown steadily with the passage of time. The hostility of her admirers could only become more intense. He was condemned for refusing to answer questions his wife's admirers believed they had a right to ask. He had become, in the minds of the Florentines, the villain, a murderer perhaps, a criminal certainly. The longer he remained hidden, the stronger their hatred grew; and the stronger and more violent their hatred, the more resolved he was to become, once again, private. He must have thought that publicity could only make his life more bitter. And so for a while he vanished, or seemed to vanish, almost as she had.

"In the end," Dennis said, "I thought he would have done better to come out and answer questions. If you dig a pit in your yard and leave it open, no one bothers you. But if you cover it over with leaves and branches, everyone wants to know what's in there."

"It might not have been his nature," I said, "to talk to perfect strangers. Who were they to him?"

"He's proud, he's defiant," Dennis said. "I had a guilty conscience about hunting him down."

When it came to it, Dennis told me, finding him was not difficult. He was a reporter, after all, someone who knew how to get people to give up their secrets. He knew people who knew people, and the word went out. Soon anyone who'd met Florence began to call him. He knew Jack's face, how he moved, how he smiled, knew the timbre of his voice. He had the scent.

It took him three weeks.

The reports came in. Jack was in Thailand (but he wasn't). He was in Turkey (but he wasn't, although he had been). And then Dennis walked into a café in Goult.

Goult is a small, ancient, sun-blinded village whose whitewashed buildings cling to the hills, and the hills above the village display romantic castles of the sort seen in medieval tapestries, castles whose walls change color with the position of the sun, blinding white at noon, rose-colored against the gold skies of morning, a deeper rose against washes of evening lavenders and blues, a place no one goes who doesn't like the heat, where the light is so bright everyone walks around in sunglasses. And there Jack was, in Goult, sitting at the bar of a small café.

Dennis ordered a glass of wine, and while he drank it, he thought of what to say, watching him out of the corner of his eye, John Pine, called Jack, husband of Florence Meek for seven years, notorious for his temper and physical strength, still more famous for his attractiveness to women, who were said to follow him everywhere.

Two days after Florence's death, one such woman began sending him roses and chocolates, and it became quite a fashion, sending Jack Pine roses and chocolates, often with poisonous letters or enticing photographs.

A local apothecary gave interviews, saying that he himself had counted out sleeping pills for Florence Meek before she disappeared. He remembered Madame Pine saying, How beautiful are these pills, what a shame it is to swallow them, how full of light they are, what a beautiful purple, a royal color, wasn't this the color of kings and queens? No, not in this country, not purple. But perhaps he was mistaken? Perhaps it *was* purple?

He remembered she asked for a bottle of *essence de lavande,* she stood there holding the bottle up to the light, tilting the thick golden oil back and forth, saying, It moves like a wave. Did you ever see such a heavy wave? That was what she said. Of course he remembered every word. Did he not have an excellent memory?

She was acting strangely, the American madame. She said, In my country, they surround dead bodies with white lilies. To this day she couldn't stand the smell of lilies, though they were so beautiful, their skin so white and waxy; she hoped when it was her time someone would oil her with *essence de lavande.* That was exactly what she said, *précisément,* he would make up such things? Oiling a dead body, a corpse, with *essence de lavande?*

No, not for one instant had he been suspicious.

The week before she died, she came in for more sleeping pills. Yes, he did ask her what had become of the first pills, so powerful, surely she had not taken them all, and she said, I was washing the dishes and the cat knocked them into the sink, right into the dishwater, so what could I do but rinse the dishes very, very well? I didn't want anyone falling asleep in their dinner plates.

He laughed at that. It was funny, after all. Perhaps you had to hear her say it, see the comic grimaces. She was very gay and happy, he never saw her any other way. Why should he have been suspicious? a young woman who stays up late, gets up early, has no schedule at all. Of course there are days she cannot sleep, is lively, excitable, like all young people today probably high-strung. These young people, they ask so much out of life, they insist on having it, of course their nerves are wrecked. After all, a doctor gave her a prescription. He had it in his files. Did anyone want to see it? Was anyone accusing him of anything? He'd like to see anyone accuse him of anything.

And after all, was it a deadly combination, sleeping pills and *essence de lavande?* Had anyone ever heard of someone preparing to commit suicide by buying sleeping pills and *essence de lavande?*

You bought *essence de lavande* to perfume your house in winter when the winds howled and the windows were shut up and the shutters fastened and the air grew stale. You bought it to heal cuts and chapped lips. You poured some drops into water and put the pot on the stove and inhaled the steam when your eyes were rheumy or your nose *bouché.* Housewives bought it, tourists bought it, masons took home small vials when they bruised their hands. Why should he then have thought of suicide? Such a young girl and so happy, always laughing.

She made you feel as if you were drunk, Madame Pine. On days when she had her hair down, such wild black hair, such tight black curls, he was ashamed to say he wanted to touch them, to pull them, so shiny. Of course, there were other days he preferred not to speak of, not the behavior of a gentleman to take notice, when she came in, her face white, frozen almost, her hair pulled back by a rubber band, pulled back so hard and tight her scalp showed through. It looked oily. You couldn't talk to her when she pulled her hair back. She wouldn't look at you.

Moody? She was a customer. They kept to themselves, she and her husband. You must keep to yourself here. It's wisdom, isn't it? I used to see them walking at all hours, up and down the lanes, holding hands, or their arms round each other. She was almost as tall as he was. That's all I know about them. I know I said she was always happy when she came in. I meant that's the way I remember her, the way I like to remember her. Most of the time she was happy. No one is laughing and giggling all the time, not even you, not even me.

Jack was unaware of his wife's disappearance until someone heard of it on the BBC World Service, and then he packed his things and flew home, drove home from the Marseilles airport.

The man who rented him the car remembered that, how Monsieur Pine filled out the paper, eyes streaming, how he took the key, eyes streaming, how he drove off, his face a sheet of water. You are safe to drive that car? the attendant asked him. He remembered asking. He was a responsible man. Monsieur Pine drove off at a terrible speed. The attendant thought, They will get you down the road, Monsieur Pine! The police will get you! I will pass you on my slow way home to dinner! What more did he know about it? Nothing. These things happen. You cannot persecute every married man whose wife tires of the mistral blowing and thinks, If I could only sleep, and takes one pill, and it doesn't work, and then she takes another, and it doesn't work, and then another, and finally, her eyes still wide open, she empties them all into her hand and thinks, I'll sleep for days, when I wake up I'll be fine. If she went out into the country with her pills and a bottle of wine—couldn't it have happened like that? If she went for a walk and lost her balance? There are deep, deep canyons around Goult! People have no imagination. *Accuse the husband!* It's all they know.

When Dennis imitated the way these two men spoke, I was delighted. He was a natural mimic, just as Florence once was, and he conjured them so vividly that they seemed to be there, standing in front of us.

"Then this isn't upsetting you," Dennis asked. "I didn't want to upset you."

"Oh," I said, "no! I've been *starved* for information! I really have. If I weren't such a coward, I would have gone on a search myself."

"Instead I've searched you out," Dennis said.

"Yes. Instead."

"So," Dennis said, "I sat at the bar, I pretended not to look at Jack Pine, but I *was* looking, thinking, What's this bastard going to do to me if I try talking to him? For years, everyone's pursued him, and the same thing always happens. Someone would ask him something about Florence Meek and if they didn't stop when he said, 'She was my wife,' he knocked them down. He's a plumber's son. He put himself through Berkeley logging summers in Oregon or fire fighting in Montana. People said he was strong as a bull and at least as stubborn.

"So I wondered, could I take him on? I was raised in the Northeast Kingdom of Vermont. Life wasn't easy there, either. If I didn't split wood, the family froze. I shoveled the snow from the paths, and after a week or two, the walls of snow on either side of the path were higher than my head. I had to climb up on the roof when the snow piled up and the weight of the snow and ice threatened to bring it down. Well, you know all about that. You lived in Peru. I fell off the roof one Tuesday and broke my ankle and was back up there wearing a cast on Wednesday. My mother didn't like it, but my father said it was easier to heal an ankle than a house. Get up there and be careful. But I wasn't looking for a fight with Jack Pine. I was looking for his wife, your sister, and apparently the mere mention of her name drove him crazy.

" 'You're one of the pack,' he said, looking straight at me."

Dennis said he put down the wineglass, gestured vaguely, apologetically.

"Who sent you?"

Dennis said no one sent him. He wanted to write a book.

Jack said, "It's a dirty way to make money. Digging up dirt about the dead."

Dennis said, "Yes, well, I don't see it that way. I decided to do it after my wife left me."

"She left you?"

"Because the dog died."

"Because the dog died," he repeated. "I'll beat you to a pulp, I'll drag you outside and leave you under an olive tree. The sun's so hot you'll cook out there. Your skin will peel from your body. They won't be able to pick you up. Hornets will fly into your mouth and eat out your insides."

Dennis said, "Go ahead. Try."

"Because the dog died?" But this time it was a question. So Dennis explained. While he wrote in his office, the dog slept on the rug behind him and he never turned around to pet it or talk to it. He thought he and the dog understood one another. His wife thought it was cruel.

"The rug the dog slept on, it was the same rug your chair rested on when you worked?" Jack asked.

Dennis said it was.

"Was it round or was it rectangular?"

"Rectangular."

"Rectangles," Jack said seriously, "are more powerful than circles."

Was he crazy? Dennis had read somewhere that Jack was mystical, that he and my sister kept tame ravens which they let loose, and while the birds flew, they tried to see through the ravens' eyes. Jack claimed they did it. They saw the world from up above and wrote down what they saw and where they saw those things—a red jacket caught on a brier, a rusted chassis in the middle of a poppy field—and got in their old Land-Rover and went out to look for them and there they were. Anyone could do it, anyone willing to entrust his soul to a bird. The danger was—he said this in all seriousness—that if something happened to the bird while your soul was in him, well, that was the end of you. The papers said Jack Pine drove Florence Meek mad.

"Your wife didn't understand," Jack told Dennis.

"Understand what?"

"That you were joined in the rectangle."

"Yeah," Dennis said. "Right."

Jack looked at the barmaid, bending over to sweep something up, her buttocks straining the thin, flowered material of her dress. "Look at that," he said. "Can you guess what kind of trouble that one would be? Let's go for a walk."

Dennis got off the chair, keeping his eyes on him. Jack was strong and he might be crazy. Was there a worse combination?

"Where's your hat?" Jack asked him.

"I don't have a hat."

"You can't go out in this sun without a hat. Every day some tourist dies of heatstroke."

Dennis said they could sit out front, under the awning.

"Oh, no," Jack said. "The very stones have ears. We'll take my car. I have a little house. You ought to see the French Grand Canyon."

Jack had a small blue Peugeot whose driver's seat had been moved back and riveted to the car floor. Only a few inches separated the front seat from the back wall.

"Is it air-conditioned?" Dennis asked him.

Jack said they didn't like air conditioners there. People said if your house walls were thick enough, you'd always be cool. If you're stupid enough to go out in the heat of the day, you deserve to be punished. They were filming his new play, that was what he was doing here. Once the uproar over the twentieth anniversary of his wife's disappearance died down, he'd spent more and more time in Goult. No one here was interested in who he was.

"You don't talk much," he said to Dennis.

"I told you," Dennis said. "My ex-wife."

"When Florence died, I wanted to talk, but did anyone want to listen? They thought they knew the truth, especially the women."

"But now you'll talk?"

"To you. Because you'll never repeat it. You think you will, but you won't. You have an aura. You're safer than a priest."

"Is that a threat?" Dennis asked, and Jack laughed.

"Why threaten a man with an aura?"

Jack said he was a *reporter* with an aura, and reporters published what they discovered, but Jack laughed and said again, "You're safer than a priest." Well, Jack had a reputation as an eccentric and he obviously enjoyed acting the part.

And then Dennis asked him, "Weren't there letters?" and Jack asked, "What letters?" and Dennis said, "Letters that came from her. After she *died*." And then, finally, Jack was unnerved.

———

"HE SAID you had an aura?" I asked. "Unbelievable. Really, he is un-believable."

"Well, there was more to it," Dennis said. "There always is. It was the timing, that's what it was, really."

"The timing?"

"A couple of weeks before I showed up, he was sitting in the kitchen, writing, and all of a sudden he couldn't see a thing. He was completely blind. He sat there thinking, I'm going to die. I meant to talk to someone about Florence and now it's too late and I'm going to die. And then a little while later—a couple of hours later, or maybe not so long; he couldn't remember how long he sat there—he could see perfectly well. He went to see a doctor in Aix and the man said he'd had a vascular episode, some-thing like that, and gave him some pills, and he said he decided he'd talk to the next person who came to talk to him—provided whoever that was wasn't completely crazy. And I was the next one to show up. And I had an aura. So he started talking to me."

"And you believed him?"

"About what?"

"About the vascular episode, about sitting there blind."

"Why? Don't you?"

"I think he wanted to make you feel sorry for him. So you'd be more sympathetic. He was making a fool of you. He likes to make fools of people."

"I think he had it, this vascular episode. I think it frightened him. Probably he wanted to talk. And probably he liked me. I liked *him.* And maybe he was tired of being predictable. Everyone expected him to keep quiet."

"Why didn't he just write it down himself? Whatever he wanted to say about Florence? I mean, he *knew* her. He *knew* what happened. He was a *writer.* Why didn't he write it down? Why did he have to tell you?"

"Why didn't *you* write down what you knew?"

"I couldn't. I couldn't do it. You can see why I couldn't, can't you?"

"He couldn't, either."

WE WERE in my living room, in the dying light. The room was be-ginning to lose its color. Outside, the leafy trees of Central Park would be turning slate gray. "Don't ask him to come in the morning," my husband had said. "You won't be able to get rid of him. You'll have to give him something to eat." But he had come in the morning and we hadn't eaten lunch and now it was late afternoon and time to worry about dinner.

"So," Dennis said, looking at me, "that's the first installment. Aren't you tired? You look tired. I'll tell you the rest tomorrow."

He had a lovely face, strong-featured, high-cheekboned, and his coloring was wonderful, dark-blond hair streaked by the sun, and his cheeks, I knew, would always be highly colored, regardless of the season.

"Tired?" I asked. "No." I was stunned. It was as if I'd heard Jack and seen Florence's old house in France again, and still I didn't know what had happened to her. "But you're tired," I said, looking closely at him. "You've been out in the sun too long, haven't you?"

"I haven't. I'm white as milk. As my mother used to say."

"You're flushed," I said, and I got up and went over to him. "Excuse me, please," I said, putting the palm of my hand against his forehead. "You're very hot," I said. "Where are you staying?"

"I'll find a place," Dennis said vaguely.

"Oh, no. You're staying here."

"Staying here?" he said. He sounded confused.

"We have two extra rooms."

"Can I think it over?" He was smiling but also frightened. He was a shy man. I understood that. And he barely knew me.

"No. If anything happened to you, I'd feel terrible."

"I'm one of those boring men nothing ever happens to."

"You're not boring."

"Tell me something," he said. "When I tell you about Jack and Florence, how do you feel?"

"You can use my name," I said. "You can call me Doris."

"How do you feel?"

"Oh, like a half of something, one person split in half and the other half is off somewhere, God knows where. I don't feel alive in the same way you do. I don't know if half of me *is* really alive. But I feel like this all the time. Not just when you talk about them."

"And now? Do you feel worse or better?"

"Better. As if I'm drifting toward myself. But you, you can't feel well, not with a temperature."

"I thought it was warm in the room."

"Men," I said, sighing.

"I'm not very observant. My wife said that again and again. I bored her to death. Look, Doris, I can't stay here and cause you all this trouble."

"How much trouble is it? I'll tell our housekeeper to make up your room, and when my husband finishes with office hours, he'll take a look at you. All right?"

"All right." He got up, walked across the room, and looked out the window at the park. He was unsteady on his feet, not that he noticed. "Not many people there now," he said.

"It's going to rain," I said.

"Is it?" he said, smiling. "How do you know?"

"We can always tell," I said, "when there's a change coming in the weather."

He was looking at me strangely.

"I meant I can always tell," I said, flushing.

I fed him soup and toast, I gave him a pair of my husband's pajamas, and I sat in the chair near the window in Dennis's room, waiting for John. There was something about him. His face was so familiar. Probably he had one of those faces that always remind you of someone else. When he felt better, I'd ask him if he'd ever seen me before.

"You can leave me here with a book, you know," he said. "I'm not very sick. I never really get sick."

"That's nice," I said.

"You're not what I expected," he said.

"You expected my sister."

"I know you want to hear about Jack Pine, but you're being very nice to me."

"It isn't difficult, being nice to you."

At that, he closed his eyes and fell asleep.

John came in later, woke him, looked him over, took his temperature, listened to his chest, and said, "Well, it's a long time since I've examined a patient, but you've got a virus. Stay for a few days until you feel better."

"Thanks," Dennis said, and fell back asleep.

In the hall, John said, "He'll be fine in a few days."

"You don't mind having him here?"

"Why should I mind? It's a nice feeling."

"Not so boring?"

"Why are you looking for trouble? I never said you were boring."

"Will he be able to talk in the morning? We didn't finish talking."

"He's not dying, Doris."

That night, after my husband fell asleep, I got out of bed and slipped into Dennis's room. I've always enjoyed looking at sleeping people. It seems to me that you understand someone better after you see them asleep.

His feet protruded from the covers at the foot of the bed. He was very tall. I hadn't noticed that during the day. He was so hot his body had heated up the room. Light from the hall slanted in, falling like a sheet over his face. He was not much younger than I was, I saw that now, but there was something young and wonderful about him. Was he the sort of man women want to protect? I thought he might be. I thought he was. And yet you knew he would try to protect you. Is there a more deadly combination? I sat in the chair and watched him. He was sleeping the sleep of a gentle man. I wondered what he thought of me.

"So," I said, when he had eaten breakfast and was sitting up, "why, really, are you looking for Florence? I know you said you wanted to write a book, but why? About her, I mean."

"Because she vanished," he said.

"Someone vanishes every day."

"I think if I can find *one* person who vanished and bring that *one* person back, then everything will make sense. Do you understand that?"

"Not really."

"I saw so many people vanish," he said, and he made an odd gesture with his hand, as if he were brushing a crumb off the quilt that covered him. His eyes searched mine for signs of understanding. Several times he seemed on the verge of saying something, but he stopped. "People are always vanishing," he said finally. "One day my wife walked out. She vanished. More people vanish during a war."

"Sometimes," I said, "I think that every single day, everything, all of it, is a war. And in the end, no one wins."

"You have to believe you can win—to live. Under certain circumstances, you'd do anything to win."

"Would you?" I asked him. "Do anything?"

"I already have," he said, flushing. "By rights, I shouldn't be alive. I'm only alive because I was a better liar than some of the others. People lived because they had lighter backpacks. I had lighter scruples."

"Don't you feel lucky to be alive?"

"Not lucky. Guilty. I *should* feel guilty."

"Oh, yes, I know what that's like," I said.

"You've thought you should be the one who died?" he asked me.

"I *know* I'm the one who should have died," I said.

"That's the voice of guilt speaking."

"Not really."

"Really."

We both sat quietly, thinking. Then he said, "You wanted to know why

I started looking for her. Because of her paintings. There was one, I don't know when I saw it—before I left the country. I might have seen it in Chicago, in that gallery that started showing her paintings. We were sent to Chicago a lot in the sixties. You must know the one I mean. A huge painting of snow falling, divided in half by a diagonal line—do you know the one I'm talking about? On the right-hand side, there was a figure in some kind of reddish cloak and she had her hand out, and you could see her pretty well because the snow wasn't falling so heavily, but on the other side, the snow was so thick you could barely see anything, and finally you could see someone disappearing into the snow, almost gone, and you knew in another second she *would* be gone. *And* you knew the other one wasn't going to find her. She was vanishing into the snow.

"When I got over there, someone would vanish—I mean, he'd be gone, without a trace, nothing left of him—and I'd see that painting. I used to walk around in that painting. Well, the sun was so bright, you got confused. You *could* think you were walking through snow. Sometimes you were so frightened you were cold, no matter what the temperature was. Provence was like that too. Sometimes the light looked like snow. Sometimes you were so hot you might as well have been cold.

"And then *she* vanished, and I thought, Well, I'll find her; if I find her it will make up for a lot; but I didn't find her, so I didn't make up for anything. I started looking after my wife left. I thought, I owe it to her. To your sister, I mean, not my wife. She meant something to me. It's hard to explain."

"As if she belonged to you?" I asked.

"Yes," he said. "Exactly like that."

"And finding her was some kind of penance?"

"Yes. It still is. Penance."

"For what?"

"For getting out of there alive. Let's change the subject. Unless you want to talk about why *you* feel guilty."

"I don't," I said, cheeks burning.

I thought over everything he'd said. So many lost people who felt as if Florence belonged to them. And yet he was different. It was as if she did really belong to him, or he to her, and now he belonged to me as well. The three of us, on an ice floe, on our way to the falls.

"So you have to find her," I said at last. "But you know you won't. I don't believe she wants to be found."

"I want to try."

"Yes. You have to try."

"I thought," he said, flushing deeply, "she might love me. Why not? If I already love her."

"Don't make that mistake!" I said, shocking myself.

Often, at night, I'd wake up and see my husband lying next to me and I'd think, I don't love him. Not anymore. And I'd get up and sit on the living room couch and stare out the window overlooking the park and soon I'd begin to cry because I knew I was afraid to let anyone become too important to me.

"I want to love someone," Dennis said.

"Then you'll find someone," I said. "You're tired. Go back to sleep." And he obediently closed his eyes and fell asleep.

Later, he asked me, "Doris? What was it like? When you were together? Dr. Steiner said he didn't know which of you wrote that poem. Do you know?"

"No."

"Because both of you knew what the other was thinking? Because either of you could have written it?"

"Because there *weren't* two of us, not then, not when we were small. If you were ambidextrous, and you drew something with your right hand, and then you drew something with your left hand, would you say two of you drew the picture? You wouldn't. Your left hand is yours and your right hand is also yours. There weren't two of us."

"One single thing," he said.

"One spirit in two bodies. Other people saw two beings, but we weren't. Do you understand?"

"I will," Dennis said. "I hope I will."

"I hope so too," I said, sighing.

"You know," I said, "I always thought if Florence had gone anywhere, she'd have gone back to Peru or someplace near Peru. My husband and I spent one summer driving the back roads, looking for her. It was a crazy idea. A person who doesn't want to be found, well, you can't find her."

"Probably I could find her—if she were there."

"There are veterans who live up in those hills and no one knows who they are. Every now and then a hunter comes across one of them, but he never finds out the man's name or how he earns a living or keeps warm in the winter. And they never get shot by accident, either. It's as if they're ghosts. They appear and disappear when they want to. You couldn't find her."

He seemed unconvinced. "You couldn't," I said.

"You were going to tell me more about Jack," I said the next morning.

"Oh, yes, Jack," he said, as if he were having trouble remembering his name. "Jack. Where did I leave off?"

"You were going to tell me about some letters," I said. "Letters Jack got from Florence. After she died. You said they upset him."

"Oh, yes," Dennis said.

"THERE WERE letters," Jack said. "Nothing was worse than that. They came for weeks, in her handwriting. Believe me, I know her handwriting. She used to leave me little pieces of paper with lines from poems. We read each other's things. She wrote stories, you know, stories and poems, and I commented on them. I didn't touch her paintings; that was something else. She read my plays. I knew her handwriting better than my own. All of them were postmarked. Mailed from different places in France, then from Spain, then from England, then from South Africa, then from America. You know what I did?

"I took a scarf of hers down to a man who ran bloodhounds and the dog picked up the scent and began running in circles and then he was out the door and in five minutes he found one of the letters in the garden where I hid it. *She* was writing them."

"Is that true? About the dog?"

"In Oregon, where I grew up, there were mists on the road most mornings and in the valleys they were thickest, and in the valley was a cemetery and the mists there used to swirl and move like mad snow devils and my father said, 'Those are ghosts. If you don't mind your mother, they'll get you. If you kill your mother with your bad ways, they'll come for you. They'll tear off your arms and legs and throw them all over the road.' I believe in ghosts. I wouldn't lie about ghosts."

"You believe a bloodhound can smell a ghost?"

"He went straight for the letter."

"What did you make of it?"

"Make of it? I think I went off my head. They gave me shots, they put me under. But later they told me I'd get up at night and search for letters, and if there were any in the house, I found them and read them, but I don't remember. I take their word for it."

"What did the letters say? 'Take care of my paintings'? 'Call my mother'?"

" 'Call my mother'! She didn't have a mother! She didn't have a family! One of the first things she said to me was, 'I'm an orphan and it's my ambition to marry another orphan—a *happy* orphan.' I disappointed her there. I had four sisters, and both parents were still alive.

"They were threatening letters. 'You think no one will know you hit me. You think no one would believe you hit a woman but when I am finished the whole world will know. You think no one will find out what happened before you went to Sweden. You think no one will know about the woman you went to see there. You think no one will know what I told you, that if you went I would take the pills, but you went anyway, saying you were tired of my threats. Everyone will know everything. You think I can't see you but my raven is flying over your house. You think you can marry again but I will be breathing in the next room. I will be the bird pecking up seed in the garden. I will be the dead vine that blooms in the spring. I will be the wolf howling on the hill. I will be the apples on the trees. There are more than one of me.'

"But I loved her. And those letters came so soon after she disappeared, so of course I didn't think she was dead. Now I think so. Over twenty years—if she were alive, she would have come back to see if I was suffering enough, wouldn't she? There were two letters waiting for me when I came back from Sweden and I knew she was writing them and the *dog* knew she was writing them. You can't fool a bloodhound. A bloodhound doesn't care for art or feminism or crazy Florentines. They stopped coming about nine months after she disappeared. You'll think it's funny—it is funny—but I'm afraid if I destroy them, she'll start writing again. She said she knew I'd marry again, I'd find a way to do it, she said her shadow would fall over me the rest of her life. She said, 'Don't look in mirrors because you'll see me there.' She had a lot to say. Well, you asked about the letters. She cursed me."

"You believe in curses?"

"I'm *living* one."

They were driving along a winding mountain road not wide enough for two cars. They were up so high that in the canyon below they could see a hawk circling, his shadow flashing black against the gray cliffs, which looked as if a giant hand had just molded them out of wet, gray clay. It occurred to Dennis that Jack could open his door, push him out, and no one would find him.

"Don't worry," Jack said. "You're safe with me." Could the man read minds?

"Another mile and there's a place where we can get out and walk.

There's a dam you ought to see. You can walk across the bridge and look down into the middle of the canyon."

"Look," Dennis said when they got out, "I want to ask you some questions."

"Who's stopping you?" Jack was mocking him and protecting him, and Dennis was fascinated. This, he thought, is what they mean by charm. Dennis was charmed and he was uneasy. Jack cast a spell, one man drawing another man in. He didn't like it.

"What was she like?"

"She was my wife. I loved her."

"Loved her how?"

"The ordinary way. You know how."

Dennis said he had the impression, from things Florence had written, that it wasn't an ordinary love affair.

"In what way not ordinary?" Jack asked him.

"More intense."

"I can't breathe without you and you can't breathe without me? That sort of thing? Yes. It was that sort of thing."

"She was jealous?"

"Yes."

"Possessive?"

"Yes. Possessive."

"Were you jealous?"

"Yes."

"Possessive?"

"Yes."

"But everyone is possessive and jealous," Dennis said.

"We were tied. She described it. In those damn journals. She didn't do such a bad job. You probably read it. They keep printing it."

"I've read whatever there is."

"It's simple enough. *I loved her. She was my wife.* That's the whole story."

"You believe she's dead?"

"I have dreams. She's standing in front of a white house with black shutters. There's a red barn. There's an old mower rusting in the grass, tall grass, purple milkweed, white butterflies on everything. She's there, in front of that house on a steep hill. The path is overgrown with weeds. You have to step carefully. The surface is uneven, the ground is rocky, and she's waiting. If I were awake and saw her like that, I'd call it a hallucination, but I'm asleep. Last night she said, 'The wrong person's telling the story. Start the play again.' Even dead, she's a critic.

"She tells me her dreams. Last night she dreamed someone took all her clothes and she found clothes heaped up in the theater dressing room, and she began taking everything back, but everything was so old, she didn't know what belonged to her and what didn't, so she took back what she thought was hers, but a voice kept saying, *They aren't yours.* 'I want to stop having this dream,' she said.

"She used to say I was one wing of an angel. She was the other. She was given to hyperbole. Normal life wasn't enough for her. Of course at the time I didn't think it was hyperbole. You don't when you're very young. You're flattered, aren't you?

"I could work with someone else in the room. She couldn't. She used to tell me, 'If a shadow falls across the page, that page is dead.' I came in once, suddenly, and my shadow fell over a sheaf of pages and she tore them up, into tiny shreds, like feathers. I never saw such tiny pieces. And she said, 'Can't you knock?' In a voice that would freeze water. 'Can't you knock?' Her face went stiff. I didn't know her. You wanted to hit her. It was my house! Who was she to say that to me?"

"Did you?"

"Did I what?"

"Hit her?"

He chuckled. "I gave her a black eye. Once. What a martyr she was, going up and down the stairs with a piece of ice big enough for an ice-house, dripping water everywhere.

"My mother used to get after me. 'They have to be trained. You can't let her get away with it! Get out of the house! Go into town and eat something there! Treat her like a child if she acts like one! She'll get hungry! She'll cook something!'

"My sister said, 'She's not the trouble. *You* are a wimp.' They were going to talk to her. *Why* did I stop them? Because if they'd said *anything,* Florence would have gone upstairs and days would have passed before she'd move on that damn bed and her skin would go cold and blue. 'A man, to be so afraid of his wife!' That's what my mother had to say. And according to Florence, we were the only two people who belonged in our lives and anyone else was trespassing. Unless she happened to find someone interesting and dragged him in the front door, half chewed, as if the cat got him.

"I never talked back to my mother. I wasn't raised to talk back to her, but I had to warn her off because if I didn't, she was going to call Florence. So I said I wasn't afraid of Florence, I was afraid *for* her. 'It's not a normal state of affairs here, you know.' That's as much as I told her."

"Not a normal state of affairs?"

"I thought she might harm herself. That's what I meant. I thought *I* could live like that. That's how stupid I was. Then Florence would say, 'Can't you knock?' She stayed in her room and wouldn't cook, so I cooked, always the same thing, sausages and lentils, I still can't cook anything else, and pretty soon my whole family was fighting with me. You tell me. Was it worth it? *I* thought it was—for the first five years. She took it for granted! You'd put up with anything she did."

He was agitated, his face flushed, fists clenched, as if it had happened five minutes ago, not over twenty years.

And Dennis was astounded by clearly seeing her deep beneath the ground, the rain and the leaves and the snow coming down toward her, gravity's endless gray hands pushing her deeper, and then he thought how wonderful it would be if she could go down deeper still, down to where the earth itself ran liquid, if she could be burned up once and for all, her bones flashing white and pure like lightning, and Jack looked at Dennis and said, "You see? She's taking you over," and Dennis thought again, He's mad. Probably he and Florence were both mad. Who can know mad people? And then he remembered how young they were when they married. The young *are* mad. That's what it means to be young.

"Do you know enough?" Jack asked him. "Come home with me and I'll give you some dinner."

"Sausages and lentils?"

"What else? No one makes sausages and lentils the way I make them."

Dennis wanted to know more. He was hooked, hooked by Jack Pine. He liked him. And he was flattered. The man who, as far as he knew, hadn't talked to anyone in over twenty years was talking to him.

Dennis was hungry and the lentils and sausages and his own curiosity tilted the balance. They began the drive back to the house in Goult along the narrow roads, through the melting mountains plunging crazily down under the blazing sun, coming down onto more level ground, the patchwork fields, lavender fields black and burned in the sunlight, fields of sunflowers all facing the sun, past the vineyards in their neat rows, everything stunned by the sun, everything dusted white by the brilliance of the light, past groves of olives, their green leaves dusted white. It was almost eight o'clock but still there were few signs of sunset, only a faint green tinge and then a greenish-gold tinge to the horizon, and Dennis thought, The sun never sets here. What a place!

How could Jack have come here, brought Florence here, after the winters at home, the snow-covered winters, the dark-green pines casting their blue and violet shadows on the gray and white fields of snow? Here, bees buzzed over everything, fat gold bees, and patches of lavender grew under windows, scenting entire houses, the smell especially strong in the evenings, when the air cooled, if it cooled at all. Florence was haunted by it, that smell, as if it granted protection against decay and death, even in this heat.

Then they turned off the main road and were driving up a cobbled alley, a narrow passage between white stone walls of houses, up past the one restaurant in the village, and the one café, to the topmost house in the village, when the car slowed and Jack pulled in his side mirror so he wouldn't lose it against the stone walls. He pulled up in front of an ancient white house built in the shape of a square U.

"You'll feel better soon," he told Dennis. "It's cool inside. The walls are a foot and a half thick and I shut the blinds this morning."

He likes taking care of people, Dennis thought. Until he gets tired of it.

He thought about the sausages and lentils boiling on a stove and his head spun. He wiped his forehead.

"They're cooked," Jack said. "All I do is heat them up."

They got out of the car and walked in. Dennis took off his sunglasses and waited for his eyes to adjust to the dim light. At first he thought he was looking at plain white walls. Then he recognized what he was seeing. The White Paintings. The walls were covered with white paintings, paintings of objects seen through snow, mysterious paintings whose perpetual fascination seemed to have something to do with the texture of the paint, so that when you looked at them you strained your eyes, as if you were trying to see through falling snow, and eventually it was as if something came clear, and once it did, you wondered why you didn't see it immediately.

"These are the ones the museums don't have," Jack said. And he went down a flight of steep gray stone steps into the kitchen.

In the first painting, a white, black-shuttered house was barely visible through thickly falling snow, but through a top-floor window a small face peered. Dennis looked at it a long time before he saw that the house was not resting on the earth but was separated from it by a thin ribbon of intense white light. The house was floating in the air just as the snow was floating toward the ground.

In another, a tiny house fell through snow toward a foundation dug for it in the earth. In still another, a young girl stood on the crest of a hill next to a gnarled apple tree while an identical young girl fell through snow toward her outstretched arms.

The White Paintings were an almost endless series, and everyone had his favorite. And in them, snow covered everything, the barn blending into the field, the trees into the mountains, the mountains into the sky, the river into the riverbank, the animals into the fields, the birds into the sky, and the faces of the animals and the humans, all identical. The White Paintings, which Dennis had always adored. And here was a houseful of ones he had never seen.

They reminded him of Vermont.

He found himself looking at a painting that was a variant of the famous *Golden Rope,* only this one differed from the one everyone knew because two figures clung to the lower portion of the rope, and above them, on the upper section, a small figure dressed in black held a clawlike hand out to them. The one above could only have been the mother of the two small children below.

Jack came in with two plates of sausages and lentils, set them down on a corner table, and went back downstairs for silverware, wineglasses, and wine. Their seats were to be benches built into alcoves in the thick whitewashed walls.

"I've never seen these before."

"No one has. Well, I have."

"And everyone who comes in here."

"No one comes in here."

"No one ever comes to the house?"

"Not to this floor. To the third level, up there. To the kitchen, down there. I keep this level locked."

"Then why me?"

"Because you won't tell anyone."

"I'm a journalist," Dennis said. "I told you that. A reporter. One who reports what he finds." If he was in danger, if there was to be some kind of attack, he wanted to bring it on before he began drinking and was too drunk to care what happened.

"I trust a man with an aura," Jack said again, and began to eat. "A man with an aura causes no harm." He broke off a thick piece of bread and heaped it with lentils and slices of sausage. "Go on," he said. "Eat. Ask questions."

"These White Paintings. She painted them back home? In America?"

"No, she painted most of them here. She'd start in the spring and paint them all summer and all through the autumn and then kept on painting them until it began to snow. Then she stopped."

"She stopped when it began to snow?"

"It only snowed once, and she stopped the minute she saw the first flake."

"Why?"

"I suppose she couldn't see it as clearly when it was falling right outside her window. You can understand that."

He couldn't.

Jack finished his glass of wine, poured another, got up, and took down a stack of portfolios from the top bookshelf.

"Sketches," he said. "Hundreds of them. For more White Paintings. You want to see them?" He slid them down the bench.

Dennis piled a piece of bread high with sausage, ate it, wiped his hands on a thick linen napkin, and opened the first folio—a night scene, snowy fields, a halo around the moon. The halo was formed by tiny spiders spun out of ice.

"She liked that one," Jack said, chewing. "She would have painted that one—if she'd stuck around."

An empty winter sky, snow falling, a small, gargoyle-like animal flying just beneath the moon.

"I don't know about that one. I don't think she'd have done that one. But the next one, maybe."

A village composed entirely of churches, cruelly thin steeples piercing the skin of a plum-colored sky that seemed to bleed its light into the falling snow.

"Pastels. Chalk. That was a short phase."

"You think she would have painted it?"

"I know she would."

"How?"

"I always knew. We always knew what we were going to do."

"Everything?"

"In the beginning, anyway."

"What happened?"

"What always happens?"

"Another woman?"

"Maybe there was another man. No one ever thinks about another man."

"Was there?"

"I don't know. I don't think so, but who knows? Maybe she just got tired and walked away. People get tired and walk out the door and you never see them again. It happens. But there was someone. Or something. Someone or something who had her attention."

"No one ever said anything. About another man."

"No one knew anything. I wasn't saying anything. Horns on my head, people laughing when I came into rooms. It was quite bad enough."

Dennis turned a page in the folio. A child walked along the edge of a pond. On the bottom of the pond, another child, identical to the first, was walking underwater.

"Sometimes," Jack said, "they give you the creeps."

Dennis said, "I'd sell my soul for one," and Jack said, "I expect you will."

Later, they stood in the doorway. The air was cooling. Outside, the sky had gone a milky lavender, the air smelled of lavender, the bees were gone, and here and there, a bright star shone. The air was cool on the skin.

"If you really want to know about her," Jack said, "look for her family. All these paintings of soul mates, all that talk of two souls in one skin, and she never said one word about her family. I never did buy that orphan business. She wasn't an orphan. I thought she'd tell me. She told me everything. Not one word. I couldn't trick her. She'd tell me her dreams and I'd think, Aha! There's the mother! The sister! The brother! You couldn't get your hands on anything. Maybe they knew something. I didn't want a wife with blue lips lying on that damn bed. They could have told me something. Look for her family. If you find them, let me know. What an odd bunch they must be. None of them ever came to look for her. I understand there's a sister somewhere. I hear rumors. People see to it that I hear them."

Dennis said he owed him one.

Jack said he didn't. He needed to talk to someone, but who could he talk to? Every word he said ended up in the papers and then the Florentines stayed up nights studying. After Florence disappeared, he got a letter from someone she knew. "Dear Murderer." That was the friendly part.

He offered to drive Dennis back to the café, but Dennis said he'd just as soon walk.

"Don't pet the dogs. They're not tame," he said. And then he closed the door and he thought Dennis was gone. But Dennis thought he'd push his luck. He'd always done it. Why not do it again? And he came back in the morning.

"W E L L," my husband asked, "did you learn anything from Dennis Cage?"

"She's made Jack miserable," I said. "I was happy to hear it. But I didn't recognize her," I said, and it was true. My sister, the one I mourned for after her disappearance, had nothing to do with cults, with strange women who called themselves Florentines, nothing to do with fame. She was not—to me—Jack Pine's wife. She was my sister, the one who looked like me, the one who spent an entire day sitting outside my window one winter when I had the measles because my mother had forbidden her to come into my room.

"If I talk to Dennis about her—about us—he'll be very disappointed. We were normal children."

"I don't know about that," my husband said. "And didn't he tell you you couldn't possibly disappoint him? It will do *you* good to talk to him. That's what *I'm* interested in. That's *all* I'm interested in. Talk to him."

"About toothbrushes? About how Florence always used mine and dried it on a towel and swore she hadn't touched it? He wouldn't be interested in toothbrushes."

"He might be interested in how she stole her paintings from you. When you get around to telling him."

"I don't want to talk about that!"

"Why? You're afraid of speaking ill of the dead?"

"She isn't dead!"

"Then speak to him. Tell him whatever you want to tell him."

"Florence wouldn't like it."

"Then let her come back and complain."

"He's going to London," I said. "And to France. To talk to Jack again."

"Then he can look after you in London," my husband said.

"I don't need looking after."

"You're not sorry you agreed to see him?"

"I'm not sorry. I suppose I'm not sorry," I said.

But I wasn't sure, and I had reason to doubt the wisdom of what I had done. Within days of his leaving our apartment, I received my first phone call from the young man I called the Impostor, the young man who insisted he was my son.

Right after Dennis's visit, a man began calling, but when I picked up the telephone, he didn't speak. There was only the sound of someone breathing, breathing normally. And then one day when I picked up the phone, the voice said, "I know all about you," and this frightened me enough so that I told my husband. He said if we received any more calls, we would call the police. I wasn't terribly frightened by this. Everyone who lives in a big city expects these calls. But then, a week later, I picked up the phone and the voice said, "I know all about your sister."

I sat in my study chair for hours, looking out the window. How did he know about me? How did he know about my sister? *If* he knew. Did he follow me? Was he outside even now, watching our apartment windows? When a car backfired on the street, I jumped. My husband called the police and I called the phone company and had our number changed to an unlisted one. And then the next month, the man called again. "Can I see you?" he asked me, and I banged the phone down. And then he called once more, this time on our new unlisted number. I was in a panic. Someone we knew must have given it to him, but who? Only my husband and I—and my mother's nurses—had it.

After a while, I refused to answer the telephone. Either the housekeeper or my husband answered it and then called me.

But one day when they weren't there, I picked it up myself and it was the same voice I had heard before. This time he said, "You ought to want to meet me. I'm your son, so to speak."

"My son, so to speak?"

Why didn't I immediately hang up the phone? Why did I continue speaking to him? I listened because if he was insane and meant me harm, I wanted to be forewarned. And I was accustomed to deferring to the wishes of others.

I said that if I had a son, surely I would have known it. He said, "But I *am* your child, your *biological* child. If your sister had a child, wouldn't that child also be yours? You're identical. You have the same genes she had. Biologically, I *am* your son. Does it really matter which womb I grew in?"

As if my genes were the only things about me that mattered, as if my sister and I were utterly interchangeable, as if I existed only to take my sister's place, as if I were not a person at all but a biological understudy for the important one, the talented one: Florence.

Why was I shocked by what the Impostor said? He was only saying what I already believed.

I asked him, "Do you mean to tell me you are my sister's child?"

He said that was exactly what he meant.

"Then you know what happened to my sister," I said. "You know where she is."

He said, "I know that she gave me up after I was born."

I asked him how old he was now. He said he was twenty-one.

"Then you saw her last? You're the last person who saw her?"

He said no, the man who raised him was the last person who saw her.

"Wouldn't you like to meet me?" he asked, his voice both wistful and furious. "Wouldn't you like to see what I look like? You *are* my mother," he said. "In a way. In a way, she *left* me to you."

"I am hanging up this phone," I said. "Don't call me again." He was a lunatic, a hoaxer, the worst sort of fraud. Then I went about my business as if nothing had happened. I didn't tell my husband about the Impostor.

Instead I thought things over, and as I thought, I could hear Florence's voice as clearly as if she were in the room. "It really is amazing," she said, "how long it takes you to react. Now, if it were me . . ." Yes, if it were her! She would have hung up the phone, gone to my husband's study, lined with walnut bookshelves laden down with psychoanalytic works, and she would have picked up one at a time and thrown it across the room. She would not have stopped until the Oriental rug was completely buried. I could see her quite plainly, picking up a book, saying, "Fly, little book, fly."

Of course, I did nothing of the kind. I went into my study, got down on my hands and knees in front of my old wooden chest, felt beneath for the little key I'd taped there, pried it loose, opened the chest, and began sifting through a loose pile of old photographs until I found the one I wanted. It was a photograph of Florence standing in front of her house in France, the wind blowing her hair back from her face, her cheekbones un- naturally highlighted by the brilliant Provençal light, that light that made the hollows of her face blacker than shadows on flesh ever are. I picked up the photograph, stood up, and held it out in front of me. Then I let it go. It floated to the ground, circling, as leaves sometimes spiral when they fall from trees. When it reached the floor, I picked it up and looked at it, and when I saw the face had not changed in falling but was still my sister's face, or my face—how could I ever be sure which one of us was pictured in a photograph?—I dropped it again. I became quite absorbed, picking up the photo, watching it spiral down, picking it up, dropping it down, until I heard my husband's voice behind me.

"What are you doing?" he asked me. Evidently he had been watching me for some time.

I told him about the Impostor. "Well, that *is* upsetting," he said. Psy- choanalysts must take courses in circumspection and self-restraint. I said it was all nonsense, it couldn't be true, and he said, if it couldn't be true, I wouldn't be so upset. And then I began to shake and it seemed to me that I would be happier anywhere else than I was in my own home.

There are some people who are sticky with chaos as some flowers are sticky with pollen, and perhaps Dennis was one of these. And I believed I would never have heard of the Impostor and he would never have found me if Dennis hadn't first sought me out. I'd given Dennis my phone number. Mightn't he have given it to the Impostor?

After the Impostor called, I had nightmares. Now I was sure Florence was back, that she wasn't dead. I had thought all that was over. I had thought none of that would ever happen again. I told myself, I refuse to relapse.

"It *is* because I spoke to Dennis, isn't it?" I asked my husband. But then I would never have seen him sleeping, asleep in a bed in one of our rooms, so angelic.

"Don't be ridiculous," John said.

LATER THAT NIGHT, I heard someone rap softly on our bedroom door. I got out of bed quietly and after I looked back at my husband and saw he was still asleep, I opened the door, and there she was, her finger to her lips as if to say, Don't wake him up. It was Florence.

"You're back again, are you?" I asked her when we were out in the hall.

"Oh, you know I always come back," she said.

What on earth was she wearing? Why was she such a mess?

"There are *leaves* in your hair," I said, reaching up and pulling one free. "A brown oak leaf. Don't you ever comb your hair? What are you wearing? It looks like a nightgown. Can't you dress properly? You'll freeze to death out there."

"Don't worry about me," she said. "Come *on*. I have something to show you."

"It's cold," I said. "I don't want to go."

"Put on your coat. Hurry up," she said. "Let's take the elevator."

We went out into the apartment house hallway and pressed the button and waited for the elevator.

I asked her where we were going and she said I'd see.

"Should I press the down button or the up button?" I asked her, and she said, "What you do is turn the bulb in the fixture like this"—and she twisted it—"and then we go out through the door."

She turned the bulb and I saw the back wall of the elevator was also a door, because it slid back and opened into a little room, and Florence said, "That's it. You can always do that, even when I'm not here. Let's go out."

We walked into the little room and went out the door on its far side and we were standing in the town graveyard and I said, "Oh, someone will see us out here and tell Mother," and Florence said, "Don't worry, no one will see us. Come *on*, Doris."

I followed her, thinking, I've looked for this door so many times when I'm awake. Why can't I find it unless she's here? If there's a door, I should be able to find it during the day. I should be able to find it whenever I want it.

"I think the stone's around here somewhere," she said, and I asked her what we were looking for.

"Oh, a hole in the ground they haven't filled up yet," she said vaguely, and I said, "Florence, I think I want to go back," and she said, "No, you don't, you just think you do. Believe me, I know you better than anyone. You don't know yourself at all." I said I did want to go back, I knew myself well enough for that, and I'd go back through the little room we just came through, and she said, "You know you can't find it without me," and I asked her why she hid from me during the day and why I never could find her, and she said, "I'll tell you all about it, but let's find that hole."

Then she grabbed me by the shoulder and said, "There it is! You almost slid into it! Look at that, Doris! Isn't that something?"

I looked down, but I couldn't see the hole, much less what was in it, and Florence said, "Wait a minute. I have a match," and she held it up and lit it and suddenly there was light around us and light poured into the hole. "Now can you see?" she asked me. "Go on. Look!"

I looked down and in the hole was a coffin, or I assumed there was a coffin, because in the bottom of the hole a young woman was lying and she held a baby to her chest and as I watched, the infant raised its head as if it wanted to see its mother's face and he put out a fat little hand and touched her cheek.

"There's a mother down there," I said. "With a child."

"Oh, yes!" Florence whispered. She was quivering, she was so excited. "She thinks the child is alive!"

"The child *is* alive," I said.

She shook her head at me, as if to say, No, you're wrong. The child is dead.

"But look," I said. "He's moving. He's trying to creep up closer to her face."

Florence stared at me and I knew she wanted me to look more closely at the woman's face, and when I did, I saw the woman had Florence's face—and my face—only her face was bloodless and white and her eyes were shut and I knew she was no longer alive. I turned to Florence. I wanted to say, Let's go back, take me back, but she shook her head, and I looked down into the ground and the baby sat up on its mother's belly, holding its arms up to me. All I had to do was climb down into the hole and I could have him.

"Florence," I said, and now I heard how I was sobbing, "go down there and get him for me, go get him!" But when I turned to look for her, she was gone. I turned back to look for the room that led to the elevator, but there was only the sound of the wind in the few dry leaves, and the sound of the stream running over its stones. I had to find the little door or I would freeze out there, and how would I explain to my husband why I had gone out again in the middle of the night, and how would I explain that I had left the baby down there, reaching his arms up to me?

I began walking rapidly, looking for my sister, but I knew she was gone. She always did this. She came for me, took me somewhere, and then she left me there alone. I leaned against a tree, thinking, If I'm going to freeze, I might as well stay right here, but then I heard footsteps, and I knew it was the baby following me, coming after me. He meant me harm. He was not so small.

I walked quickly but in front of me was a stone fence, except that when I reached it I saw it was not a fence but a bier, and on it a woman was lying, obviously dead, and yet she was pushing a baby out of her body. And when the baby was out, she picked him up, looked at him, and set him back down on the wall, and then she sat up on the wall and looked at me, and I saw she had my face. I saw she was me and she was dead, but she was climbing down from the wall and beginning to walk toward me, and when I looked down at her feet I saw they had rotted below the knees, and I was afraid to look at her face, because it might be rotted too.

And suddenly my eyes opened and I was back in bed, next to my husband, who was bending over me, frightened. I was shivering so violently the bed shook. I could hear the headboard creak. I could still smell the damp odor of rotting leaves, so strong, as if I had slept in them.

"It was a dream?" I asked him. "Another dream?"

It had been so long since I'd had one of these dreams.

My hands were beneath the quilt. I was afraid to draw them out, to look at them. They were cold. Were they covered with leaf mold? Had they begun to decay? And I thought, as I always did after these dreams, If she is dead, aren't I also dead? How can I be alive?

"Only a dream," he said, and he told me to turn over and he put his arm around me, and gradually I stopped gasping for breath. The smell of the leaves grew fainter and finally disappeared, and I felt my hands grow warm and I was no longer afraid to look at them. I listened to him breathe, rhythmically and deeply, and I must have fallen asleep.

In the morning when I got up, I said to myself, I'm going to London.

I'm *escaping* to London, where I won't have these dreams. It's because of the Impostor calling me. It's all his fault.

But later in the day, I went out to the elevator and stood inside it without pushing the button for the lobby and looked up at the lightbulb in the fixture, and if someone else hadn't gotten on, I would have climbed up on the little stool the elevator operator used when he was on duty and twisted that bulb. You see? I said to myself. Go to London before you get worse once more. You were happy in London. Go there.

"You don't mind?" I asked my husband later. "If I leave for London before you leave for Prague?"

"Mind? Why should I mind?" In fact, he sounded absolutely delighted.

PART TWO

And It Was
Very Early in the
Morning

A ND IT WAS very early in the morning, and the grass was still wet, and the sun was not up, and I heard the latch. It clicked into place. And I heard the sound in the rooms of the house behind me, a hollow sound, and echoing: the sound of rooms that have suddenly been emptied. And in that instant, the house was emptied out and hollow, startling, as skulls are emptied out and hollow and startling, and I thought, How strange, when death is only the closing of a door.

And as I walked down the street toward the village, my feet scattered gray pebbles, shiny with dew, and I heard it everywhere, that hollow sound as if cavernous, empty rooms were once more speaking to me. And then I thought, This has always been my music, my true music, this is the sound I listened for all my life, a hollow, echoing sound in my body, my body, that empty room. I heard it in my sister, also in her. That hollow sound was our song. And then I thought, I heard that sound for so long, I grew used to it, I forgot to listen for it, one day I stopped hearing it, and now I hear it again. Inevitable, yes.

And I thought, People speak of divorce with such dread. For years, I thought of it with such dread, but the click of that latch behind me, that was the divorce. I left everything behind, there in those empty rooms. I thought, So it is possible—to divorce the world.

The road felt soft beneath my feet. Within hours, each of the bones in my feet would make their complaints, make themselves known. I thought of our leather boots against the frozen ground in Peru, my sister's and mine, in the winters, the sound they made as they struck the earth, frozen and hard, that sound of struck metal. I thought how I stood in our garden when I first came, and it was hot, always hot, and in a far garden, under the huge oaks and willows, a lawn sprinkler was sweeping back and forth in great silver arches: from where I stood, like the liquid silver-mercury tail of an enormous peacock, raising itself to its full height, then lowering itself, first to the right, then to the left, while the hot sky darkened, turned violet and gray, blue at the edges, precisely the colors in my stained-glass window. And the rain began falling lightly and it seemed so prodigal, so splendid, so plentiful, this beautiful watering of lawns while it was raining.

And then I told myself, This is the last happy thing you will think of. Now you will put everything away.

It is surprising how little you need, really.

There is always water, and sooner or later the sun always shines.

Then came a terrible clap of thunder, enormous, and the sky went dark, and wind whipped the trees and rain poured down heavily. My dress was thin and plastered to me. I might as well have taken off my dress and walked naked through the rain.

After a short time, the sun came out, and steam rose from my clothes as I walked. I would soon be dry. I looked at the houses in the hills above me. Surely one would be empty. I always know an empty house, by its sound, its smell, by the way it seems to wait, patient and doglike, but expectant. It is surprising how many empty houses there are. It is shocking how easily people abandon their outer skins, their houses. It is amazing how many empty houses litter the landscape like empty shells of turtles. I wonder where they've gone, the turtles without their shells. I wonder what keeps them going.

As for me, it is my stubborn body that drives me along. It is my body that strains toward the sun, that lies languid in the heat. I am an empty house. I have gone off, leaving this body behind me. I am like the empty houses, but not waiting, not expectant. You can be cured of waiting. You can be cured of hope. A good thing to be washed clean of hope, and disappointment and fear.

Once I saw a thin dog. Its rib cage protruded sharply. The dog behaved oddly, and I thought, Probably he is rabid, probably he will bite me. I sat down and extended my hand, but the dog looked at me and whined and ran off. It would have been so easy, if he had bitten me.

I have always been attracted to madness. As I child, I looked out the window, looking for them, the women who roamed the common in their nightdresses, crying strange names aloud. I thought they saw wonderful things. My father, whose heart was bad and whose skin was blue, said madness was a country like death. No one returned to speak of it. How can you be so silly? How can you be so foolish?

The next year he died.

How wonderful to end that way, unaware of the world, walking into a strange town, your mouth covered in froth, everyone running from you, crying, *Madness, madness, death and fury.* No longer human. How splendid that sounded: no longer human. You can say anything, if you have anything to say.

If I wanted something, it was that—to become no longer human. I suppose some sharp splinter wanted to remain alive, the long bone of my arm or the small bones of my ear. I wanted to become something other than what I was, an animal, a lion, a tiger, a plant, a ginkgo tree. Not a human spirit alive in two bodies, not a person with two minds, four feet and four hands, a two-headed monster. I wanted to undo myself, to exist as if I had died and come back.

I would get what I wished for. You usually do, if you wish carefully enough, if you wait long enough. And this time I was careful.

It was so hot in the sun, so dazing, walking and walking, bareheaded.

And my dress and my jacket were quite dry. As if the sun had pressed them. And the first empty house I found was dry and fragrant with lavender. And I told myself, This trip has begun well. One foot after the other, hayfoot, strawfoot, why did I ever think there was more to it?

W E S A T in the café in London, and sometimes he touched my shoulder as he talked, and sometimes I put my hand on his, his hand was so warm, and I was immensely grateful to him for taking me through the scenes of my own life. I couldn't do it alone. We had become good friends, Dennis and I. I told him about the Impostor. Dennis said if he called me again, I was to let him know immediately and he would come straight over, but since I had come here, the Impostor hadn't found me.

"I've put the telephone in a cabinet so that I don't see it, and when it's out of sight I forget about it," I told Dennis. "But of course every time it rings, I jump three feet in the air. And I have such dreams!"

"If he calls, let me know and I'll come right over," Dennis said again.

C A N I T A L K about mirrors? Can I talk about lovers? I asked him that.

You can talk about whatever you want to talk about. You're her sister.

And I tried to think back, to the beginning, to the first thing. He would not let go of my hand and so I would not be lost. And after all, what a relief it is to go back, to begin putting things together. How strange it is, to see your young selves, as if you were watching from the topmost branch of a tall tree, to finally see yourself as others must have seen you.

The girls—we are the girls, my sister and I—are walking down a lane and the grass grows high on both sides and the goldenrod is high and waves in the breeze and in the warm air white butterflies flutter and the two girls, the two of us, are dressed in white and both wear yellow sun-bonnets and their long black hair curls wildly where it escapes from beneath their bonnets and their feet are bare because neither of them like to wear shoes and, a few minutes ago, they sat down on a log and Florence helped Doris pull off one shoe, and then Doris helped Florence pull off one shoe, and then they repeated the process.

The first girl raises her hands and the second one raises her hands, and the butterflies fly farther down the lane, and the girls move down the lane, side by side. One raises her left hand, the other raises her right hand, as if a mirror reflected one of them, such perfect synchrony the little crowd watching them falls silent, there are tears in their mother's eyes, in their grandmother's eyes, and their grandmother says, Did you ever see anything so beautiful? Their grandfather shakes his head. No, he never did, he never saw anything so perfect.

At that instant, two orange butterflies appear, one on either side of the road, and each twin turns, one to her left, one to her right. They try to catch the butterflies. Each gesture, each reaching out of the arm, each standing on tiptoe, each cry of disappointment, is identical and synchronous. The adults who see them tap one another on arms or shoulders, put a finger to their lips and point to the twins and then watch as if hypnotized. The butterflies fly away and the two girls turn to each other with identical expressions of disappointment, and then, as if by mutual decision, they begin walking down the lane. If the longing in the spectators were heat, everything would waver in heat lightning, everything would burn up.

One person after another thinks, Aren't they beautiful? And they are filled with desire, but what they yearn for is not known to them, that state of perfect closeness, of wordless understanding. They envy the twins, as if the twins lived in a dream they themselves once dreamed. But when the others awakened, they found they could not go back into the dream, could not have it again.

"It is not what it seems," their mother says wearily.

The butterflies flutter away, the girls turn back, see everyone watching, enraptured, turn to one another, sit down in the middle of the path side by side, staring at everyone who is staring at them, look at one another again, get up, run down the lane until they come to a tree, run behind the tree. Now they are out of sight, no one can find them, their laughter one laugh, the same sound, the same sound precisely.

But this path, the butterflies, the girls laughing, was not the first thing.

This was the first thing: When there were two who didn't know there were two, Florence and Doris, before they knew they had names, before they knew they had bodies, when they touched one another's face: *my face.* When they saw each other's arms, legs: *my arms, my legs.* When they heard

a word again and again: *twins*. A sad word; someone is crying: *twins, twins*—
behind it will be the sound of their mother, crying, the slow sad sound of
her breathing deeply, as if she were sleeping, but she is not sleeping, she
is thinking, Twins, *twins*—what did I do to deserve it?

When Mother was the first thing, when there were planets in her eyes,
their faces in her eyes. When she read, she wore glasses, their gold stems
cold to the touch, the two little windowpanes over her eyes cold to the
touch, their hands wavering toward the white suns shining in the panes of
her glasses, hiding her eyes. They wanted to see her eyes. Like the tree outside the window, black-haired, a dark cloud of hair, crackling. Sometimes
it sparks, blue-black, her face a moon caught in the black branches of hair,
white suns in her eyes. They have torn up pieces of paper. Her voice storm-
ing against the walls, the white walls full of cracks, the ceiling full of cracks
(they must be older to remember this). One day she comes in, climbs some
steps, waves her arms at the wall, the walls change color, glow pink, but
tomorrow will they be white again? No, she has waved her arms. Tomorrow they are pink.

They like this color, press their mouths to it, a taste like chalk, a cold
taste, a smell they don't like. They cover each other's noses with their
hands.

The sound of her voice like running water, the sound of her voice soft
like the wind in the white clouds at the windows, the curtains billowing
in, the sound of her voice like the rustling of taffeta. Her scent floating before her. She is coming! When she leaves, the scent lingering. She is still
here! Why can't they see her? Their fingers on each other's faces: wet. My
tears. They are crying.

We, me. Are these words different or the same? You cry. It's your turn.
Bring her back.

Mother sees it, how they talk to one another, yet they have no words,
they are too small to have words, they should have only her, every mother
deserves this, a new thing who loves only her. What has she done, why is
she punished?

Two against one, it is inevitable, how can it not happen? She says she
loves them, she tells them she loves them, probably she does love them, but
there is something else as well. Jealousy, resentment, anger. Thunder
crashes. They cling to each other. The snow falls and falls. The night sky
is white tinged with violet, a sky with thin milk behind it, an unnatural
sky. It frightens her. She takes the children from her bed to the window,
shows them the falling snow. They turn to one another, turn back to the
window; they forget she is there.

They grow older, she tells them stories. As soon as they can understand, she tells them about her own mother, who began coughing, who coughed up blood, was sent to Saranac Lake, wrote her letters saying, Elfrieda, enjoy your life, Elfrieda, life is not long. She thinks she tells them both stories, but really she tells them to Florence, the plump child, the child who cries for her until she picks her up. She can't tell them apart.

What kind of mother can't tell her daughters apart? She spends the days searching out differences. Florence is stronger, Florence weighs more, eats more, sleeps more soundly, and yet she ties pink wool around Florence's ankle, green thread around Doris's. Otherwise how can she be sure?

And then their aunt Lotte stays with them and bathes them and she takes off the woolen anklets and now both girls are the same weight, and now which is which? But of course she is holding Florence. Florence screams when she puts her down.

Doris waits quietly, quiet because she is unnecessary, wants to make as little trouble as possible, already second nature, before she has the words, something she knows, takes for granted.

Elfrieda tells them, My father, coughing up blood, taken to Saranac. A year later, my mother, coughing up blood, taken to Saranac. My mother's letters speaking of dances, *Imagine, even here we have dances,* telling this to Florence again and again, This is how I became an orphan, I was alone so long, before the priest came to the orphanage, he didn't know I was a Jewish child. He sat on my bed and asked me, Will you work hard? and I said, Oh, yes, will the lady in the country be my mother if I work hard? And he said, Yes, she will be your mother, you must do what she asks you, and she will love you, I am sure she will. And she did love me, more than her own children, but I did not love her, not as I should have, because she was not my mother. I remembered my mother. And later the priest told me he picked me out because of my hair; it was long, like yours, and tightly curled, like yours, and well brushed, and he knew the nuns had no time to brush it. He knew I brushed my own hair. He thought, If a child so small can comb her own hair, can pull through the tangles, can make her hair smooth and shiny, she will work hard. She will fit in.

She tells Florence (she thinks it is Florence, but sometimes it is Doris), You see why? You see why I am a bad mother for twins? An orphan is a bad mother for twins. All my life I wanted someone who was mine. I thought when I had a girl, one would be mine, but when there were two, when I saw you belonged to each other, when I saw I was shut out, I turned away from you.

She tells herself, I'll go back for Doris, when she cries I'll go back for her, but Doris doesn't cry, not often, and when Doris does cry, Elfrieda thinks, I'll go for her in a minute, in a few minutes, and in a few minutes Doris stops crying, pulls her sister's blanket to her, goes back to sleep.

But the twins have a sense of justice, of fairness, and Florence comes back and tells her sister the stories. In the beginning, she repeats what she's heard, but she's a child. She misunderstands, later she embroiders, how can she help it? Her imagination is vivid, she is intelligent, her sister as intelligent, they consider the story, they change this, add that. Finally, they have their own version of the dances at Saranac, and this story haunts their lives. They will never be free of it. Would Elfrieda recognize it if they repeated it to her? Would she say, But I never told you that!

As she did say when Doris published her first stories. I never told you that! How can you write such things about the family? As she said when Florence painted the dancing women. I never told you anything like that! I never said any such thing! You girls conspire against me! Your grandmother was a good, plain woman, a hard worker, she didn't enjoy dying out there in the cold! The patients slept outside on sleeping porches, beneath bearskins, hot-water bottles down near their toes, or heated bricks, they were too sick to move, Doris, what are you saying! You two get together, you go into your own world, you change everything beyond all recognition! The woman in your story is not my mother!

They turned away from her, they looked at one another, they shrugged.

This is what happened: Their mother told Florence the story. Florence heard something beneath the words. She told everything she heard to Doris. Doris heard something beneath Florence's words. When it was her turn to tell the story, she changed it so those words were there. And so it went on, and so the story grew, and in the end, they were sure their version of the story was true. The story no longer belonged to their mother. Their mother's story was proper and uninteresting, as their mother wanted to be, as she had been ever since they were born. Their aunt had said that. After you girls were born, your mother settled down. Before you were born, she was wild. She was such a good dancer, she had all the social graces, gentlemen were always interested in her. She was always up to some mischief. Not anymore. *Of course* it isn't your fault, people change, people settle down, she's not so much fun now she's settled down, but that's my opinion, don't pay any attention to me. Your father's happier. He used to say, One of these days she'll be standing on a street corner with a red pocketbook. How she cried when he threw out her black stockings, she wouldn't wear them now! Not since you were born.

Tell me the story, Doris said, and Florence would tell it to her. Tell me the story, Florence said, and it was Doris's turn. Until they had it perfected, until they had it down, until it stayed as it was, until it explained life to them, the purpose of life, its meaning. And then they forgot it.

B U T   N O W, sitting in the café, I remembered it and I told it to Dennis, Dennis whose hand has closed over mine.

"And they used to dance when the attendants were gone for the night, she wrote me letters every day when she was strong enough, she said they used to dance, she said, 'You should see us, with our bright-red cheeks and our bright eyes and all our bones showing, except for the ones who are really getting better, they have so much flesh on them it is hard to know how they move at all, their flesh shakes when they raise their arms, they have no waists. Anywhere else but here you would pity them. Here, everyone envies them their pounds, begrudges them their closets full of skinny-melink clothes they can't fit into.

" 'They're generous, though, they lend us whatever we want, we thin ones. Someone who can get his breath humming the song, that is our music, that is the only orchestra we have, in our white gowns, not even so well fastened. There's not much modesty here, you don't think about who sees you, not when you may not be around tomorrow. I'm sorry to tell you all this, Elfrieda, but otherwise how will you know me, how will you know what happened to me, our warm robes thrown over the beds? We have an attendant who pushes the beds back against the walls; if the doctors ever found out! After a few hours he comes back and pushes the beds back where they belong, the exact place, their legs over the dents in the floor. He doesn't scrape the paint, or if he does, he sweeps it right up, or he wipes it away fast with a wet cloth.

" 'Everyone dances close. Last night someone said, We are all everyone's husband or wife. You must understand, when you're dancing on your own grave, then you can have whatever you want, there has to be some compensation. Sometimes I pretend I'm dancing with you, I'm holding you to my breast, you are my own true baby, the only one I ever had, I never wanted another one, and a good thing it was, too, and how lucky I was, a perfect baby the very first time. Did I tell you that you were born with hair, it grew right down to your eyes, everyone said you looked like a monkey, my mother and her sister saw you and were laughing out in the hall. I was so angry! How I shouted at them and said I never would forgive them, but after two weeks that hair fell out and you were the most beautiful baby in the hospital. Everyone stopped to see you, you had such big, big eyes. They said you looked like me, but you didn't, you looked like your father, what a beautiful man he was, but it wasn't enough to protect him.

" 'The neighbors said the angels were jealous and came to get him, but I don't believe it, the angels are beautiful enough as they are, your father said I looked like an angel, Elfrieda, there are no angels here, I dance with any man, I like the tall ones, they remind me of your father, but if they cough, then I change partners. When I dance there's nothing wrong with me, I'm not sick, I'll never be sick again, I'm hot, my cheeks are burning, my skin smells like hot iron, I smell like metal. Even when I put on someone's perfume I smell like metal. Do you know I have a fur coat now? A woman who left last week wanted me to have it. Sometimes the women dance together, I danced with her. I have two beaded dresses she gave me.

" 'When I first came here she was so fat she couldn't wear them, then she grew thinner, she couldn't eat, she couldn't come in from the porch. She wanted to dance last night but she couldn't get up from the couch. Two men carried her in. They held her up, she didn't weigh anything. They said it was like carrying a dried-up leaf, they whirled her around twice, someone was humming, quite loud that night, they put her back on her sleeping couch, they tucked her up in her bearskins, in a few minutes she was gone. When the doctors came they remarked on her face, how happy she looked. By then the beds were back where they belonged. They don't know what goes on here. You shouldn't, either, probably you shouldn't, but when I'm gone, what will you have to remember me by? Will you think, My mother was a sad woman who coughed and filled a basin with blood and never in her life had a merry moment, will you think that of me? I want you to have more, I want you to know I wanted to live. I had a fever to live.

" 'When I saw what was coming, I said, "No, there is more to it than this, while I last, I will have it," and I danced in the cold in my white gown, my cheeks burning, held by thin-armed men, their cheeks as red as mine, their eyes glittering so that I knew mine glittered also, we sat on the floor drinking wine straight out of bottles. We couldn't infect one another, not anymore, and outside, the snow was falling or the leaves were falling, it didn't make any difference. We never looked up at the stars. We were sick of stars. We spent so many nights on our sleeping porches. We danced and danced, our feet bare, we liked the feel of the floor, well, some of us did, I did, we lay in men's arms, even women's, another body is a wonderful thing, you grow so thin one body is not enough. You think, I barely exist, I barely cast a shadow, you need someone else.

" 'You will lead a good life, a long life, I know this, I hear this when I hear someone humming a waltz and someone else whirls me about and my feet leave the floor and my eyes close and the night spins around me like a top and the wind blows the stars down like leaves.

" 'Elfrieda, you understand why I tell you this, Elfrieda, be a good girl. Wherever I am, I will watch you, I will be like a small bird on your shoulder. You will live to see your children grow up, you must not worry about me. Whatever happens, I shall not mind it. I have had these dances. Elfrieda, I remember every day, every minute with your father, but I hope he danced as I am dancing. Never think, If she had not danced she would be here now. We only danced when we knew we would not be here long, the doctors made it quite clear. We knew how it was when they came to see us less often, when they looked at one another and shook their heads, we knew how it was when we coughed and ruined our white gowns and they took them off to be boiled and gave us another one, quite clean but with faint pink spots. The boiling and bleach can only do so much. Do not think, She should not have danced, she might have been here, Elfrieda, I knew I was going, Elfrieda. Say, She had her dances. We all looked so beautiful at those dances, Elfrieda, we did, Elfrieda, tell yourself it is true, tell yourself, Elfrieda, I danced for you.' "

And Elfrieda told the story to the family in Vermont who took her in, the family to whom the priest brought her, good Lutherans. When she first told it, Mr. Hewitt, her foster father, sat forward, his elbows on his knees, his fists pressing into his cheeks, supporting his head, which suddenly felt so heavy.

But Hilda Hewitt, his wife, was weeping, tears were streaming down her cheeks, dripping from her chin, dropping onto the starched white bib of her apron, and she held out her arms to Elfrieda, who got up and went to her. She drew Elfrieda down onto her lap, and she pulled Elfrieda's head to her chest and stroked her hair as if she were her own child, and she said, "A mother must give her child something, a mother must say something to her child, probably they were very nice dances," while she stroked Elfrieda's hair and stroked it, and Mr. Hewitt looked up at his wife, so round and so healthy, wondering, would his wife have danced while someone hummed? Do all women want to dance?

And he saw Elfrieda, so natural and so comfortable on his wife's capacious lap, and he said, "Hilda, there were such dances and they were not very nice dances," and his wife said, "A dying woman ought to dance!" and Mr. Hewitt was struck dumb by his wife's defiance, by the passion with which she spoke. She was not a log after all, not any of the things he silently called her when she disappointed him. She was a woman who wanted to dance like Elfrieda's mother, what was he to make of that; he would lie awake nights working it out, he would never make sense of it, but his wife was weeping. Would she ever stop weeping? From that day forward, his wife loved Elfrieda, loved her best, said to herself, I will give this child back her childhood.

Elfrieda, raised by a woman who loved her more than she did her own children.

"I'm telling this story to *you*," she told Florence. "It's our secret." And then the girls would change the story. Why tell her, when she would argue, correct them, insist she was right? When she would say, Women dancing with women! As if that were natural! As if that were right! As if everyone was like you! As if everyone took baths together, walked around naked together! Do you think other women are like you? Other women aren't like you!

She hates us, Florence said. She thinks we're beasts.

And I said, She's only jealous.

And Florence said, She's more than jealous!

And I said, She loves you, Florence, she loves you best.

And Florence said, Hating me less isn't loving me, Doris! What's wrong with you?

But before that, we ran through the fields, the sunflowers were so tall we had to tilt our heads back to see them, our feet were bare, there were black-eyed Susans and daisies we grabbed at, running, and sometimes they streaked and stained our hands green, and the wind was blowing the Queen Anne's lace this way and that way, through the apple orchard with its red apples and gold apples, the crooked-women apple trees, I remember that's what we called them, past Darlington's Funeral Home, out where the houses thinned out and the mountains rose up like a wall, dark green, dusted white by the heat.

The sun beat down on our heads, and the earth was sandy and full of pebbles and the pebbles pressed into our feet, and we stopped and stood on one foot and looked at the sole of the other, and the soles of our feet were red and warm and the skin of our feet was dented by pebbles, and I said, Let's let the birds go, right, Florrie? Let's go swimming in the creek, right, Florrie?

Florrie said, Right, Dorrie, and Florrie looked at me, and I said, Yes! In our clothes! and we ran to the creek, and Florrie looked at me, and I said, Yes, jump off the bridge! and we climbed onto the outside of the covered bridge, the planks brown and warm and splintery in the soft parts, holding on to the planks of the wall, edging along until we got to the deep part.

The sky was down in the creek and the clouds were moving fast across the water, they must have been pouring out from behind the mountain. There was pollen floating on the water, and bits of green leaves, and blades of grass. Someone had been here before us but now he was gone.

A frog jumped into the water, we knew that sound. Later, we could follow the creek where the frogs grew big enough to jump in a canoe and turn it over. Once, a big frog jumped in our canoe and tipped it, and then we let go and fell into the water, both at the same time, always at the same time, I always thought someone watching would have seen two showers of silver splashes rising up from the deep place we made deeper, diving down for stones, digging them out, holding our breath, watching the frog-mottling sun pattern the creekbed, staying down until our lungs forced us up, always at the same time, always breaking the surface at the same instant, right, Florrie? Right, Dorrie?

"s o," I asked Dennis, "is this what you want to know?"

"Anything you want to tell me, anything you can remember."

"If we could settle it, one way or another. If we knew what happened to her."

"I believe she's alive," he said. "I'm sure of it. Aren't you?"

"I don't know, not anymore."

Dennis said, "I think she's alive and wants to watch her husband suffer. Don't you think so?"

"If she's alive, she wants *me* to suffer," I said.

"You?" he asked. He raised his eyebrows.

I thought back to the fields, the covered bridge, the water. "I thought it would be like that forever," I said. "I didn't know what a catastrophe love is."

"A catastrophe?"

"Well, it wouldn't be if each one loved the other equally, but they never do, do they?"

"Not in my experience," he said.

I sat still and quiet and thought about the words: *lover, beloved,* the saddest words in the language. Noah was my favorite character in the Bible, the man who filled his ark with couples, who must have believed only couples were worth preserving, who saw to it that the whole world would begin again, from couples, who, along with God, decided that nothing singular, no matter how beautiful and unique and priceless and heartstop-ping, would be preserved, who dismissed the single, unique thing as an aberration, a dream, only momentarily sketched on the air.

"Always," I said. "Someone always loves more. And you never know which one that is."

"Usually you do know," Dennis said. "I loved my wife more."

But had he? Hadn't his wife complained she wanted more attention? Hadn't she grown bored when he disappeared into his own room and his own world? If you could measure love by the depth of disappointment, then his wife had loved him more.

"Think about my sister," I said. "She *showered* Jack Pine with love. What if that wasn't a particularly loving way to behave? What if she knew that kind of love would drive him away and that's what she wanted, that's *really* what she wanted? To be alone. Suppose he had matched her passion for passion and she had *still* run off? That might have happened—if they'd stayed together. Who knows why anyone falls in love? Maybe she saw he was frightened of her and she wanted to marry someone she could frighten. We don't know."

"I don't think Jack frightens easily," Dennis said.

"Well, he wouldn't let you see it, would you? He'd wait for a woman and then he'd let *her* see it. That's what women are for, isn't it? Women love strong men with weaknesses. It makes them feel needed."

"I didn't realize you were cynical," Dennis said.

He smiled at me. I stirred my coffee and was silent.

The lover, the beloved. Sometimes the lover is fleeing from the one he seems to pursue. It happens all the time. I know. You have a couple, but which is which? How can you know?

It's the way of the world to sympathize with the one who suffers. The lover, that tortured one. Who thinks of sympathizing with the other one, so beautiful, so indifferent, so without conscience, so invulnerable—the beloved? The beloved's the strong one, infuriating, frightening, the one who uses your love to trap you.

"It is terrible," I said, "to be the one who loves more."

"It can't be wonderful to be the beloved, either," Dennis said.

"Why not? *Everyone* wants to be the beloved."

"Because *everything* the lover does makes the beloved feel inadequate and unsatisfying. It would have to, if the beloved didn't love in the same way as the lover. Every kiss would be a reproach. No one likes to be told how disappointing he is. What else would the lover be telling the beloved?

Look how I love you but you can't love me back. See how disappointing you are? Who wants to hear that day in and day out?"

"But there are many kinds of beloveds," I said. "There's the enraging kind who says, 'I love you, but not as much as you love me. I love you *this much*,' and between thumb and forefinger he measures—what?—an eighth of an inch. And the lover says, 'I love you *this* much,' and throws her arms wide, saying, 'See if you can match this.' Isn't it possible that the beloved loves the most after all, but he's frightened, he tells himself, No, I don't love her at all, or, I love her today, but I won't tomorrow. There's nothing steady about me. For her own good I have to leave her. Isn't it possible that fear makes him say—and he's afraid of how much he loves her—*This can't go on, this has to stop?*"

"I think you've just described Jack Pine," Dennis said.

"Or there's this kind of lover, the one who says, 'I'm not sure, tomorrow I may leave.' Doesn't she know she has to seem ready to leave, ready to pack up and walk out, because otherwise he'll grow too comfortable, too sure of her, and then he may leave her? Isn't she the one who loves more? Even though *she's* the one threatening to go, she'd be the lover. Wouldn't she? And him—he complains, he says she's unpredictable, she's unreliable, her affections aren't steady—doesn't she keep him there? She makes him afraid: today I may leave, today I don't love you, what will you do to make me love you once more? And he never has time to wonder if *he* loves *her*. But he *thinks* he loves her more—because she's made him think so. You see? One always loves more, but which one?"

"Does it matter?" Dennis asked. He seemed uncomfortable.

"It does," I said.

He shifted restlessly in his seat. "You and your husband?" he asked me. "Which one are you?"

"I'm the beloved," I said. "My husband loves me more."

"And you and Florence? Which one were you?"

"Florence was the beloved. I was the lover. I loved her."

And he asked me: "Are you sure?"

W E W E R E B A C K in the café—Eva's—the next day, and as soon as I sat down I was irritable. The sight of Dennis annoyed me, and when he touched my hand I moved it away.

"Is this all you have to do?" I asked him. "Don't you have to make a living?"

"Actually," he said, "I don't." He cleared his throat. "I'd like to talk to your mother. I'd like to try. She might have a clear day. You never know. Do you think that's possible?"

"Oh, I wish you wouldn't try! She's never gotten over it, Florence disappearing that way. She was confused *before* Florence disappeared, probably all those years of drinking. You'd come into the kitchen and she'd be standing there holding a wooden spoon in the air and smoke was pouring out of the oven and she didn't see it, she didn't seem to know why she was coughing. That's why John and I put her in that home in Florida. She always wanted to go to Florida—she hated shoveling snow, she was always afraid of falling and breaking something—and she used to wander off even there, and they'd find her walking along a road, but if someone stopped her and asked her where she was going, she didn't know, or she'd say, 'I'm looking for my daughter. Have you seen her? Florence Rice?' "

"I'd like to talk to her," he said stubbornly. "You never know."

"No," I said. It was the first time I'd refused a request.

We sat there in silence, and after a while I began drumming my fingers on the table and I heard Dennis push back his chair. I saw his elbows appear on the table. Finally, I looked up.

"Dr. Steiner had quite a bit to say about her," he said.

"Dr. Steiner! You talked to Dr. Steiner?"

"I told you I did," he said. "I found you," Dennis said, "because I found Dr. Steiner. I found him when I found Peru. I went to the post office and asked the man who worked there if he knew who the town doctor was thirty years ago and he said, 'That'd be Dr. Steiner. He lives in that red brick house next to the Lutheran church. He doesn't take patients anymore.' I asked the man how good Dr. Steiner's memory was, and he said it was as good as his, as good as anyone's, and what did I want with him, so I said I'd promised my mother I'd come to see him, and the man said I ought to keep a promise I'd made to my mother. That's how I found him. It wasn't hard."

"You lied to the man in the post office," I said. I shouldn't have been surprised, but I was. He was a reporter, after all.

"I could have said, 'I'm looking for information about someone named Florence who grew up here,' and then everyone would have closed ranks the way they do in small towns, and everyone would have been suspicious of me and no one would have talked to me. Is that what I should have done?"

"Of course not," I said. "Of course you can't always tell the truth."

"Oh, you're a person of high moral standards. You tell part of the truth and let everyone assume it's the whole thing. Sometimes keeping quiet is even better than lying," he said. He'd slapped me down. He didn't think I was too fragile to argue with or insult. He respected me. I hadn't expected that.

"Tell me about Dr. Steiner," I said. And I could see them, those old Vermont houses. They never changed, porches loaded down and sagging, the yards overflowing with wrecked cars, mattress springs that once had looked so promising as trellises for morning glories, old headless dressmakers' forms, some still wearing their wire hoop skirts, rotten wicker rockers, rockers made of willow wood left out so long they'd taken root and turned back into trees, houses that announced, We've kept everything we ever had, and this is what it's like.

It had been so long since I'd been back. Peru, the common, the enormous elms in front of the pink brick house, Mrs. Mudd, who said, "I want these elms to last as long as I do," the mountains behind the pink house, Dr. Steiner, who gave us lollipops, who told my mother, "Elfrieda, let them go away to school. Even as newborns they were intelligent. Let them go, Elfrieda."

When enough time elapsed, you stopped believing the town was real. It seemed to sink beneath the surface of the earth. You thought, Why go back? Everything will have changed. And you thought, I can't go back.

Everything's gone. Everything's disappeared. There's no one left alive.

"Was it raining?" I asked him.

"It was raining. And you won't like everything he had to say."

"Tell me anyway. Everything. Where did you park?"

"I parked on the common and it was misty and the ground was damp."

"And your boots sank in, and your clothing was covered by little beads of rain." It was remarkable, how quickly I fell into the old game; remarkable, too, how well Dennis played it with me.

"And I twisted a bell handle and no one came and I rang again and this time feet came shuffling along, and an old, white-haired man came shuffling along, and I told him I'd been looking for someone, and I told him I came from Athens, and I asked him if he could help me out, and I showed him a picture of your sister when she was about eighteen, and I said, 'Maybe you would recognize her,' and he said, 'Well, you better come in while I get my glasses. Wipe your feet.' "

"And he took you into his study. I remember that study!"

"I followed him into the study and he sat down in his chair and looked me over, and I wondered what he was seeing—you know, the onset of liver disease, bloodshot eyes meaning high blood pressure, he saw *something*. I always thought these old country doctors saw straight through you, and then I had trouble getting him to talk about anything but what the fishing was like in Athens. He used to go fishing in Athens. That's what he wanted to talk about. So I said, 'If you don't mind, take a good look at the picture. I think she comes from Peru.' And he said, 'I think her name is Florence Rice. What did she do? Murder someone?'

"I said, 'Her name's Florence Meek.'

"And he said, 'Maybe she's called Meek now, but she was born Florence Rice. When the girls graduated from school, they took their mother's maiden name. Meek. They did it legally. They went to a lawyer in Lofton who did it for them. It was Florence's idea. I know that. Elfrieda Rice, their mother, lived here in town until something happened to her daughter, no one would ever say what. I thought maybe she got pregnant and she didn't have a husband, something like that. Now she lives in Florida—the mother, I mean.'

"Well," Dennis told me, "that's when I first found out Florence had a twin. I kept saying, 'Girls? What girls?' And he looked at me as if I were an idiot. 'You mean to say you didn't know she had a twin?' he asked me. 'But you *did* know she changed her name?' I said I didn't really know anything and would he mind starting from the beginning. Is it true?" Dennis asked me. "About changing your name?"

"Yes. It's true. Florence wanted to get away and stay away. She said she never wanted anyone from Peru to know where she was or what she was doing. I didn't think anyone knew. I didn't think my mother told anyone."

"And you went along with it?"

"She didn't want *me* to change my name! She wanted us to have *different* names. I couldn't stand the idea. So I changed my name too. Then we were both named Meek."

"Why?"

"It was important to her. I don't know why. What else did Dr. Steiner say?"

"Well, *I* couldn't believe *he* didn't know what happened to Florence. But he said the idea that the girl in the papers was the same one in the town never entered his head."

"Of course not," I said. "No one from Peru thought Florence Meek had anything to do with one of the Rice *twins* they knew. I mean, no one ever saw one of us without the other. Half the time, if someone saw one of us alone, they didn't know which one of us they were seeing, so they *thought* they saw us both. At least that's what *I* always thought. I'd go to the store and later someone would say, 'I saw you girls shopping for a dress,' and I was the only one who'd been there! He didn't recognize her? From the picture?"

"Not at first. After he looked at it awhile, though. He said, 'That triangle face, once you look for it you can't miss it.' Then he asked to see the clippings. I said, 'You know, she's probably dead. At least that's what people think.' He said she couldn't be dead. She wouldn't be more than forty-seven or eight! And then that marching band starting tuning up on the common. The annual parade of Dr. Steiner's babies. Remember?"

"Of course! The Parade of Babies, when the town decorates the common and ties streamers to the gazebo. We used to ride at the head of the parade. The famous Rice twins of Peru, Vermont."

"He asked me what I wanted with her, so I had to explain. And he showed me a poem. He said years ago one of you wrote it for his birthday and he had it in the file somewhere and he asked me if I was interested."

"A poem about a tree?" I asked.

Dennis said, "No, it went like this:

"If you would tell the world
Don't tell it all you know
For words will change the world
As fields are changed by snow.

> "And though sunshine melts the snow
> And washes green fields clean
> Pour words must stay to stain
> And blister your old age.

"You should have seen that piece of paper, all yellow around the edges, and whoever typed it hit the keys so hard all the *o*'s and the periods cut out little holes. But he'd saved it. He had it in a special folder."

"I think," I said, "I wrote it. But it might have been Florence."

"You signed it. Doris Rice, ten years old."

"That doesn't mean anything. We were always signing each other's things."

"Well, that's what he said. He also said he thought you were the talented one and that if one of you was going to wind up famous it would have been Doris. I thought he'd mixed up your names. I said, 'You mean Florence, don't you?' And he said, 'Young man, I mean Doris. I always thought she was the nice one. She held back and let Florence do the talking. *That* was one way to tell them apart. Doris would stand there and watch Florence and she'd smile and keep on smiling! I can still see them! You never saw anything like it, as if the sight of Florence made her happy. It *did* make her happy.'

"He said your mother thought you were coldhearted, but he never thought so. And he said the two of you surprised her. She thought she'd keep you in Peru forever, but on college night you got more offers than you could handle. He said you took the painting scholarship and Florence went in as an English major."

"He got that backward," I said.

"He wanted to know if you were all right, and I said I'd heard rumors about a sister, but no one ever said anything about a twin sister, and no one was even sure there *was* a sister. People said Florence Meek was an orphan, because that's what she'd told everyone. He was taken aback by *that.* He said your mother was alive and kicking and he couldn't imagine why Florence would want to tell people she had no family. He said he'd been against your going to Chicago, a city built on swamps and slaughter-houses. He said he didn't recommend the place but of course you two didn't pay any attention to him—or anyone else. You listened to each other.

"He said *you* had the real talent. He kept coming back to that. He told me stories about how your mother mixed you up, and I said your mother sounded interesting, and he said she was. He said the entire time she was pregnant, she kept on insisting she was having a two-headed baby. She said she could feel the two heads, and he used to say, 'Elfrieda, you mean to tell me you'd rather have a two-headed baby than twins?' and your father used to say there was no talking to her and he shouldn't bother. And when you were born—both of you—she said she couldn't manage two at once and didn't want to take you home."

"Ever?"

"He didn't think she ever wanted to. He said she talked about putting the second baby in an orphanage."

"She meant it?"

"He thought she did. Then it was, 'Two babies, how wonderful!' and the next thing, 'I can't manage two babies,' and she'd start in about the orphanage again. He said, 'Elfrieda was more trouble than the twins.' He was a nice old gentleman.

"I asked him if your mother was a good mother once she got you home, and he asked me, 'Look here, how much of this will see the light of day?' and I told him that I'd been looking for Florence Meek for more than a year, Florence Meek was all I thought about, and I'd give anything for any crumb I could get. I didn't have to publish everything I knew, and if he told me something was off the record, I wouldn't print it, and that was what he wanted to hear. After that you couldn't stop him.

" 'What kind of mother was she? She tried, but I never saw anyone make such a muddle. After about two months, you couldn't tell the babies apart. I remember when they came for shots, I put an ink mark on the bottom of the first baby's foot. I wouldn't be the first doctor to give two sets of immunity shots to one identical twin. So Elfrieda tried the same thing, but she didn't use ink. They had plenty of hair, so she put a pink ribbon in Florence's hair and a green ribbon in Doris's, but the trouble was, the babies managed to pull out the ribbons and then she didn't know which was which.

" 'And then one day she brought the two of them in and I couldn't believe it. One was skin and bones and the other was so fat she didn't have a neck. So I said, "Elfrieda, what's going on here?" and she said, "That's why I brought them in. My husband doesn't like the look of this one." And I was alarmed, well and truly alarmed. You know how it is with twins. Sometimes one is strong and the other is weak. One is born with the umbilical cord wrapped around its neck and doesn't get enough oxygen, or one takes up the blood first and doesn't pass enough on to the other one—

that's what happened with these two—and you get one fat red baby who looks almost black and one small white one who looks half dead, and I thought, I've missed something here.

" 'So I told Elfrieda I'd have to examine them both, and they both started crying and Elfrieda said it was nothing, they were only wet. I went out of the room, and when I came back in, she was changing one baby, and I stood up there in the doorway watching and she turned around to get another diaper and when she turned back to the babies, what did she do? She picked up the same baby and changed its diaper again and the other one, the thin one, was crying, and I said, "Elfrieda, you see what you've done? You've changed one baby twice!" And she didn't have the least idea. So I knew what happened. She was feeding one baby twice and the other baby wasn't getting fed and I forgot about serious diseases and I said, "You need a way to tell which baby you've been feeding. You should always pick up the one in the crib nearest the window and feed that one first."

" 'And she was furious. She said, "In the middle of the night, I pick up the one who's crying the loudest. Otherwise my husband won't get any sleep." So I said, "Well, it isn't working, is it? You better put an ink mark on the back of the baby's hand when you feed her," and she wasn't happy about that. She said a mother ought to be able to tell her own babies apart, and I said she could tell them apart now, because one was thin and one was fat, but when the thin one fattened up, only God could tell them apart, so she'd better get a pen or a crayon and start marking their feet or the back of their hands. I don't think she could ever tell them apart.

" 'A lot of the townspeople could, though. And her husband could. Not on first sight, even he couldn't do that, but after he'd watch them for a second, he knew which one was which. And she didn't protect them from their half-brother, her son from her first marriage. Albert. He's dead now—pneumonia. A miserable thing. He said the twins ruined his life. He certainly made a misery of theirs. That's a long story. Come back tomorrow, and whatever I remember I'll tell you. More than you want to know, probably.' "

And Dennis said Dr. Steiner must have thought that was the end of it, because he got up and looked out the window, and he said, "The baby parade. They're back. I know more about every one of them than their husbands and wives. It's a burden."

"So that's how I found out your sister had a twin," Dennis said. "That's how I found you. Dr. Steiner delivered you up all over again. Well, he didn't give me your address. Your mother did. Well, not your mother. The woman who takes care of her in Florida. I was afraid he wouldn't speak to me, but when he found out I came from Athens and started talking about fishing, you'd have thought he'd delivered *me*."

"Tell me about Jack. He didn't say Florence had a twin? Doesn't he know?"

"He knows Florence had a sister. He didn't know she had a twin. He knew she talked to you every day. I don't know how he knew that. Probably from the phone records, because the police checked them afterward. Probably he got someone to look into who she was calling every day. But he knew *something* about you."

"And you didn't tell him?"

"I'd like to tell him. He ought to know. Don't you think he ought to know?"

I stared out the window. What did Jack deserve? What, really, did he deserve?

"You might want to think about meeting him yourself," Dennis said carefully. He cleared his throat. "I might have mentioned that Florence had a sister. I don't remember. I'd heard that rumor before I went to see him."

"I really don't think I want to meet him."

"Will you give it some thought?"

"Did you understand? About Dr. Steiner and my mother?"

"Understand what?"

"They were lovers. For years and years. He lived across the common. I don't think my father knew."

"They weren't happily married? Your parents?"

"My father was what they called a cardiac invalid. We weren't a happy family, or we shouldn't have been happy, but Florence and I were. Florence and I had one another. We saved one another. That's why our brother hated us. Oh, he was horrible, Albert. We called him the Cloud. We didn't need anyone else, nothing really touched us. Our mother was so miserable when our father died, and we weren't. She thought we went on as if nothing happened. I think she wanted us to suffer the way she suffered. Not that we always got along. Once, I had a high fever—I think I had chicken pox—and I passed out on the bathroom floor. I couldn't get up, I couldn't call out, and Florence came in, I saw her looking at me, and she stood still, she stared at me, and she kicked me. She kicked me and said—well, she didn't *say* it, she *hissed* it—she said, 'Doris, get up!' I still remember it, how cool the tiles were, how shiny her shoes were, black patent-leather shoes, we both had them, metal taps on the soles so they wouldn't wear out so fast, and she saw me lying there and she kicked me."

"Maybe she saw herself lying on the floor, maybe she was frightened. Maybe that was it."

"Then she wasn't kicking me? She was kicking herself? What a good explanation! You really are an admirer!"

"You're angry."

"I hate remembering," I said.

We sat in silence, thinking.

"Have you heard from your husband?" Dennis asked finally.

"Oh, I've been calling him every day. I've got to stop. What's the point of leaving home if you're going to do that? I know everything going on there. He hasn't found anyone to live in the apartment and take care of the cats. My mother called and thought I might have gone back to college. He told me to call her. Do I want anything put in storage? I might as well be home."

"Don't call so often," Dennis suggested.

"But if I don't call—"

"You're calling because you feel guilty."

"I *love* my husband."

"I know that, Doris. But you're calling because you feel guilty."

"Oh, I don't think so," I said.

The silence grew heavy. "I'm tired," I said. "Let's come back tomorrow."

"Tomorrow, fine," Dennis said. He got up, touched my shoulder, paid the bill, and came back.

"I'll just sit here for a while," I said.

"I'll see you tomorrow, then," he said.

I sat in my seat and looked out the café window. The world was, to use my father's expression, down to the tail end of the day. I imagined I was back in Peru, walking down the main paved road toward the narrow dirt road that led up into the hills above the town. The branches of the berry bushes were reddening. Some were already blood red. Every now and then I thought I heard a splash in the narrow brook running along the left side of the road and a blue jay flew a few inches above my head and up into some high branches and then watched me. A slithering, a snake. A sound near the stream like a snapping turtle. I looked up into the greenish light and saw a porcupine's nest caught in the topmost branches of an aspen. I could hear my grandmother's voice saying, *What's wrong with porcupines? They sleep nearest to heaven,* and all these things were like letters in an alphabet I knew and everyone else who lived here knew. And I was sorry I had ever left Peru, and I thought, If it hadn't been for Florence, I wouldn't have gone so far away; if it hadn't been for Florence, I would have gone back. For a long time we were so happy, and then everything she did . . . It's hard to believe it. She poisoned the well.

So Dr. Steiner thought I was the one with the real talent.

But *Florence* was the good one, the perfect one. I'd always believed that. Worlds rest on these assumptions, made in childhood.

And I thought, Dennis Cage is a dangerous man. What he says is not truth. He only repeats what other people believe to be true.

I shouldn't have told him about Florence, how she kicked me, how she watched me from her bed. He loved her. He oughtn't to know such things. If I couldn't understand them, how could he?

But what *would* it be like—to see yourself unconscious on the floor? Why was it so terrible?

Doris, comb your hair! I can't stand to look like that! . . . Don't try that on, Doris! We look terrible in green. . . . I already used the dictionary. You don't need it. . . . And I said to ourselves, no matter what, we will not go to the prom with him.

Oh, yes, I suppose I understood, after all.

"YOU LOOK TIRED," Dennis said the next day.

"I'm not tired."

"Are you sure?"

"I'm sure."

"What do you want to talk about?"

"What happened when you went back to see Jack? After he told you not to pet the dogs?"

Dennis went back the next morning. He had bread from Lumière, cheese and wine from Goult. He said, "It's hard to throw out someone who arrives carrying food." We were all taught not to waste good food, to think about the starving children in Europe. He thought that underneath everything, Jack Pine was like him, a simple man. He thought the cheese would be his ticket in. If Jack didn't take it, it would spoil in the heat. He wasn't wrong.

So Dennis came back to Jack Pine's house, looking for an answer, wanting to know why Florence had stolen out of her life so silently and efficiently, like a thief. And Jack took him back into his house and into the room hung with her paintings—"Don't you want to see that room?" Dennis asked me. "You must want to see that room!"—and there were more paintings stacked against the wall, some in large canvas rolls, and this time Jack said, "I suppose you want to know what she looked like then; I suppose you've seen the two or three pictures they always have in the papers, but they don't really give you the idea," and he crouched down near a sofa bed and pulled out a cracked red leather-covered album.

"Here's Florence," he said, handing it to him, and then he went out onto the terrace and stood looking toward the Alps, his back to Dennis.

"And there she was, Doris," Dennis said.

There she was, holding a spoon shiny with spaghetti sauce in the kitchen, and her head was thrown back, her black hair in those wild curls about her face. Her back to the camera, painting, but she must have heard someone coming, what a beautiful straight nose, what a long, graceful neck, these were pictures no one had ever seen before. There she was, the living girl, coming up the steps, her arms full of oranges, her eyes surprised, she hadn't known he was there; sitting on the terrace, buried in a book, her feet up on a white wicker chair; the two of them standing together, heads turned to one another, smiling, always smiling, two extraordinarily beautiful, astoundingly happy people. Florence in a bathrobe, her hair wet, her face still wet as if she'd just come in from the rain and perhaps she had; Florence in a thin, flowered dress, the sun behind her, turning the edges of her black hair reddish gold; Florence bent over the dining room table, writing in a thick notebook, the kind of red notebook Dennis used to buy in England when they all lived there, all the correspondents who covered the war in Vietnam and didn't want to go home; Florence brushing her teeth, the toothpaste foaming around her lips; Florence brushing her hair; Florence in every conceivable pose, in every possible activity. Page after page.

He must have loved her.

"Do you want one?" Jack asked him when he came back in. "I have duplicates. Of some of them. Those in the beginning, they're all duplicates. Take one if you want one."

He picked a photograph of Florence holding an apple in her hand, studying it, as if to decide whether to eat it or to paint it.

"That's a good one," Jack said. He took up a rolled-up painting and spread it out. "Self-portraits," he said. "She went through a phase. She went through many phases."

And there she was again, more vivid than in the photographs, menaced by oversized furniture that threatened to topple against her, her hair spreading out through the room, not like hair but like a vine gone wild.

"The shadow's face is as detailed as hers," Dennis said. "It's the same, only fainter."

"She loved shadows. She loved doubles. She loved trees over water, cats reflected in mirrors, her reflection distorted by a car hood. Those are pretty good. If I can find them."

"She never painted you."

"She painted me," Jack said, but he didn't offer to show him those paintings, so Dennis prompted him.

"Were they good?"

"Everything she did was good. I'd show them to you, but she slashed them to ribbons. It looked like Mardi Gras time in here."

"She cut up the paintings?"

"That's what I said."

"She was angry?"

"She had a terrible temper. I told you. I never knew, not for the first five years. After that, all she did was lose it. And she sulked."

Dennis said his wife had sulked, but the sulking was like the quiet before the storm. The storm always followed.

"I can't say I know all that much about women," Jack said. "I know my reputation. It's true I love them. Probably I loved one too many. I never understood any of them. I thought I understood Florence, but there you are. I would have sworn she was the last person to take her own life, but there you are again."

Dennis asked him if he looked at these pictures often, and he said not often, once a year, usually on March 25, the only date he remembered, the date she disappeared. He couldn't remember the date of their wedding unless he looked it up, although articles and books announced it often enough. And Dennis thought, She'll always be twenty-seven.

"Dying young," Dennis said to Jack Pine, and sighed.

"Forever beautiful and forever fair. *Brightness falls from the air. Queens have died young and fair.* I should have sold her to Gypsies. She'd be alive today."

"Gypsies?"

"White slavers, then."

"Today she'd be almost fifty. Maybe wrinkled. With gray hair."

"And what's wrong with that?" Jack asked.

"As long as she was alive?"

"As long as she was above the earth and not under it. And you," he said to Dennis, "you're after a woman who's still the same as she was more than twenty years ago. You understand that?"

Dennis said he understood it.

"And if, by some miracle, she were still alive, you realize how disappointed you'd be? Because you never loved *her*. You love this myth about her. They all do. If she walked through the door now, her hair full of gray, or completely gray, that white skin of hers puffy and quilted the way it gets, the little lines at the corner of her eyes and her mouth, her chin wobbling, you'd be disappointed. Tell the truth. You'd be sorry you saw her."

"I don't know."

"But I do."

"And you?"

"I'd give anything," he said. "Anything." He struck the table hard with his fist and then rubbed one hand with the other. "We're none of us as young as we used to be. She'd be forty-seven. I'm fifty-two."

"You mean you'd want her back?"

"I'd want some answers! I'd have a thing or two to say to her!"

"But you'd want her back?"

"If she were the same? Yes. At least for a while." And he grinned at me, that mischievous grin of the early photographs. "I'm not sitting here pining away," he said. "I'm not some crazy Heathcliff waiting for his Catherine. I've kept busy."

"But you never married again."

"What was the point? In the beginning, she didn't see the point. She didn't see the point of a lot of things—like children, like travel. If she had me and a roof over her head, she had what she wanted."

"It must be wonderful to be loved like that."

"Another myth. That's the one that drives all the others, how wonderful it is to be loved like that, how wonderful to have someone who lives only to see you. In the end, that was her great gift, wasn't it? Persuading people that no one else in the world loved as well as she did. As magnificently! Those few excerpts from her journal—I don't know who got hold of them, but they did it. They cast the spell. People read what she said about how wonderfully she loved me, and if I didn't appreciate her, what was I? A monster. They would have appreciated her. They would have loved her the way she loved them. Their love would have saved her! They wouldn't have made her suffer. But they didn't live with her. They don't know what it's like to be loved like that.

"In the beginning, I told you, when biographers came here, I wanted to talk to them—you have to talk to someone—and then I'd realize. They came to find out what was wrong with me for throwing away this wonderful love. I didn't throw it away! She threw it away. No forgiveness in her, none. Love like that, it's claustrophobic. It's a demand. You're always as intense as you were at the beginning, or you're disloyal."

"But you never found anything like it later."

"I never *wanted* anything like it later. I told you that."

"I never had it at all."

"Better to have loved and suffered the torments of hell than never to have been tortured at all?"

"Something like that."

"Think before you ask for something," Jack said. "I didn't. I saw what I wanted and grabbed it. Very romantic, my image of myself in those days, like a cossack swooping down on a village, sweeping up the fairest maiden, throwing her across his saddle. But we might have been all right."

"If?"

"There was always something wrong. On her side. I don't know what it was. Oh, I don't mean I was an angel. Everyone in my family was half cracked, why should I turn out any better? She hid things. I was out in the open. The whole world saw my misdeeds. You can read about them anywhere. She didn't trust me, not from the beginning. *Never marry an orphan.* That's what my sister says now. I'll go down to the kitchen. You're hungry?"

Dennis said he was always hungry. Jack pushed the album back under the sofa bed. The paintings shimmered on the walls. "If anyone broke in here . . . ," Dennis said, and Jack said he had an alarm system and three very vicious dogs, Dobermans. Right now they were in a pen in the back of the house, but if he called them, they could clear the fence. "They'd tear up their stomachs on the wire but they'd be in here before you could count to two. If Florence were alive, they'd be useless. She couldn't say no to an animal. She made me jealous of her dog. She painted that dog fifteen times, maybe twenty. Sam. He was a great dog. He'd have died for her. She didn't take him with her when she left."

"You sound bitter."

"Wouldn't you be? Thousands of women vanish or kill themselves every year, and the world doesn't persecute their husbands, the world doesn't sit around inventing stories about them. I can't poke my nose out of a door without some crazy Florentine coming up and reading out a list of my crimes. I'm not speaking metaphorically, don't make *that* mistake. They arrive here God knows how, and they stand in the village in front of the church and they denounce me. It's the Middle Ages I live in here! There was a hammering at the door one day, early in the morning, and by the time I got down there, a sheet of paper was dangling from a nail telling me why I ought to be crucified. Any woman I take up with gets stopped on the street by some birdbrain who tells her what I'm really like. On March twenty-fifth last year, they burned me in effigy in the churchyard.

Wouldn't you be bitter? And worse than that, *I* don't know why she did
it. It's hard to live with mystery."

"There's another mystery."

"What's that?"

"Why you're talking to me."

"I told you. You had an aura."

"Come on. That's not why you're talking to me."

"Well, there was another little thing," Jack said.

"What?"

"I recognized you."

"*You* recognized *me?*"

"Let's not be modest," Jack said. "We used to wait for your columns in
the *Times*. You did interviews when your book came out. I have a copy in
my study."

"That's why you're talking to me?"

"I admired the book," Jack said.

"You mean you felt guilty because you weren't there and I was."

"I don't feel guilty but I always thought I missed something."

"You didn't miss anything," Dennis said. "Take my word for it."

"There are questions I'd like to ask *you*," Jack said. "Turnabout's fair
play."

"Not in this game."

"We'll see," Jack said. "Won't we?"

"I said everything I had to say in the book."

"Oh, I doubt that," Jack said. "You left out a lot. How you got out when
everyone else in the platoon was killed. A few small details like that."

"Maybe some other time," Dennis said. "What about Florence?"

"Time passes. By now she might be dead of natural causes. Did you
ever think of that?"

He hadn't.

Jack said, "Everyone thinks he knows the meaning of these simple
phrases: *Time passes. Everyone dies. We're all growing older.* Not many do."

"People in the valley I come from," Dennis said. "They do."

"What makes you think so?"

"They do," Dennis said. "It's the winters."

"AND AFTER THAT," Dennis said, "I thought I should leave
him alone. Until I had something to tell him. Until I could be of some
use to him."

"Are you going to tell him about me? Meeting me?"

"Not unless you say I can. Aren't you running out of tissues? Your nose is all red."

"I'm fine," I said. "Fine."

It was so quiet. I couldn't hear the sounds of traffic. The world outside the café seemed to have disappeared. Then I heard the sound of wind howling around the building. Dennis heard it too. He looked at me and smiled. The sound of the wind shrieking in chimneys in Peru.

CHAPTER

EIGHT

M Y SISTER had one vision of heaven, I had another. In my heaven, there was a world of angels, all
the same. And now she is laughing at me and saying,
"A world of identical beings, that *is* what you want! Why won't you know
yourself?" And now she is blaming me for everything that happened,
everything, since the minute we were born. She has that expression, the
one that means, If it weren't for you, I would have been like everyone else.
If it weren't for you, I would have had my own life, I would have known
what to do with it. It was you, your fault.

She means to say, If you hadn't existed, I would have been happy. I was
happy once, for a while, when I believed I was free, when I thought I had
shaken you off.

Would she have been happy? Without me? If someone had foresight-
edly and obligingly smothered me in my crib? Is that what she wanted, all
the years of our lives, for me to vanish, or if I could not simply vanish, to
stop breathing so she could stop listening for the sound of my breath,
rhythmic and endless, in the next bed, in the same room? So she would
never have to look up and see me again? Or did she know it was far too
late for that, and even if I disappeared, nothing would change, could
change, our essential natures having already been formed?

I did try, once—to vanish, to set her free. I couldn't go through
with it.

She always said she believed in imagination, its power. She would
imagine the person she wanted to be and she would become that person.
She could be whoever she wanted to be. She could be, against all odds, utterly unlike me.

She wanted, in other words, to destroy me, my nature, which was, after all, her nature; my face, which was, after all, her face.

"How can you think of it that way?" she asked me. Crying. In the days when she still cried—because we were bound so tightly together, because we were still almost the same. "You see why I say it's your fault! It *is* your fault!"

"But, Florence," I said. "I *want* to be like you. I'm happy looking like you."

It was the worst thing I could have said. How could she not think of me as her enemy—after that?

Still, it was true. There was nothing I wanted to change. I never wished her out of my way, never wished her dead. The thought of death terrified me. I drove blocks out of my way to avoid passing the funeral home. If a line of cars with their headlights on went by, I held my breath and my skin went cold. If people could die, then Florence could die, and I could not live without Florence. I always believed that. Probably I still believe it. When I was a child, I used to dream that one of us had died and was lying in a coffin in Darlington's Funeral Home, and when the one who was still living went to look at her sister in the coffin, she looked down and found herself looking at herself, and she thought if she reached out and touched herself, she could wake herself up, but she was afraid, because she knew the body would be cold, and she was afraid that the dead body would reach out for her hand and grab it by the wrist and pull her in also. It was the worst of my dreams and I always woke from it shaking.

"Monster!" said Florence. "Monster! Look what you've done!"

But what had I done? Must I be blamed? For loving her? For being born when I was?

She stared at me. "You still think you love me?" she said. And then she turned her back, so enraged she couldn't look at me. Or she was crying and wouldn't give me the satisfaction of watching tears varnish her face, making it shine in reality as I always see it shining in my mind's eye, her perfect face. Which is also my face, exactly and precisely my face, although I don't think my face is perfect. But then I don't love myself. Not as I love Florence.

"Florence cries *tiny* tears," my mother said, "while you, you cry large, round tears."

I would pinch myself, think of sad things—a kitten crushed by a car wheel, our dog bleeding at the side of the road—until I began to cry, and then I would lean in to the mirror and it was true. I cried large, round tears. But if I practiced? If I cried long enough and hard enough, couldn't I cry tiny tears? Wasn't that what our mother meant? That tiny tears were better, so delicate, so ladylike? Whereas my tears splashed down like rain from the roof's edge. Ugly tears. *She* was the beautiful one. *She* was the perfect one.

And then one day she said, "Why do we have to wear the same things? We don't even look alike."

And my mother stared at Florence, dumbstruck. "That is just ridiculous," she said. "I can't tell you apart. No one can tell you apart."

"We don't look alike," Florence said, fists clenched, one leg crossed over the other, fingers drumming on the white enamel of the kitchen table. "We don't." I thought, So that's what I would look like if I were angry. If I could ever be that angry—at anyone.

I started to cry, large tears, ugly tears.

"Now look what you've done," my mother said.

Florence got up from the table, she knocked over her chair, she ran from the room, she stomped up the stairs. That night, she sat upright on her bed, suddenly, the blankets falling from her, and said, "You don't even know the meaning of the word *I*."

"And you do?" I said.

"I will!"

"We never will, we can't," I said, and she lay back down, and I pretended to sleep, and later I heard her crying, and when I heard her crying, I was happy. Did she know I was awake, listening? Did she know how happy I was because she was miserable? Of course she knew. We always knew. She could be miles away, in the next town, in another country, and I knew. As she always knew about me.

Were you envious when your sister became so famous? Were you jealous? Of her?

No. How can you be jealous of yourself?

Didn't you ask yourself, Could I have done it? Could I have done the same thing?

No. We knew. If one could do something, so could the other.

Why did her marriage fail? Everyone wants to know. She was so happy for a long time. Whose fault was it? Her husband's, wasn't it? Infidelity, wasn't it? His, of course, his. But she loved him, didn't she? Everyone wants to love like that. Didn't you envy her that? How could you not?

How can you envy yourself? It was as if I had also married him, wasn't it? It was as if I also loved him. Wasn't it? Wasn't it, Florence?

———

IN THE CAFÉ WINDOW, she shakes her head at me. Sadly. She smiles in exasperation. How long can I go on believing such stupid things? *You don't know the first thing about him. You can't imagine what it was like. You don't have the least idea. Don't talk to people about me!* But I do have an idea of what he was like. I do. I turn my back to the window and she vanishes. These days I can control her appearances and disappearances. It's like having her with me, only better.

Idiot! she says. *You believe I am here! With you! Why would I want to be here with you?*

These are the conversations of nightmares.

But I am getting ahead of myself.

I was thinking about love and the many ways it goes wrong. That is my subject, really, the unthinkable ways it goes wrong, and the separation that takes place after it goes wrong, and I considered this every day as I sat in Eva's Café, the little café in England's Lane where I would come when I finished writing or making a new piece of jewelry because it was exactly one mile from where I lived and I needed the exercise. Or so the doctor said. *We all need exercise, don't we, Mrs. James?* And when I got there, I would sit down at a little table, a small round of marble atop a wrought-iron base, every table in the café the same. I notice such things, doubles, duplications, surfaces that reflect, identical buildings joined together into a huge crescent. These are beautiful to me. Salt and pepper shakers in pairs, a bunch of daisies, every one the same, two gloves flung down on a tabletop, two damp shoes set over a heating vent, the peacocks across the street, eight of them, four males, four females, the males the same, the females the same, eight peacocks out for a walk, eight of them, like eight peasant women out for a walk, stopping at every flight of steps, tilting their heads back on their long necks, staring up at the front doors of the attached buildings.

I'm disturbed by too much difference.

I dislike my own jewelry. No two pieces are ever the same. But if I put a lizard in front of a mirror, then it seems there are two of them. Then I can decide if I have done well or badly.

There is no consistency in my attitudes. Don't look for it. How could I be consistent? A *person* can be consistent. I'm not a person. I never wanted to be a person. *In her own right. Secure in herself. Me. My. Myself.* None of these expressions ever made sense to me. I expect they never will. Not now.

I am a half-sister. Under a half-moon my watch measures half-time while I am living my half-life.

This is my mathematics. What is one and one? One (because each one is half). What is one divided in two? One (because each one is half). What is a half? Nothing human.

Of course, what seems simple to one person is not uncomplicated to another. How many hours in the day? Forty-eight. How many presents for the two of us on a birthday? One. You see yourself reflected in a mirror. How many of you are there? Two. Which is real, the mirror or the reflection? Both.

ᴛʜᴇ ᴄᴀꜰᴇ́. Eva's. I love it as if it were a person. And what is it but one huge, soaring room fronting on the street, a room with its front wall knocked out and replaced by an enormous window. The right wall is mirrored, and if you sit at the best table, you see yourself reflected twice, once in the window overlooking the street, and once in the mirror. And I sit there for hours, looking at myself doubled, the reflection in the mirror vivid and solid as flesh, the reflection in the window vivid when the street darkens and the rain comes down, wavering and flimsy when the sun is out—a ghost.

I love the wide, tall window, its generous view of the street, I love the street, connected houses half hidden behind trees, I love watching the weather change outside the café, I love to sit at my table, eating a chicken sandwich, watching the people across the street wait for the bus, watching the dark umbrellas begin to flower as the rain begins to fall, the water on the window streaming, someone opening the café door and coming in, soaking wet, shaking himself slightly, smiling ruefully at whoever looks up from the newspapers the café provides, by now smudged, here and there translucent where greasy fingers have handled them, then sitting down, looking at the hopeless menu, trying to decide what is least expensive and least dreadful, ordering finally—as everyone new to the café does, as people in this situation always seem to—an egg sandwich. These events keep me busy and as happy as I ever am. The world doesn't have to entertain me. I sit at the café table for hours, thinking.

Once upon a time there were twin sisters. They were very beautiful and very intelligent (or so everyone said) and they should have turned out well, but they didn't. They loved one another and should have been able to protect one another, but they couldn't. What happened?

Sometimes I think of Dennis and what he looked like asleep, and sometimes he turns into Jack Pine, asleep, and sometimes he turns into the Impostor, asleep, and then I am afraid and can't get my breath and my hands grow cold and my nose is cold to the touch. And then I think of my husband, sleeping his hot sleeps that always warmed the bed for me, but I don't wonder what I'm doing here and why he's not here with me.

LAST NIGHT when I went to bed the rain had just begun falling. It left little sequins of light on the windows. It fell without sound. Several hours later, when the lightning woke me, the small rain had become a downpour. It hammered against the skylight and sounded like hail. It streamed over the windows in a solid sheet of water the streetlights turned to silver.

In the morning, the sun was out, streaming into the room, which seemed, nevertheless, to hold on to the thunderous darkness of the night before, but by noon the light was triumphant and then it was difficult to remember the storm, how the house shook with the thunder, how the furniture leaped out when the lightning flashed, not the same as it was in the daylight but drained of color and detail. How hard it was to believe that when the light came back, everything would be as it had been before.

THE CAFÉ, run by an older, thin, voluble Serbian woman, was a haven for refugees—for the Serbian community who lived nearby or who traveled long distances on the tube to get there, for South Africans who had lived first in France and then came to London—for American expatriates writing screenplays and plotting to stay on longer, local writers and painters, stage and TV actors and actresses who came here to be interviewed if their apartments were beyond cleaning, old age pensioners who had little money and less to do with their time. Some were regulars and some were people who lived in the neighborhood and came in before a film began at the Screen on the Hill. And everyone could stay as long as he liked, spending three or four hours over a single cup of coffee, while others, who had money to spend, who did not regard the café as the final setting for the last act of their lives, went down a short flight of steps into a large back room, which no one noticed the first few times he came in and probably never would have noticed if Eva hadn't looked up and seen a new customer hesitating just inside the doorway, looking from one table to another, disappointed when he saw they were occupied, turning back to the door, ready to leave, until Eva came up to him and said cheerfully, "Would you like a table downstairs? There's smoking downstairs."

And after a while one could distinguish the regulars from the others, the ones who came in and picked up menus and ordered quickly, ate quickly while they read their newspapers, were unaware of the elaborate system of etiquette that governed behavior among the regulars in the café, each of whom had a table he regarded as his own, so that if you came in and found one such table unoccupied, you didn't sit at it but sat at another table, which was often empty for days, smiled apologetically at the "owner" of *that* table if he came in, never asked someone would he mind if you sat at his table, not unless every other table in the café was occupied, and then got up as soon as another table was empty.

Privacy was important. Privacy was respected. The café was so small. You caught on quickly. If you came in and saw someone you knew, you pretended not to see him until you had ordered your coffee and gone through at least one daily paper. Then you looked up, pretended to be surprised, happily surprised, to see someone you knew there, made tentative and ambiguous gestures of invitation, which, just as tentatively and ambiguously received, permitted someone to get up, come over to your table, and say, I was just leaving, so good to see you, and how is your hip?

Unless you said, Oh, please sit down, unless you were insistent, whoever it was would say, No, no, I really have to go soon, oh, look, I've left my books at the other table, I'll just go back there and finish my coffee, will you be here tomorrow? Not tomorrow, but Wednesday? Good! We'll have a long talk Wednesday.

At Eva's Café, people took no chances, did not make scenes even outside the café window but walked down the block to the corner, crossed over to the pharmacy, and shouted at one another to their heart's content. There. But not in front of the café.

The crippled artist sketching in the corner knew better than to sketch the South African woman in the red shawl. She had made a scene, not in the café, oh, no, she knew better than that, she had waited for him outside on the sidewalk and then told him she didn't like people drawing her, with or without her permission. Would he please stop or she'd have to sit at the table near the counter because there he couldn't see her from his table.

He promised her, he swore, never again would he sketch her, but from then on she was alerted. If she saw him looking over at her, she paid attention, if he looked at her and then down at his sketch pad, she stood up, paid the bill, stopped at several other tables, whispered pointedly to people she knew there. They looked at the artist, shook their heads, stared at him until he became uncomfortable, until Eva herself came over and asked what was the trouble. The artist stopped sketching the South African woman, at least in the café. If he could remember her features well enough, he could sketch her when he went home. What could she do about that? But not here.

O N C E, when the rain came down steadily, I began doodling on a piece of paper. I sensed someone watching me, a very thin woman, about twenty-five, her long, dirty-blond hair oily. She pushed her hair back repeatedly, and each time she did this, she stared at me from beneath her hand. In that second that her hand was poised at her forehead as if she were saluting, I wasn't sure. Did she think she recognized my sister?

So I got up, paid my check, came back to the table and put on my raincoat, and went out the door, and the girl thought I was gone, and when I looked back in, she had gotten up, gone over to my table, picked up the sheet of paper I left there, looked at its scribbled triangles and squares, shaken her head, sat back down. And I thought, Well, they're more polite here than at home. They wait until they think you're not looking, until you've finished your coffee. I shouldn't mind. She wasn't a reporter, that girl; an admirer, a worshiper, probably.

I wanted to come into the café to think, but most of all to feel *alone,* to feel, finally, that condition everyone has so much to say about—aloneness, loneliness, how awful loneliness is. I've noticed that people tend to say this after someone has died, usually a husband or wife, and then, usually about fourteen months later, the same people—usually women—go on about the joys of solitude, how they're discovering things about themselves they'd never known, as if they'd never lived in their own bodies, as if the houses of their lives had been full of locked rooms they only now dared to enter, and I listen to them and think, The euphoric stage. When it passes, they will look enviously at couples, any couples, not only human ones, even ducks on a pond, animals in pet shop windows sharing the same cage, and if they had seen me standing next to my sister, they would have been ravished by jealousy and envy. How could they not have been?

If Eva hadn't spoken to me first, I never would have spoken to her. But one day when the café was almost empty, she came up to my table and said, "You're not from this country, are you?" and when I said no, she said, "Oh, you can always tell, but what confused me was how at home you seemed. You must have spent a lot of time here," and I said I had, and she said, "I'm not from here, either, almost no one in this café is, although I'd be hard put to say where I am from, well, I'm from Serbia, originally. So I should say, I'm from Serbia, shouldn't I?" And I asked her to sit down. And she said, "There! You see? If you were a Londoner, you wouldn't ask me to sit down, not a woman you weren't properly introduced to. Last week I was walking along, it was late at night, and you know the joke here? If you see a well-dressed man, and he's walking along smoking and says hello to you on the street, he's a psychoanalyst from South Africa. I saw a woman walking in front of me, and she stopped to look in a window, and since it was late and dark, I went up to her and said, 'Would you mind if I walked along with you, for safety?' And she said, 'Oh, no, what a good idea,' and I thought, *Not* an Englishwoman! So I said, 'Shall I guess your nationality?' and she said, 'By all means,' and I said, 'You're a psychoanalyst and you're from South Africa,' and she stopped dead and said to me, 'How did you know?' and I laughed and told her the joke, and we walked together until I turned off. Someday she'll come in here. Sooner or later everyone does."

Well, she had commandeered me. That's the way to handle me, after all. I am the half-sister, and it was never my job to make the first move, to make friends, to say, *This is what I want.* Don't leave me to make my own decisions. I expect other people to make them.

"What do you want to do?" my husband would ask me, and this was how a fight would begin.

"Whatever you want to do."

"I want to do whatever you want to do."

"You decide."

And it would always end the same way. "Can't you make up your mind about anything?" my husband would ask me. "I know why you want me to decide! Then if anything goes wrong, it's not your fault! It's my fault! I'll be the one to blame!"

And I would cry and say I *never* accused him of anything. If we went to the wrong movie, if *he* thought we'd gone to the wrong movie, it wasn't *his* fault, was it? He hadn't made the movie, had he? But he would accuse me of selfishness when it wasn't selfishness at all. What did I want to do? I had no idea. And even if I did know, did I want to do anything *desperately?* Did it matter to me one way or another? And if nothing mattered, not really, why shouldn't we do what my husband wanted to do? In every possible way, didn't I try to please him? Would he have been happy if I had said, "No, I don't want to go out. I don't want to go for a walk, you go"? If I had begun to rebel? If I had suddenly—at my age—developed preferences of my own? Become, in other words, my sister?

"At least," he said, "at *least* Florence never had trouble making up her own mind. At least you didn't have to sit there for hours guessing what it was she might possibly want to do," and I would cry out, "Tell me what you want to do! How can it be selfish to ask *you* what *you* want to do?"

And the last fight, when he said, "We're not going anywhere, we're not doing anything, until you tell me what you want to do, if I have to take three weeks off from work, or two months, or three months, we're sitting right here until you decide what you want to do." And I said, "I want to go to London." And he said, "Alone?" As if he'd never heard the word before. And I said, "You told me you wanted me to tell you what I wanted to do. I told you. Happy now?" And he said he was—very happy. And afterward he looked at me differently. He *flirted* with me. He was *suspicious* of me. I knew what he was thinking. Is this really my wife? Or is this Florence? Did they change places? They're capable of it. No one knows where Florence is, everyone says she's disappeared, maybe she's here, maybe this is how she's hiding.

"I am not Florence," I told him. "I'm Doris. And I'm going to London. I intend to escape from the Impostor."

"Of course you're not Florence," he said.

"Then who am I?"

"You're Doris," he said, but now he was suspicious again. How did he know? Really *know?*

"You'll just have to take my word for it," I said wearily. He was so unreasonable, so ridiculous. Better than anyone, he knows who I am. Still, the suspicion is always there.

If I were sitting there saying, We'll do whatever you want to do, he'd know which was which. No one would tell Florence to do whatever she wanted to do; he might find himself rappelling down a sheer cliff in Nepal or photographing rats scurrying over a hotel roof garden in Vietnam.

My mother told him, "She wants to go somewhere where no one knows she's a twin. She wants to go to London because Florence didn't like London."

What nonsense!

My mother, who could have saved us.

Although it was true. I had no intention of telling people I was a twin. What possible business was it of theirs? If she were here, that would be one thing. But to tell people I'm a twin and to have them ask, "Identical?" and when I said, "Yes, identical," to watch them begin their calculations. Oh, I see. There are two of them! And watch them change, nothing obvious. They're careful not to make it obvious. Now when they looked at me I'd be transformed—into something like a plate in a department store, a very nice plate, but there are identical plates. Why settle for this one when the other one may be nicer? But everything twice! What a torment that is.

"Doris," my mother said, "your father is dying." If she hadn't told me then, she wouldn't have been able to tell me at all. But Florence wasn't home.

"Can't you tell her for me?" my mother asked. "I can't go through it again."

No, no, I couldn't. She had to tell Florence.

"But she'll only wait until I'm gone and then she'll ask you, 'Is it true?'" my mother said. "Tell her!"

I said I couldn't.

"The two of you!" my mother shouted. "Selfish! Selfish! Selfish! From the beginning! Selfish!"

"I'VE BEEN THINKING about death," Eva said, as she was sitting down at my table. "Do you ever think about death? You're American, aren't you? They say Americans don't talk about death, but one or two must *think* about it. Well, I think about far too many things, some people say so. But it keeps you alive and young, doesn't it? Especially things no one else thinks about, although in this place people must think about death; there's hardly anyone English in here. But you must tell me if talking about death upsets you. You've been sitting so quietly, I thought, Perhaps someone has just died, perhaps that's what she's doing in here, getting over it. When my father died, I sat here for two months without saying a word, just staring out at the bus stop on the other side of the street."

I sighed a great, silent sigh of relief. This woman wouldn't wait for me to begin a conversation. No, she was one of the people who always made me happy, a woman satisfied and pleased with her own thoughts, existing in a perpetual state of delighted surprise that she herself, without benefit of reading or conversation, had come to such interesting conclusions. Such a woman was wonderful company; she would value me, the perfect audience, so happy to listen, so unwilling to interrupt, much less contradict her. She would be better than Dennis, because she wouldn't ask many questions. She wouldn't want much from me.

First Dennis had commandeered me, and now this woman. Perhaps together they could make something of me. A person. I was always optimistic.

Eva, this possible sculptor of souls—my soul.

"Well, then, Doris," she said (I had told her my name almost immediately, my name and where I lived on Perceval Road), "death. You're sure this subject won't disturb you?"

"I'm too old to be disturbed by death," I said. This wasn't true, but I wanted to know what she had to say about it. She was so excited. She had the energy of a very young child, and I thought, She may have found out something. It's always possible.

"Well, you know what they say, that we can't imagine ourselves dead, that we can't even dream we're dead? That when we try to imagine what the world would be like when we're dead, what we're really doing is imagining ourselves looking at the world—so we can never picture our own death? You've heard that? I don't believe it, I won't accept that, it's all hogwash. Because you could practice. You could imagine this café without you in it. You could imagine this street, the cars, other people walking up and down the block, couldn't you? Try."

I tried. And for an instant, there was the world going on without me, the café full of people, none of whom remembered me, the street full of strangers, none of whom I knew. And then I couldn't continue. I shuddered and looked at Eva.

"It's generosity to the world that makes us incapable of imagining our own deaths, yes, generosity! To destroy all these buildings and all these people and all the apple strudel in the case over there, all the umbrellas outside, and the cars and the buses and the rain clouds and the rain and the dark-green leaves like porches in the air, how can we imagine it? If we imagine it, might it not happen? Yes, yes, that's what I think about death, that's why we fear it, I think. We're not selfish and cowardly, no, we simply have primitive minds, we're all savages, but kindly savages! We're . . . what's the word I'm looking for?"

"Altruistic," I said.

"Exactly! Altruistic! How did you know? No one ever knows what word I'm looking for. That's most extraordinary."

"I wish it were more extraordinary," I said.

"Why? Can you read minds? I've known people who can. I can, not all the time, of course, not if I have a headache. Then I can't read anything, not even a newspaper headline, but I don't admit this to everyone, people are so ready to say you're mad. Just now I looked up and thought I saw you sitting at another table! Probably I am a little mad, don't you think so? I think most refugees are."

"I really don't know you very well," I said.

Eva put down her coffee cup and started to laugh. "Well, that's refreshing, not to be told, 'Of course you're not mad,' when I could be, you know. Every other person's entirely mad these days. Last week two women came in here and sat at the next table, and one asked the other, 'Do you and your husband have this hate thing between you?' and when the other said they didn't, the first one said, 'You will. Give yourself another ten years.' You hear the most amazing conversations. Well, you can't help it, can you? There's only a few inches between tables. And when people don't know you, they think, Well, she has no reason to listen to us, and even if she listens, she doesn't know who we are, so what difference does it make?

"But I think it makes a difference, other people picking up pieces of your soul and looking them over and taking them home and weaving them into their own nests and suddenly you're part of other people's lives. No, I think you should be careful. Strangers are not always benevolent. There was a sad young man in here last week, something about your eyes reminded me of him, very dark hair, like yours, and I thought, That sad young man is not benevolent. He's looking for someone, and when he finds her he means her harm. I haven't seen him for days, that angry man, very young, much younger than we are. He looked like you but he had an accent—Spanish, I think. I listened when he gave in his order. Tell me, do you think about such things?"

A sad young man who looked like me! Could he have come to the café? Could he have been here, watching me as I peacefully drank my coffee? I felt light-headed and then I realized I had forgotten to breathe.

"Do you think about such things?" Eva asked me again.

Forget about the Impostor, I told myself. He isn't here. You'll never hear from him again. Answer this woman.

"About sad young men stealing my soul?"

"Not stealing! Knowing it! Drawing conclusions! Letting their lives be influenced by your life, people you don't even know!"

"There are so many mirrors in this room," I said.

"I don't like them," Eva said. "Not anymore. The things they have to say to me! So rude! But they make the café seem large, don't they? And brighter. They multiply the light. Do you mind mirrors?"

"Not the kind you hang on the wall," I said.

"What kind of mirrors *do* you mind?"

I made a motion with my hand, as if I were about to brush away a fly. "Oh, I don't mind about mirrors," I said.

FLORENCE MINDED mirrors, she minded them very much—Florence, who didn't want to look like me, Florence who opened the door when I went to see her in Goult, who took one look at me and saw that I had cut my hair just as she had cut hers and now we looked identical once more, Florence who looked at the black dress I wore and down at the dress she was wearing, the same dress, only dark purple, who said, "It always happens! She goes shopping in Manhattan and I go shopping in Aix and we come home with the same dress! How is it even possible to buy the same dress in different countries?" Who asked me had I been ill, I looked so much older. Who stared at me and then walked over to the mirror and touched her own face in horror, who said, "I never know what I look like until I see you; if it weren't for you . . ."

The old song—if it weren't for me, she'd be different, she'd be a law unto herself. Even snowflakes, tiny, mindless, cold things, no two of them were the same. Wasn't it everyone's birthright, wasn't it the point of evolution?—new combinations, uniqueness, something new and precious on the face of the earth. How many times had I heard this, how many times had I said, Those people you envy, those unique people, they spend their lives looking for someone who's just like them, half the tragedies on the planet, *all* the tragedies on the planet, don't they come from one person trying to force another person to be just like him, isn't that what happens? Isn't that what you're doing to your husband, Florence! Isn't it?

But I didn't say any of this. She'd heard it before. It would only madden her. Instead I said, "If it weren't for me . . . ?"

"If it weren't for you, I'd be . . ."

"Happy?"

"Yes, happy!"

"We were never happy. You're a child, a baby, you're *hopeless!* You weren't put on this earth to be *like* someone else!"

"How do you know that? How do you know that wasn't exactly why we were put on this earth? Because we were meant to be alike! Because we were meant to be happy! Together! Because we weren't meant to waste our lives looking for soul mates! Because we already had our soul mates!"

And now (as I stand in her doorway in Goult—no one knows I went to see her there, not even my husband) she says, "Not again! Not this drivel!"

"Florence! It isn't drivel!"

She says, "Will you come inside? I don't want the neighbors to know about you!" She grabbed me by the wrist, she pulled me in, she pushed the heavy wooden door closed behind me. "Do we have to stand here arguing like fishwives? The neighbors listen to everything. Do you want something cold to drink?"

The neighbors. If they were looking out the window while Florence and I argued, what would they have seen? They would have seen me and thought I was Florence. They wouldn't have seen Florence, standing back in the dark doorway. They would have thought Florence was arguing with someone inside the house, and if they understood English, and I doubt that they did, they wouldn't have known what to make of what they heard. I might as well have been invisible, as I always was when Florence was there.

"Were you painting?" I asked her. On her arms and hands were smudges of blue paint, a grayish blue, the color of the skies over our house in Peru before the snow came.

"Oh, yes. I paint every day. You know that."

"Do you mind if I look?" I got up and walked from painting to painting before she could answer.

"Don't think you could have painted the same things," she said. "You couldn't."

"If I had wanted to," I said.

"You didn't have the ambition. Why can't you admit it?"

"The ambition to do what, Florence? To take it back from you? I let you be the painter."

"You *let* me be the painter?" she repeated incredulously. "You *let* me keep something I'd stolen?"

"The truth is too simple for you," I said. "It always was. Tell me, Florence. Who started painting first?"

"Who *stopped* first?"

"I stopped because you started!"

"What is the matter with you?" she shouted. "Why are you fighting with me? I thought you came here to help me! You *never* fight with me!"

"We should have spelled out these rules, Florence! Every few years we should have gone over them and decided if we wanted to keep them the same or change them."

"What are you talking about? What rules?"

"What rules? The rule that says I'm not to visit you unless you invite me? The one that says I can't come here unless Jack is off somewhere? The rule that says you can call me or visit me whenever it suits you? The rule that says I'm to pine for you and I'm to pretend I don't mind it, I like it! The rule that says you're the talented one and we all have to defer to you because you're delicate and special and valuable and I'm a copy! No one has to bother about me! I'm tired of it, Florence!"

"It's because you know I'm weak, isn't it? It's because you know I'm in trouble. That's why you have the nerve to turn on me like this! For no reason!"

"What do you mean—weak? What do you mean—in trouble?"

And she said, "He doesn't want me anymore, I don't feel like a woman anymore. I don't know what to do!"

"You've had a fight; everyone fights. My husband and I fight. For heaven's sake, you and I fight. Where *is* Jack?"

She said she didn't know where he'd gone. She thought he'd gone to Sweden with the troupe. She thought he was in Stockholm staying with friends. They were rehearsing his new play. It was all because of the red dress; they'd argued about the red dress. She couldn't let things go on this way. She couldn't live with a man who treated her like that. She couldn't live *at all*. He was her world, he'd been her world for seven years. Don't talk to her about how life changes! She didn't want her life to change! Don't talk to her about compromising, accepting the way things were. She didn't want to compromise, she wasn't *accepting*, she'd rather die. He'd always been frightened of her, that's what he said: *I've always been frightened of you. You won't be happy until you swallow me up. No man could live like this.*

"What did he mean, he was frightened of you? What did he mean, no man could live like this?"

"I don't know!"

"You do know."

"I don't!"

"If you're too afraid to tell me—"

"I'm not afraid! He's the one who's afraid!"

"Of what, Florence? Of what exactly?"

"Oh, who pays attention to what he says? He gets carried away by crazy ideas. He's afraid of things and he blames it all on me. What he says doesn't *mean* anything."

"Exactly *what* does he say?"

"Oh, nonsense, Doris! Four arms and four legs! He's not a woman, he doesn't want to become a woman, he doesn't want to *feel* everything I feel. One of these days he's going to look in the mirror and he'll see my face, growing a beard! He's entitled to his own skin, isn't he, that's not asking too much, is it? He says I don't understand skin. What is he talking about—his own skin? How can anyone *understand* skin? I don't want his skin! It's mad stuff, he doesn't mean any of it!"

"He doesn't want to become a woman? What does he *mean*, Florence, what does that *mean*?"

"That I'm swallowing him up! That I *chew* on him! That I won't be happy until we've digested each other. That we ought to get into a Waring blender together, that's what I really want. His soul isn't his own, I take him over, I overpower him, all kinds of stuff like that. He doesn't believe it! He *wants* to be close. It's what he always wanted. I know!"

"But he says it isn't what he always wanted?"

"Oh, he says he wanted it once, but he didn't realize, he didn't see what it meant, he didn't realize it meant burying yourself alive. There's not enough air for him when I'm in a room, I'm a fire burning up all the air. Doris, who can listen to such nonsense! He means he's tired of me, that's what he means, he means he's not strong enough to be faithful, that's what he means. Well, that's clear enough. God!"

"Florence," I said, "he may mean what he says."

"He doesn't!"

"Florence, remember what happened before we went to college? Remember what *you* were like when we were in college? How is he behaving differently? Isn't he behaving the way you were then?"

"It's not the same! He's not my twin!"

"Oh, well," I said, "I don't know about that!"

"What are you talking about? You see twins everywhere! Mother says she always knows who a card's from before she reads it. Yours always have two cats on them! I always have one large cat. A tree over water, it's from you. You don't know what you're talking about!"

"He feels like he's turning into you. Doesn't he? Didn't he say that?"

"So what, Doris? He'll say anything. He feels guilty because of that blond slut, Tobie. It doesn't matter what he says!"

"But he did say it? He's turning into you?"

"So what! So what! Tomorrow he'll say he's turning into a porcupine, and *that* will be his excuse. I'm not listening to him!"

"Maybe you should."

"You're taking his side! How can you take his side? You're *my* sister!"

"I'm on your side, you know I'm on your side."

"You're not! You don't care what happens to me! You're just like everyone else. You used to say you'd die for me, remember? You'd rather die than live without me? Remember that? And now you're taking his side!"

She was crying, hysterical, digging at her eyes with her fist, picking up the hem of her dress, wiping her streaming cheeks with her skirt, and I thought, Any second she'll jump up, she'll be out that door, and God knows what she'll do. There are *precipices* in back of this house. Don't try to reason with her. It only makes things worse. She's just like our mother.

"He's my whole world, *he is my whole world,*" she said. Her voice was forlorn, worse than a bell tolling late when someone had just died.

Of course I forgot I was angry at her. Her face was swollen, not just her eyes but her entire face, as if she'd been underwater for hours, as if she'd drowned.

I said, "Forget about him and what he says. It isn't important. Tell me about the red dress, and I'll comb out the tangles in your hair."

"Don't touch my hair! You see that dog? That dog's the only reason I'm alive! There's no one else to look after him. What a reason to live, to keep the dog alive! I took *six* sleeping pills last night. Six! I wanted a good night's sleep. They didn't work. Nothing works!"

"Tell me about the dress."

"Doris, I have an idea," she said, grabbing my hands. "Wait for him! Wait until he comes back! Pretend you're me! *You* don't care about him!"

"I think he is a deplorable, despicable person."

"You don't even know what he's done."

"If he's done this to you, he's deplorable and despicable."

"He is! I know he is. But he controls me. Doris, he does! I've started to leave fifty times in the last month, and then he comes home and talks to me while he's cooking, and the sound of his voice . . . ! He says, 'You're hysterical, you'll get over it, you'll feel different in the morning,' all the things you said! He picks me up and swings me around, he says how middle class I am and it's not *all* his fault. Nothing is *ever* all one person's fault. He *still* doesn't know about you. He thinks I'm an orphan, he doesn't know anything about the family. He doesn't think there *is* a family."

"Why not, Florence? What did you think we would do? Did you think we'd come camp out on your doorstep?"

"Oh, I'm *sick* of it! Sick of it! He doesn't know the meaning of the word *fidelity*. It's not important to him, that's what he says. *I'm* important to him. But not important enough to leave that blond slut alone! He was bringing her here! Into this house! He had every intention of bringing her in. Here! He expected me to serve biscuits and jam and make coffee and politely discuss our *situation*. I wasn't going to do that! You wouldn't do that! Would you do it? I went out the back way and sat down in a café. I'd like to see him bring her to me there, with all the good men and women of the town watching. After all, he has to go on living here. He *wants* to live here. He says he'll never go back to the States.

"He wanted to sit her down in *my* living room and discuss separation, he intended to say, 'Florence, I want to be fair. As if he knows what the word means! As if he had the right to say my name! To speak to me in front of her! He wanted to ask if I'd agree to a trial separation and he'd live part of the week with her and part of the week with me. We'd have joint custody! Of him! The current arrangement—*arrangement*—isn't working, is it?

"I can't face him! You do it! You can see why I can't face him! If you'd stay here, pretend you're me—it wouldn't be hard, Doris, we used to do it all the time. It wouldn't take too long. Tell him you're leaving and you never want to see him again. You can do it!"

"How can I do that, Florence? I'm a terrible liar. How can I stand here and tell him I don't love him and I don't want to see him anymore? Think about it, Florence. He'd *think* I was his wife. He might just decide to take me to bed. How would I stop him? If I said, 'Look, Jack, put me down, you have the wrong twin,' he'd think we'd lost our minds, he wouldn't listen, and then what? I'm not going to bed with your husband! And he'd *know*. He'd know I wasn't you."

"He wouldn't. Can Mother tell us apart? Even now?"

"Florence, I'm not going to be raped by your husband!"

"He's not a rapist."

"I don't want to find out!"

"You won't do it?"

"No."

"Not even if it would save my life?"

"*Why* would it save your life? Leave a note. Say cold things in a note. Florence, this is a lunatic idea."

"I want to see his face," she said.

"But you won't be here!"

"*You'll* tell me what he looked like. You'll tell me what he said."

"What difference does it make what he said? What difference does it make what he looked like? If you're leaving."

"You don't understand," she said hopelessly.

"Oh, I understand. You want to torture him and you don't have the nerve to do it yourself."

"He'll be back soon, he'll want to discuss his reasonable requests. 'We're stuck, we can't get out of this, we're a car spinning its wheels in a ditch. If we lived apart, if I lived with her for a while, I might come back, probably I would come back'—he'll say that, very reasonably, Doris! And I'll start to scream and shutters up and down the street will start slamming and in the morning I'll be too disgraced to go out."

"Why should you be disgraced? *He's* the one who ought to be disgraced. When did you start worrying about what people think?"

"I don't care what people think. *You* care what people think."

I wasn't going to argue with her. She was a frightening enough sight, her face red, her eyes streaming, her hands clenched into fists, her black, wildly curling hair matted and gnarled as if she'd been sleeping in the woods for weeks. And *I* was frightened. What if she was serious? What if she couldn't think of a good reason to stay alive? I hadn't seen her in seven years, but always I knew she was there. Always I knew I could find her— as she'd found me.

"How many sleeping pills have you got?" I asked her.

"Sleeping pills?" That innocent look, that bland voice, *my* innocent look, *my* innocent tone. So she did have them.

"You have two hundred," I said.

"Two hundred and four."

My scalp went cold, and my hands. "I'm tired," I said. "Give me a couple. For the jet lag."

"You'll look for them when I fall asleep and you'll pour them down the toilet. I know you, Doris."

"Two pills. That's all I'm asking for. I'd give you two of mine if I had them."

"Do you really expect to fool me?" she asked.

Even then—facing my sister, the strong one, the one who always knew her own mind, who made all the decisions for us, the leader—even faced by her, shaking and hysterical, her face bloated, the skin beneath her eyes smudged and grayish blue—even then I was happy. We were in the same room and I was looking at her face, which was my face, still my face, I was listening to her voice, which was my voice.

My sister, my beloved creature.

"WHY WON'T YOU kiss each other?" our mother asked. "It's a birthday party, isn't it?" And my sister said, "It would be silly, like kissing myself."

"You kiss your sister," our mother said to me, and I said, "No, I don't want to kiss her," and our mother said, "Why not?" and I said, "Leave me alone! I don't have to kiss her if I don't want to kiss her."

"They won't do it, not ever," our mother said, exasperated. " 'I'm not kissing a mirror,' that's what she said." And Dr. Steiner was there (he was always there), and he said, "Elfrieda, we don't know what it's like for them. Really, we don't. How can we know?"

Our mother said, "As long as they don't start fighting again. I can't stand it when they fight. It's a nightmare! The same person, attacking itself!"

"Don't talk that way in front of the girls," Dr. Steiner said.

"I came in last night and they had each other by the hair and you know what one said? She said, 'She's trying to rip our head from our necks.' "

"They always did murder the language, Elfrieda," he said.

"Remember? 'Personally, I ourselves don't remember that.' Remember when Florence said that?"

"It was Doris."

"It was Florence!"

"Does it make any difference?" Dr. Steiner asked her.

"It *should.* Shouldn't it?"

"Ask them," Doctor Steiner said.

Florence was right. She'd always hated us.

"Florence," I said, "the red dress."

"Didn't I tell you? I didn't? No? I took too many pills last night. I shouldn't take so many."

"Florence!"

"It's a long story. It's hot. Don't you want something to drink?"

I said I wasn't thirsty. My tongue was dry and stuck like cotton wool to the roof of my mouth.

"He said he was going to Sweden for a week and I asked him—I couldn't stop myself—I asked him if Tobie was going, and he looked at me as if I were a madwoman, and said, 'Actually, no.' And I said, 'Actually, no? Why not? Is she busy? Shopping for her trousseau?' And he said it wasn't anything like that, and I said he was lying, and he began sighing deeply. Doris, he has the most wonderful sighs. You're sorry to suffer because your suffering upsets him! And I asked when he was going, and he said in the morning, and I asked how he'd get there, and he said he'd take a taxi to the airport, and I said, You'll never pay for a taxi all the way to the airport, and he sighed again and said Tobie was driving him to Marseilles and then she'd come back and I'd see her in the village. And I said, 'Oh, good, where would I be without Tobie?'

"And he wanted to know if it was all settled and he could pack in peace, and I said of course he could, I'd have the dog to look after me, and then he wanted to know, was he worrying about the wrong person? Should he be worrying about Tobie? He asked *me* if *I* meant any harm to Tobie—I mean, Doris, how stupid! Would I tell him if I did?—and I said Tobie was a punishment to herself, she didn't need help from me, and he said, Then it's me you're after, and I said I wasn't after him. All I wanted was for him to go. And then he went off somewhere with his suitcase, and he came back in with it and he said he wasn't going to Sweden after all—not for another few days. But I'd had a drink and taken a few pills and I was beyond him. There wasn't much more he could do to me, and he said something, and I started laughing at him, I don't remember *what* he said.

"He wanted me to go to a party they were giving for him, for his play *Three Raven Wood*. I didn't want to go. I never want to go. I'm happy home alone. He said it wasn't a matter of my being sociable or not sociable. I was making people unhappy. I had to go. So he was giving me an ultimatum. I understood that. You know, Doris, I didn't even read the play. It's been lying around here for weeks and I haven't read it. I can't concentrate, that's what I told him. If I read it, I'd know—if he was thinking of leaving, if he's thinking of moving that dreadful Tobie in here. I wouldn't put it past him. I wouldn't put anything past him."

I asked her, "How did this happen? The last time I saw you, you were so happy."

"Maybe he knows. Sometimes I think he knows. About you. If he did, he'd be angry, wouldn't he? He told me everything but I never told him about you. He wouldn't forgive that so fast, not when he thought there was no one else important to me. Maybe he does feel it. Maybe he thinks

I'm unfaithful. You think that's it? He senses something? He knows you're there?"

"Florence," I said, "I was *always* there. I don't think it's my fault."

"Oh, I didn't mean that. I didn't mean you'd *done* anything."

But I did get myself born. Born pale and frail. In the birth pictures, Florence looks like a black baby, fat in body and cheek, while I am small and white and look dead.

She didn't return all the blood. Contemplating warfare, initiating it, even in the womb.

"I think, He's sick, it's some kind of illness, he'll wake up one morning, he'll open his eyes, and we'll be back to the way we were. He'll stop humiliating me, that's what he wants to do, and he's good at it. He's worn me out. I wish you'd take my place, I wish you'd talk to him, but you won't. Once you say no, that's it. You're worse than Mother! How is Mother?"

"The dress," I said. Wearily.

"Oh, the dress. He said, 'We're going to Aix to buy you a dress for the party,' and I said, 'It's a waste of money, I'm not going,' and he said, 'If you don't go I'll go, and I won't come home.' And then he said he'd already been to Aix and he saw the perfect dress in a window. So we went. I tried on the dress, a typical French dress, absolutely simple, beautiful fabric, red wool, long sleeves, deep décolletage. He said, 'That's the dress. Take it off and let's go.' I said it was March, still winter, and the wool was fine now, but when it warmed up I wouldn't put it on. He said, 'We'll worry about that in the summer.' As if he didn't expect there to be a summer, as if he didn't care what I did with the dress as long as he wasn't around.

"I was getting dressed—I was looking for a pin to wear at the neck—to hold the neckline closed a little and he was sitting behind me, I could see him watching me in the mirror, and he said, 'Florence, let's treat this as a date.'

"A date, Doris! What was he talking about? He said, 'Wouldn't you like to date?'

"I said I couldn't date, I was married, and he said, 'Never mind that. Wouldn't you like it, though? To feel young again?' and I said, 'I am young.' And he said, 'No. You aren't. We'll go to the party as if we were going on a date.' I didn't know what he was talking about and I didn't want to know. I said, 'Fine,' and put on a necklace and he said, 'Maybe a black scarf,' and I said, 'I hate scarves.' And he said he liked them, and I said he meant Tobie liked them, and he said, 'When we get there, we can dance with whoever we want to dance with. We can leave with whoever we want to leave with.' And I said, 'Why are you doing this?' and he said, 'Doing what?' and I said, 'Doing this!' and he said, 'We need a change.' And I said I didn't need one, and he said it wasn't what I needed that he cared about just then.

"And I asked him, 'Why? What have I done?' and he said, 'Why is it always something *you've* done?' and I said, 'I don't feel like a woman anymore,' and he said he was sorry to hear it, and was I almost ready? So I took off the beads, those jet beads you gave me for our birthday, you remember? And I put on my black jet earrings and he said, 'You look terrific. Very sexy,' and I pulled off my earrings and threw them on the floor.

"He said, 'If you think having a fit will do you any good, think again. I'm going in five minutes, with or without you.'

"I kept thinking, if I had time, more time, I could talk him out of this, I could make him stop, I could make him come back to me. How could he mean it? But he did, Doris, he did! He said, 'Well, I'm leaving,' and he meant it, he started for the door.

"And I grabbed up my earrings and my necklace and pushed my foot into one shoe and ran after him, hobbling, one shoe on, one shoe off, God knows what I looked like. But he was out the door and so was I, and I was still holding that shoe, running after him, and I said, 'What's the hurry?' and he said, 'No hurry. Meet me there.' And like an idiot, I put on my shoe and ran after him, putting the beads back on, and I was trying to get the earring hooks through my ears, all at the same time, and I must have started catching up with him, because he walked faster. I couldn't keep up with him.

"Down there where the street ends? You see it? That's where the party was. Emmeline—she was a new actress in the troupe—she opened the door and said, 'Oh, Florence, we're so glad you could come. Doesn't she look beautiful, everyone?'

"*Everyone.* Who was everyone and what did they have to do with me?"

" 'What a beautiful dress, I love dark red,' Emmeline said. She was little and dark, her hair was cut like a boy's, he likes that type, and I knew she had picked it out. *She* showed it to Jack. *She* said, 'Wouldn't that be perfect for Florence?'

"So I walked away from her. I didn't see Jack. Probably he was out in the garden, leaning over some woman, very romantic, out there in the moonlight—all he has to do is look at someone. You can't even blame them. You can't blame him, either, can you, Doris? They throw themselves at him. Look what happened to me! I took one look at him and there wasn't anything else I wanted. You *can't* blame him."

"You *can* blame him," I said. "I do."

"You wouldn't. Not if you knew him. Anyway, one of the other play-wrights, Tony, came over to me. He asked me to dance, and after all, I was on a date, and we danced—very close. I had no idea, no idea what I was doing. I saw Jack dancing with Emmeline, and I saw Tobie, glaring. So who was his performance for? Me? Tobie? Emmeline? All of us? Which one of us was supposed to end up with him when the party broke up?

"And Tony said, 'Look, Florence, he's not behaving well. If you don't want to go home, come with me. I won't bother you. I'll sleep on the couch. You can lock yourself in the bedroom.' And I said, 'Let's go.' I left first, and then he came after.

"And I thought, He won't know where I am, and then I thought, What if he's arranged this with Tony? What if this was part of his plan? From the beginning? If he put Tony up to this? So I asked Tony if Jack had asked him to take me home, and then *he* was insulted, and I said, 'But he'll know,' and Tony said, 'He'll figure it out. Let him. I don't give a damn.'

"Later, he said, 'Why are you sleeping with me, Florence? Is it to get even with him?' and I said I didn't think so, but of course that was what I was doing, you never admit that, of course you don't, and he said, 'Don't you want to take off that dress, it's a beautiful dress,' and I said, 'Let me take off this pin. I want to keep the dress on,' and he said, 'Why? Are you shy?' and I said, 'No, I want to ruin and stain this dress,' and he said, 'I'm not asking any more questions.'

"And I'd slept in it all night, and in the morning the dress wasn't ru-ined or stained, only crumpled, and I walked back to our house wearing that damn dress. I was sure everyone in the village knew exactly what I'd been doing, and I wanted them to know.

"And he wasn't in the house, and I locked the doors and fastened the shutters. I lay down on the couch and fell asleep; the dog's head was in my lap and I didn't care—he could stay at Emmeline's or Tobie's or shuttle between *both* their houses.

"But he must have decided I wasn't unhappy enough, so he came pounding on the door until the neighbors started shouting, and then I opened the door and let him in, and he wanted to know where I'd been. He had the nerve to ask me where *I'd* been, so I said, 'On a date.' And he asked me what happened to that damn dress. I hate that dress! I asked him what he thought happened.

"Then he wanted to know where the beads were! I said I didn't know where they were and I didn't care where they were and if there were any other inventory matters, let's get them over with now. And he said there was another party tomorrow and he expected me to go. 'You will go,' that's what he said, and I said I would not, and he said, 'You know what will happen,' and I said yes, I knew he'd leave, and if he was going to leave, he ought to go now. And he said he was going to Sweden, and I told him to have a good trip, and he said he meant it, he wouldn't come back, and I said, 'Just don't expect me to drive you to the airport,' and he said, 'Take off that dress,' and I said, 'I'll take it off when I damn well please,' and he said, 'I bought it for you,' and I said he bought it with my money, and I made more money than he did and I was more famous than he was. Well, Doris, I'd had enough! And he said he was leaving. Right then.

"And he left. And I sat there, drinking glass after glass of red wine, the same color as my dress, and I thought, He's gone crazy and he wants to see how far he can push me, but he can't, not anymore.

"I thought about our father and all the sweet-natured men I'd known and how Jack once seemed perfect because he was so different and I used to feel sorry for you because you were stuck with the same kind of man— plain, nice. And I tried to figure out how much of this was my fault. And I thought, Somehow or other, it will work out, but I didn't believe it would. And I drank another glass of wine, and then another, and when I woke up, I was still wearing the dress and I went into my studio and took a brush and dipped it into white paint and began painting it over with white paint, in dots, like snow. I was standing in front of that mirror, painting my dress with snow, and when I was finished, I unzipped it and walked out onto the terrace half naked and threw the dress over the back of an iron chair. I said, 'Let it dry there.' I said, 'This is the end of the world.' Then I took some pills, then I drank some more wine, then I called you. What do you think?"

"What do I think? What do *you* think?"

"I can't stay here and wait for him."

"Then leave. Come back with me. You've got a passport."

"I've got to go somewhere he can't find me."

"Why? Florence, why?"

"I don't want him to know if I'm dead or alive. I want him punished. He acts as if nothing can touch him, but he can't stand guilt. I know he can't."

"Don't do it. Lead a normal life. We're only twenty-six. The women in our family live a long time. You could live to be eighty. You'll find someone else."

"But if I leave, if no one knows where I am . . ."

"If you do?"

"I can always come back."

If I had stopped her there, if I had called a doctor, if I had found her husband, if I had called my husband—if I had done any of those things, everything might be different today. Didn't she know I would go along with her, wouldn't stop her? Didn't she know she was safe with me, that she had nothing to fear from me? And does she blame me now for not stopping her? Because if I loved her as much as I thought I did, I should have stopped her.

Instead, in the morning, I took my suitcase and went to the airport and then waited—for news of her mysterious, inexplicable disappearance.

But I thought she'd be back. I thought she'd tell me where she was. I couldn't believe she'd leave me behind, not forever. I don't think she would have. If she were alive, I'd have heard from her. And after so many years isn't it reasonable to believe she's dead? But I don't really believe it, not all the time. After all, I pinch my own arm and it hurts. After all, I'm alive. And so is Jack, if you can call the existence she left him a life. *Devastator. One of the Furies.* As Jack, who clearly hasn't forgiven, referred to her in his most recent play.

It is not wise for me to think too long about my sister, because if I do, she gains strength as a storm does and, on the grass, white lawn tables spin past like giant hoops, the roof leaks and the walls shake, and if you're given to wild imaginings, someone's hand closes over your wrist and you can't shake her off. The red dress is always a dangerous subject, but as time passed, I saw that I had an antidote—the pages in her journals describing the time in Goult when she was happy.

In the beginning, I needed to read the actual pages, but later I could summon them up in my mind, whenever I missed her, whenever I sat up, frightened, in bed. It is like walking into a happy house, reading the journal entries from this time, like waking up and finding my sister sitting on the edge of my bed.

⎯☙☙⎯

I AM in France, in a little village called Goult, installed as a housewife. Almost all of my canvases came with me, still rolled up, but Jack says as soon as we find the framer in Cavaillon, we will hang them.

I want to burrow into Jack! It isn't enough to press up against him. I said I would tunnel in through his belly button and begin biting around it, and he said, Go ahead, come on in, and I wanted to know where I should lie when I was inside, behind his spine or in front of it, under his heart, and he said in front, he was no lightweight, he had heavy bones, he remembers the doctor said that about him—*This child has heavy bones. He's going to be tall.* So I have been tunneling and I believe I've gone through, am in, am a white and cloudy powder in his blood, a bone shadow for each of his bones, and I lie there letting his heart beat for me, his lungs breathe for me, I look out through his eyes, nothing is required of me, not even breathing in and out, and what a rest it is, what perfect peace! I've never felt so relaxed. My bones have turned to wax and melted. I have grown quite fond of my skin, which lets me in and out as easily as a perfectly fitted door on well-oiled hinges. Jack says, Now it is my turn to get in, and nibbles at my belly button, but I don't like the game played this way and find ways of changing it. We are very happy.

He says he never knew he could be so happy.

I love my daily life because that is exactly what it is—daily, quotidian, ordinary, every day the same. In the mornings, we get up and fly through the house, closing the shutters, and then whoever finishes first jumps back into bed, and the dog jumps in after.

Sometime in the late afternoon, I begin cooking dinner. I am not an ambitious cook and never will be. But now that I have Jack to feed! I love to watch him eat, I love to watch his jaw move in its sockets, I love to think that he is eating my food and no one else's. I adore watching this huge man sit tamely at my table and eat my food, as if a lion or a tiger came down from the hills and for a while took on human shape, and I treacherously think of the old saying about cats, how they love whoever feeds them. But often I continue painting too long and then I begin to smell the aroma of food wafting up the stairs and it is Jack who is cooking for me, and there is no question about it. He is the better cook.

After six, I begin to wait for him on the terrace overlooking the village, a glass of anisette in one hand, a dry cracker in another, my hand on the dog's head, and I love this waiting, watching the men return to their homes, the women rushing out to take in the last of the clothes or to hang one last thing on the clothesline, watching the sky dim, although it really doesn't dim here, it merely loses its brightness. I love waiting because I know he is coming and the anticipation is the most exquisite thing, so fierce it's hard to believe there is anything better, but there is—his arrival, and when I see him coming, usually walking up the steep main street, I wave slowly and he stops and slowly and grandly waves back. I bow and he bows. And when the dog sees me wave, he barks, two barks, sharp and loud. It is quite a ritual.

Why do I never date these entries? I believe it would be tempting fate, as if admitting that time was segmented, had seams, could be divided, would be conceding that the future might be different from the present. I want things timeless, unchangeable.

I think of my life now as taking place inside an enormous white-sheeted tent and outside the sun shines and the tent is forever filled with a pure white radiance. I am the only bride under the eye of the sky. I am the only woman with a perfect husband. I am the lucky one who paints white paintings while her husband writes plays that are sensationally successful. There is nothing more to ask for. This is paradise. Goult is paradise. Its turnips are paradisal turnips. Its apples are paradisal apples. The lavender I dilute in water and sprinkle on our sheets is celestial lavender. It is a perfect world.

A strange memory keeps coming back, but it's fuzzy, it doesn't seem like something *I* saw. Still, I remember looking in the window of Darlington's Funeral Home and a man in a white coat came in and Mr. Darlington stood against the wall, and the man in the white coat started up a saw—a small saw, one he held in his hand—and sawed through the body on the table, through the ribs down to the waist, and then stopped. Then he pried the bones apart and cut out the man's heart and held it in his hand.

Did this really happen?

I remember the color of the heart and the four stumpy things sticking out of it. I remember its texture. It is a dreadful memory but I hope it's mine. Why waste time shuddering at memories that don't belong to you? Why wake with nightmares that belong to someone else?

Do they put the heart back before they stitch the body up and bury it? They must. What on earth would they do with it?

I STOP here. Because these days I remember, although I usually refuse to do it—everything she wrote, not only the passages that comfort me. I remember her account of her miscarriage, how she reacted to the news of my pregnancy, which also ended in miscarriage. I remember how desperately she wanted to escape me. The journals were never the simple record of happiness I wanted to believe them to be.

CHAPTER

TEN

THUNDER in the morning, and the sky lead gray and silver, and I thought, A rainy day, fat raindrops falling, splashing onto the casement windows, striking the fat green leaves like piano keys, so many porches in the air, didn't Eva say that?

And they are, they are like porches, and the air soft and cool on the skin and the skin itself soft with the silvery damp. A rainy day and the regulars will come in at one and settle in for the afternoon. They'll start coming in at one o'clock and by one-thirty the café will be full. They won't come at twelve, no.

Then, the café will be almost empty. They'll think, Eva has her eye on me, she saw me come in, she knows how long I've been here, she'll cut a small slice of cake for me, she'll come over and smile and say, You won't mind if this nice gentleman shares your table? Look how wet he is! Then I'll have to make conversation, then I'll have to endure the man's curious looks. What am I doing, sitting there all afternoon? Don't I have anything better to do? I'm the reason the country is in such poor financial condition. Safer to come in at one, when the café is crowded, when Eva has all she can do to take the new orders and run up the little flight of steps to the kitchen to ask what happened to the liver and onions.

So I went to the café early, knowing I would be alone, hoping Dennis might be back. I didn't want to become part of what Eva called the café's ecosystem. To become part of it meant, I thought, that you had given up your belief in a future. If you came to the café every day, you believed nothing would change, or things would change only for the worse, and I was coming more often than I intended.

I was fascinated by Eva. There was something between us, and whatever it was, it was important. I will leave it alone, I thought. I will wait. Sooner or later, that thing hiding itself on the forest floor, camouflaged by fallen leaves, will stand up and reveal itself for what it is. That is one of the advantages of growing older, isn't it? Being able to wait. If I had learned nothing else, I had learned to wait.

And all at once I saw what it was: it was so obvious. Eva was like my mother, a teller of stories, and when she spoke of her life in Serbia, I felt once again as I had always felt when our mother told us stories, as if I were floating in the green waters of a great bay surrounded by white bonelike hills, and in that water I was absolutely alone and entirely unafraid. Whenever my mother began to tell us one of her stories, I would begin to feel as if I were floating, and then I would see that bay and myself in it, no one else near me, its green waters, its white hills. How long had it been since I last floated in those waters? Five years? Ten? I lay back on my pillow and smiled up at the ceiling; I was so happy to be back in the water once more, alone and unafraid of being alone, brave little Doris who was otherwise never very brave—when all at once I understood that the bay was my sister's eye, her bluish eye, and the white bony hills were the white bones of her skull that surrounded that eye, shimmering beneath her delicate skin which was also my skin, and I understood that I had never floated alone in an empty expanse of water. I had only floated safely in the green sea of my sister's eye.

There is not very much to you, is there? I asked myself sadly. And then I understood that this time I had been floating, not in Florence's eye, but in Eva's. Surely everything would come to look different if I could only begin to float in someone else's eye! When I turned back to look at the bone-colored hills, surely they would change color. When I came out of the water, the world would have changed. I would have changed. Nothing would be the same.

A new bay, a new eye. Anything was possible!

Isn't that you all over? Florence said. Now your ambition is to be a mote in someone else's eye. Doris, you are hopeless. Leave the poor woman alone.

E V E R Y   Y E A R, on Florence's birthday, reporters turn up on Jack Pine's doorstep. Has he heard from her? Does he expect to? If she's dead, does he think they'll ever find the body? Is he still suspected himself? How many times has he been arrested? For assaulting reporters? For smashing their cameras? For firing a skeet gun at a man hiding in a bush in the yard across the way? Is it true that his mother drowned herself when she read the papers? Did his mother believe her only son was a murderer? What does his current lover think? Doesn't she mind Florence Meek's paintings hanging on the walls of the house? What kind of woman was Florence? But now that Dennis had found me, I was afraid that soon they would be asking him, Is it true that Florence Meek had a twin sister? Had he ever met her?

Or the reporters would say, of course he wouldn't be asked any questions about Florence Meek, that was so long ago. No, all the reporter wanted to do was ask him about *Three Raven Wood,* and perhaps a few questions about his earlier plays, but when they arrived, they asked, Is *Three Raven Wood* a play about your marriage? The dead child lying on the table in the third act—are we meant to believe your wife had a miscarriage? Did the miscarriage break up the marriage? Is it true you told her she was less than a cow because even cows could have children?

His nerves, they said, were shattered.

I didn't believe it.

Not of Jack Pine, the man with whom every woman on campus fell in love, the wild man of the math department, who made his reputation as a theoretical mathematician in his early twenties—the topology of H-spaces, whatever that was—who, by the time he was twenty-three, had begun writing plays and decided to give up mathematics, who took my sister, in the middle of the winter, the temperature below zero, on a camping trip to Starved Rock, where they pitched their tent in the snow and rescued a dog who began scratching at the tent, Sam, the dog they took with them to France. Jack, who called my sister at her dormitory room in the middle of a blizzard and asked her to meet him at the Hobby House and proposed to her after knowing her three months, and most of that time she never knew where he was or if he was going to call her.

Jack Pine, who had been engaged the summer before he met Florence, and who so enraged his fiancée, whom he took on a canoe trip, nearly drowning her, that she took off her engagement ring and threw it into the rapids. The whole campus was preoccupied with him; the whole campus knew these stories. Jack Pine, who proposed to my sister after she walked to the restaurant through the blue early-morning light, past the snow-covered cars like hibernating animals, skidding every other step—proposed to my sister, who had no idea what he wanted to talk to her about, who asked him what was so important. Jack, who was so astonished she didn't take him seriously. She told him he proposed to everyone. He wanted to marry everyone.

And when he said again that he wanted to marry her, she said that wasn't funny. She asked, "Why me?" and he wanted to know, how could he answer that, did she expect him to answer that? And when he saw she was cold, he got up and put his coat over her shoulders and said he had bought that coat with his first paycheck, a sheepskin coat, he had never worn such a warm coat. And she said she thought he never wore a coat, and he said of course he wore coats, and hats and scarves and gloves, and it occurred to her that she wasn't being particularly helpful.

All this is in her journals. That's how I know.

And he said, "I'm not the type to go down on my knees," and she said, "I don't want you to go down on your knees. Besides, the floor's wet." He said, "You don't think I mean it," and she said she wasn't sure. He said he was serious and he did mean it. He wanted to leave the country and live in France. He wanted to try making a living by his writing and it wasn't even a risk. He was still working on math theory, but he could do that anywhere, he'd keep on doing it, it was second nature, not work, and if the writing didn't succeed, he'd come back and teach again, but in the meantime, he said, if she came with him, she'd have to leave school. And she said, "Leave school? I haven't even finished my second year."

But a few minutes later, she had agreed to go with him, and he asked her if she was happy, and she said she was, she was ecstatic. But she knew she didn't sound ecstatic. She sounded stunned. And a few days later they were married, and my sister left me a note saying, "I've gone to France with Jack. Don't worry. I know what I'm doing. I'll call after a while. Don't worry."

Don't worry! When I had never been separated from her and now she was gone. My sister, who said, much later, I thought life would get you by the throat and shake you and you'd forget about me.

Jack Pine, who had taken my sister away from me and then grown tired of her.

"TELL ME what she was like," Dennis said. He was back—from Provence, from Spain—he wouldn't say where he'd been.

And I was furious. How could he be so stupid? Asking me what she was like when he was sitting at the table with me, in Eva's Café, when all he had to do was watch me and listen to me. But he could be stupid beyond words. No matter what I told him, he believed Florence was different, not only from me, from everyone. A special halo enveloped her, a magnetic field surrounded her. Something. Florence would have liked him. You always like someone who shares your delusions.

My mother's nurse liked him. Dennis is the sort of man everyone likes, the kind of man who sits down in a cafeteria and finds himself listening to a perfect stranger's life story. She'd talked to him about her, about my mother, who would wake up with a headache on the morning of our birthday and begin drinking, first sherry, then vodka, and by noon she was crying, "What did I do to deserve this? Was I such a bad mother?"

She was.

And then, later in the day, the phone would ring and my mother would say, "Doris, if I could find her, if I could only find her! It's the not knowing that's so terrible! You can't imagine how terrible it is!"

I can't imagine!

There are times when I think my mother blames me, when I see her watching me through narrowed eyes as if she were trying to answer the incredible question she asks herself. Doris was there, Doris was one of the last people who saw her. Did Doris have something to do with her disappearance? Did Doris do something to her? And then she remembers. Florence was the one. Florence was the one who turned on her sister.

So I saw he'd fallen in love with her. I suppose I knew that, even in New York. Everyone falls in love with Florence. First they see one of her paintings, usually *The Golden Rope.* They buy a print. They hang it on their wall. Then they buy *The Paintings of Florence Meek.* Then they begin to study the White Paintings. They go from museum to museum, studying them. They sit on the little upholstered benches in front of them. They find themselves in bookstores, where they buy a dreadful, sensational volume called *The Riddle of Florence Meek.* In it they read my sister's account of her first meeting with Jack Pine and they learn how hopelessly she fell in love with him, and then *they* fall in love with Jack Pine, and this too is natural. It's part of falling in love with Florence. You love what she loved. Next they read the account of the marital breakup. They pore over the list of Jack Pine's considerable—and to some men enviable—infidelities. In short order, they turn against the husband she turned on, but theirs is no simple hostility. No. It is one part hatred, one part curiosity, and one part love. And one part envy. Her few published descriptions of her married life undo her readers entirely.

They say to themselves, *That's what I want. Of course, it didn't work out for her, but for me . . . !* And so the fascinated ones make a pilgrimage to Jack

Pine's house. He shoots at them with a BB gun or he gets his slingshot and sails pebbles at great velocities over their heads.

Then they change their tune. *If he won't talk to me! Who does he think he is! I'll show him!* This is the final stage. Florence's admirers love her, hate her husband, and they are, they think, at one with her. If they had only been there, in Aix, she would never have disappeared. They would have understood her. They would have rescued her. They were, after all, just like her.

But Florence wouldn't approve of them. She certainly wouldn't like them—she liked so few people. She would deplore their existence. She wanted to torture Jack herself. She wanted revenge. And then she wanted to take him back. This is what no one understands. She never stopped loving Jack. She would be more indignant than Jack is. She would say, "What business is it of theirs? He was married to *me!*"

"She disappeared and left all the paintings in Jack's hands," I said to Dennis. "What do you make of that? He's the one who decides whether or not to lend them to museums. They had to get his permission to send them to Russia last year. *We* can't get them back. We haven't even seen all of them! And *The Golden Rope* was meant for me. She always said she painted it for me. That was the first of her White Paintings. In the absence of a body," I said, "these things are important."

He stopped eating. He put down his fork. "Then you believe she's dead?" he asked me, and I said, "No, I don't," but my throat was tightening as it always does when I speak of her, so I didn't say, There's nothing to touch, nothing to look at, you want something solid, something that belonged to her. Isn't it natural? I didn't say, Dead or not, I fully expect her to come in through that café door. One of these days. She will. She'll come in through that door.

And then I asked Dennis about Jack and he told me how bitter he was, how nothing he did or could do would change the way the world looked at him. Was he the first unfaithful husband in the history of the planet? All he was doing, *all* he had ever done, was try to free himself. You had no idea, Jack said, what it meant to be caught by her. You could feed yourself to her bit by bit and you'd only increase her appetite. And she had been incapable of telling the truth. That was maddening, how she lied about simple things that made no difference, the kind of lying that meant this world wasn't complicated enough for her or beautiful enough, but all the same, it was *your* world, and it was the best you could make it.

"What kind of lies?" Dennis asked Jack.

"Unbelievable lies, ludicrous ones! Once she hit me and I hit her back, and with my bad luck she fell and cracked the side of her head against the fireplace mantel. Half the village was walking around with black eyes. The butcher's wife had a perpetual black eye and the butcher usually had two. Well, he was a scrawny man and his wife was the one who hacked through the sides of beef and if anyone asked her what she was doing with a black eye, she'd say, 'A present from my husband.'

"But not Florence! No, there was a tremor, a definite tremor, everything shook. Didn't they have earthquakes in this part of France? No? Well, Goult had its first earthquake. And she was standing near the grandfather clock when the house began shaking—only our house, mind you—and the clock came down and struck her there, right at the corner of the eye. An inch higher and she'd be wearing a black patch. She'd have no depth vision, and her painting days would be over. Did anyone believe her? Of course no one believed her. Everyone lived in houses. There were plenty of men and women with black eyes and most of them didn't blame them on earthquakes, and if Florence was telling such stories, who knew what really went on? *Something* must have gone on if she had to make up such crazy stories.

"A woman in town—Hélène—she came into the bar one day with a big black eye, a real shiner, and she sat down on a stool and told the world, 'I deserved it. I chased him around the house with a knife.' Not Florence. A doctor she went to thought she had a split personality. She was quite pleased with him after the first session. She came home and said, 'He said it's as if I have to live two lives, one for myself and one for someone else, and if only we could find out who that other person was!' What a laugh she had! The doctor didn't have the first idea of what he was talking about. He didn't know *who* he was talking to.

"But after a week or so, something went wrong and she came home quiet and sat at the table thinking and drawing on the tabletop with her finger. For a while, if she was late, she'd come home and say, 'I'm sorry I'm late.' Fine, good. But then she stopped going to see the doctor. No warning, no explanation. And now if she was late, she'd say, 'Oh, the neighbor's chimney blew down and a brick hit her husband on the head and I had to stay there and clean up the mess.' Or, 'I was sitting at the bar and the man on the stool next to me started twirling around and he knocked me down and I don't know how long it took before the room stopped spinning.' Or, 'I got my shoes wet on the way to Elizabeth's and wore a pair of her shoes home, and the soles were leather instead of rubber and it was wet out and I slipped on the cobbles and twisted my ankle and thought I sprained it but then it felt better and I limped home. I felt better enough to pick daffodils!' And she'd stand still, *maddeningly* still, in front of the kitchen cabinet, deciding just which vase she ought to put them in. Then she'd go helpless and say, 'I can't make up my mind. Which vase do we want to put them in?' and I'd say, 'I don't give a good goddamn about the daffodils, you can throw them in the trash!' And she'd give me that look—*now* you've really failed me—and she'd stalk off to her room. Never mind what time it was, dinnertime, lunchtime, nothing was going into a pot that I didn't put in it. Nothing was appearing on that goddamn table that I didn't cook."

"She hit you?"

"Oh, yes, she did. With a book. With the Webster's unabridged dictionary. I swear to God! How could I forget? I didn't think she could pick it up! She meant to bring it down on the top of my head here—the way you'd squash a bug—but I moved, well, I *tried* to move, and the corner of the book caught me on the side of the face, right here." He pointed to a thin, pale scar. It traveled from the corner of his left eye into his hairline. "Well, it's not quite a dueling scar," he said, "but the doctor who stitched me up said I was a couple of millimeters away from losing that eye. She was very strong, Florence was."

"Something must have made her mad."

"I think it would be fair to say that in those days we were both mad almost all of the time," Jack said.

"YOU DON'T SEEM surprised about the lies," Dennis said to me.

"Oh, I do the same thing. I don't think of them as lies, that's all. They aren't, not really. We used to make up stories about the day, about everything that happened during the day. You can see why. We were always together. The same things always happened to us. We would have bored each other to death if we'd told the truth. We already knew the truth. So we made things up. But there were *rules*. If we went out and got caught in the rain and got wet, we couldn't change *that*. We couldn't change something anyone could have seen. We invented reasons—why it rained, why we got wet. That's all she was doing. He should have known that."

Dennis asked me how he would have known that, and I said, "I suppose she *should* have told him, but *we* never had to explain things to each other. We knew what we meant."

I told Dennis, "She must have been annoyed by him—if he didn't know. We weren't mad. How did Jack get such a crazy idea? We knew what really happened, but we liked our own versions better." Dennis asked me when it started, and I said, "Oh, as soon as we could talk, I think.

"We made up stories about the Land of the Twins. Everyone had a twin there but the other twin died. We were sure that was how it was. Everyone started out a twin—like us. Then they had to come here—you know, to this life. We invented deaths for the twins who died.

"When we saw our grandmother, we made buzzing noises. That was the bee, buzzing in the rose, then biting our grandmother's twin. It killed her, the bee. When we sat at the table, we made rumbling noises. That was the train, running over our mother's twin.

"And when our mother heard us—probably she knew what we were up to; we were always so pleased with ourselves we couldn't keep quiet—she'd shout, 'Will you girls stop that noise! Stop it now or leave the table!' "

"You know," he said, "this is wonderful."

I WASN'T listening to him. I had traveled back to the house in Peru. I was watching the twins, Doris and Florence, who didn't stop when their mother shouted at them, and so they were sent upstairs, and as they slowly climbed the stairs, holding hands, in perfect step, they heard their mother say, "Look at them! It's no punishment sending them up there together! They like to be together!"

They change the story and decide their mother's twin was never buried because the train splattered her all over the station, like paint. In their room, they lie down on their beds, their white-enameled beds, thickly coated with white paint. Beneath their fingertips the painted iron is a relief map. They like to imagine the country beneath their fingers. They like to press their cheeks against the cool metal when the days are hot. They lie on their beds and imagine that the cracks in the ceiling form maps of other places. Here is the Land of the Twins. No Mothers Allowed. They make up many stories about the Land of the Twins. Yes, that's probably where it started, really.

Dennis is fascinated.

My eyes are stinging. I'm eavesdropping on my younger selves, whom I love now as if they were entirely separate from me and from Florence, as if they were not our younger selves but our children, and I think, This is what happens as you grow older. You become the parent of your younger selves, you become everyone's parent. No one is as old as you are, but you as you *were*—that is who you love best.

Of course I understood Florence's lies. Of course I understood why Jack said he fed himself to her bit by bit and it was never enough. Of course I understood why she didn't know she was harming him. Did either of us ever believe we could consume the other? And it seemed to me that now I knew absolutely what had gone wrong, and it was what I always thought.

Poor Florence. She loved him, and all she wanted—*all* she wanted—was to be loved as she had always been loved. How could he possibly do it? Is it any wonder he came to hate her? Or came to believe he did? Because I don't think he hated her any more than she hated him. They feared one another. That's different. If some time had passed—if they hadn't both been such strong characters, so extravagant in their emotions. If something had distracted her, taken her attention from him. If she had had a child—but she didn't want one, not then. If one of them had come down with malaria! Or tuberculosis! Something curable that took time. Anything to calm the waters, just for a while, while they grew—only slightly—older. Tamer and older. It's possible, isn't it?

In the first volume of Florence's journals, I found loose sheets covered with thick black-ink letters, Jack Pine's handwriting. The sheets were carefully smoothed out, carefully placed between the front cover and the first page. Somehow Florence got hold of them. I doubt if Jack knew she had them, but he might have known. There was a time when they shared everything, and they might have shared even these. Since she vanished, no one but me had ever seen them. Probably no one ever will. They complicate everything, and I want her story made simple. She loved him. He stopped loving her. A simple story. But these pages hint at another one.

I think she must have shown him a few passages from her journals, and he thought, I'll match her, perhaps outdo her. Competition and imitation. They're hard to tell apart, I think, and sometimes one becomes the other. I always thought it odd that when he described their early days together, he spoke of himself in the third person. He was writing of the time when he was seduced by her, but probably even then he was fighting for distance.

He wrote about how greedy she was. He wrote that he found she loved his body, she knew how to love bodies, and he thought, I never want to get out of this bed even if she's crazy, but later in the evening he thought, If she's not crazy? If she's right? If we belong together?

He would understand her. She would see to that. She would open herself, split herself open as a butcher splits open an animal. She would do that for him if he asked her.

But she was possessive, he wrote. Odd things, meaningless things, would frighten her. Then he would sit her on his lap and stroke her hair, but eventually, he knew, he would grow impatient. He wouldn't want to reassure her. He would tire of reassuring her. He would tire of watching her make grand opera out of trivial and tiny things—like turning over in bed and turning away from her.

And then he would want to punish her. Who could endure such unending, such protracted, such senseless inquisitions? Silent inquisitions—she wouldn't have to say anything. He would know what she was thinking. He had a cruel streak. He knew that.

And she was not without claws. He remembered the night of the dance at school and how she danced with another man, how provocatively she danced when she knew his eyes were on her. All the room noticed. How seductive, how shameless. Everyone watched. But it worked, didn't it? He was caught. At the time, he had no idea how sharp and vicious was the hook she'd use to catch him. She could be merciless, cold-blooded. She was the kind of woman—he had no illusions—who avenged herself. Were the insults real, were they imaginary? It made no difference. She believed in evening the score. She believed in balancing the books, and she kept the books open. She looked at them every day. There would not be a past sin she forgot, not an indiscretion she forgave. Living with her would be like living with a firecat, this woman in his bed, promising to love him as no one else would ever love him. She would hate him as violently as she loved him—they always did—he had enough experience to know that.

She was different from the others—in the fierceness of her will, her passion, her worship. What frightened him, warned him off—all that drew him close. A high-gravity planet, that was what she was. He couldn't escape her. The longer he stayed, the less he cared to escape. Her will leached his. Her will became his. And for a time, it was wonderful, giving himself up, for a short time. And then he would rebel. He knew he would. How could he not? It was in his nature. It was in everyone's nature.

No one had ever desired him like this woman. No one would ever love him as she did. Didn't she keep repeating that? No one will ever love you as much as I love you? Wasn't he beginning to believe it? No one would ever love him as she did. She needed nothing but him. Everyone else, everything else, was a distraction. Anything they couldn't share was distress, anguish, misery, a burden, something to be driven off. He would write. She would paint. They would have what they wanted. She was young. She would be happier with him than without him.

They were happy now. They would be happy for a time. What more could they ask for? Nothing more. Why push her away, why lose her—because he could see what was coming.

And yet he felt guilty.

And then there is one more page, and on it he has written:

—◦◦◦—

I OUTSMARTED myself. I love her. I cannot imagine life without her. Will she stay with me? Forever? I thought that word didn't belong in human vocabulary.

It is more painful than I thought anything could be.

I ASK YOU —who can read this and not feel *something* for him, some faint stirring of sympathy? I read it and asked myself, Where are we now?

Perhaps Dennis is right. Perhaps I ought to go to Goult and see him. Who knows? Something of her may linger in the stones of that house.

PART THREE

When I Came
to the Cemetery

WHEN I CAME to the cemetery, I thought, I'll stay here for a while, I'll rest. There was a little house, a marble house, and the sun struck it hard and thin silver blades of light leaped from it like knives. I put my hand to my eyes. Somewhere there would be a marble bench, I would sit on the bench and eat my apples and drink my bottle of wine.

I had plenty of money. For months, squirrel-like, I'd stored away what money I'd need. I kept my hair covered, I carried my red dress, I wore my jeans and a T-shirt, every day I looked more and more like a peasant, every day I grew browner and thinner, my jeans were shorter, my ankles and shinbones were sunburned, was it possible I was growing? And if I was growing, was my sister growing?

She would grow, if she knew I was.

I slept in the angular shadow behind the mausoleum. The heat no longer touched me. I was always cold.

Later, I heard voices. I sat without moving. The sun was going down. I walked through the cemetery, idly touching stones. I thought, I'll stay here until dark, I am so tired, he's not to know about this, he doesn't deserve a child, neither do I, I'll give it away, when the time comes I'll give it away, I'll leave it on a church step, yes, that's the right thing, that's a good idea.

Surely everyone was gone. Surely the cemetery was empty.

At the cemetery's edge, I came upon them suddenly, in the dark, in the moonlight. At first I didn't understand they were alive. At first I thought they were two marble carvings on top of tombstones laid flat, two identical girls lying on their backs, hands crossed over their breasts, effigies, carved effigies, that was what they were, surely. But when I bent over the nearer one, she opened her eyes and said something to me and I asked her what she was doing there, and she said, We sleep on the stones of our grandmothers and ask their spirits to fill what is empty, and when we are filled, suitors will come for us. We will have babies who will run in the fields and splash in the streams and golden apples will rain down on our heads and we will eat the apples and watch the crows eat the apples and there is nothing under the sun or moon that will frighten us, not even a ghost like you.

And I asked her where she heard such nonsense, and she said it was all true, every word. She was not afraid. Her sister was not afraid. They had each other. They slept on long tombstones pocked by rain, laid flat in the earth. They sat up to speak to me. They thought I was a ghost. I was frightened to see them move. I was more comfortable when I thought they were stone, when I thought I had become mad, hearing the voices of stone girls prostrate on stones.

Also, said the sister, we come here because the stones are so cool. In the summers, even at night, the house is hot.

In the morning, the girls were gone from the stones. I had slept all night at the feet of an enormous stone angel. I slept in its wing-shaped shadow. I gathered up my jacket and my backpack and walked on. How quickly the soles of your shoes grow thin, how quickly you come to feel the small stones of the dirt through the thinning layer of leather. Soon it will be easier to take off the shoes and walk barefooted.

CHAPTER

TWELVE

THIS MORNING an odd crackling sound, like small nails striking the windows. When I got up and looked out, I saw little beads of ice striking the glass and, on the windowsill, chunks of rough ice like rock salt. Mists swirled in the garden. The cream-colored castle next door was dissolving in fog, and even the tops of its slate-covered turrets were hidden. Hail in June! But this was London. Hadn't everyone told me? Bring warm clothes.

The phone rang. It was my husband. His cousin was coming to London and did I want to see her? I said I didn't want to see anyone from my old life.

"Your old life?" he said.

"You know what I mean. It's different here. I keep hoping *I'll* be different here. I'll see things differently."

He said he hoped I would and did I think I was making progress?

"Oh, yes, I think so," I said. We were in two different countries. I didn't want him to think I'd made a mistake in coming.

"But you'll come back to your old life?" he asked me, and I said, "Sometimes I miss you so much I wake up crying."

"For me or for Florence?"

"For you!"

"Good," he said. "I'll call in a few days so you won't worry."

"Fine," I said.

After I hung up the phone, it was very quiet in the room. No street sounds reached it. The telephone sat on its table and was again silent. It was three weeks since I'd come, three weeks since I'd heard from the Impostor, and at odd times a wave of anxiety would catch me at the base of

my throat and I knew I was still afraid of him. Was he the one walking behind me in the street when I went out to buy bottled water? When the
phone rang and I picked it up and no one was on the line, was he the one
who had dialed the number?

Fears have to be pushed down, hammered back in, like nails that rise
up out of the wood in the heat.

When I got to the café, I hesitated at the door, watching my reflection
in the glass, and then went in. Eva came to take my order, and I asked her
what had happened. "Oh, the artist who sketches over there against the
wall, he couldn't breathe. It happens every few weeks. He'll be fine tomorrow." Would I like a cinnamon roll or the usual scones?

I said I'd like a slice of apple strudel.

"And your sister?" Eva asked me. "She's coming?"

"My sister?" My hands had gone cold. "I don't have a sister."

"The lady who came in yesterday, I thought she was your sister, such
a resemblance," Eva said.

"I don't know who you mean," I said.

Eva regarded me dubiously.

"The artist, he thought she was your sister. He said the coloring, the
hair, everything but the shape of the faces. Well, so we are mistaken. All
the time we are mistaken. You will want your strudel now?" Eva asked. Eva
brought me the apple strudel.

The sun had come out and people were lifting their heads from the
daily papers and looking out the café window. One or two people folded
their papers, gathered their things together, paid their bills, and left.

"I had a sister," I told Eva when she sat down, "but she's gone."

"So many people dead," Eva said, and we sat in silence, looking out
the window.

I said yes, and after a while Eva said, yes, she could see I was a person
who turned things over. Perhaps that was why she liked talking to me.

I said I hadn't done any thinking, not for years. I'd stopped thinking
altogether. Of course, I said, I might have been thinking and didn't know
it, the way you think you haven't been dreaming and later in the day you
remember you did have a dream the night before. And now I'd started
again, because of her; really, I thought so.

"Try to think properly, not like me," Eva said. "You'd think I'd never
heard of a straight line."

I touched her shoulder, paid the check, and went out.

Outside, everything was still varnished and shining with the recent
rain. There was the smell of wet leaves and wet concrete, a slight chill in

the air, the smell of glassy blue skies in the spring—although it was not spring. But it was blue, blue and beautiful, green leaves shining, as if it were still very early in the morning and they were still covered with dew, and as I walked, one leaf after another sent down a little shower of silver, and for the moment, I was happy.

WHEN I CAME in, the phone was ringing. I picked it up and a familiar voice said, "It's your son again, so to speak," and I put the phone down and started to laugh. I could hear my husband saying, *It's a paradoxical reaction to a shock. That's all it is.* I waited to see if the phone would ring again. When it didn't, I dialed Dennis's number. I was still laughing. And shaking. I couldn't hold my hands still.

"What's wrong?" he asked me.

"Wrong?" I couldn't stop laughing.

"You don't sound like yourself. What's so funny?"

"Who do I sound like?" I asked, and suddenly the question struck me as hilarious and I laughed until I couldn't get my breath, until my eyes filled with tears and I had to rub them with my free hand.

"What's *wrong?*" Dennis asked again. He was more insistent.

"The Impostor called," I said. I was shrieking with laughter.

For a moment, he didn't say anything. Then he asked me, "Are you sure? Are you sure that's who it was?" I said I was absolutely certain.

"What did he say?" Dennis asked me. "He didn't frighten you? If you're laughing like that, he frightened you."

"He *always* frightens me! He said he was my son, so to speak."

"I hope you hung up," Dennis said. "I hope you didn't talk to him. You'll only encourage him."

"I did. And I changed my mind. I think we should go to Goult."

"When?"

"Tomorrow."

"I'm coming over there. I'll sleep on the sofa. All right?"

"Fine. Can we go tomorrow?"

"If Jack's home," Dennis said. "I'll call him."

"When you come," I said, "ring the bell and I'll throw down the keys. I can't buzz you in from my flat."

"Wrap them in a paper towel first," he said.

I threw the keys out the window and he came up the stairs and let himself in—as if he lived there, as if there were nothing out of the ordinary about his having my keys. I asked him if Jack was home, if we were going in the morning, and he said we were. Then he turned on the television and we watched a film in which an old doctor revisited scenes of his youth, and after that Dennis went to sleep on the couch. Later, I got up, pulled the duvet up to his chin, and sat down on the love seat and watched him sleep. Asleep, he was beautiful in his transparency, someone you met and immediately knew—almost angelic, but haunted by guilt, and the guilt was what made him so attractive, so utterly beautiful.

Angels are not always good, my mother said. *Angels can be bad and have very dirty hands and feet.*

You could look at him and see the small boy he must have been and the old man he would eventually become. He was not someone who would dramatically change with age. When you spoke to him, you would always feel as if you were speaking to someone who was still, somehow, very young. You knew that as a boy he would have helped anyone who asked for help. He loved his mother and his mother loved him, and when she baked bread, she made small loaves for him. In the spring, he followed his father into the woods and helped gather up deadfall for firewood. His father taught him to hunt, and he was a good hunter. He didn't leave bleeding and limping animals behind in the woods. You knew that his mother and father had loved one another without effort. They had that gift and so did he. You looked at him and you looked into clear water and you could see straight down to the bottom. You knew everything about him you needed to know. I felt as if I knew him well. I'd felt that from the beginning. When he slept, it was as if he'd never been to Vietnam, as if he'd never been touched by the world's bruising hands. What had he done? Why did he suffer from such guilt? I couldn't believe he had a good reason to feel such guilt. But then everyone thought I was angelic, incapable of harm.

Even kittens have claws, Doris, my husband once said. He was trying to persuade me to grow some talons of my own.

Dennis reminded me of someone, probably of myself.

I looked at the print over the fireplace, a reproduction of one of my sister's paintings, and thought, I should put that away. I thought that every morning and every evening, but one day succeeded another and still the print stayed where it was. Dennis must like it, I thought. That's a good reason for leaving it where it is.

I went to bed intending to leave for Goult in the morning, but when I called my husband's office, no one answered. I shouldn't go, I thought, without telling him. He'd want to know. And yet it was becoming harder and harder for me to picture him. I'd taken his picture and put it in the bottom drawer of my bureau. Now I called him every three days. Soon I'd call once every week. He shouldn't mind. He wanted me to believe I could manage on my own.

"I'VE CHANGED my mind," I told Dennis.

"Doris, sit down," he said. "I want to talk about this Impostor business. Whenever he calls, you can't decide to leave the country. Are you going to hang up every time he calls? Maybe we should call the police."

"And tell them what?"

"Tell them to trace your calls."

"He's probably harmless," I said, "and crazy."

"If he's crazy, he may not be harmless. For one thing, he has no trouble finding you."

"Oh, well," I said.

"What does that mean?" he asked me. I didn't answer. "Look, you understand that even if he was your sister's child, he still wouldn't be *your* child? At most, you'd be his aunt. That's clear, isn't it?" I stared down at my plate. I didn't say anything. "It *isn't* clear, is it?"

"If he were Florence's child, he *would* be half mine," I said.

"No, he wouldn't. He'd be her child."

"I don't want to talk about it."

"You mean he'd be the child you might have had?"

"Exactly."

"And she'd want you to take care of him?"

"Oh, I don't know about that," I said. "But if he *were* her child, I'd want to meet him. He might know something about what happened—after she left Provence."

"Then you ought to talk to him. Make him prove who he is. Ask him to tell you something only he could know. Ask him how he knows he's Florence's child. He'd be a pretty important person if he were her child, wouldn't he? And if Jack was his father."

"He doesn't *have* to be Jack's child. Do you think he's talked to Jack?"

"Jack didn't mention it to me."

"Probably that's why I wanted to go to Goult," I said. "To meet the child's father. If there is a child. If Jack is the father."

"Doris, that's not a good reason. I don't have to tell you that."

Just then the phone rang. I picked it up. "You are my mother," said the voice at the other end. I nodded to Dennis, who got up and stood next to me, his head pressed against mine, listening through the receiver to the voice on the other end.

"Look here," I said, "either stop calling me or give me some reason to believe you're my sister's son."

"My father saw her passport."

"That's not good enough," I said.

"I don't know much about her, and my father didn't, either. She had long curly black hair and she had a red dress. That's all he could tell me."

"A red dress?"

"She took it with her wherever she went."

"Why?"

"*I* don't know why. He said he had the maid clean it, and she was restless until she got it back. He said he couldn't do anything with her until she had it back again. That's all I know. I can't *prove* I'm her son. You should meet me and look at me."

A hole was opening in the floor in front of me. A few feet from me, the floorboards ended, broken and jagged. If he did know the truth! And if it was a truth I couldn't accept—what then?

In a few seconds, you can grow colder than the dead. And still, when I spoke to him, I sounded calm, unmoved, untroubled.

"Where did your father meet her?"

"In Spain."

"Spain!"

"He said she'd walked. And hitchhiked. Do you believe me?"

"Believe you? Don't expect me to believe you. Don't expect me to act like a mother. How old are you? Twenty-one? You don't need a mother."

"Everyone needs a mother."

"Well, at best I'm your aunt," I said, looking at Dennis. "I don't even know your name."

"My name is Antonio Mercado, and an aunt is better than nothing," he said.

"Where are you?"

"In London."

"What are you doing in London?"

"Looking for you."

"If you're not busy, we can meet at the end of next week," I said. "At Eva's Café in England's Lane. Next Friday at two o'clock."

"I could make it today."

"I want time to think this over."

"You'll change your mind!"

"I won't. I'll be there. Don't be surprised if I come with a friend. I'm going to hang up now." For the first time since he'd called, I wasn't frightened by him.

"All right," said the Impostor in a small voice.

"Well?" I said to Dennis.

"What convinced you?" he asked me. "Why are you seeing him?"

"Something he said about a dress," I said. "It's amazing."

IF HE WAS Florence's son, what was I going to tell him? Wouldn't he want to know what kind of family he came from? And what would he think then? And what was I going to tell myself as I waited, shaking sometimes with fear, sometimes with excitement, laughing for no reason at all, or violently weeping for no discernible cause? How was I going to exist until I saw him? How would I survive meeting him, listening to what he had to say?

Everyone, everywhere, trying to understand Florence, and now Dennis and the Impostor, trying to understand me, as if by understanding me they would learn about her—a natural mistake, one we made ourselves, always turning to one another, dismissing the rest of the world, underestimating *her,* our mother, who had, as I came to realize (it was too late, it's always too late), a strange affinity with death. Her father was dead before she had time to remember him—of tuberculosis. Her mother died of the same thing when she was ten. But then perhaps it was not strange, how death-haunted she was. Perhaps all orphans are.

Still, not all orphans marry two husbands who die young. Not all orphans buy a general store next to the town funeral home, or have daughters who find dead bodies when they go into the woods, or have a daughter who disappears and is believed to be dead, or tell their children stories in which death is forever the main character, the most interesting character, or are irrational and unpredictable and irresistible, and given to fits during which they sleep as if dead. Not all orphans have children who come home after weeks away at their grandmother's and find their mother unable to get out of bed or speak to them, so that the children turn to each other and cling together and later say to themselves, We saved each other.

And in the end, she was loyal, and as confounded by us as we had been by her.

Our mother would come into a room and find us sitting facing one another, our eyes locked together, time passing slowly for us if it passed at all. We had left her alone in her world: disappeared. She could see us but we were not there. Once again she was the orphan. Once again she was alone. She called us. We didn't answer. One day when she called and got no answer, she picked up a cut-glass pitcher and threw it at the wall. Our eyes uncoupled and we turned to her.

"Look what you made me do!" she cried. "My favorite pitcher! Ruined! What will Hilda say?"

We looked at one another. We had done nothing. Why must we be blamed because our mother threw her favorite pitcher at a wall?

"If you would pay attention when I talked to you!" our mother shouted at us.

She calmed down when she got older but by then we were grown-up women ourselves. We were her death-haunted daughters.

She was unlucky and she was thrifty, and when she was young, life and death twined tightly together, and in the stories she told us it was as if the angel of death himself put the wedding ring on your finger. And it was Florence, her favorite, who heard these stories most often, and it was Florence whom she loved more and who loved her more, who was most affected by them. And her stories were not happy ones.

Our grandmother told us how my mother fell in love with Albert Land, her first husband. They had gone through school together and never taken much notice of one another, until one day Albert looked up from his book and saw our mother, Elfrieda, staring out the window at the old apple tree that had stood there far longer than the school, and our mother thought she felt the sun on her neck but realized she felt Albert looking at her, and when she turned around, she smiled, and after that it was not possible to separate them.

Our grandmother told us how happy they were and how, when our mother would wake in the night, she would prop herself up and look at her husband and think how lucky she was, because among other things, she finally had something she could call her own, and later, when we were born, she would tell us what she'd already learned. Find a man who worships you, find someone who will put you on a pedestal, someone who is always faithful because he can't imagine anything better in the world. Don't be any man's dishrag. She was lucky, she was more than lucky, and she knew it.

Everyone knew it. They were the sweethearts of Peru. And then one day the townspeople noticed our mother stop in to see Dr. Steiner and leave looking puzzled, her eyebrows drawing together, and when she got home, she told Albert she wanted to go for a walk in the apple orchard because she had something to talk over with him, and he stopped splitting wood and went off with her, and they drifted aimlessly up and down the hills while our mother pointed out which trees she liked and why. This one resembled an old woman tearing her hair, look how the branches grew out and then grew back in toward the top of the tree trunk, and that one with its arms spread out looked like a dancer or a gymnast, you could imagine a wind picking it up and sending it down the meadow doing handstands, and that one leaning down to the earth was like a mourning woman, it seemed to be listening to the earth, oh, she always felt as if she had plenty of company here.

And it was as if Albert had never seen anything until she described it. Because of our mother, he knew that poor Mrs. Nightingale resembled a rabbit, and our grandmother, whom he regarded as his mother-in-law, bore a distinct resemblance to a basset hound, and when he looked at the river after the snow melted and the river lay peacefully in its bed, he saw that the bottom of the river was speckled like a frog, and it amazed him that he could have lived here all his life and not noticed that the hills encircling the town resembled great humpbacked beasts peacefully sleeping, or that if he glanced down from a high hill when a cloud passed over, the meadow below looked as if it had been burned black.

There was nothing he would not do for our mother, but what? He wanted to do something as enormous as what she did when she described ordinary things and made them shine out, but what could he do? And here they were, nearing the end of October, married almost three months, and it came to him. Oh, it was small, but it was something she didn't know. Apples! How good they tasted after the first frost pierced them and then the sun thawed them. No, apples never tasted better than they did after a frost followed by a warming sun. His own mother had taught him that.

And it was true that it was harder and harder to remember someone dead and gone, his mother and how she had looked standing in doorways, shading her eyes, waiting for the school bus to honk when it dropped him off. But she had taught him some things. She had taught him about the apples.

"You sit down," he told our mother. "Sit down here. Lean against the trunk of this tree." And she was tired and dizzy, very slightly dizzy, and so she sat down and as soon as her back touched the rough bark of the tree she felt her eyes grow heavy and begin to close, and when she opened them, she saw Albert high up in the apple tree, and he was sitting on one of the upper boughs, beginning to edge his way along toward a cluster of fat red apples for some reason ignored by the raccoons, and she saw how gray the tree bough was and she was about to shout, "Come down! Come down! That bough is brittle!" when Albert reached out for the apples and turned to look at her, and called out, "Catch them in your skirt!" and just then they heard a faint cracking sound, and Albert stared at her and began edging back along the bough, this time more quickly. But now the cracking sound was louder, and he shouted, "I'll be all right," and the breaking branch snapped with a sound like thunder and he fell through the air along with the branch of the great tree and lay perfectly still.

And our mother got up, thinking, He's had the breath knocked out of him, just the breath, he wasn't so high up, and she struggled to stand up and walk over to him. The small, snapped-off branches were all around him. The thick bough rested on his chest. His arms were wrapped around it as they must have been when they both began to fall, and he lay so still, looking up at her, lying on his back. And she said, "Albert, get up now, it's not funny," but he didn't move, and she bent over him and picked up his hand but it didn't return the pressure of her own. And then she began frantically pushing the branches that littered his body from his chest, but the big bough was too heavy. She couldn't move it. She said, "I'll go for help. Don't move," and ran through the meadows until she came to the road, and then ran all the way to the Hewitts'.

And when our grandmother saw her face, she moved her pot from the stove and ran outside and called for her husband and her children and all of them got in the truck and drove quickly to the orchard, and there he was, Albert, her husband, still lying where he had fallen, and our grandfather made a gesture, *Stay where you are,* and our grandmother held our mother while he and the children went closer. When they surrounded him, when our mother could no longer see him, when it seemed to her his body had been encircled by crows and was shut off from her, she began gasping as if there were not enough air in the world for her, and Hilda, our grandmother, held her and said, "It will be fine, everything is all right," and then our grandfather turned and walked slowly back to them and said, "Elfrieda, he is dead."

"Then," said our mother, "I will go and sit with him."

My grandmother held on to her, but she pulled loose easily, and when she reached the Hewitt children they stepped aside for her, and she sat down next to her husband and began speaking to him in a low voice, so softly that they couldn't hear her.

"I think," my aunt said, "she is telling him that story about the girl who got lost and went to sleep in the snow," but they didn't know what she was saying, only that her voice went on and on, curiously intent, as they had never heard her before, as if she believed she could wake the dead, as if nothing could be easier, as if she merely had to wait long enough or think of the right words. And the Hewitt children looked down at Albert, lying so peacefully on the ground, not ground really, but a great gray slanting rock onto which he had fallen, and thought they saw him move.

"She will have to come home with us," our grandmother said.

One of her sons went to telephone the doctor and then Mr. Darlington at the funeral home, and when he was through, Mr. Darlington was to stop at Old Mrs. Land's house, Albert's grandmother, and let her know what had happened. Perhaps she would know what to do with our mother. "And you," our grandmother told my aunt, "you go home and tell the boarder what's happened and tell him the house may be disturbing to him and he may want to stay in the inn for the next few days and of course we won't expect him to pay for it."

"Mr. Rice!" our grandmother said. "Why did we ever take that man in?" But she knew why they had taken him in. The minister said the man's health was not good and unless a good family could take him and keep him warm and feed him good food and let him sit in the sun and the clean air until he regained his health, he wouldn't last out the year. And our grandmother thought, Just this way was Elfrieda brought to us, and she said yes, of course they would take him. And now she wished him at the bottom of the river.

"You will not get that girl away from him until he is in the ground," our grandfather said. "Perhaps not then." And at that moment, Albert's grandmother walked up the hill through the dimming light, walked toward them and through them until she stood over her grandson's body. She looked from his body to the apple tree and, nodding her head, said, "The damn fool knows better than to climb dried-up trees. Elfrieda, get up. He is dead and that's the end of it. He climbed up a tree and he fell down onto a rock and now he is dead. How I outlive everyone," she said. "Elfrieda, get up," she said again, and when our mother didn't move, but went on speaking to her silent husband, she raised her stick and struck her grandson across the knee. "You see?" she said to our mother. "He doesn't move. Get up before I take this stick to you." Our mother got up. "Did anyone think to call the doctor?" the old woman asked. "She is pregnant, you know."

And she was pregnant with Albert, our half-brother, who died of pneumonia soon after we left Peru.

Our grandparents looked at one another, then at Albert, lying on the ground, then at our mother, who now stood staring up into the tree.

"I believe," our mother said, "he went up there to get me some frozen apples."

"Eat one," the old woman said. "He went to a lot of trouble to get it."

"It is delicious," our mother said, chewing. "But we should save some for him."

"I won't have craziness around me," said the old woman. "Elfrieda, wake up. He's dead as a doornail," and at that point our mother began to cry. "I'll be the one to wash his body," the old woman said, but our mother shook her head. She would do it. "You won't do it," the old woman said. "We're going back to your house, all of us here. Come with me, Elfrieda." She held out her arm and our mother took it.

"See how Elfrieda obeys her," our grandmother said. "She didn't listen to a word I said."

"The sun and the moon obey Mrs. Land and her stick," Mr. Hewitt said.

She could have returned to our grandparents' house, the Hewitt house, but instead she married again—our father, Frank Rice, the boarder the Hewitts had taken in, a man who needed to regain his strength.

Did she love our father?

"Oh, she loved him, I always believed she loved him," our grandmother said. "Not like her first husband. But enough. And she grew to love him more. You always do, if you don't grow to hate them, but I said, 'Elfrieda, don't do it, he isn't a healthy man, he isn't strong, you don't want to bury another husband.' She didn't listen to me, of course she didn't, because here you are, and I used to say to her, 'Elfrieda, you wouldn't have the girls if you hadn't married him, look on the bright side,' but she wasn't one to look on the bright side, not in those days, and how could she have known he had a bad heart, *he* didn't know he had a bad heart. It was Dr. Steiner who found it out, after your father fell down a flight of steps.

"When he came to, he remembered how dizzy he'd been, and it was Dr. Steiner who found out your mother was pregnant again, two patients fainting away in the house. At first he thought they'd caught something, but he knew better fast. He was a good doctor, Dr. Steiner.

"He asked them what they wanted first, the good news or the bad news—you girls were the good news: that was when Elfrieda started in saying she knew she was having a two-headed baby, she could feel the two heads—and your father's heart was the bad news, and in no time at all his lips were blue and his fingernails were blue and he was forbidden to climb stairs, and my boys helped in the store and they carried him up and down stairs. He didn't struggle. He didn't complain. He wanted to stay alive for your mother. And you girls, the sun rose and set on the two of you, and he knew your mother didn't know what to do with you. She used to say it was a sign, having twins, it must mean she didn't have much time. That was why nature gave her two instead of one. It was trying to make up to her for having so little time. He must have told himself he had to stay alive, and he lived longer, much longer, than anyone expected, eight years longer. That's how old you girls were when he died.

"But of course he did die," our grandmother said, "and that was when the trouble began. Before that there was no trouble. You two girls were so wrapped up in each other, your aunt Lotte used to say she felt you were on loan. You could have settled anywhere, in any house, you didn't seem to be *ours*, you didn't seem to be *anyone's*, only each other's. Your aunt Lotte used to say, 'Poor Elfrieda! She's like someone in a book and from the first page you know the author's after her.' She was right, too."

And it seemed the whole town knew the story of our lives from the moment we were born, the two of us, the wonders of Peru from the moment of our birth, slightly famous, people turning to look at us, famous not for what we did, famous simply for existing, for resembling one another.

TWIN GIRLS BORN TO PERU, read the paper's headlines the day we were born, and our father indignantly asked our mother what the *town* had to do with it.

And after we were born, everyone told our mother what a good mother she was, and how brave, taking care of three children and the store and her husband, and doing so well with each. And everyone told our grandmother what a good mother she had been to our mother, and everyone said how good Lotte and Fritz were to Hilda, their mother, and all of them knew they owed their celebrity to us, the twins, who were a constant source of fascination. Surely everyone was happy.

My mother had her children. Our grandmother knew she was needed. Our father watched us with delight. If he had to die young, he'd leave behind two children, two in the time it took to produce one. We were like extra time, weren't we? We were a measure of grace. The two of us had one another. And the town, which previously had only the gazebo to distinguish it, now had the twins who rode in the first sleigh or horse drawn cart in every New Year's Day parade together with the oldest citizen in the town, Old Mrs. Land.

But our mother was beginning to complain, and our grandmother said, "Of course two are harder than one," and our mother said, "When they were tiny and we first put them in separate cribs, they screamed all night. We thought they would stop after one night, but they screamed harder. So we pushed their cribs closer together and in the morning we found them pressed up against the bars, their hands on each other's heads.

"Then they learned they could climb on each other. One would get up on all fours and the other stood on top of her and got to the top of the railing and fell out onto the floor. I left them alone in the bathroom and one of them nearly went out the window. They get into everything. I don't do it to be mean, but when Frank is upstairs and I'm alone in the store, I tie them to chairs, and they *walk* with their chairs and get into the flour.

"When they were not even two, if I gave them a glass of milk, they pushed the glasses together to check and see they both had the same amount. One might have more! I came in to give Doris some milk because she was crying, and in her sleep, Florence said, 'Me, too.' Sound asleep and she said, 'Me, too.' It isn't what it seems."

S H E   H O L D S Florence up to the mirror. "Who is that?" she asks her.

"Dowie."

"No," our mother says. "*That* is you. That is Florence. Who is that?" Elfrieda asks, pointing to Doris, who was playing on the floor.

"Dowie."

"That's right," our mother says. "That is Doris. And who are *you?*" she asks, holding Florence back up to the mirror. Florence shakes her head, meaning, I don't know. Quite contentedly, quite happily.

Our mother begins to cry. Both babies turn to her with identical looks of concern. When she puts Florence down, both babies crawl over to her, try to crawl together into her lap, settle for pulling themselves up by the sleeves of her dress, touch her wet cheeks and look at one another in wonder.

Later, our father will teach us to call out, "We're home," and we will come back and call out, "We're home," and go up to our room, and our chattering begins.

But we are already at home whenever we are together.

Walking down the street in Lofton, people stop my mother, on the way to buy us boots and dresses, and say, "Are they twins?" and she says, "Yes, they're twins." She is proud of being the mother of twins. At that moment she doesn't mind the exhaustion, the way we shut her out, the way we ignore her when she calls out, "Girls! Pick up those papers!"

We would answer only if she called us by name, and she is never sure which is which, and so she doesn't call us by name and eventually she picks up the papers herself.

"You are just tired," people tell my mother, who does not go on to tell them that when she told Florence, "Stop that!" Florence first looked at me and in that instant we decided whether we would obey her. If the decision went against her, both of us would do the forbidden thing and then which twin did she slap and how do you slap her when the other one distracted you, doing something else just as you were about to grab hold of her sister, so that you feel like an animal taunted by two buzzing flies, both flying in different directions?

And who can she tell that it is always two against one, that she envies the twins as much—more!—than anyone else does because we are hers, we resemble her, and yet we shut her out. She would like to join us, she would like to wander down the lane with us, pursuing orange butterflies, but we don't want her. She would be out of step. We would have to stop and wait for her. We would need words to talk to her.

Oh, yes, we wanted our mother, all children do, but she hated it, our perpetual, horrifying cry: *Me, too!*

And yet we were not jealous of one another, not really.

And after all, we were twins. She and her daughters were not triplets, although she knew that's what she wanted to be. Triplets. To be part of us.

At night, she heard us chattering to one another from our youth beds, a stream of gibberish punctuated by screams or shouts of laughter, and suddenly the chattering stopped, and when she went into the room, both of us were asleep, hands through the railing bars, fingers clasped tightly together.

They do not need me, our mother thought.

IT IS quite amazing, said our father, that two fifteen-month-old infants can intimidate you simply by glaring. Two infuriated faces! Instinctively you feel you are wrong.

Two infuriated, identical faces, our mother murmured.

As if a whole town had turned against you, and yet they are only two babies.

She noticed his lips were blue, conspicuously so, as were his finger-nails. She hoped we would not notice and make blue fingers and lips part of our games.

THEY HAD a game called the Dead Game. It was one of their favor-ites. First one went into their room, lay down on the floor, her arms at her sides, her legs tight together, her eyes closed, breathing shallowly, and the other came in and put her hand to her chest and pretended to faint away, collapsing on the cot near the window. Probably this was the best part, the fainting.

The twins practiced this at every opportunity, alarming visitors to the house and the store.

Only the doctor was critical of their performances, saying, "When someone really passes out, it's like six bags of groceries hitting the floor at once. A fainting person can make quite a lot of noise, and they're almost always clumsy." The girls ignored this and went on fainting—simultane-ously. "I've heard of synchronized swimming but never synchronized faint-ing," said the doctor, at which point they both sat up and asked him, "Was that better?" And because they were children, and who could resist them, he said, "Oh, much better."

In the Dead Game, the one who fainted "came to herself" (somewhere they had heard that expression, and how they loved it), got up, walked sadly over to the dead body, went to the dresser and took down a plastic mirror, held it to the mouth of the dead one, dug at her own eyes as if she were violently weeping, went to her cot and, pulling off a flannel blanket, covered the dead one with it, waited a few minutes, looked around the room (for what? no one knew), and then threw herself upon the rigid, cov-ered body of her sister. For a few seconds, they lay there quietly, and then the dead sister rolled over and they began tugging at the blanket. One of them was stronger. Which one? And the struggle turned serious. One hit the other, who returned the blow, and soon they were rolling over and over on the floor, kicking and biting and punching, and when Elfrieda or Lotte came in to stop them, they were oblivious to her presence.

It was as if no one else were there. They were deaf to Elfrieda's shouts or slaps. They responded only to one another. Elfrieda had learned—as had their aunt Lotte and their father and anyone else who had to deal with them—that they would not kill one another, and so she gave up and let them settle matters. Downstairs, she could hear them thumping against the floor. She heard the high-pitched, outraged shriek that meant one had pulled the other's hair. And then it was quiet and the chattering began, the endless giggling, and then the sound of a soft thud, and their mother knew the Dead Game had begun again, but this time the other twin was the dead one, and her sister had her turn fainting, covering up the body, and lying down on it.

Where did they learn this game? Darlington's Funeral Home was not one hundred yards down the road, but Mr. Darlington took endless precautions to keep his corpses out of sight of the living, having long ago called in a carpenter to reset his first-floor windows so high that no one, especially not children, could see into his workrooms, and on most days, thick draperies shut the rooms from sight. But of course some children were curious and would persist, although most attempts were foiled because of the noise made by dragging up a stool or a ladder or a particularly large log.

The twins, naturally, got away with murder.

They were a tiny, perfectly coordinated team of two who seemed to communicate with one another through the ether. Did they steal out of the house at night in the cold when Mr. Darlington believed no one would possibly be watching? Did they wait for a night when snowdrifts were already high against the wall of the house, and solid, the snow having thawed and then frozen into a thick crust of ice that would support their small weight? And did they then go to the back of Mr. Darlington's house, one of them crouched on all fours, the other one climbing on her sister's back, silent even if one fell and hurt her hand and cut her lip, because they had agreed they would be silent before they left the house or because they agreed at the instant it happened? Blood or no blood, they would remain silent. And did the first one look into the workroom and see a dead body lying on the table?

And after she had seen all she wanted to see, did she climb down and crouch on the crust of the snow and let her sister climb onto her back? She must have. If one had missed her turn, she would have come to their mother for revenge. They had a passion for justice, the twins. From the time they began school, their cry *It isn't fair!* rang through the classrooms.

"They will grow up to be lawyers," said their aggrieved, besieged teacher, who often thought how nice it would be to separate them if only there were more than one class for each grade.

They added to the Dead Game. They took their jar of blue tempera paint and in turn painted each other's lips and nails blue. How nice! Now they looked exactly like their father. Then they would look at one another, exactly as if they were looking in a mirror, and nod. Simultaneously.

The first time Elfrieda saw this, she was standing in the hall holding a stack of towels, which she promptly dropped, and screaming, *Monsters! Monsters!* she rushed into the twins' room, where she was, it seemed, everywhere at once, and this time neither of them escaped her. She hit them on the head, on the breast, knocked one down and held her down with her foot while she grabbed the other one, who was shrieking *Help! Murder!* trying to roll under the cribs they still slept in (but now with the bars down), and held that one (which one? which one?) and slapped her face again and again although the child tried to twist away, tried turning her head from her mother, who hit her on the stomach and across the buttocks, and would have gone on until she was exhausted except that Lotte ran into the room and grabbed Elfrieda from behind and dragged her away and then fought her way through the storm of Elfrieda's flailing hands, catching her hands and pinning them behind her back. But not before Elfrieda had slapped Lotte's face and left a handprint on her left cheek and a red mark on her upper arm (it would turn blue later), while the hysterical twins sat up and fell silent, staring entranced at their mother who was fighting with Lotte—as if they were watching the best performance in the world.

"Frank," Aunt Lotte said to their father, her chest heaving, "please give me one of your sedatives. And a glass of water. And call my mother. Don't go down. Use the intercom and tell Fritz to call her."

"Elfrieda, what happened?" Aunt Lotte asked, but it was the wrong question. She knew it was, because Elfrieda sat up on the cot and pointed at the twins and begin whispering, *Monsters! Monsters!* at which point the two girls looked at one another and dove under their cribs.

"Their lips and fingers!" Elfrieda gasped.

"What did you girls do?" Lotte demanded. Her fingers tightened on Elfrieda's wrist. "What on earth did you two girls do?"

"We were playing our Dead Game," one of them said.

"We always play it," they said together.

"Come out in the open where I can see you," Lotte demanded, and when she saw their blue lips and fingers, she said, "Oh, Elfrieda, I am so sorry," and she told the girls to wash their hands and faces and not to come back until every bit of blue paint was washed off, and they were not to do it again.

"Lie down here, Elfrieda," she said, giving her the capsule Frank brought her. "Drink this water."

"Come in here, girls," she said, seeing them in the doorway. "Look what you've done. This painting yourself blue upsets your mother. You promise me you won't do it again!"

"Why is it bad?" asked the two together.

"Because I say so," said Lotte, and the twins looked at one another, seemed to discuss the matter (although they said nothing, did not even nod), and then turned together to face Lotte and said, together, "All right."

"Lotte," our grandmother said when she arrived, "those girls can drive you crazy. One day last week I could have picked them up by their adorable twin arms and dropped them out the third-floor window onto their adorable twin heads."

"They seem to have no human sympathy," Lotte said, reflecting. In those days Lotte wanted to become a nurse and she placed an even greater value on compassion than usual.

"Oh, Lotte, they are perfectly normal little girls. When you were just under three you had a kitten you loved so much you strangled it. You didn't know what you were doing. You were interested in all the noises it made and how it jumped around. I cried for days. But imagine if there had been two of you and you had strangled two kittens!"

"I killed a kitten?"

"Not deliberately, Lotte! Not knowing what you were doing! You kept looking for it for an entire week! You nearly drove me crazy! You emptied out cupboards and drawers!"

"*I* killed something? A living thing?" Our aunt, our grandmother's perfectly sensible daughter, had drifted off into the preoccupied sort of trance our grandmother knew so well in our mother.

"Oh, for heaven's sake!" Hilda said. "You two!" she said to the twins. "Is it your ambition to upset the whole world?" Whereupon the twins began weeping and sat at Hilda's feet and encircled her legs with their plump pink arms, and Hilda tried to pat the top of their heads and at the same time stroke our mother's cold, gray face, and she thought, Only an octopus is fit to have twins. No one human is meant for it.

It seemed to their mother that they cared about no one but each other. They counted the peas on their plates. Florence had twenty-six peas and Doris had twenty-eight, and Florence told Doris she had to give her one pea so they would both have the same amount, and when Doris said no, she was eating all of her peas, they started hitting one another and Florence picked up a fork and stabbed Doris in the arm with it, and she bled all over her clothes and dripped blood on the floor.

And all Elfrieda could do was send them to their room, and they loved to go to their room. What did they talk about all the time? Once, she stood in the hall and eavesdropped, and Doris was telling Florence every single thing she did that day and then Florence said it was Doris's turn, and Doris told her everything *she* did, and when they were finished, one of them said, "Well, I guess we got a lot done today." They didn't know there were two of them!

And they sat facing one another and played the mirror game. They were never lonely. There were times she hated them.

At night, our parents sat in the parlor. Our mother crocheted squares for a maroon and rose afghan and our father read *The Pickwick Papers*. *Always read a long book, because God won't let you die until you finish the story.*

"What do you suppose they're talking about?" he asked, looking up from his book.

"I know what they're talking about," their mother said. She wound some rose wool around her left hand and went on crocheting. "Their favorite game. They've decided everyone once had a twin but everyone's twin died. Now they walk around making up stories about how they died. They have horrible imaginations, really morbid. Florence must have started it. She starts everything."

Our father said, "Some of your stories are quite as bad, Elfrieda."

"Oh, I don't think so. I know about this game," she said, "because I eavesdrop. A wineglass works very well—if you press it to the wall and then put the stem to your ear."

"Elfrieda! They have little enough privacy in there, two of them in one room!"

But our mother said it was cheaper than bugging the room; she needed to know what went on in their evil little minds.

"Their minds are not evil," said our father, and Elfrieda said, "I'm their mother, and if I didn't eavesdrop, I'd never know *what* they were thinking," and their father said, "We should get a television. Then everyone would be too busy to bother about everyone else. Then they wouldn't sit at the table for an hour counting their peas." But they were hemmed in by mountains. They could barely tune in the radio.

"There must be a way. There must be a big enough antenna," their father said.

"A television won't cure those girls."

"They don't need curing. They need distraction."

And Elfrieda asked what they needed distraction from, and their father said they needed distraction from everything that went on in the house. They didn't know there was a world out there. Elfrieda said they knew as much about the world as any children their age.

"If only we had a television," their father said. "We'd forget about them. For a while."

"No one can forget about the twins."

"At least they get along."

"They love each other. They're each other's great love," their mother said, but their father said, "Don't say that!" and Elfrieda asked him why.

"Because it can't go on. You know it can't. What happens if one of them decides to get married?"

"It would be bigamy," their mother said, laughing.

"Bigamy?"

"Because he'd have to marry both of them. He *would* marry both of them, whether he knew it or not."

"I wish we had a television," Frank said. Did he look down at his hands and see his nails were shockingly blue, that even his skin had a bluish cast? Did it occur to him that the bluish glow he sometimes saw through the windows of farmhouses on flatter, more open land resembled the color of his nails—the blue of a television screen? Did he think it was the color of nostalgia, of perpetual sadness, of loss, of souls wandering the earth, of people whose spirits left their bodies at night to look for those who had sunk beneath the earth? Did he think it was the color of mortality? Did he ask himself why he wanted such a thing in his house?

There was a sudden crash in the twins' room, and shouting, harsh and strident.

"A television would be wonderful," our mother would have said, sighing.

CHAPTER

FOURTEEN

I T WAS still raining and I was still sitting at the table, watching my reflection in the café window. Everyone in the café came in dripping, and Eva rushed out and mopped up the new puddles, and for an instant, the thick black linoleum tiles shone and reflected the ceiling lights and I was astonished at how happy I was to see Eva, a woman who didn't come in trailing threads from the spiderweb I lived in. She came over to me when it quieted down.

"Tell me, what have you been doing?" she asked, and when I made a vague gesture, she said, "I've been thinking about young love. There was a couple in here yesterday after you left—I daresay the entire café was thinking about young love—and they weren't *doing* anything, they were looking at each other, only looking, you see. When he got up, she stared after him, such a drama, that separation! Two minutes while he went for two cups of tea! Well, separation is the drama of our lives, isn't it? Oh, you felt so young, they made you remember, they really did!

"And then you felt so old, you asked yourself how long it had been since you first fell in love, and my God! I never thought I'd *live* as long as that! Forty years since I first fell in love! I remember when I didn't think I'd live to be thirty! When I was forty, I cried all day, and the man I lived with was distraught. He didn't know what to do for me. He went out and bought sherry. He bought red wine and white wine. He bought chocolate roses—you know, those Cadbury chocolates they call roses, all different kinds. Well, he's English, he thought they were fancy chocolates, the very best chocolates. What can you do with an Englishman? Tell me, what are you thinking about?"

"I was thinking," I said, "about first love. First love and what a mess it always is."

"We don't think about it correctly," Eva said, rapping the table with her knuckles. "We don't. Do you realize that I still dream about him, that boy—he was only a boy, only nineteen—after all these years? And whenever I dream about him, we're always the same age I am now? We're not seventeen and eighteen and nineteen anymore. We're in our sixties and we have an understanding. We know everything there is to know about each other, as if we've been together all this time, growing old together, you know, somewhere behind the curtain, while the play went on in front and we've never let on, not even to ourselves.

"Isn't it strange? And the dreams always end the same way. He says something and I know he means to say he's leaving all over again, just the same as it really was that first time, but it doesn't make me unhappy, not at all. I wake up very happy. And then this morning I woke up and thought, Eva! As old as you are now, you're old enough to be the mother of that young boy! You're old enough to be your own mother! In another ten years, you'll be old enough to be the grandmother of that young couple! For heaven's sake! How can you still go on dreaming about them? A pederast, that's what you are! Well, it is something, isn't it? Would we be interested in two children, two seventeen-year-olds? At our age? But we're still in love with them, we still want them, we dream about them. It's what I've always thought, you see. It's not only ducks who imprint on the first things that walk in front of them. We all do it. The first things that happen to us are the important things. They make up the immortal memories, that's what I call them. The first people, they're the immortal people. Oh, our mothers have a lot to answer for."

"Mine does," I said absently.

"They all do," Eva said sadly. "Look over there, Doris. Who is that young man who keeps staring at you? Do you know him?"

"What young man?"

"The one on his way out the door."

"I've never seen him. Was he staring?"

"He doesn't take his eyes from you! But you must know. He's been in here before."

"God knows who he is," I said uneasily.

"You don't know him?" Eva said. "Then you have an admirer! It's been a long time since I had an admirer strong enough to walk his own dog! But you know who I mean? That young man who just left?"

"I didn't get a good look at him."

"Next time I'll point him out." The bell over the door tinkled. "I'd better get back to work," Eva said.

I sat at the table, I ordered another coffee, I thought about the young man who stared. Was it the Impostor? But I was to meet him at the end of next week. He wouldn't want to scare me off by appearing early, without warning. I thought about first love and how we made too much of it and how it was doomed. Wasn't it doomed by its very nature? The poets knew better. *His first minute after noon is night.* Everything caught in time, the one you love dragged by time from his pedestal, changed by time—but was I thinking about first love, or love at first sight?

First love could accommodate change, couldn't it? But love at first sight was love at a precise instant, love in a specific slant of light. How could you keep it, how could you hope to see the same thing again, even one minute later?

That description of Florence's meeting with Jack Pine, in Chicago, so famous. What do people make of her, I wonder, people with their tidy lives kept small? What do they make of her extravagant emotions?

I had passages from her journal with me, I always had them, I kept them at the bottom of my handbag always: even though I had them memorized. But I might forget. One day I might try to summon them up and my mind would have erased them. I couldn't take that chance and so I carried them with me everywhere. My husband used to see me open my handbag and he said, "If I didn't know better, Doris, I'd think you were in love with him too, I'd think you were wondering how to do the same thing," and I said, "The same thing?" and he said, "Fall in love with him yourself. Just as she did."

And I said, "No, no, I want to *understand.* I never thought she'd fall in love like that. I thought that was *my* fate. She always said she'd never get married."

That's what she wrote in her journal—

—↶↷—

DORIS WILL get married, she already has a married look, as if she already had a husband but didn't quite know it, not yet.

But not me! I want to be unique, I want to be special, although how I'm to manage this with Doris on the same campus is beyond me, but there's a solution to everything. *She* wants to get married. Maybe some boy will carry her off before Thanksgiving. I hope so. I'll egg on anyone who takes an interest in her. I'd *seduce* them, pretending to be her. But I mustn't think about that! We've agreed to take different classes and keep out of each other's way. From now on, she will be just another person on campus. I won't look directly at her and I won't see her great moon-cow eyes gazing at me with such love that I feel as if I'm drowning beneath a wave that's knocked me down.

The truth is—the truth is—I want more than to begin over. I want to be *born* again. I want to go back to wherever it is we came from and come into this world stunned and blinded by the light, and when I open my eyes I want everything to be itself and nothing to be like me. I want a mother who looks at me as if I'm the most remarkable creature in the world and who doesn't believe there's anyone on this earth as beautiful as I am. I want parents whose glances rest on me and whose eyes don't flicker back and forth between two children. *I am not Doris. I never was Doris. I never will be Doris!*

As for me, I don't want any husbands. I don't want to be anyone's wife. I don't want to ask anyone his opinion of what I buy and I certainly don't want anyone's permission to do anything. I don't want children. Why don't I want them? Isn't it obvious? They might resemble me. I've seen mothers whose children look like shrunken versions of themselves. I've had enough of resemblances. And if you don't want children, why do you need a husband? I don't want anyone watching my every gesture and expression, trying to determine what my mood might be and grilling me about my state of mind. I've had closeness and I've had enough of it. A surfeit, that's the perfect word.

FINALLY, alone! A summer alone in Chicago! I have been ecstatically happy in the tyrannical heat. My roommates are both working and I am often alone in the apartment or in the studio and there is no one at all to answer to when I wander around the campus waiting for the carillon to begin playing while the organist practices ringing the bells (he does both), no one to ask if it is safe to walk out to the lake in the middle of the night, for I go when the other two are already asleep. Last night I dragged my mattress out onto the fire escape and slept there and had no one at all to explain to.

And today when I walked past International House to the lake, a gust of damp, cool air almost knocked me over and I wondered what that signified.

I found out when I was about to cross the footbridge leading to the point and a policeman was stationed there to stop people like me who didn't know a tornado was heading in from the lake.

This freedom brings back memories, things I thought I'd forgotten, things I didn't know I'd seen—of a man who used to come in when Mother was cutting up a bar of naphtha soap to do the washing and as the chips fell into the water, he grabbed her from behind and said, "I'm going to boil *you,* I'm going to throw *you* in with the clothes," and how delightedly she would laugh before he put her down. The end of another wonderful day.

It is so glorious, this freedom, so unutterable.

AND THE NEXT DAY, the very next day, she took one look at Jack, and then what? Well, the whole world knows.

Her first sight of Jack, her first account: was it ever published in its entirety? I don't think so.

I always thought it was written especially for me.

And now, sitting in the café, the light less bright but gilded—how lovely human flesh always looks in this light—I took it out and read it again, the way some people read their Bibles, not really looking at the pages, already knowing the words, moving their lips, but happy. Happy to know the words are there on the page, like secret money, like dreams of extra rooms in a house you've lived in all your life, this account of a grand passion that came for you like an astoundingly fast express train and somehow you had your ticket, you knew you had to get on, you knew you wouldn't have a second chance. Grand passions aren't in my nature. I had one grand passion, my sister, the sister of my childhood. But in this world there's no place for such a passion, is there? The world allows sexual love anything. But the rest—love of parents for children, children for parents, sisters and brothers for one another—in the end, their claims are not even recognized.

This is what Florence wrote—so melodramatic, so love-struck, so extravagant. She was only eighteen.

_____

WONDERFUL, catastrophic, splendid, incredible, marvelous disaster! The summer ended, the days already cold, gold leaves falling and blowing, scudding across the street like animals desperate to escape the wheels of the cars, and this is what happens.

I fell in love. Today. Oh, ring the bells for me. Let them toll! I fell in love in the terrible way one might fall in love with a killer, knowing full well that he could take everything I had, including my life, hoping that, if he was a killer, he would take my life, because what larger thing could I give him? And my soul. It is barely worth speaking of my soul, because that flew up from my chest and out of my mouth the moment I saw him and when he opened his mouth to speak to me, my soul, that small, insignificant, incomplete thing, had its chance and flew in and found his soul and twisted itself about it so that no one, not even God, could disentangle them again. No bird that finds its nest after a storm could be happier. And I never knew there was a storm! I never knew I was lost! In a moment. Before I knew his name. Before I knew his circumstances. Had he been married, I might have turned killer. Had he had children, they might have died at my hand. I saw him and it was as if something tore in the fabric of things, and behind the sky I saw our two forms and I knew we had been searching for one another and nothing was going to separate us. And I had not yet spoken to him. He had not yet seen me.

Everything I had known before—gone. Everything still to come in front of me—in him. All decided—by that one glimpse of him. When your fate comes to meet you, when at last it steps forth from the crowds of gray-faced men and women, you know it. It extends its hands and you take it. What choice do you have?

What now of my precious independence? What now of my solitary, unique splendor? In the trash! Gone! A fever dream!

I want to explain how it happened, how extraordinary it was, but what is truly phenomenal, stunning—in the way a victim must be stunned when a mugger strikes him in the back of the head—is the way it comes, that thing that changes your life forever, disguised as the most everyday, ordinary moment, so that someone watching would turn his head aside in boredom, or continue to stare, as people always stare into the middle distance because nothing remarkable is there, because their

mind is elsewhere, as if nothing could arrest their attention, as if fate
knew that instinctively you would step aside, not out of dread, not out
of fear, because, after all, isn't this what you have been waiting for, as I
was waiting, all my life a moment preparing for this? And I didn't suspect! I thought I was preparing for something utterly opposite! So we
are humbled.

I should have rushed toward it, but I did not. You would not. You
would do as I did. You would step aside, sensing danger, sensing change,
for aren't the two the same? No matter who or what we want, however
much we want it, at the last moment we don't hear a great rush of wings,
we don't see a great gold light promising heaven. No, I felt the hot wind
of the passing train on my ankles and I jumped back. But not far
enough. You can never go far enough.

I felt very young and ancient—all at once. Present, past and future,
all settling on me, lightly, like butterflies.

This is what I saw. This is what changed my life. All so ordinary! Tell
me, was there anything marvelous in it? Is there any way to describe the
moment that divides life into what has gone before and what will come
after?

Everyone will think I have gone mad.

I was standing outside the college cafeteria, splendid in my solitude,
enjoying it, but frightened, all my friends gone off for the weekend, all
invitations to visit declined. I stayed, saying, Oh, the paper is long,
you're the organized one, you know how I procrastinate, you go home.

It was chilly, very chilly, the first of those days Mother made so
much of each year in Peru, saying, "This is when the spirits begin stirring, this is when your soul grows restless and has its own ideas and
you'd better breathe it back in! Breathe it back in or it can go off forever!" I used to believe that. Perhaps I still do. And the sky was very blue
and very thin, as if at any moment it might crack and let the dark stars
through. A small wind shook the leaves on the oak boughs, and dry
leaves hissed like snakes.

The cafeteria is a modern building, its walls made of glass. I sat on a
small cement bench and looked at the street reflected in the great glass
wall, and then I saw him, walking and talking with a friend. There was
nothing more to it than that. But the way he walked, the vividness of his
gestures, the eagerness with which he talked, the shirt he wore—a yellow
and brown plaid flannel shirt—the way his muscles shifted beneath the
fabric of that shirt, how indifferent he was to the cold, while everyone
else shivered, chattered their teeth in their jackets and corduroy coats.

That was all there was, but he might have been wearing a sign; a bird should have flown overhead, a banner unscrolling from its mouth, reading, in gilt letters, *He is the one. Stop him.* A golden arrow should have pointed down from the sky. Am I being ridiculous? I suppose I am ridiculous. But *something* to confirm this—this *what?* This annunciation. This inability to get my breath, to stop my eyes filling with tears, spilling stupidly down my cheeks. I was cold beneath my coat, quaking, but I didn't know I was cold, not until later. I told myself to get up, I told my feet to take me into the cafeteria, to take me up the steps. I watched myself move as if I had split in two, as if a tiny version of myself watched me from just under the ceiling.

In the cafeteria, I stopped at several tables and spoke to various people I knew from my classes. Someone said something and I laughed loudly, and he looked pleased, and his friend looked puzzled, so I knew what he said hadn't really been funny. I knew where he—He!—was sitting, that revelation in the brown and yellow plaid flannel shirt. I knew the instant his eyes fastened on me. I put my books down on an empty table and hesitated as if unsure. Should I stay or should I go back to my room? How to explain, as I stood there, his eyes on me, that I was filled with the most elaborate visions, visions of ironing his shirts, especially the one he now wore (I, who had never ironed a shirt in my life!), visions of setting a table, looking out the front window, waiting for the first glimpse of him, amused at my impatience, interested by my irritation, as if I had never before felt such an emotion, filled with admiration for my own tolerance, because I have never been tolerant or patient, oh, quite the contrary. At the table, leaning my cheek on my fist, watching him eat, marveling at the way his jawbone moved in its socket, leaning on my elbow at night, watching him breathe in the moonlight, thinking, What a miracle it is to breathe, how easily one could stop, in my imagination tracing with my finger the vein prominent between his eyes, that throbbing vein running down his forehead, so blue. Did it portend a short life, was it dangerous, so close to the surface, so visible? (Never sleep in moonlight, Mother used to say, moving our beds back against the wall farthest from the window. Moonlight can kill you! Never sleep at night in an open field! Always sleep beneath a tree! Now go to sleep. Don't get out of those beds again!)

All this in a part of a second. In the rest of the second, I thought, White Paintings! The White Paintings have always been for him! They are *his* paintings. And then I saw the red pomegranate, bright red, but its skin faded to beige here and there as pomegranate skins do fade, its texture like the earth itself, irregularly veined, and as I watched, the pomegranate split in half, and inside were the countless, the infinite seeds steeped in shining red juice, and then, before my eyes—in the cafeteria!—each seed became a tiny person, complete, fully dressed, but so tiny, and each one precious, and I knew I had seen this before, in dreams, in a recurring dream from which I would wake, terrified, sweaty, saying, "They're all the same! They're not worth *anything!*" And my sister would comfort me. My sister, who was she? I had no sister!

Now the pomegranate, the great red planet, the enormous brain-world, was back, hovering here in this almost empty cafeteria that sheltered this man as an empty great cathedral shelters the one precious relic it was built for, and I saw the painting it would become, the floating pomegranate burning its way through thickly falling snow. I put my books down. A second had passed—if that. I had his attention. I knew that.

I took off my coat. I put my hands under my great tangle of curly hair and threw the curls into the air and felt them fall back against my furry green sweater. I thought, Good, in this light, in this sweater, I will look as if I have golden eyes. I knew his eyes were on my body and it was as if I understood its use for the first time—to draw his attention.

And then I, the skittish, the shy *(Stand up straight! Look at people! What will they take you for? A frightened rabbit?),* did an amazing thing. I settled my coat over the back of my chair and walked over to his table. He was still watching me. Smiling. Slightly ironically. Slightly alarmed, as well he should have been. My shadow fell over his friend's plate, and whoever he was—that human pillow, that uselessly beating heart in its anonymous, unnecessary body—looked surprised. But He did not look surprised.

"Are you the one I have a letter for?" I asked him, and he said something: *I really don't know. Who gave it to you?* He must have said something. And I said, "Marie Reiter's letter. Is it for you?" And he must have said, "I don't know Marie Reiter." And we must have stared at one another. And he must have asked me to sit down. And the friend, that linen form stuffed with dead cotton, faceless, he must have gotten up, excused himself. We must have said things to one another. Time *must* have passed, because the bright blue sky had been replaced by a night sky and stars and our reflections were brilliant in the plate-glass window. Something must have happened, because we got up and left together. We walked out to the lake. He walked me back to my room.

———

AND THEN I spent two days, two interminable, torturous days, two desert days, one dune of sand after another and no oasis, sitting on a folding chair next to the one telephone on the dormitory floor, reading Proust, not out of choice, not that first time—it was assigned, the subject of a paper—listening for the phone. And on the third day it rang and it was for me. Could anything be more ordinary? More banal? Could anything be more astonishing, more final, more exalting, more *alchemical?* Because I had been turned—the world had been turned—from lead or pewter to the purest gold.

And I had no misgivings. None. No warnings, no hints, no intimations, no premonitions, no omens, no shiverings, no swiftings, no quivering of flesh, no harbingers of danger. And I *would* have had them! If everything had not been as it should, as it was meant to be. The pomegranate, the planet, the earth seed, had risen red in my sky. I felt its weight in my hand and its weight was good.

AND THEN the waiting began. Where was he? Would he call? The two questions that *mean* youth and beauty and hope, when even one's fingertips become smooth, fingerprints erased. Life is trackless and mapless and it seems impossible that your life could ever come to resemble anyone else's.

THIS IS how my days go on now. In despair. In humiliation. I have found the one I want, I want to rush up to him and take him by the hand and lead him off to some place no one else can follow, because, after all, our *souls* are married, but where is he? I don't know where he is! At this very moment he could be in a justice of the peace's dingy office, marrying someone else! Someone with long blond hair!

Is there anyone else on campus who studies on her fire escape wearing a square-shouldered raccoon coat and gloves and a raccoon hat (gift of my mother at Christmas)—looking for him? Is there anyone else on campus who is foolish enough to spend more than two minutes running from building to building when the wind blows in from the lake this way? Last night I sat outside in the snow watching for him and I let snow cover me until I was entirely white and when I came in I was so cold I took a hot shower and stayed in there until I was lobster-colored and even then I was shivering for an hour afterward.

Nothing is wrong with my body. That can't be it.

My mind! I barely have one. I will improve it. I resolve to read more. I will pick books by the thickness of their spine. I will ask people what are the most difficult books in the language and I will patiently read them until I understand.

AND THEN she worried. Did he know she had a sister? She wouldn't tell him. She'd tell him she was an orphan. Did he know she painted? Did he know how talented she was? She felt, she said, as if someone had ripped away a great sheet of skin from her stomach. She said she thought I would feel better if I knew how she suffered. She said she knew she would have to make me suffer. She said she knew I never enjoyed making people suffer. She remembered a photograph of us on the mantel at home. We wore our identical red dresses. She was grinning so hard into the camera that her gums were exposed and her eyeteeth looked like fangs, but I was smiling with my eyes shut. I looked soft. She didn't. But she had softened up now.

She didn't know how she would study for exams or how she would write papers. She discovered she didn't have any paper to write on. She told herself that if she failed exams, it would be Jack Pine's fault. If she was thrown out of school, if she went to Midway Airport and waited to hear if planes could take off in a snowstorm, if she took her life in her hands, it would be his fault.

And then he called her and asked her to go camping at Starved Rock and she was once more ecstatic.

ᥲ᷐ᥲ᷐

THE SUN has come up, the real sun! Jack was out in the Quadrangle early this morning, calling my name. He must have awakened the entire campus, because all day long people have been glaring at me as I go by. I put on my raccoon coat and ran downstairs and there he was in nothing but a red flannel shirt and his jeans (and his shoes and socks, of course), his cheeks red with cold, but otherwise as comfortable as he would have been in front of a wood stove. We will go camping. He will come for me on Friday at two-thirty, after his last class. He didn't ask *me* when my last class was, but I don't mind. I don't mind anything he does as long as I'm there when he does it.

He is so beautiful! He has the cheekbones of an Indian chief. His eyes are green like a cat's and glitter in the sunlight. His head is perfectly shaped. He moves beautifully. I know him by his walk well before I can make out his features or his clothes. And he is so tall! He has to stoop down to kiss me and often he tires of bending over and simply lifts me up to him and holds me against his chest, my chin even with his. When we walk together, other people turn to look at him. I'm used to people turning to look at me, but when women turn, I know who they're looking at.

HER FRIENDS were afraid that if they went camping in such weather, they'd freeze to death. She wasn't. If they did freeze to death, would that be so dreadful? She asked herself if life could ever be better than this, and decided that, yes, it could. They could spend years and years together, grow old together. What an idea! She'd never liked it, thinking of herself in one rocker, her husband in another, the two of them listening to their joints creak and feeling their teeth rot. But he would always be beautiful (if his hair didn't fall out, said her friends), and if happiness made people beautiful, she would always be beautiful (if *her* hair didn't fall out, said her friends). When he didn't call, she walked down Fifty-seventh Street and stopped at the used-record store and bought three records, the most lugubrious things she could find—Gregorian chants, Te Deums. What she would have liked was an album of four records entitled *Great Funeral Music of the Ages*.

She came out of the record store and saw the sky had come down, resting heavily on the tops of the brick buildings. If it started to snow before she reached Dorchester Avenue, she would see him that night. Dorchester Avenue—no snow. If it started to snow before Woodlawn, she'd see him tonight. No snow. If it started to snow tonight, she'd see him tomorrow. In the morning, the quadrangle was white, not with snow but with frost. She asked herself what she could use to make him jealous.

She asked herself how long someone could survive without sleeping.

After she met him, that's what she was like.

And then he proposed to her and she forgot she never wanted to marry. She forgot she never wanted to have children. She forgot she'd once had a sense of humor. She'd known him for a few months and she packed her things and left for France. And with that, her life stepped off into myth.

And my mother and our grandparents, and I, the identical sister, and the common with four churches at its four compass points, and the hills above Peru, and Peru itself, and the countryside, and the snow in winter and the blazing leaves in the fall and the muddy roads in spring and, in the summer, the river running over its speckled stones, and the gold light through the trees splashing the high grass waving in the soft winds, and the tasseled rows of corn, and the raccoons who picked up the chain-link mat in front of the door and dropped it down, and the porcupine hanging upside down from the aspen boughs—everything shrunk down small enough to fit into the room of a dolls' house or into a glass globe in which two stuffed yellow-breasted birds are protected from dust, small enough to fit into the palm of Florence's hand.

Which is what she wanted and what she would now have, all of us like trophies, toy people safe in a glass globe she could pick up and upend when she pleased, sending the snow swirling about us, a tame world, tame storms—unreal, safely forgettable, far away, quaint. She was done with us. Or so she thought.

I drank my coffee, I paid my bill.

I've always paid my bills.

He Took Care
of Me

H E TOOK CARE of me.
He woke me from a dream to give me water. He asked what my dream was because I had been speaking in my sleep.

I said I dreamed of my sister, who told her husband she didn't want children. Her husband couldn't understand it. I said I could give my sister my child, it would really be her child, he could see that, couldn't he? If we were identical, even in our cells, wouldn't the child be her child, exactly as if she'd borne it herself? Of course it wouldn't have her husband for a father, but otherwise it would be her child, we were both the same, wasn't it plain?

He said I was delirious, he thought I was raving, he held my head up with one hand, with the other he held the metal cup to my mouth, he said, Twenty sips, not less than twenty sips, and I fell asleep seeing faces, as I always do, faces I've known, my sister's face, multiplied again and again, swarming through the air like a cloud of gnats, then new faces, faces I'd not yet seen. They traveled from left to right, always from left to right, like soap bubbles drifting by, all these faces bubbling up from the inexhaustible well, each one different from the next. When I saw those faces, I fell asleep, as if into deep water, as if into a thin web covered with dust, I fell into happiness, into my own world, where no one could follow.

He said he would show me the exuberant stone angels—yes, exuberant!—who cast their shadows on the town's violet church wall. If I would grow stronger, if only I would get better.

One day I saw a stone angel standing in the doorway. Great rays of light shot from her wings. She was flirtatious, a coquette of an angel, a tease. Another day I heard hooves beyond the window. I saw stone horses tethered to the gate. Once, he took me in his car to the top of a mountain and from there we looked down at a cemetery. Each lot was square and hemmed in by a stone wall. From up above, the tombs were chess pieces on a chessboard, and I thought, It can go on even after death. There was a stone angel bending over as if to pick a flower and in front of her were two empty lots, two empty spaces, and I thought, She is not trapped, she can move forward, and then I saw she was stalemated. And then I dreamed that the world was a chessboard and that she was following after me, my sister, the queen. There were no kings on the board. There were no kings anywhere in the world.

He was pleased when the fever subsided. He didn't mind my sleeping. He said I had to sleep. When I awakened, he would change my clothes and the sheets on my bed. He mixed a white powder into my water. The water was cloudy as it dissolved, it smelled like garlic. After I drank it, I was cooler, and then one day I opened my eyes and reached for the coverlet and my fever had broken.

I stayed there, in that white stone house on top of a white stony mountain. I was pleased by the soft curves of the house wall, the gentle arches over the doors, the round deep portholes of windows, the stone angels on either side of each doorway, the stone horses rearing in the garden, the stooping angel in the garden.

His mother loved angels. His mother had ordered the angels. The stone horses: the death of his brother. The stooping angel: the death of his sister. There was a saucy angel who stood with her hands on her hips. She had always been there. She was pitted by rain, stained by moss and by weather. From a distance, she was perfect.

CHAPTER

SIXTEEN

THE SOUND of waves rising and falling, and I thought, How did the water get up so high, up to the third floor of the house, and I thought, I don't mind swimming, I like water, and then I opened my eyes and turned on my side in my bed, in my precious rented rooms, and the light was mercury-colored, and the wind was blowing, moist, almost wet, very strong, and the curtains were blown in, potbellied, shaped like the round-bellied stove in my mother's old kitchen, all the way back in Peru. Peru seemed a long way away now, all my life before renting these rooms seemed a long way away, not unreal, but smaller, tiny, small enough to place on the glass shelves of a china cabinet, mementos of something, as a sequin is part of an evening dress but is one thing among many, can fall off and not be missed, is not the dress, is not the same thing.

And for the first time, I thought, *I* am the main thing, I am what holds everything together. And that struck me as the most remarkable, most singular idea, as if I had bumped my nose against one of the facts of the universe, and I was so delighted I held up my hand and examined it and its five fingers as if I had never seen them before. I raised up my foot and examined its toes, and the wind blew the curtains way into the room and now they were bell-shaped in the air and for the first time I saw that the patterns were not abstract but were flowers, tropical flowers, and outside I could see the wind lifting and dropping the thick green-skinned oak leaves and it felt like spring, not summer. I could see the leaves turning their silvery sides toward me and I thought, More rain.

And I thought, I'm hungry, I should go early to the café, eat when none of the regulars are there to see me. But the air was so soft and moist and the curtains floated so on the palpable air and the oaks behind the glass were so full of meaning I could not make myself stir, and then I heard carillon bells and I wondered which church they were coming from, and I told myself I ought to get up and look. Was it the church I saw from my front window? But I thought that church was abandoned. Was there another church, behind the house? Here the churches were so massive and solid, huge gray blocks of stone, gray and blacker with each passing winter, more and more somber, a sermon in themselves.

In Peru, the churches were built of wood, white-painted, thin steeples like needles piercing the rose-streaked blue skies, blazing, when the sun struck them, like angels' wings. Seashells that wash up on the shore and bleach out in the sun are that color when the sun hits them, our mother said. She was not always bad, was she? Yes, that was the trouble—she wasn't always bad. And the curtains blew in, rang in the room like enormous bells, and I thought, I have to get up.

If we hadn't begun talking, if we had remained infants forever, if she could have gone on imagining whatever she pleased about us, then she would have been happy. Then *we* would have been happy. And probably all parents wish for it, a child who is forever their child. Probably all parents mourn the grown-up child who might as well have eaten the small child they so loved, and it is an odd world, an unsteady world, a discontinuous one, isn't it, when the small thing changes as it grows—as houses in Peru change, two-hundred-year-old houses. Every year clapboards rot in the weather and are replaced. The wind shakes stones loose from the chimney, tears slate shingles loose from the roof. The chimney is rebuilt, the roof is repaired, the floors warp and new planks are put in. Finally, everything has been replaced. Isn't it a new house? A different house? But no one says so. Everyone says, Oh, yes, it's a very old house. It's always been there.

I don't change. I am a plain person, a simple person. All I ever wanted was to love the people around me. I loved my mother and my sister and my husband and I still love them. My husband—I don't speak about him now. He's so far away. They are all so far away. Or to put it another way: I am so far away from them. But I don't want to feel guilty. I don't want anyone else to know about them. They are my own private treasure, what I will go back to. They are not part of the life I live here, and I think often that my life is, in spite of everything, basically happy. Everyone knows the happiness of a settled life, the way the river bears you up and lets you float when you are tired of swimming. It is what you are left with that you don't want to lose or leave. I have been so much more fortunate than my sister.

But I'm deeply superstitious. I don't like to think about it. She was the one supposed to have turned out well.

Was I still a twin—if my sister had been gone for so long?

The curtains billowed into the room again. Downstairs, my landlady was cooking. Was it lamb? The odor was drifting up through the hall, under the door, and the moist wind was blowing, and I was so happy here, on my own for the first time.

I wondered if my husband would call. I hoped he had taken enough warm clothes. He never packed sweaters. It was as if he never expected the weather to turn cold.

The last time I saw Dennis, in the café, he told me that Jack had long ago had my sister declared legally dead, and I began shaking so violently that my body shook the table and coffee sloshed over the rims of our coffee cups. "Of course," he said, "that doesn't mean she is dead," and I asked him what it did mean, and he said it meant that Jack Pine was free to remarry, free to make decisions about my sister's estate, free to sell his house—things like that.

And I thought, How dare Jack Pine think of selling that house! My sister loved that house! They bought it with her money! If he's thinking of selling that house, I'll stop him. The sight of me would be enough to put the fear of God into him.

"He doesn't know about me yet, does he?" I asked Dennis. "He doesn't know Florence had a twin?"

"He's going to have trouble believing it," Dennis said. "How much she kept hidden."

"TELL US a story," we said to our mother, and she began a long story about a little girl who had a magic shell, and when she rubbed the shell she could travel wherever she wanted, to any country, into the desert, to the top of the highest mountains in the world, into the throats of the deepest volcanoes, and even backward in time, into the past, or forward, into the future.

And we wanted to know what she saw there.

Our mother said, "When she went back in time, she saw herself, not as she now was, of course, but as she was long ago, as a very small child."

"You mean," Florence said, "if I went back in time I would see myself? I would see another Florence?"

"Another, younger Florence."

"And if I went further back in time?"

"*Another,* even younger, Florence."

"Two more Florences," my sister said.

"And if you went forward, *another* Florence!" our mother said merrily.

"Three Florences," my sister said.

I knew something was wrong. "Florence," I said, "let's go catch caterpillars."

"If I went back five minutes, there'd be one Florence, and if I went back ten minutes, there'd be another Florence, and if I went back fifteen minutes—"

Her face was white, her fists were clenched, their knuckles showed white under the skin. "And if I went forward five minutes, there'd be another Florence, and if I went back ten minutes, there'd be another Florence—"

"And another Doris! Don't forget Doris!" our mother said.

"All those Florences and Dorises," my sister said. Pale, shaking, breathing rapidly like little Emily down the road, who had fits and fell.

"Yes, and if you went back, you'd recognize the very little Florence, but she wouldn't know *you.* She'd think she'd never seen you before. Oh, how I would love to go back to the old rooms in New York and stand there and see my mother before she started coughing and watch her cook and peel carrots and potatoes! Oh, I'd go very far back so I could see my father as well, before *he* started coughing, I'd go back invisible, so they wouldn't see me—Florence, what's wrong with you?"

"Florences and Dorises everywhere, a whole world filled with Florences and Dorises. Which Florence is *me?* Which one is *me!*"

Our mother said, "Florence, calm down! What is wrong with you?"

My sister was glaring at me, thinking, That's how Doris got here, isn't it? You went back in time and got one of the Florences and brought her back and now there are two, only one's named Doris. And then she stared at my mother and she thought, Maybe you went back and got another Doris and you named that one Florence and I'm not really Florence at all. I'm another Doris. I'm not the first one, I'm not real. And her head kept turning. She stared first at me, then at my mother, and I could read what she thought as clearly as if she'd written it on paper. *But I was born first, I must be the real one, there was no one before me, you had to have me before you could get her, why did you get her, why did you want her, a world full of us, everyone will turn into us, my God!*

She was beside herself.

"I don't like this story," I said.

"And if there were so many Florences and Dorises, what would be so wrong with it?" our mother asked.

"I hate you!" my sister shouted. "I hate you!"

"Go to your room!"

"And *I* hate *you* too!" I shouted. "You're mean and rotten and you hate us!"

Our mother got up and slapped me.

"Leave her alone!" Florence shouted. "Don't touch my sister!"

"You don't understand anything," I shouted at my mother. "You shouldn't tell her those stories!"

"Are you telling me what to do? Are you?"

And I said I was. I kept it up, defying her, because Florence would protect me, Florence would take my side, and when she did, she would forget about those endless Florences and Dorises swarming like mosquitoes through the air.

And even then I must have known how unhappy I made her, how I spoiled the world for her, that the sight of me meant confusion, meant madness. And yet there was no one in the world she loved more than me. And it's possible, isn't it, that even then she was planning her escape?

Always I'd thought that if she hadn't heard Cecilia sing, if we hadn't followed Bill Stubbs and his dog into the woods, into Three Raven Wood, we would still be together.

We would have been like the twins we met in Chicago who both became nurses, both married firemen (oh, yes, I was the kind of twin who wanted a double ceremony), both had two children, cut their hair identically, used the same hair dye, shopped for the same clothes, weighed each other once a week, and if one weighed more, she went on a diet until she was the same weight as her sister, who said, We have four children. We think that's enough.

I envied them.

Florence said, "I can't stand the sight of them! They're freaks! Why do you talk to them?"

I refused to see the signs. I kept telling myself, After all, no matter what she says, we are both the same.

MY MOTHER came to Peru one cold night in February, at two in the morning, on the night train, on its way from New York City to Montreal. Amidst clouds of steam and with a great hiss of brakes, it stopped at the station on the Vermont side of the river and a young girl appeared in the doorway of the first passenger car and, making her way carefully, because the steps were coated with ice, climbed onto the platform. She stood beneath the indigo-blue sky and the brilliant stars, looking down first at the thick ice beneath her feet, gray ice so thick and so irregularly patterned it resembled melted wax, and then at the mountains that rose up in a black crescent to the left and right of her. She would have been frightened by all of it—the bright stars, never visible in the city, the enormous spaces, all of them empty, a great silence woven of many sounds, each of which began to make itself known to her: the rustle of wind in the bare branches, the sound of water surging over rocks and under ice, the sharp snap of a branch cracking under the weight of snow that had thawed and turned to ice, the rustle of dry leaves that still clung to the trees, the striking of steeple bells marking the hour—all this would have frightened her had she not been so cold even though she was wearing two pairs of leggings, three pairs of socks and a thick pair of boots, two sweaters, and a heavy man's woolen coat that ended just above her shinbones. The town, she knew, was shut up tighter than a tomb; the complete, inhuman silence surrounding her made that clear. If the man who was to come for her did not appear, she would be found somewhere between the platform and the town, frozen solid, her lips and fingers blue. This pathetic vision—she could see herself quite clearly, lying on her side, one arm stretched out, her head resting on her outstretched arm, her cut-velvet carpet bag lying just beyond the tips of her fingers—comforted her, comforted her even when the first snowflakes began to fall, and as they fell, she was so caught up in contemplating her small, frozen body stretched out on the ground that she began to revise her imaginary painting so that it more accurately reflected the recent change in the weather. She still lay on the ground, this time on a carpet of fallen leaves, but now the snow began to cover her. At first it collected on the outline of her shoulders, hips, legs, and thighs, as snow first collects on the top railing of a fire escape; then, slowly and steadily, it began to cover the ground and climb higher until it covered her entirely. As she watched, people of the town, all wrapped in black shawls, began to approach the sleeping girl, who was not sleeping, who would not again awaken, and the hands of women flew to their mouths. Tears leaped to their eyes, spilled over, froze halfway down their cheeks. Well, she thought, stamping her feet (her toes were beginning to freeze), tucking her gloved hands beneath her folded arms (the tips of her fingers had gone numb, as had her nose and the tips of her ears), if I must die, then let people take notice. Let them ask what this girl was doing alone on a night like this, in a man's coat and a boy's earflapped hat. How she had protested against that hat, although now she secretly gave thanks for it. The women would take off the hat, they would pull it off by its hideous earflaps, they would say, "Oh, but she is beautiful." They would wonder who she was. They would tell their children, "You are lucky to have a home. Don't you see how lucky you are? Let me tell you about the little girl who froze to death one night in February." She would become a legend, here in this empty place, here where the snow was now almost impenetrable, slanting down in thick chalk-colored streamers. "What was her name?" the children would ask; "what was she called?" And their mothers would say, "She was called Elfrieda Meek. Did you ever hear such a name? Elfrieda Meek. *Poor Elfrieda Meek.*"

"Poor Elfrieda Meek," one child would say. "May I name my doll Elfrieda Meek?" And the mother would reply, "What a kind thought! And isn't it time for you and Elfrieda Meek to go to bed?" Hundreds of children would name their dolls Elfrieda Meek. If they had dolls here: hadn't her father told her that in the country children had dolls whose heads were made from dried apples? Hundreds of dried-apple-headed dolls named Elfrieda Meek. It was most satisfactory. Except, of course, that she didn't want to die, and so she was enormously relieved (and frightened as well) when she saw what seemed a square shape, a kind of thickening in the snow, advancing toward her, waving, shouting something: was it her name? It was her name! "Elfrieda Meek!" shouted the shape, and out of the snow it came, a tall man in a huge, thick fur coat, a shaggy black fur coat, who swept down on her, picked her up, and tucked her under one arm as if she were a small parcel, who held her carpet bag in his other hand, and who began talking to her as if he had always known her: the train was early, had she known the train was early, and not only was the train early, he was late, the nearest bridge washed out, the storms had been dreadful, such rains during the warm spell, the rivers were swollen, he had to drive to the next town, where the covered bridge was built up high. They had foresight in that town. She must be frozen right through. She needn't worry. He had bearskins in the sleigh. She wouldn't be able to move under their weight, not breathe even, but she'd be warm, she'd be warmer than anyone inside, and when he got her home, oh, when she got home. There was a cot in front of the big kitchen stove, heaped with blankets. There were foot warmers and bricks set in the cookstove. Poor sad little thing with no parents, she could leave off worrying now. She was coming home with him; no one ever froze, no one ever starved in the Hewitt house. Here's the sleigh, isn't it grand, did you ever see such horses, Clydesdales, the biggest in the valley, we breed them, they send for them all the way to England, one even went to India, he said, tucking her in, heaping the bearskins upon her; is three enough? he asked; I have more; and she said,

Oh, thank you, Mr. Hewitt, three is enough, more and I shall go numb with the weight, and he laughed and said, They told me you were a smart little thing; are you a smart little thing?

And he gave the reins a shake and they started off and later she remembered skimming along under avenues of pines, snow-covered, laden with snow, past houses glowing ghostly in the deep-blue dark, ice-colored columns of smoke rising into the thin air above the rooftops and then thinning, a bridge that looked like a house, the sound of water like rain falling, and in the morning she woke up in a small cot in front of an immense cast-iron cookstove, covered in thick, heavy blankets, surrounded by staring children, one of whom cried out, "Ma! She's alive! Come see! She's alive!" And she thought, My new life has begun. She would have cried, so happy was she for having survived her previous life and awakened in this one, so grief-stricken was she for having lost her former life, which had just yesterday been so precious to her, but she did not believe in crying before strangers. Even then, at twelve, she had an iron will, an iron will and a great capacity for self-pity. Even then she remembered what her mother had taught her: Elfrieda must always do what is best for Elfrieda.

That was how my mother saw herself as a child—an orphan, alone, slightly heroic, and completely dedicated to her own survival.

CHAPTER

SEVENTEEN

I HAD PLANNED things carefully. I thought I knew what
to expect. On Friday morning, Dennis and I would walk to
the café, and I would finally meet the Impostor. We would
meet for exactly one hour. That was Dennis's idea, and I admired it. It was
what my husband would have thought of—a meeting an hour long.

The night before, I threw down the keys and Dennis came up and
slept on the couch. He had often slept there before, and there were nights
I slept on the couch in his small flat in Chelsea and then took a bus back
to Hampstead.

I didn't tell my husband about these arrangements, because I was sure
he wouldn't understand and I wasn't sure I understood myself. I was attracted to Dennis and he was attracted to me, but when we spent the night
together, we were huddled together, I thought, like two babes in the wood.
And then the morning we went to see the Impostor, I looked up and said,
"We're being faithful," and he said, "You are. You're the one who's married," and I said no, we were both being faithful. I was being faithful to
my husband and he was faithful to Florence. "That's a lot of nonsense," he
said, and I said it wasn't. He still hoped to find her—the living woman,
not only her story, not only an account of what had happened to her, and
I said, "You've fallen in love with a woman you've never met, who might
not even be alive. That's a very strange thing." And then I thought that it
wasn't so strange, because after all, hadn't he been drawn to the story of
the couple swept over the falls? Hadn't the painting *The Golden Rope* become the image he always saw shimmering just beneath the surface of
things?

The sun had come out early and the air was warm and would soon be hot, and two women passed us, and we heard one of them say, "I came out today because if today was to be the only hot day, I didn't want to have to say I missed it, and if today is to be the first hot day, I don't want to say I missed that, either." It was a lazy day and we drifted along slowly. Dennis asked me how my book was going and I said it had turned into a journal. His first screenplay, he said, had turned into a paperweight. He should never have tried it, never should have begun. Then I felt him stop walking, and I turned back to him, and he was staring past me, and when I looked in the same direction, I saw a tall young man with very curly black hair, and I recognized him as the man Eva had pointed out, the one she said had been staring at me in the café. With Dennis next to me, I was confident.

"Who are you?" I asked the young man.

"Well, you know who I am. I'm Antonio Mercado," he said, and so I knew he was the Impostor.

"We agreed to meet at the café," I said.

"I was restless and came out for a walk," he said.

"We might as well walk back together," Dennis said.

"Let's walk to the heath," the Impostor said. "No one can overhear us there."

"I don't care if they overhear us," I said recklessly. "I don't have anything to hide."

We began to walk, and whenever I could, I stole covert looks at the young man. Did he resemble us? His black, curly hair—that could be his legacy from Florence, although if he was from Spain, if his father had been Spanish, the thickly curling hair might mean nothing. The eyes, though, the way they slanted at the corners, the way he had of looking away when he spoke—all that reminded me of Florence, of myself. Even the way he put his hand up to his mouth, partially covering it, reminded me of her. But if, for some reason, I was tempted to see Dennis as a kind of relation, I asked myself, wouldn't I also see similarities between myself and this boy?

We sat on the grass in front of one of the ponds. A heron stood on the edge of a raft and watched us. People went by, walking their dogs.

"What is it you want?" I asked him.

"First ask him what he knows," Dennis said. "You want to be sure he's who he says he is."

"I told her. I don't know much about my mother. My father found her hitchhiking on a road and picked her up and took her home. She wasn't well and he took care of her and after I was born she left again. She told him she didn't want a child. She said she could barely take care of herself. She said I'd do better without her. My father said all she had when she came was a backpack and a red dress that she held on to all the time, the way children hold on to a toy. I don't know anything else." His voice was sullen.

"The red dress," Dennis asked me. "Is that important?"

"Yes," I said. "And your father?" I asked the Impostor. "He—he had an affair with my sister?"

"She was pregnant when he found her."

"So he's not your real father?" I asked.

"He is! He is my real father! He raised me! Which is more than *she* did!"

"Of course he's your father," I murmured. "If he raised you."

"He was a wonderful man!"

"Was?" Dennis asked.

"He died two years ago, and that's when I found out about my mother. He wrote it all down and left the letter for me in his will. He said, 'If you want to look for her, go ahead, but I don't think she's anywhere to be found. She didn't have the look of a woman who'd be living very long.'"

"So you have some money?" Dennis asked.

"I have plenty of money!"

"Oh, yes, we all do," I said, sighing. The boy looked at me curiously. The *boy*. "How old are you?" I asked him. "Didn't you say you were twenty?"

"Twenty-one."

"Then she had you right after she left Goult," I said. "Only six or seven months later."

"She left me the minute she could walk!" His cheeks had flushed with anger.

"Tell me," I said. "If you're so angry at her, why meet me?"

"I want to see where I come from, I want to see what kind of woman you are, what kind of person leaves her baby outside a church when he's still black and blue from the delivery. He told me about *that!* I want to see what she'd look like today so if I walked into a room and there she was, I'd recognize her. I wouldn't let *her* get away without answering a few questions!"

"You would tell her off. You would tell her what you think of her," I said. "You wouldn't let her go on her merry way. You'd ask her what right she had to lead a happy life—any life—after she gave you up."

"I would!"

"I suppose," I said, "I'd ask her some of the same things."

"Why are you in London?" he asked abruptly. "You can't be very happily married if you're here and your husband's somewhere else. Why don't you stay on here?"

"Stay on here and do what?"

"I'm not bad company," he said, staring out over the pond. "I'm your son. You never had one. You could find out what I'm like. I could take you to Spain where my father found her. You'd want to see that. Or I could take you to Las Flores, where he took her, the last place anyone knows she was. You'd want to go, wouldn't you?"

"He wants to break up your life, that's what he wants to do," Dennis said. "He can't get even with Florence, so he'll get even with you."

"Everything Florence did to you she did to me," I said. "At least you didn't know until you were older."

He said, "I think what she did to me was worse. She was my *mother*."

"Perhaps that is worse," I said.

"Perhaps!" He snorted contemptuously. "Well, now you're my mother and you're stuck with me, or I'll go to the papers."

"Don't threaten me," I said. "I'm not threatenable." And it was true. It was one of my few virtues. *If you don't do what I want,* Florence would say, *I'll tear up these paper dolls and say you did it,* and I would say, *Go ahead, go ahead and say that.* I could defy Florence, but only if she first threatened me. "And I'm not your mother," I said. "I'm your aunt." I could feel Dennis's approving eyes on me.

"How would you like it in the papers? Your sainted sister and her abandoned child! And you, the *aunt,* refusing to have anything to do with me! Wouldn't everyone love it?"

"If everyone loves it, you'll be very happy," I said, standing up.

"You *want* to be my mother!" he said, standing too. He towered over me. Dennis also stood up and stood next to me. "She doesn't need protection from *me!*" Antonio said to him. "She needs protection from *you!* You didn't tell her you knew me!"

"You *knew* him?" I turned to Dennis.

"Don't you see what he's trying to do?" Dennis said. "He's trying to turn us against each other."

"You knew him?"

"He came to me when he was trying to find you. I gave him your phone number in exchange for information. Before I knew you, Doris!"

"You gave him my phone number? And all the time you knew who was calling me?"

"I should have told you."

"Yes! You should have!"

"I knew you didn't have to be frightened. Not of him."

"But *I* didn't know! *I* didn't know."

"Look how happy he is," Dennis said miserably. "Look how he's smiling now that we're fighting."

"Were they so important?" I asked Dennis. "Those bits of information?"

He nodded miserably. Yes, yes, they were important.

"And as for you," I said to Antonio, "if you thought I was your mother, or even your aunt, what were you doing, calling up and trying to frighten me to death? You could have put me in a mental hospital!"

"You're very melodramatic, aren't you?" he said. "Just like she was."

"You don't feel *any* remorse at all?" I asked him.

"You'll pardon me, but I'm accustomed to feeling sorry for myself," he said.

"Oh, please!" I said. "Plenty of people are adopted! Millions of people are adopted! And they don't turn out to be the son of an identical twin! I don't know what you're so unhappy about!"

"Yes, you do," he said. "You do know."

"What *is* it you want?" I demanded. "And don't threaten me! Don't tell Dennis! Tell me! If you want to get anywhere, tell me!"

"I want you," he said. "I want to get to know you. I want to understand you. Is that too much to ask?" And his eyes began to fill and his Adam's apple bobbed up and down and I could see he was fighting back tears. Either he was a wondrous actor or he was sincere. I looked over at Dennis, who was avoiding my eye. He was flushed with embarrassment.

"Do you believe him?" I asked Dennis. "*If* I can trust you about anything?"

"I do believe him. I always believed him," Dennis said.

Of course. That was why he had given him my phone number.

"I can't be a mother to you," I said. "You're already grown."

"Grown people still have mothers."

"I suppose they do." I stood still, thinking.

"What are you thinking about?" he asked me, and I said I really didn't know. I said if he was Florence's son, of course he would be precious to me.

"Yes," he said. "If you could stop hating her."

He took me by surprise. "I don't hate her!" I cried. "How could I hate her?"

"Of course you hate her," he said. "We both do."

"I think the hour's more than up," Dennis said. "Why don't we stop here?"

We both turned and glared at him.

"Exchange phone numbers," Dennis suggested.

I said Antonio already had *my* phone number, and he took a card from his wallet and gave it to me. "I'm going to be an architect," he said, and his voice sounded very small and very young.

"Oh, yes," I said. "When we were little, we built dolls' houses. Florence built beautiful ones, dripped all over with mud, like Gaudí." I'd forgotten the dolls' houses. "Who will call whom first?"

"I think you should call me, since you get so angry when I call you," the boy said, and I said, "Fine, all right, I think that's fair."

"I'll go now," he said. He bowed to both of us and strode decisively off. Dennis and I were left staring at each other.

"What do you think?" he asked me.

"Oh," I said, "he's a beautiful young man. And very angry. And as for you! What you did wasn't right!"

"I know," Dennis said.

"I didn't expect this! Not of you!"

"I told you," Dennis said. "I'm no angel."

"Yes, well, it's different when someone does something to *you,* isn't it?"

"I told you I was a reporter."

"Even reporters have morals!"

"Will you forgive me?"

"I forgive everyone, sooner or later," I said.

"Make it sooner," Dennis said. "I want you to come with me to Goult."

"Did you tell him? That she had a twin?"

"I promised you I wouldn't."

"But did you *keep* your promise?"

"I did."

"How can I believe you? You knew Antonio for a long time, you knew his name, you knew everything about him the whole time, and I was so frightened!"

"I'm sorry about that, Doris, really I am," he said. "But in the beginning, I didn't know *you,* and I wasn't sure *what* to tell you. You seemed so . . ."

"So fragile?"

"Yes. Don't keep secrets from me," he said. "I'm sorry."

"People are always sorry—when they're caught."

"I *am* sorry. If I'd met you now, I'd have told you. You don't seem frag-ile now."

I hit him on the arm and we walked back. The day had turned very hot and we went along slowly. "It really is a lovely city, isn't it?" I said. Probably I *was* someone's aunt. It would take me a while to call Antonio, I knew that. I should have told him that, but probably he already knew. Probably he'd worked that out for himself.

And So I Stayed
with Him

CHAPTER

EIGHTEEN

AND SO I stayed with him. It was easiest.
"You must stay with me forever," he said. "Oh, yes,
forever. With me you will be happy. It is what some
people want, after all, to make someone happy. I will make you happy.
What a challenge you will be."

Oh, yes, forever. There was no such word, I knew that now. Forever
and ever and ever, the hopeless chant of little children.

He was talking about one world. I lived in another. At night, I left
the house and walked into the woods, and once I saw a flight of stairs
between the trees, leading down to a train, and I thought, I will take
that train, that train will take me where I want to go. And once I saw a
small table set up beneath the trees, and on it was a gas lamp and the
light it cast was brilliant, and a woman sat at the table wearing nothing
but her skin and a huge black hat covered with enormous curling feathers, and her arms rested on the white tablecloth and there was a glass of
wine in front of her but she didn't touch it. She stared straight ahead as
if sightless and I thought, Perhaps she is blind. And a man in a long
gray flannel coat watched her and the white moon was caught in the
black branches and I knew she would be there night after night and the
wine would remain untouched and leaves would drift down and settle
on the tablecloth and catch in the feathers of her immense hat.

There were telephone kiosks in the woods, bright red, and always
the phone was swinging from its cord, and there were times I thought I
heard a voice speaking through the receiver and then I was frightened
and hurried on. But by this time I knew. There were doors everywhere,
doors in the woods between the trees, trapdoors in the floors of tele-

phone booths, doors in the clouds, doors in the smooth plastered white walls; you could walk through any one of them and disappear. It was comforting to think that, how many doors there were, how simple it was to disappear.

Probably he followed me when I left the house and went into the woods.

I explored all the empty rooms of his house and some rooms had bare wooden floors on which sat brown rocks that cast reddish shadows. I never asked him about those rooms. I never asked him about the missing wall, and why some of the rooms were open to the weather so that, at night, you could see the trees and the moon and the pebbled path shining whitely in the moonlight. I knew these were visions, I knew none of this was real, yet it seemed best not to speak of it.

I cut up pieces of paper and built a paper house.

When he saw that, he sent someone into town and later a dolls' house arrived and day after day I glued it together, I watched it take form. He bought me little porcelain dolls' heads. I took the fabric he gave me and sewed little dolls for its rooms. He seemed pleased. But you must sleep, he said. You cannot work on this dolls' house day and night.

At night, I went to bed, but when I knew he was asleep, I got up and finished one doll and began another.

Their faces were all the same. He couldn't find any others. One morning I was up early. I smashed them. I ground them beneath the heel of my shoe. He sent the old woman in. She swept them up without comment and so I knew he had instructed her. He must have said, Whatever she does, treat it as normal.

I will have to go, I said. I'm strong enough to go. But he said, Don't go, come with me in my plane, come with me to my other house. And I said, What other house? And he said, My house in the North, in Las Flores.

Why not? What difference did it make where I went? When, in fact, I was nowhere, ever. When every day I grew thinner and less substantial, like a shadow as the sun goes down. And yet when he looked at me, he saw a solid woman. He saw flesh and blood, something three-dimensional, a person in a body.

Africa, lions and gazelles and unending sun. Wild beasts.

I said, Somewhere in Africa, there is a huge tree in the middle of an endless plain. Will you take me to see it?

He said, There are hundreds of such trees, hundreds of such plains, I will take you to see all of them. I thought, I want to see elephants and lions, under the hot sun I want to be chewed on by a lion. When I closed my eyes, I saw narrow cobbled streets, completely flooded, and in them, porpoises and small whales swam. In Africa it would be dry, footprints in the sand would blow away in the hot wind.

I will go to Africa, I said. Is it beautiful?

Oh, yes, he said. It is very beautiful. Such flowers, silver flowers! And brindled crows, tame crows! I will give you a crow, I will give you a parrot. It will speak to you in your own voice! Such colors, in the parrot and the sunsets. If only you could paint!

Yes, I said, if only.

The plane crossed water, aquamarine and blue, silver when the sun hit it, so easy for water to change its shape. I envied the water.

The house was large and cool, a wooden house baking beneath the sun. He brought animals to the fields around us—an elephant, a small giraffe, an orphaned rhinoceros. The elephant commanded the others. I watched them for days, the elephant spraying itself with dust, lying on its side in the dusty field. And the colors of the flowers and how long the light remained, and yet I was not better. Often he carried me back into the house because I could not walk.

I could have stayed there forever, but before I had the child he took me back to Spain. A boy, you could tolerate a boy, couldn't you? he said. A boy wouldn't remind you, how could it remind you, but it did remind me, not of my sister but of my husband, how could it not? How could I not see his face in the small face of the child? When I had the child and said, No, I can't keep him, then he turned from me.

You are sorry now you nursed me, aren't you? I asked him, and he said no, he was not sorry. And if I leave the child, I said, you will go back for him, you will bring him back here, won't you, isn't that what you'll do? And when he said yes, he thought he would do that, he thought he would bring the child back to the house, I said, I really must go on, and he said yes, he supposed I must, he said, Why don't you leave the child here? Why bring it to a church when I will only go after it? And I said I didn't want to be sure, I didn't want to know what happened to him, let me have a few spaces on the chessboard, did he understand? And he said I was beyond understanding. He asked me, wouldn't I feel empty?

When I left, he had stooped down to pick up the baby in his basket on the warm church step. He had dark hair and dark eyes. He spoke Spanish. He didn't know my name. I didn't think he knew my name. Although when he found me, when he changed my clothes, he took my passport from my pocket, its pages wet from the streams of sweat that poured from my body in its fever. He dried it on a windowsill, a dry gray slab of stone. He spread out the bills from my pockets, also wet. They were dry and puckered when I left.

When I was so feverish he didn't think I would live. Nor did the doctor. The old lady who had raised him arrived with herbs and boiled them up into teas. She stewed beets and fermented them. She ground raw rhubarb into the gruel she fed me. She shredded the poisonous rhubarb leaves and demanded I chew them. Later, she said, "I gave her my strength."

He said I laughed when the doctor said he thought I would die within days, a pitiful laugh, weak, more like a cough. When I tried to speak, I made the sounds of a sick cat.

There were curtains around the bed. He tied the curtains on the outside edge of the bed into knots. They swayed in the wind. I stared at them for hours. The hanged ones, the knots were their heads, the fabric their bodies. They were hung upside down.

The doctor said I had drunk bad water.

He soon discovered my love of cemeteries, of tombs, of carved angels. Whenever I asked, he took me up the mountain to look down at the checkerboard of tombs.

What cured me? The stubborn will of that old woman, she was the one I had to thank. *Chew the leaves,* she said. *Is your tongue numb? No? Then chew longer.* Cured, in South Africa, in Las Flores, at the end of the world. Where could I go that was farther away?

They wanted the baby. The old woman wanted it and he wanted it, a baby, a new life, a fresh start. He believed in such things, new lives, fresh starts, life's long fingers to unravel the knot on its way to the heart.

Whereas I didn't, and never would again.

WHEN OUR FATHER DIED, we were taken to see him. In the funeral home, he slept quietly, flat on his back, and Florence said, "He never slept like that at home. He always slept propped up on pillows," and I said, "Look! His lips aren't blue! He's wearing lipstick!" and our mother grabbed us and dragged us out of the funeral parlor, and when we got home, our mother slammed shut the door to our bedroom, and Florence said, "Good. Let's play the Dead Game. I'll be Mama and you be Daddy," and our mother, who was listening, heard us.

There was the sound of bare feet on the floor's wood planks and then Florence's annoyed voice saying, "If you are dead, you have to lie down. What are you sitting up for?"

"Sometimes the dead can come back to life," I said.

"The dead don't come back to life. Not in their same bodies."

"Then how do they?" I asked.

"Dressed in sheets."

"Or like mists in the cemetery. There are always mists and clouds and fog in the cemetery."

"If you won't lie down, I'll be dead," Florence said.

"I could really be dead. And then I'd be cold and they'd have to bury me but I'd still look like you."

"I wouldn't want to be buried," Florence said uneasily. "You better not die."

"If they buried me by mistake, would you come and get me?"

"Of course I'd get you."

"Because they might bury me by mistake. Mother says I always sleep like the dead."

"They're not burying us," Florence said. "They only bury old people."

"Was Daddy old?"

"Of course he was old."

"They won't bury us until we start having blue lips and blue fingers. Are my fingers blue?"

"Our fingers are as pink as can be," Florence said.

"I'm lying down now. Start crying. All right, that's enough crying. It's my turn now."

"Talk to me," Florence said. "I'm a dead person and maybe dead people can hear."

"What am I supposed to say?"

"Tell me you're sorry I died."

"I'm sorry you died because now no one will call us by our names," I said. "You always called us by our names. You didn't call us the Twins. Mother is sorry you died because now who will help her in the store? *Everyone was quite shocked.* Old Mrs. Land said that. You were quite shocking, Daddy. If you're not really dead, you'll be warm and the snow will melt over your grave and if it does, we'll run to the police station to get you dug up, so don't worry."

"I'm happy to hear it," Florence answered in a quavery voice. "Come look every day. Do you promise?"

"I promise."

"Do I sound like a dead person?" Florence asked.

"I'm sure dead people sound like that."

"But maybe they sound like the wind. I think they sound like the wind."

"Not when they're still in Mr. Darlington's funeral home. Then they sound like you did. Let me try. 'Oh, what will I do without my dear husband?' " I quavered.

"Don't give Mother a dead voice! Mother's not dead!" Florence said. "She wouldn't die and leave *me*. She might leave *you*."

"She won't leave me," I said in a high, trembling voice. "Oh, sorry," I said. "Wrong voice."

"You mix everything up," Florence said. "You be the dead one."

"She will never see him again," I said. "But if I died, you could see me again. Look in a mirror and there I'd be. No one could ever separate us."

"Unless I had plastic surgery, like in that movie."

"Would you do it?"

"No, would you?"

"Not unless we both had it."

"I wonder, if I had it, would your face change and be just like mine?"

"It might," I said. "We'll always have the same face."

"Which bed do you want to sleep in? The one near the window?"

"No," I said. "He might come and knock on the window."

"In his sheet?"

"Yes."

In the hallway, our mother heard the white cast-iron bed pushed until it came to a stop against the bedroom wall. Then there was silence, and she thought we had fallen asleep until she heard a voice say, "You know what we look like? We look like those dolls in the case in Lofton. They make dolls the same, not people."

"Not usually people," said the second voice. "Why do you think they made two of us?"

"One wasn't enough. That's what Daddy said. He said we'd do special things."

"Like what things?"

"Go to sleep. Aren't you sleepy? I'm sleepy so you must be sleepy."

"Yes, I are sleepy," said the voice, and then it was completely silent.

They will never be alone, our mother thought. They would always have one another. *But, Elfrieda,* our father said, *that is a wonderful thing.* But where are my children? she cried. They were supposed to be for me! *They are yours, Elfrieda,* he said, *but they are each other's as well.* They leave no room for me! Only Albert leaves room for me! *They will leave you all the room in the world,* our father said, *as long as you leave them alone. They love you.* They don't! said our mother. They really don't. They don't love you, either. *You are wrong there, Elfrieda,* he said. You believe what you want to believe, she said. *As you do,* our father said. But this time I am right, she said.

The morning of the funeral, our mother said, "Don't play any of your dead games while Grandma and Grandpa are here. It will upset them and make them cry. Promise!"

We looked at one another. How did she know about the Dead Game? She spied on us, but how? We would have to be more careful.

Our mother saw our identical eyes flicker back and forth in our identical faces. We were speaking to one another. "Do you promise?" she asked. We promised.

At the cemetery, it seemed to our mother as if she were seeing everyone for the first time. There was her son, Albert, who had such a mean look. There were frown lines between his eyebrows, and the corners of his mouth turned down. Something had harmed him. We—the twins—had shut him out and made him envy us, and so we had harmed him. And then she saw us, two beautiful girls who resembled and did not resemble her, the same triangular shape to our faces, but our eyes were light blue and our hair was black and we were slender and graceful and either one of us would have drawn a spectator's eye, but two together were irresistible. We had edged forward until we were only inches from the opening in the frozen ground.

It had taken many men armed with pickaxes several days to dig out the grave site and our mother wondered if they had dug down deep enough, and if not, would they have to dig up the coffin in the summer and dig the hole deeper before replanting it? It had happened before, caskets buried in a shallow grave until the ground began to thaw and then the casket was thrust up, briefly exposed to light, and then shut up in the dark once more. One winter the snow was so deep and so constant, Mr. Thorp had stayed aboveground on his wife's porch from the end of December until the middle of April, and everyone who spoke of it said that Mrs. Thorp was never in her right mind again.

The sky darkened and snow began to fall, large fat flakes like pieces of torn paper, half the size of our mother's little finger. The coffin was going into the ground, lowered by ropes that slipped over pulleys, slowly going down. Our mother looked up and saw Mr. and Mrs. Rice, our grandparents whom we had never before met, standing in back of us. Mr. Rice had taken out his enormous handkerchief and was clumsily wiping his wife's cheeks under her veil, but it was impossible to say if people were crying or if their faces were streaked by melting snow, and the sky, which had been gray, had now turned a mild, pale lavender. The Rices wore black coats, as did the two of us, whose coats had come from Lofton, ordered and paid for by Hilda. We wore black wool hats that covered our ears.

But the snow, now falling so heavily, was turning everyone and everything white, positively bridal, and our mother saw that everyone standing at the grave site was turning white, as were the trees and the cars and the roofs of the houses and the gazebo and the common itself.

A storm of white confetti was turning the funeral into a celebration, a party. Was it a wedding or a funeral? It was impossible to tell, but life was like that, wasn't it? The snow was exciting us. Our mother could feel it where she stood. We could only, she thought, sympathize with others for so long and then we looked into one another's eyes and we were safe in our own world.

She wondered what we wanted to do now. Build a snowman? Probably build a snowman. As soon as we thought no one was watching, we would be off, building a snowman, probably right next to the grave, part of our Dead Game. She saw Albert glaring at us, as if to say, He was *your* father too, and *I'm* the only one who's unhappy! I'm the one who's left alone and you two have each other! I hate you two for that!

And now the Rices were thanking the minister, and Mr. Rice was taking his prayer book out of his deep pocket and chanting his own prayers over the grave, and then the Rices turned to Dr. Steiner and thanked him for giving his son so many more years than he'd expected. Dr. Steiner said he had nothing to do with it, but it was time to look after our mother before she became the next patient, and Mrs. Rice turned to our mother, her eyebrows and eyelashes coated with snow, and said, "You were very good to him; if you ever need anything, you will come to us, won't you? We didn't think you were right for him but we were wrong, no one could have been better to him. Everyone's told us, and he told us, every week in his letters. Elfrieda, you're not our daughter, but if you could think of yourself as our daughter . . . Well, it may take some time." And she clumsily hugged our mother, who stood stiff as a tree but finally bent forward toward her tiny mother-in-law, and then Florence said, "Can we be your granddaughter?" and Mrs. Rice said, "You are my granddaughter, Florence, you and Doris both are!"

And Florence said, "Can we go off now?" and Mrs. Rice said, "Go ahead. This is no place for children. Have a good time."

Later, from the living room window of the house, our mother peered out through the snow. It was coming down, thick and fast, blown straight at the windows by the wind, melting and running down the panes, and if we were outside—she could not see us, but she was sure—twin snowmen were growing up near our father's grave, and each of us was pretending our snowman was our father, and each was talking to him as if he were, somehow, still alive.

It Was Amazing

CHAPTER

TWENTY

I T W A S amazing, how many cars stopped for me, how
many trucks, how far away I went, how no one tried to hurt
me, how I was unharmed by anything human, how nothing
could touch me—except for the sun. My skin reddened and blistered
and peeled and finally browned. There were times when I saw myself in
a car window and didn't recognize my own face. Those were wonderful
times, small miracles.

I thought, I must be very young, I must have grown very young once
again. The world spares the very young and the foolish.

The countryside was mountainous, dry and flinty, gray and dust blue
in the sun, dry dust over everything, the silvery-leafed acacias, the dark-
gray stones. The dust was beige-colored, the faintest possible color.

In the beginning, I paused frequently. I rested on the dusty stones,
huge boulders set down here and there as if by a purposeful hand. Then
the muscles in my legs swelled and grew strong, and each day I went
farther. My bones grew sharper, pushed at the thinning flesh. I thought,
I must eat more. I must not collapse, must not let myself be found.

I passed houses like castles, perched on the edges of cliffs, as if
carved out of stone. There were fields of sunflowers. They turned their
faces up to me, as if watching. On the edge of cleared fields there were
brambly bushes, huge ferns dustily waving. There was dust everywhere.
When I took food from my knapsack, it tasted of dust. There was dust
in my water. I coughed as I drank it. I coughed afterward. Swirling dust.
Floating dust. Dust dropping gently from the sky, weightless. When rain
fell, the drops fell like stones.

When I stopped by the side of streams, I moved tall rocks away from the water so that the water could not reflect them. The rocks and stones thanked me. I would look at the stream and at the rocks, moved back from the stream's edge, and think, The world is better for these changes. I felt contented and peaceful. I hoped the rain when it came would not swell the rivers. I said to the stones, You are saved, and the air quivered with happiness.

I CAME to a blue town. All the houses were blue, all the roofs were orange. A man in a black car took me to a red town where the roofs were black. He said, Tell me stories, tell me stories while I drive.

I told him about a king and queen who lived happily until, one greenish dusk, a strange angel walked up to the castle gate. He taught the king and queen to move through walls. He showed them the bones beneath the skin of their hands when they held their hands up to the sun, and their skin glowed orange and their bones traced black branches beneath the skin. And then one day the angel grew tired. He began to pluck the feathers from his wings. He looked for a deep-blue shadow, a navy-blue shadow, and he lay down in it, and in the morning there was nothing left but dust. Then the king and the queen stepped into the malachite sea and swam out to the great orange wings the rising sun spread out on the quilted water.

He asked me why they were unhappy, why they drowned.

I said, They assumed their kingdom held one immortal.

He said, The king, the queen, and the angel. One too many.

Yes, one too many, I said.

A sad story, he said, and I said, All stories are sad stories in the end. That was the last of their stories. In their first stories, they all are happy.

Tell me the first stories, he said, and so I did.

I don't remember them now, the first stories.

I remember telling him that all the stories were true.

A man in a red car stopped for me. The sun painted the car with white dandelions gone to seed. In the back seat was a priest wearing a black robe. In one hand was a black book, in the other, a gold globe attached to a wand.

Later, the man said, The priest is an exorcist. A demon possesses my daughter. Of course you won't understand that, you will laugh at us; you people who speak English, you are all so modern.

And I saw her, his daughter. She was a church steeple lined with furry bats, sleeping upside down. Her throat was a church steeple and from it poured thick, soothing music, black and thick, like black jam. The church was her body. She was possessed by the voices of people praying, by their souls, buzzing like flies. She could smell the dead meat of their bodies, and so she sang and her voice poured from her throat, the church steeple.

I said, We are all a cauldron of souls, we are possessed by generations, what nonsense it is to think there is only one of us, that we are pure, like gold, like an element, no, we are all mosaics, isn't it true, isn't it obvious? That I am a crowd and he is, and his daughter, she too is a crowd, and if the crowd is driven out, what will be left? An empty building, insane rooms.

I said he must send the exorcist away.

He said, We all have our beliefs. I know my soul is given me by the one God.

I said, Our souls are like windows of stained glass.

The exorcist drove out the daughter's demon. She never spoke again, not while I was there. She would never speak again, that was plain to see. Her eyes slid this way and that over the brightly colored world. Occasionally we took her for rides in the car. Her eyes lingered on red doors, her pupils narrowed, hesitated on red-painted stones in front of yellow houses. Otherwise they were flat and gray, like stones from the dry bed of a river.

I envied her. I never envied anyone as I envied that empty-eyed girl.

She will be cured one day, her father said. One day she will speak.

I prayed for her. I prayed she would remain as she was.

CHAPTER

TWENTY-ONE

As I GOT UP to leave the table, the sky darkened, thunder rattled the windows, lightning lit the leaves, and the rain poured down, thick mercury-colored droplets snaking down the big plate-glass window, and I sat back down. I thought, I'll stay until the rain stops, and someone came rushing in followed by lines of slanting water, and I thought, This is what I want, to talk to Eva, who is older than I am, ten years or more. I don't want to talk to Dennis. I don't want to feel as if I'm in my twenties again. I don't want to rush off to Goult! Looking for my sister! Again!

The Impostor—Antonio—came in and I told him to sit down. "You're dripping wet," I said, and he said, "I don't mind water."

"What are you doing here?" I asked him, and he said, "Looking for you." I said he had agreed to wait until I called him, and he said, "I couldn't help it. I was in the neighborhood," and I said, "Well? What do you want?"

"We could sit here and get used to each other," he said. "We could do that."

"Yes, we can do that," I said.

"Do you paint?" he asked me.

"No, but I used to."

"I can paint."

"Good for you," I said.

"Why are you so angry?" he asked me. I said I didn't have the slightest idea. Probably because he intended to ask me all sorts of questions about things I'd rather not think about or couldn't answer and so I knew I'd disappoint him.

"I'm used to being disappointed," he said.

"What a wonderful beginning," I said with a sigh.

"Do you know my father?" he asked me. "My real father? Jack Pine?"

"No. I don't know him."

"But you will know him. You'll go to see him. Take me."

"Oh, no," I said. "If I'm going, I'm going with as little baggage as possible."

"So that's what I am to you," he said. "Baggage."

"Dennis can take you. He gets along with him. You'd be better off with Dennis. You can't come with me."

"I'll follow you."

"No, you won't. I'll call the police and I'll hit you with my umbrella." We both started laughing. "Well," I said, "we could sit here for a little while and get used to each other."

"Yes. We could do that," he said. He picked up a salt shaker, examined it, and put it down.

"Where did you go to school?" I asked him.

"Here. Oxford. The Spanish think very highly of Cambridge and Oxford."

"Do they?"

"I have to go now," he said, flushing. "I'm late meeting someone."

"You're going to see a girl, aren't you? What's her name?"

"Rose."

"I *will* call you," I said. "I promise. Don't worry, I'll pay for the coffee. Aren't aunts supposed to do that?"

He nodded, got up, and left. On the tabletop his wet arm had left a dark shape. Rose. So it was starting all over again. There was a next generation after all.

THAT NIGHT, I got undressed in front of my mirror and spent a long time looking at my body. I imagined myself with a swollen stomach and then an enormously round one. I lay down on the bed and tried to imagine a living child pushing its way out of me. In the mirror, my body looked hopelessly seamless and self-contained. But soon enough, I would be dreaming I was pregnant again, dreaming I was giving birth. Then I would begin to dream about Antonio's childhood and in the dreams he would begin growing up under my eye and my husband's eye, and the dreams would go on until it would seem as if I had raised a child—as if I had raised him.

What was my husband going to think of this?

If Antonio was really Florence's child, my husband would make room for him. I didn't doubt it for an instant. And then I thought that if Antonio grew in my dreams, if, in my dreams, he was mine from the first, he might replace her. And then I thought no, that was not possible. I didn't want to dream of him. And that night I slept well and was altogether free of dreams.

The next day, I went to the café and he did not come. Life took up its normal, predictable shape.

To OUR MOTHER, our father's death made it seem as if someone had come into the house and speeded up the clocks and that time flowed more swiftly through the rooms, and although she herself appeared unchanged, we seemed caught in the rapidly moving currents and daily we changed before her eyes.

Before our father's death, we were not popular with our teachers. We annoyed them by our giggling, our glaring at one another across the room after we fought in the schoolyard, our tendency to exchange places, so that Florence took my math test and I took her essay exams, and although teachers suspected the wrong child was taking a test, they could never be sure, and so they felt they were constantly mocked and made fools of, and since no one likes to feel a fool, we were both resented and wondered at, as if we were moving paintings, rare beings who had come to rest in human bodies and annoyingly had to be taught and scolded and fed like everyone else.

But after our father died, we were fatherless children, and Miss Winter, who taught painting and drawing at the Hunter and Moffit School, began to take an interest in us, and astonishingly, only I seemed to respond to her. Florence wasn't interested. When Florence saw me sitting at a table with Miss Winter, drawing trees or cats or dogs, and soon after, sketching the other children in the classroom, the trees outside the window, the houses blurred by snow, she would come closer, look at my drawing, and wander off, ending up either at our house or at Hilda's, where she settled down with a book and a large glass of lemonade that Hilda kept ready for her.

Hilda was delighted to have one child to herself. So was our mother, and when I stayed after school in art class, she began to tell Florence stories, some of them the same ones she had told the Hewitt children, others she invented especially for Florence, stories about women who formed when the snow whirled, crying because they had lost their crowns or because their husbands had run off, and now, when the snow swirled, they could fly up and find them and take their revenge, and their revenge was horrible. If you tilted your head back and looked at the church steeples when a snowstorm was raging, you saw them holding hands, flying in a ring about the steeple, and if you listened carefully, you heard them shriek as they always did before they flew off, and in the morning, when the snow stopped, certain men came to their windows and when they looked out, women made of snow whose eyes shone red and furious glared at them and they knew their peaceful life had come to an end, and everyone in the village who saw the women on the men's lawns knew those men had done something dreadful for which they needed to be punished.

There were stories about devils who hid themselves in fogs that clung to the roads in damp weather and who, hidden in the fogs' thick skirts, made their plans to kidnap small children; toads who hopped across the dirt roads and looked like blowing leaves in the headlights but who were really messengers from the forest king on their way to ask for help from his brother who lived in a far-off forest, and that was why, if you were driving, you must never run over a toad hopping across the road, because the forest king's brother might not get his message.

"There is a whole world living in the small spaces of this world," our mother said, "in the cracks between floorboards, in the footprints your boots make in the snow, in the spaces we can't see between the clouds and the sky, no thicker than a sheet of paper, in the knotholes of trees, in the wrinkles in your sheets and blankets, between the springs of your mattress, everywhere!"

When she was finished, she would say, "Now you tell me a story," and Florence would say, "I don't know how to do it. Tell me another," and our mother would tell her another story, until one day our mother said to her again, "Tell *me* a story," and Florence said she was no good at stories but she wrote poems that weren't about anything particularly. For instance, she wrote one about someone who died and his adventures underground and the best part was that every line rhymed. Did our mother want to hear it? She did.

"But you have to promise you won't tell Doris," Florence said. "I don't want her starting to write poems. She paints pictures. *I* write poems."

Our mother promised. But she wanted to know why it was so important to keep the poems secret from me, when after all, I showed them my paintings.

"Yes, but how can she help it?" Florence asked. "She can't paint in a closet. She can't paint holding a flashlight. She has to paint out in the open."

"She could paint at Hilda's and not let us see them."

"I want *my* things just for myself," said Florence. "I don't want to share. I have to share everything else."

"I didn't think you minded."

"I didn't," Florence said. "But now I do."

All the same, I knew what stories my mother told her. I knew about Florence's poems.

"Doris paints the most beautiful pictures," Hilda told our mother. "She paints people so you think they'll start speaking to you. She painted a lace collar so real I wanted to buy one for myself. Here, see this crocheting? I'm copying it from her picture."

And then we began to fight. And even now, looking back, I can't say what happened. There were no differences between us. At least I saw none. We were exactly the same—or so I thought.

But I was uneasy because for a long time I sensed that Florence wanted to break free. She was the one who had objected to wearing the same clothes. She was the one who had asked for a doll and wanted to keep it for herself.

These, I thought, were small things. They didn't matter. They were too insignificant to matter. Really, we were the same.

And I didn't see that when I began painting, when Florence watched me and saw that one of us could have something the other didn't have, when she saw that people looked at us differently—I was the one who painted, she was the one who wrote—I didn't see that I showed Florence how to escape me.

One morning when our mother was brushing her hair, she heard shrieks from our room and, brush still in hand, idly wandered down the hall to investigate. She stood in the doorway and saw us facing one another, apparently taking turns slapping one another's faces. Both of us were in our white nightgowns. Both of us had our long, curly hair down, and to our mother it seemed as if a single being were attempting to destroy itself.

Suddenly one of us grabbed the other by the hair and began to pull it violently as if she hoped to pull her sister's head from her neck.

"Stop that!" our mother shouted, but we didn't hear her. Now one of us, her hand in the other's hair, was yanking the other one's head back and forth.

They can't hear me, our mother realized, and so she ran into the room and interposed her body between the two of us, both of us still unaware of her until one of our hands struck her cheek and she cried out, and her voice, so different from ours, seemed to wake us and we stopped, suddenly.

"What is this all about?" our mother demanded. "What's going on here? Who started it?" We didn't answer. "You *will* answer me," our mother said. "Florence, tell me what happened!"

"I was going to cut my hair," Florence said. "She wouldn't let me."

"You *can't* cut your hair if I don't cut mine!" I cried. "We had an agreement!"

"An agreement not to cut your hair?"

"An agreement to stay the same!" I said.

"I don't want to stay the same," Florence said. "I'll cut my hair if I want to. I'm not you! I don't want to look like you! Every time I see you and your hair's all over the place, I think, *I* look terrible! I pick up a sweater in a store and you say it won't look good on us. It's not for *us*. It's for me! What difference does it make if I cut my hair? We'll still look the same!"

"I want to look *exactly* like you!"

"We don't *really* look alike," Florence said in an evil voice. "It's our hair and our clothes. If I cut my hair and we wore different things, no one would know we were sisters."

"Don't be ridiculous," our mother said.

"No! I don't really look like her! I don't!"

"Why are you saying that?" I asked. I was crying, my face wet and shining. "Why?"

"I'm not doing anything to *you*," Florence said. "I'm cutting my own hair."

"Because you don't want to look like me!"

"And *who* are *you*?" our brother, Albert, asked from the doorway. "You think you're Doris, but you're not Doris. You're Florence. Mother mixed up your ribbons when you were a few weeks old and she didn't know which one was which, so you don't even know your right names."

"Will you get out of here!" our mother shouted, turning on him.

"But I'm the older one and she's the younger one, no matter what you say."

"You are not Florence," Albert said. "You are Doris."

"I'll kill him!" Florence screamed. "I'll tear him limb from limb! Doris, give me the scissors!"

"Don't give them to her!" our mother said. "Hide them! She doesn't know what she's doing!"

"Give them to me! I'm the oldest and you have to listen to me!"

"You both listen to *me!*" our mother cried. "Albert, get out of this house! Put on your coat and sit in the car until school starts. Lock the doors!"

"Oh, Mother, she won't do anything to him," I said. I was still crying.

"Don't be so sure," Florence said. "Give me the scissors and we'll *see* if I do anything to him."

"You are both out of your minds," said our mother.

"It's her," I said. "She's the one who wants to ruin everything."

"I want you in different rooms until you calm down," our mother said. "You, in here. Florence, you in the living room."

"I have to comb my hair!" Florence said.

"Take your comb and go into the living room or I'll get your father's belt and you'll get a beating you'll never forget."

"Don't hit her, Mother!" I cried.

"Why are you defending her?" our mother asked. "She wants to cut her hair."

"Don't hit her!"

"Out," our mother said to Florence, who left the room, walking as slowly as possible, pausing in the doorway to look triumphantly back at me, as if to say, You see? I've won. I'm the oldest and I always win.

"What on earth," our mother said, sitting down on one of the twin beds. She was shaking. She looked around the whitewashed room with its sloping ceiling, its two metal beds that we had amateurishly painted white, its rag rug given us by Hilda, the rose and pink afghans on each of our beds, the flowered curtains at the window, the polished wooden floor beginning to shine like honey in the early-morning light.

For years, she had wanted to separate us—not completely, of course. That seemed unimaginable. Still, if she could move us apart just enough so there would be room between us for her ... and yet, now that we were fighting, now that Florence was trying to pull loose (it *seemed* to be Florence, but you never knew), she was terrified, as if the integrity of our bodies, our very lives, depended on our remaining identical to one another, and if we began to change, to look like two people instead of one magically doubled, we would begin to decay and crumble. We would die.

She thought, *They have to stay the same.* And then she knew she had *always* believed that. All along she had been telling herself a story about two girls who were really one, who had only one soul between them, which was the same as saying they had only one heart between them, and many creatures tried to pry them apart, but the girls, who knew they would cease to exist if they were separated, fought off all the creatures, both good and evil, who tried to part them. Had she told these stories to Albert? She thought she had. She must have.

"You two have to try and get along," she said.

"I do try," I said. "This wasn't my idea!"

It had to do with our father's death, I knew that, as if his death was an omen, as if, by dying, he said, See? This can happen to you. One of you can be put in the ground and the other one will be left to walk around alone. Florence understood this first and was frightened by it, and, being more practical and cold-blooded, as she had always been, she was moving away from me before I could be taken from her.

"She tried to tear my head from our necks!" I said, weeping, and in spite of herself, our mother smiled.

"You have only one neck, Doris," she said. "I'll talk to your sister."

In the living room, Florence was violently brushing her hair with our mother's hairbrush.

"I thought you needed the comb," our mother said. "What is this all about, really? Your sister's hysterical and you're pulling your hair out with that brush."

"I could paint if I wanted to!" Florence screamed. "I tried it last week! I'm just as good at it as she is! But I don't do it! *She's* the one who paints! *I'm* the one who writes poems!"

"If you want to paint, you have every right to paint. If she wants to write poems, she has every right to do it."

"No! She doesn't! When I come home from school today I'm buying a large roll of red adhesive tape and I'm measuring the floor and making a line down the middle and she'll stay on her side of the room and I'll stay on mine!"

"You'll do no such thing."

"Then I'll live in the little room at the end of the hall."

"It's not a room, it's a closet. It's not big enough to live in."

"I'll put the cot in and I'll live there. All I need is a lamp."

"Get dressed and come down to breakfast. The doctor should take a look at you."

"At me!"

"Is this normal behavior?"

"*You're* the one the doctor takes a look at!"

"I don't know what you're talking about and I don't want to know. Clean that brush before you put it back."

When breakfast was ready, we came in and sat down to eat as if we were looking at our plates, but each was inspecting the other.

"Are you sorry?" I asked, finally.

"No."

"Will you cut your hair?"

"Yes."

"Then I'll cut mine."

"No, you won't."

"I will."

"Then I won't cut mine," Florence said, and in so saying understood that I had outmaneuvered her.

"I DON'T KNOW what's wrong with them," our mother said.

"Don't you?" Hilda asked her. "*Your* mother shouldn't have told you those stories about dancing in Saranac," Hilda said. "Look at the effect they've had on you."

"My mother! She didn't have anything to do with it! Living with a man whose lips and fingernails were blue, that's what did it!"

"Let's change the subject," Hilda said. "Florence comes here after school. You should send her more often. They can't fight if they're in two different places."

"MOTHER," I asked her, "is it true that when we were small I was a fighter?"

"Yes; if anyone came near Florence, you went for them. You threw stones, you hit a boy with a stick, you pushed a girl down so hard she cut her forehead. You always protected your sister. You were a ferocious little girl."

"And I stabbed Florence with a fork?"

"No, I think she stabbed *you* with a fork."

"I remember I stabbed her with a fork, but she says she stabbed me."

"I think she's right."

"I want to know who stabbed who!"

"What difference does it make? One of you must have a scar. One of you stabbed the other in the arm."

"Why?"

"One of you had two more green peas and you wouldn't divide them up."

"We stabbed each other over *green peas?*"

"Green peas," our mother said.

"Why did I stop fighting?"

"I don't know," she said, flushing.

But she did know. I fought Albert when he tried to force us to make his bed. I fought him again and again, but Florence wouldn't fight him and she wouldn't help me, and one afternoon when he was threatening to smother me with a pillow, when the pillow covered my face and I was choking, breathing in feather dust through the cotton covering, Albert was suddenly gone, the pillow was gone, and our mother was shouting at him and going after him with our father's belt, the belt buckle lashing at his arms and his back, and when she was through, he was covered with raw, red welts.

"You don't have to make his bed," our mother said that night. "Your brother will make his own bed."

"He *has* made his own bed," our father said. "If he ever does it again, he won't live in this house. Do you hear me, Albert?"

But the next day Albert was back. "Make my bed or when you're sleeping I'll set fire to the house with you in it," he said, and Florence said, "Doris, let's make his bed. It's not worth it." But I said, "No, I still won't make the bed," and the fight began again, but this time our parents were on the common, listening to a string quartet playing in the gazebo, and there was no one to stop him.

He seemed to know exactly how long he could hold the pillow over my face before he would really kill me, and when he let me up, gasping, I turned on him and bit him above the elbow, and his arm bled and the blood soaked his shirt.

"If you say what happened, I'll set the house on fire," he said. "I mean it."

"Why are you bleeding?" our father asked him when he came back.

"I fell against a nail," Albert said.

"Did he fall against a nail?"

"Yes," Florence said.

"Did he fall against a nail?" he asked me. I looked at Florence. "Don't look at her! Look at me! Did he fall against a nail?"

"Yes," I said. "Florence said so."

But our mother understood. "If you ever, ever touch either of those girls again," she said, "I personally will call the orphanage and have them come get you. Or I'll call the police. That's your choice, the police or the orphanage. Don't think you can fool me! No one can fool me! You threatened them! What did you threaten them with?"

"I said I wouldn't help them with their homework."

"They don't need help with their homework. What did you tell them? Tell me!"

"I said I'd burn down the house with everyone in it."

"Are you out of your mind? You know where they put people like you? In lunatic asylums!" And suddenly she realized that what she was saying was true. If he continued as he was, he might very well end up in a lunatic asylum.

"Don't cry," Albert said.

"You tell me not to cry, but you smother your sister and threaten to burn the house down!" she said, outraged.

"I didn't threaten *you.*"

"Is that supposed to make me feel better? And if I were in the house and you didn't know it when you set fire to it?"

"I wouldn't hurt you," he said, starting to cry. "I didn't mean it."

"I wish I could believe that. I wish I could."

"I hate the twins!"

"Hate them! But don't lay a hand on them. Your father won't let me keep you. He'll send you away and I won't have any choice. I'll have to agree with him."

"He's not my father," Albert said sullenly. "He's my *step*father. *He* hates *me.*"

"No, he doesn't, Albert," our mother said wearily. "But I'm warning you. Don't make me say it again."

After that, he made his own bed, but he began taunting us. It was always the same thing, and he knew what to say because he had heard the other children. "You're not Florence, you're Doris. You're not the real child, you're the shadow. How do you like it, being littermates?"

And then Florence asked our mother, "Mama, what are littermates?" and our mother asked her where she heard that, and once more Albert was under a cloud. We began calling him the Cloud.

"YOU STOPPED FIGHTING," our mother said, "because of Albert. He hit you and he frightened you and you decided fighting was no use."

"Where was Florence? If Albert fought with me, she would have helped me." And then I saw Florence, as at the end of a long tunnel, immobile in the doorway while Albert hit me or smothered me, and I remembered. So, I thought, I was not always so peaceful, and this idea was wonderful to me and gave me hope, although why I needed hope I could not say.

I WAS PAINTING and Florence watched me intently. "Why are you watching me?" I asked, and Florence asked me if I was ashamed of what I was doing. "Why are you watching me?" I asked again. "You always have a reason."

"I have nothing better to do."

"Florence, I want to talk to you," our mother said. "Why are you watching her?"

"I'm learning to paint," Florence said. Our mother said that she could only learn by doing, and Florence said no, when she watched how I moved my arm, she knew how to move her own arm. She could feel her own arm moving. When she saw how I mixed my paints, she knew how to mix the same color. One day she would sit down and start painting. Why should she learn the hard way, when she could watch me?

"I hope you're not going to start painting. Your sister thinks she's the painter and you're the writer. You're the one who said you wanted it like that. She thinks you'll write stories and poems and she'll paint pictures to go with them."

"If anyone paints pictures from my stories, it will be me," Florence said.

"Then teach her how to write stories."

"You can't teach someone to write stories. She can watch me write them if she wants."

"Isn't that generous of you," our mother said.

The next night, I came in and said, "Florence is still going around telling everyone we don't look alike, and everyone laughs."

"It *is* laughable," our mother said.

"She talked to Rodney Putnam and he's bringing his prize bloodhound here this weekend."

"Why?"

"She said, 'I'll show you. Even a stupid dog can tell us apart.' That's what she said."

"The dog is going to hunt for you?"

"We'll each give Rodney something and then we'll hide and the dog will sniff it and he'll find the right one. I don't want to do it. It's a freak show! I feel crazy enough now! She says I don't look like her! She keeps saying it! She thinks this stupid bloodhound will prove something."

"Don't do it."

"Then everyone will say I'm afraid."

"Such nonsense! You're identical and you'll always be identical. There must be something special about you or God wouldn't have made two of you. Your father always said that."

"That's not what Florence says. She says we're stupid typing mistakes."

"Typing mistakes?"

"Like when you make a mistake and type the same word twice."

"Why do you listen to her? The more she upsets you, the more she keeps it up."

"But *why* is she doing it?"

"I honestly don't know. Ignore her."

"When Rodney brings his bloodhound, will you come?"

"If I don't have to be in the store."

"It's going to be in the paper."

"The paper!"

"On Sunday."

O N   S A T U R D A Y, Rodney Putnam brought his prize bloodhound, Sandy, who was regularly lent to the valley police when a child was missing. Locally, Sandy was a famous dog. He could find a quarter buried in leaves in the middle of a four-acre field. He had found a small child who had fallen into a narrow ravine in the middle of a thick pine forest, even though the child had slipped in the mud and was thoroughly coated when the dog picked up his scent and triumphantly began barking.

"All right," Rodney told us. "Choose a hiding place in the woods. Go as far in as you want. Then I'll give him the handkerchief—that belongs to Florence—and he'll find her. He won't go looking for Doris. He's got the best nose in Vermont."

We disappeared into the woods. Rodney held out the handkerchief and Sandy sniffed at it. "Go get him, boy!" he said, and he let the dog off the leash. The dog ran into the meadow and began circling, then stopped, sniffing the wind, and soon he headed straight for the woods. Rodney and the others ran after him, and within a few seconds, they heard the dog's urgent loud bark.

"He's found Florence!" Rodney called out. "Come out, Florence!"

"I'm not Florence, I'm Doris," I said.

"Doris! Sandy doesn't make mistakes! You're Florence pretending to be Doris."

But before I had a chance to answer, the dog raised his head and began sniffing the air and then ran back and forth as if completely bewildered.

"What's wrong with him? He never acts like this," Rodney said. And then for the second time, they heard his jubilant bark, and when they followed him, they found him pawing at a tree trunk, and up in the tree was Florence.

"Well, he found me," Florence said smugly. "I knew he would."

"He already found you," Rodney said glumly. "He found your sister."

"What are you talking about? He can tell the difference between us! Anyone can!"

"He can't tell the difference," Rodney said. "I don't believe it. He could always do it before."

But now the dog was heading deeper into the woods, and when Rodney called him, he paid no attention. "I'm following him," he announced, and the two of us, by now standing together, decided we too would follow the dog.

The woods were damp and buzzing with mosquitoes, and the sunlight, so strong at the top of the trees, was pale and weak as it lost itself in the tangly undergrowth. Blackberry branches caught our bare skin and thistles stuck to our shorts, but when we looked at one another we knew we would continue following the dog. We were careful as we walked to hold the branches we pushed aside, so they would not snap back into the other's face.

"We're going very deep in," Florence said uneasily.

"The dog knows how to get back," I said. "Don't worry."

"I'm not worried," she said, but she was. We both were. There were bears in the woods and coyotes and mountain cats. "We should go back," she said.

But I said if we went back without Rodney and the dog, we would certainly be lost and we'd end up waiting for the dog to find us while the mosquitoes drank all our blood.

"The dog," Florence said, stopping beneath a low pine bough, "thinks we're identical. But he's only a dog."

"Watch out for poison ivy," I said, and Florence said, "We're not allergic."

Not far ahead, we heard the dog howl and then howl again, this time louder and more anguished, and it was an eerie sound, it made us shiver, and we heard Rodney shouting, "Sandy! Stay! Stay!"

"What's going on?" Florence said.

Rodney came crashing out of the underbrush. "You twins better stay where you are," he said. "There's something in there."

"What?" I asked.

"People," Rodney said. His face was red, his eyes were wet.

"I want to see them," Florence said.

"They're dead."

"Dead!"

"Who are they?" I asked. "Do you know who they are?"

"A girl from Islington's been missing. I think it's her."

"Who's the other?"

"Her boyfriend. I think."

"I want to see them," Florence said.

"You don't."

"We do," I said.

Probably it was because we were all three deep in the woods, far from anyone else; probably we were all maddened by the mosquitoes, so thick and vicious and persistent; probably because the air was also thick with yellow jackets and we kept looking down at our feet for a yellow jacket's nest buried in the grass or hidden by the ferns; probably because Rodney was angry at us for making a fool of his dog; but Rodney, who ought to have known better, who later said he did know better and how could he have been so stupid, told us to follow him, and we went in single file, slowly, pushing the branches back carefully, holding them until the next one could push them away with her hand, and I was walking behind Rodney when I said, "There's Sandy!"

And we came to a little clearing where enormous boulders of granite were buried deep in the earth, preventing trees and ferns from growing, and at the edge of the clearing, Rodney tried to stop us. He said, "You don't have to look," but we said we had come this far, we wanted to see what was there, and we walked past the still-howling dog into the clearing and there they were, a young man and a young woman, lying side by side staring up at the sun, their chests dark with blood, blood staining the rocks on which they lay, their faces and hands white and gray, the color of nothing human, dead, unquestionably, incontrovertibly dead. A shotgun lay next to the young man.

"My God!" Florence said.

And I thought, They're beautiful, and I moved closer, bending down to look more closely at the bodies, at their faces. "They look so happy," I said.

"They're not happy, they're dead," Florence said.

"Don't get so close," Rodney said nervously.

"Why? They can't hurt me," I answered.

"They've been here for days," he said. "Decay. Germs."

"They're swollen," I said, "but their faces are beautiful."

"Their faces are horrible," Florence said. "Let's get out of here."

"I want to paint them," I said.

"What *is* the matter with you?" Florence asked. "Let's get out of here."

"He was wearing a red plaid shirt and she was wearing a flowered dress, lilac-colored."

"Doris, shut up," Florence said. Chill after chill was sweeping over her body, I could tell. The top of her scalp was tingling; when she pressed her fingers to it, the places where her fingertips touched prickled, as if with needles. She was telling herself, I'm not going to disgrace myself, I'm not going to throw up. I'll take deep breaths.

"Take deep breaths," I said, walking behind her. "Give me your hand." Florence thrust her arm out behind her and I took her hand.

"Follow me," Rodney said. "I'm following Sandy."

"I'd like to go back and see them again," I said.

"Shut up!" Florence said, turning to face me. "They're dead! They don't need company!"

"Sandy, halt!" Rodney shouted. "You two have to keep up with me. He's hurrying. He knows we found something. He wants to tell people."

"The dog wants to tell people?" Florence asked. "That stupid dog?"

"He's not stupid," Rodney said. "He found *them.*"

"Any dog can find dead bodies," Florence said. She was angry at Rodney. She was angry at the dog. She was angry at me.

"All right, Florence, that's enough," I said.

"When we come out, don't say anything. Their families don't know. Let the police talk to the families first."

"I'm not saying a word and neither is she," Florence said, and I smiled. This was how it used to be, my sister speaking for both of us. This was how it still should be. And for a short time it was, because we had seen something no one else had, and that night, and for many nights afterward, we sat on the porch and talked about the young man and woman dead in the woods, and wondered what had happened to bring them there. Had they loved each other very much? Had they run off when their parents tried to separate them? Did they come to understand that they could not survive apart, did they conclude that they didn't want to survive? Had they decided that this was the happiest moment of their lives and that they would never be happier? Was that why they had shot themselves?

And how had they decided? Who had made the decision? Had they made it together? Did one of them change his mind at the end but the other remain steady? Was it the boy or the girl who shot first? It might have been the boy, the gun was next to him, but the girl might have lived long enough to bend over him, and if she was holding the gun, she might have put it down next to him. Did they both know what was going to happen when they went into the woods? Were they sure? Did they have any regrets, any second thoughts? They must have been sure or they would never have picked such a secluded place. The police had been searching for days and no one had found them. The woods were on the far side of the common, but no one knew of the clearing. They must have planned it in advance. They must have picked out the spot. But perhaps they found it accidentally. Perhaps they only intended to go deep into the woods.

We used to call it Three Raven Wood, remember? There was a song Daddy sang, "There were three ravens sat on a tree"—what was that song about? About a knight who died and his dogs kept watch over him and wouldn't let anyone near. Wasn't that what it was about? Do you think they died happy?

I think they died happy, but if they'd lived, they might have been still happier. Yes, but they might never have been happy again. People don't shoot themselves because they're happy. They must have been unhappy. Perhaps she wanted to leave him but he didn't want her to go, perhaps it was the other way around. Will those faces ever go away, will I always see them, I hope I'll always see them. And so the discussions went on and on.

"What was he thinking of, to take two girls to look at something like that?" our mother asked us.

Hesitantly, she came out onto the porch. We were back together in our own world, in the Land of the Twins. She was once again the intruder. She carried two glasses of lemonade and ice like peace offerings. She noticed the water beading on the outside of the glasses. It made her think of two young people dead in the woods. She didn't know why. It made her think of leaves beading with drops of water, bending under the weight of the water, sending showers of raindrops down onto the faces of the two young people, as if they were only thirsty, as if a little water was all they needed to wake them up.

"To be fair," said Florence, "it was the dog who took us."

"You two have horrible enough imaginations as it is."

"Reality is a powerful curb to imagination," Florence said, and our mother was dumbfounded. When had the girls begun to talk like that? When, in fact, had they stopped calling her Mama and begun calling her Mother?

"I want to paint them," I said again.

"What?" she asked.

When neither of us answered, she went back into the house, sat down in her favorite chair, and shook her head. The first of many clocks began chiming the hour.

She must have thought she should have known that it was only the fright in the meadow that drew us together, that the peace was fragile and could not last, but that it would always be this way. When there was trouble, real danger, we would clasp hands and come together as if we were enclosed in a single skin.

She must have told herself she should have known a truce was temporary, that Florence had decided we were no longer to be mere reflections of one another, that I would be sacrificed to her decisions, whatever they were. She thought the two bodies in the woods were an omen, and a boy would soon come on the scene, wreak the usual havoc, turn us against one another, separate us once and for all.

But it did seem as if we had been changed, had gone back to what we were, and at the end of the day, after we helped in the store, we sat in lounge chairs on the screened-in porch and talked, and she could hear us through the living room window. She always checked to be sure it was open. She stood behind the curtain but her face was close enough to the screen to smell the dust, and if we sat there at night, she pressed her forehead right into the screen, so that when she moved away, her skin was patterned into tiny squares just as the screening was, and she hid herself in her room until the telltale marks disappeared, and it seemed to her we talked in the old way, as if we needed to work out life together before we took a step into the world beyond our own door. And Florence said, "What kind of man do you want? If you could order the man you wanted, what would he be like?" And I said, "I'd want someone who listened to me," and Florence said, "Just listened?" And I said, "No, he would have to love me too."

"Would he be like you or would he be different?" Florence asked, and

I hesitated, I didn't want to answer, but then I said, "Like me," and she said, "I don't want someone like me, I want someone who's different, and the only thing we'll have in common is that we love each other," and I said, "That won't last very long, I don't think," and Florence said, "What did our parents have in common?" and I said, "Everything; they had no lives before they met each other," and Florence said, "Looks are important, don't you think? I want to marry a handsome man," and I said dreamily, "A healthy one."

"I want an ambitious one," Florence said, and I said ambitious people were ruthless, and she said, "You don't know anything about ambition. If you did, you'd enter your paintings in some competitions. The art teacher always tells me, Talk to your sister, she could earn money from those paintings, those paintings could get her into any college," and I said, "I'm not ready, the paintings aren't good enough yet," and she said, "If you wait, nothing will happen," and I said, "I like the future the way it is, a big locked door. I don't want it open, not yet. Leave everything where it is, I'm happy where I am. You are too, aren't you?"

And she said, "This is how *I* think of the future. It's a small place with a *little* locked door at the end, and the faster you throw yourself at it, the longer you have to enjoy it. I intend to enjoy it," and I said she sounded like the birds who flew into windows thinking they saw the sky there; she should take her time, she would make fewer mistakes. When time passed, you had a better chance to know who you were.

"We will never know who we are," she said bitterly, and I said, "Don't say that; we have only to look at one another to know who we are," and Florence said, "Who are *we*, then?"

I said, "I don't think of us like that, half of a whole; I think of us as one thing, one spirit in two bodies," and she said, "I'm sorry, but I regard my spirit as my own," and I asked her, "Is that why you hide the books you're reading? Is that why you bought that locked box for your papers?" Florence said, "We're getting older, we need privacy," and I asked, "What for? Do you think I'll steal from you? What is there to steal that I don't already have, that *we* don't already have?" And Florence said, "That's the trouble, I don't see it that way, not anymore," and I said, "I do. Everything I do I can do because of you. It's because of you I wasn't frightened by the bodies in the woods. It's because of you I want to paint them."

Florence said, "What do I have to do with it? I have nothing to do with it. You're so used to thinking we're the same, you believe I know what goes on in your mind. Believe me, I don't know, and you don't know what goes on in mine," and I said, "I do know. You want to get away from me. You think if you can get away from me, everyone will love you best, the *whole world* will love you best, but it can't be done, why should we even try?"

And Florence said, her voice flat and dismissive, "It's already happened."

"I don't believe it," I said, and Florence made an irritated gesture with her hand, as if brushing away an annoying mosquito, and said, "Believe what you want."

And the truth was that Florence had glimpsed something, something like the first snowflake falling, but because it is the first and because it swirls lazily by, you're not sure it's snow. It could be a bit of ash blown from the chimney where you have been burning newspapers. And she saw it first at the cemetery, and in the woods she saw it again, but this time clearly, and every night when she came home, she thought over her life so far and asked herself what had happened to her in her fourteen years, what were her memories, what was truly hers, and it was as if she had opened a fancily wrapped box and found nothing there.

Who had stabbed *whom* with a fork? She couldn't remember. She'd always assumed she had done it, but I was equally sure I was the guilty party. And yet both of us could vividly remember picking up the fork, warm from the plate full of spaghetti and sauce, and plunging it into the other one's arm. She remembered the feel of the fork in her hand. She remembered the resistance of the skin into which she plunged it, the slight popping noise the flesh made when it gave way to the force of her hand. She remembered thinking, That is what they mean by puncturing, I've *punctured* her skin, and she remembered how the word itself lit up as if it had suddenly taken on form and light and hung in the air as mysteriously as beams of light hung there. But when questioned, I remembered precisely the same things.

She had always assumed I knew what she was thinking and so there was no need to put her thoughts into words. I simply looked at her and knew. And then there were times when she didn't want me to know, and so she avoided thinking altogether.

All the years our father was dying, we had a pact never to mention what it would be like when he was gone. What would become of our mother? Would she continue to drink? Would she continue her visits to the doctor? (Who discovered those visits first? Neither of us ever mentioned them. No one had told us, but both of us knew.)

And what *did* we think of our mother crossing the common on the doctor's day off, or late at night, leaving us a note saying she had a terrible headache and would be back as soon as she had her tablets? Did we think about it at all? Who had read which books? Who had which friends? Who was angry and why? Was *she* the angry one when *I* threw things? It often seemed to her that she felt something but I expressed it. Was she angry when she found one of our mother's notes? *Back soon. Supper in the oven.*

But I was the one who threw pillows against the wall, the one who picked up our shoes and threw them against the wall between our room and our mother's. Was Florence angry when Aunt Dorle gave all the children five dollars for Christmas but the two of us got five dollars together, as if we were only one person? *I* was the one who tore the five-dollar bill in half, in front of everyone, everyone watching, eyes wide, mouths gaping, and handed Florence one half of the bill and stuffed the other half in my own pocket, glaring.

We were experts in sharing. We had to be, two newborns, one mother, following our own principle of evolution. How little could we do and survive? After all, there were two of us. We were always together. Why should we both remember one thing? Why should both lose their temper over one thing? Why should both cry, both laugh, over one thing? Why should both find the words, both see the images, why should both think through the implications? Life went faster, went better, if we divided it up, and why not divide it up? We would always be together. *That* was the mistake. How could we not have made it? Everything alive generalizes from what it knows, and for years that was what we knew—we would always be together. If someone new came, a stranger, I came back to her, joined her, we were complete. Once I was there, she had the words, she began speaking. But if I was not there, she shrank back and had nothing to say.

But you think you will be, will always be there.

PART SEVEN

I Was Traveling Farther and Farther Away

I WAS TRAVELING farther and farther away from the world of solid shapes. There were no stone angels now, no stone horses, only forms and their colors. I concentrated on the colors, on the odd shapes of doors and windows, on the violent-blue steps ascending an outer salmon-colored wall. I thought, With time, I will forget the blue steps are blue, I will forget the salmon color belongs to the wall. I will see only the colors. I will reduce the world to a palette, a place without forms. Nothing will be trapped forever in one form, nothing will be condemned to one form forever.

I saw an arched doorway and the door was made of gray wood, and the arch itself was painted lime green and beneath the lime-green paint flaking in the sun were irregular patches of lavender. The wall of the house was blue, painted with orange rectangles. The sockets of the windows were sunken and dark and brimmed with shadows that were navy blue. I saw a blue boat with an orange anchor and the oars, still in the locks, were orange and the anchor was pitted black with rust. I saw a house painted violet and in front of its violet door were four disturbing caned chairs, enameled brilliant red, shining and loud in the sun. They seemed to scream, because of their color. I saw fishing nets spilled onto the sand, dyed brilliant red. I passed a red house with a blue door and a green arch, each window framed by a thick stripe, green or pink or purple or lime. I passed a low cement house with an orange-tiled roof, its walls painted blue but flaking in large patches to white, so that it exactly resembled the sky over the roof, the sky and its clouds.

During this time, I never saw a white wall, not anywhere. I saw boats striped with paint, red and orange and lime, their oars blue. I saw pumpkin-colored walls and windows, their gratings like elaborate bird-cages, painted purple and shining. I saw a gold wall. I saw apple trees, their trunks painted the color of coral, small bridges painted crimson over dried-up streams, the topmost stones painted pure white. I saw a lichen-covered cross over a gravestone painted bright red. I saw orange lizards whose spots were chartreuse. I saw a plain black snake, but he was dead and drying in the sun.

I gave my wedding ring to a blond man who saw me on the side of the road and took me to a farm teeming with white chickens. He went into the green wood and collected mushrooms, brown and tan and white, and cooked them into an omelet. He picked brown potatoes dotted black as if by the fine tip of a brush, and peeled them to their cream-colored insides, nicotine color, the color nicotine creates settling on white enamel, and boiled them. He stirred the sliced potatoes into the pale-yellow omelet. His hair was golden but his skin was the color of an acorn shell.

I don't remember speaking to him, but I must have said something. I must have said, What beautiful golden hair, what beautiful skin, the color of acorns.

He didn't speak English, what I said didn't matter.

It was so hot and the sun was so blinding.

I held up my hand to the sun and the sun struck my ring and I didn't like it, the way the light stabbed my eyes.

I took off the ring and gave it to him.

He seemed puzzled but pleased. He tried to hand it back, but I shook my head and he nodded and slipped the ring on his finger. His hands were longer than mine and thinner, and I thought, Good, he will lose the ring. Someday someone will see it gleaming in the grass or among gray and beige and black stones and will pick it up, thinking, How nice, a perfect circle of gold. I saw how the ring would change to a bird and fly golden through a lavender sky, back to me, settling on my wrist, covering its black eye with its gold wing when the sky had gone dark green and it wanted to sleep. I thought, This bird will have powers. When it flies over cities, stone angels will cover their stone eyes with their wings, as if they were birds who were sleeping.

I told him about the ring, about the bird, about the statues covering their eyes. He nodded and smiled. I could have said anything.

Once, a child came with me. He was amazingly ugly. His mouth was deformed and his nose had been broken and he could not speak properly, only gurgle. He must have been nine or ten. He was a strange child, and sad. Whenever we stopped, he would find a stick and draw in the mud. There was mud everywhere, slippery and shiny as a mirror. It must have rained. It must have rained constantly. I had no memory of rain. I remembered only the hot sun in the blue sky, the mud the color of milk chocolate, until we came down from the mountains and walked into a town. There, the mud was the color of rust.

Eventually, I saw he was drawing a house, a house with a tree on each side, and something on the front of the house. Was it a shadow?

When he grew tired, I took the stick, and in another pool of mud I drew a house, a beautiful brick French house. Its roof would have been slate, its walls white, its shutters slate blue. Its roof was pitched steeply. In the house's central section were two chimneys. The mud was thick, like soft clay, and held the impression. It hardened in the sun as I drew. I drew two pine trees in the shape of cones. I drew a woman who cast her shadow against the house wall. The child grew very excited. He pointed at my house in the mud and made gurgling sounds. I saw his eyes were wide with happiness. All this had happened before. I took my stick and scratched out the house and the trees. The child began to cry. For hours, he toiled over his patch of mud. He looked at me, his eyes wide and imploring. I would not be tempted again. What I saw was mine only. To paint is to double what exists, the inside weather, the outside.

The child would not stop his sketching in mud. One night when he slept, I picked up my knapsack and moved a few steps away from him. He didn't stir. I moved a little farther. He slept. The moonlight had turned him to stone. I walked down the path, away from him. When I looked back, the night had erased him.

CHAPTER
TWENTY-FOUR

IN THE MORNING, the cool air poured in, light on the skin, tinted green by the light through the leaves, the feel of water rushing over rocks in the creek in back of the house in Peru, and you know, even before you open your eyes, that the sky will be a pure, thin blue streaked with high white clouds, thinning as they go. I called Antonio. I preferred to call him rather than have him call me. When I answered the phone and heard his voice, my pulse fluttered, because for an instant it was again the voice of the Impostor. Oh, he'd meet me anywhere, Antonio said, but did it have to be in that café? Couldn't we try another place? We agreed to meet after lunch in the café in Primrose Hill. Then I called Dennis. It had been a week since he'd slept on my couch or I on his. "You still haven't forgiven me?" he asked.

"I will forgive you," I said. "I told you so. I'm getting used to the idea of your duplicitousness. I thought you were a lovely, simple man. I underestimated you."

"You overestimated me," he said. "Keep thinking about going to Goult."

"Antonio wants to come along."

"What did you tell him?"

"I said if I managed to get myself there, that was all I could handle. I'm not up to a family reunion. I can't even imagine it, how bizarre it would be."

"I'll take you to dinner," he said, and I agreed. "Just throw down the keys—if you still trust me with them." I said I would. I would throw them down.

Now I had time to wander, time on my own in the unfamiliar café, time to sit still while nothing happened, empty time, when someone might walk in and come straight over to me and say, "Florence! I haven't seen you since last summer!" And then I could pretend to be my sister, I could pretend to be an amnesiac, I could say, "Ever since the accident, I don't remember anything," I could ask questions, I could find out where she'd been. It was my fondest dream. *You're pathetic,* I heard her whisper, my sister, Florence.

Is it more pathetic to dream of her than for her to hide from me?

I thought this as I was standing at the front windows of my flat, casement windows that ran the length of the large room, looking out at the Royal Free Hospital, from my window a gray sad painting against a gray sky, floor after floor of windows like picture frames. Some windows reflected the blue sky and its white, streaming clouds, but most were poisonous lead-gray squares, empty except for the outline of intravenous stands, or vases people had placed on the windowsills, most of them empty. Patients sat at an occasional window, featureless from this distance, all robed in gray, all in profile, all staring out.

She could be in there.

I had done volunteer work at a hospital in New York, hoping to find her.

Once, a year after she disappeared, when I thought she was dead, I had been in a hospital, looking out, wearing a blue hospital bathrobe. I had an illness no one could diagnose and I asked myself again and again, if she was dead, then how could I be alive? And my husband said, "It's a good thing you're married to a psychiatrist, because if it weren't for me, they'd either operate on you or lock you up." And when I asked him, "Operate on *what?*" he wouldn't answer me; his eyes were full of tears. He said, "Doctors can't stand by. They have to do something."

After that I began to improve. At least the pains began to disappear. And the high fevers.

I shouldn't stand still looking at a hospital. I am too suggestible.

At two o'clock, Antonio was waiting for me, and when I came in, he jumped up so quickly that he almost knocked his chair over, and we both reached out for the chair and our hands touched as we straightened it and he flushed a deep, deep red.

"Well," I said, sitting down, "anything new?"

"No. But you know that house across the street from the café? The last one in the row? That's Arthur Graham's house. We could go over there and take a look when we're finished," and then he pointed out a couple sitting at the next table.

"You're surprised that I know about them, aren't you? Everyone knows everyone else here, it's such a small country. If you lived here for a few years, you'd know everyone else too. Every imaginable degree of claustrophobia, that's what people here suffer from. Every inch has its history, every bit of land surveyed and sold and resold, no waste space anywhere, nothing like what you see in movies about America, big highways, weeds all over, houses falling into marshes, miles of wilderness no one's bothered to look at, not like Devon, every square foot manicured and polished and fenced and weeded, one or two oaks per pasture, even the cows and sheep artfully arranged on the hillside; of course, cows and sheep *always* look artfully arranged somehow. Even in America they tend to pull a landscape together." I said he sounded homesick, and he sighed and said, "Yes, well, I'm not likely to find someone from my particular hillside in Spain, am I?"

"You're being very charming and sophisticated," I said. "What, really, do you want to talk about?" I sat back and looked at him. He was a very handsome young man.

"I don't know what to call you," he said, flushing. "How *should* I address you?"

"What would you like to call me?"

"Mrs. James?"

"That's a bit formal, isn't it? Call me Doris. That's my name." He sat silent and stubborn. "You don't want to call me Doris?"

"As if we were friends! As if we weren't related at all!"

"On the phone you said you were my son, so to speak. I didn't think *that* was appropriate."

"I thought it would shock you into seeing me."

"It did shock me."

"I don't know what to call you," he said miserably.

"You don't have to call me anything."

"What was she like? My mother?"

"Naturally that's what you'd want to know," I said. "Well, she looked like me, but she wasn't like me. She was very emotional and very talented, not like me at all. Intense. She was terrified of being ordinary. I'm ordinary. She didn't love many people. I suppose she couldn't; she was so violent, she would have burned herself up. It's hard to describe her. What do you want to know? You should talk to Jack Pine. I barely saw her in those last years. She called me every day, did I tell you that? Almost every single day for seven years, but I couldn't go to see her, not unless Jack wasn't home. You ought to see him yourself."

He flushed again and began drumming rapidly on the tabletop. "Didn't he drive her out? Didn't he hurt her? Wasn't she in Spain trying to get away from him? My *father!* If my *father* did those things!"

At that instant, I decided never to tell him about their fight or about the party to which she wore the dress or how they had both behaved that night. "We don't know what he did," I said. "We don't know what happened."

"They *both* sound so terrible!" he exclaimed. His voice was a wail, thin and childish, and I smiled, I couldn't help it.

"She wasn't terrible. She was only trying to save herself, I'm sure that's it, and he was trying to save himself, I'm sure he was; they were in an awful situation. They had to get away from each other. I don't know *what* happened, I don't know *what* made her leave. It can't have been easy for him, after she left. Everyone's been after him. Dennis says he's very suspicious. He doesn't trust anyone. Except Dennis, of course. He says Dennis has an aura, whatever that means. He admires Dennis as a writer, you know, so that may have something to do with it."

"She was crazy, wasn't she?" he asked suddenly.

"Oh, I don't think so," I said. "But no one ever held either of us up as models of stability."

"*He* was crazy. People say so."

"He's mystical. That's not the same thing."

"Are *you* crazy?" he asked.

"As a loon," I said.

"Well, that's good," he said. "At least you're honest."

"Not always. But while we're being honest—*why* did you call me? Why call me and say you were my son?"

"I was angry, and I thought, I can't get my hands on *her,* so . . . you know."

"You thought you'd take it out on me?"

"Something like that."

"You knew I was her twin?"

"Dennis told me."

"Oh, yes. Dennis."

"He was right to tell me."

"Yes, you'd think so."

"He said that doctor in Peru said no one ever found out where my mother came from because you were twins. He said no one ever thought of the Rice twins separately. There was Florence *and* there was Doris. An

article about a painter named Florence, no one would make the connec-
tion, not unless they mentioned you. Do you think that's right? That no
one found you because you were twins?"

"You mean, did she use me as a kind of camouflage? Certainly she did."

"A schemer," he said.

"Great unsolved crimes," I said. "She could have committed one if she
put her mind to it."

"She *did* put her mind to it."

"I suppose she did," I said.

"Are you going to do it?"

"No. Once is enough for that kind of thing."

He sat still, looking at me. Studying me. "You didn't want children,
either?"

"I did. I couldn't have them. I always miscarried. I thought the same
thing happened to my sister."

"I thought you were both too selfish to want children."

I didn't say anything. I'd wanted a child. Florence had one and gave
him away. A secondhand child, was that what he was? Why did everything
come to me like this? A used child. Still. A child was a child.

"Do you like me?" he asked.

"I don't know. I must. I'm here. Although I must be angry that you
were born to her and not to me."

"Angry? Or sorry?"

"Both."

"The worst thing," he said, "is what she did to my father."

"What did she do to him?"

"She left him."

"Were they married? Did he expect her to stay?"

"He knew she'd go. They weren't married."

"But he kept you."

"Oh, he loved me," Antonio said.

"If he knew she'd leave . . . ," I began.

Antonio pushed his chair back. "I wasn't fair to him because of her. He
deserved better. He kept me and I wasn't even his, but I'd think, There
must be something wrong with him or she wouldn't have left him. If he'd
been a little better or braver or taller or *something*, she'd still be here. I used
to look at other people's fathers and think, This one's short, this one's
ugly, but their wives are in the house. What's wrong with *my* father? I
didn't even know he wasn't my real father. I blamed him."

"And now you feel guilty?"

"Very."

"And you think if you'd loved him better he might still be here? Alive?"

"Yes!"

"He knew you loved him," I said. "People always know. Even when Florence said she hated me, I knew she loved me. They always know. Your father knew."

"Did he?"

"Yes."

"He used to lie on his back, when I was a baby, and hold me under the arms and let me walk up and down on him, and Juana used to say, 'Don't let him walk on you with his little feet. When he gets older, he'll walk all over you with shoes.' I did."

"You shouldn't feel guilty. *She* should feel guilty. My sister. She was selfish."

"I thought you'd think she was perfect."

"I loved her. I wasn't blind. She didn't give me an easy time."

"No! Cruelty and insanity run in your family."

"Why are you so angry at me? Because I look like her?"

"I was," he said. "Angry."

"And now?"

"It's not your fault, is it? *You're* not the one who left me."

"No, I didn't do that."

"Could you have come to Spain and convinced her to stay? I don't think so."

"I didn't know where she was. I couldn't have done that."

"She was responsible. She made her own decisions. *Why* do *you* feel guilty?"

"We all do, when something happens to someone we love. Anyway," I said brightly, "you didn't harm your father. Any child would have felt as you did."

"I wish I thought so," he said.

"If I keep telling you, you'll believe it," I said. "I hope."

He sat silent, thinking. "You're not like her," he said, finally. "You're not selfish."

"An unselfish person isn't such a wonderful thing."

"No?"

"People like that can be quite a burden."

"My mother told you that?"

"She didn't have to tell me. It's true. Unselfish people wreak havoc."

"What do you mean?"

"Oh, I don't know," I said.

"I look like you, I think," he said.

I smiled. It was starting again.

"Don't you think so?"

"Actually," I said, "I do."

"I've got to go," he said.

"Rose again?"

"Rose," he said.

"I'll call you in a few days," I said.

"You never call me. I always have to call you."

"This time I'll call you. I promise."

"I believe you," he said, getting up.

Then I stopped at Eva's and sat down at Eva's table. It was sunny and no one else was there.

"Was that your son you were talking to yesterday?" Eva asked.

"I don't have children," I said, "and if I did, I would be a terrible mother." I said it emphatically and Eva said, "All mothers are terrible mothers. The children are wonderful. Because they survive."

I laughed. "And the mothers have nothing to do with that?"

"No," she said.

"I HAVE SPENT *all day* in restaurants," I said later when I met Dennis.

"You need a change," he said. "You should meet Jack Pine. Get it over with. He was such a big part of your sister's life. He might know something. Something he doesn't even know he knows."

"What's that supposed to mean?"

"He might remember something she said. It wouldn't mean anything to him, but it might to you."

"Like what?"

"A place she mentioned. A story she told. Something she saw. He has rooms full of her paintings. They might tell you something."

"Tell me something?"

"I want to find her. You want to find her. Think about it. Again!"

"I don't think I could do it. Why would he want to see me?"

"Talk to him. He'll talk to you. I'm absolutely sure he will."

"About what?"

"It will come to you when you see him."

"Oh, no," I said, starting to get up. "You're turning into one of those cracked people with cracked ideas about twins! I should have known! You think if I talk to him I'll pick up mysterious emanations and I'll close my eyes and walk out the door straight to where Florence is! It doesn't work like that!"

"You know that's not what I mean."

Of course it wasn't. He was trying to follow my sister, and as he did, and as the glimmer he followed grew fainter and threatened to extinguish itself altogether, he wanted the ones who knew her to light his way. He wanted those of us who'd touched her and kissed her to show their belief in what he had begun to doubt—that she had ever existed. She was losing her dimensions. She was becoming a tracing on air. I sat still, silent and angry.

"You're very beautiful," he said. "She would have been very beautiful."

I stared and he flushed. Of course. I should have seen it, I should have known it from the start. He'd spent so long worshiping Florence, how could he not fall in love with her replica?

"I'm not like her, you know. She was ambitious, she was hard, she despised me. Dennis," I said, *"sit down*. What do you really know about Jack? He didn't have a very happy life."

"Did Florence talk to you about him?"

"I don't remember how I learned about him," I said, flushing. "But he wasn't happy. His family wasn't happy."

"Well, tell me," he said. "Tell me what you know."

"It's a long story."

"I don't mind," Dennis said. "We'll get another cup of coffee."

"Oh, yes," I said, sighing. "That makes the prospect of talking about Jack *very* attractive."

"It was a dark and stormy night," Dennis said. "Doesn't it begin that way?"

"No. It begins this way," I said, and I told him what I knew.

JACK PINE WAS the sixth child, the first boy, born into a house of women, born ten years after the last of his sisters, when his mother was forty-three, long after his mother had become disillusioned with his father. But his mother was a religious woman who could imagine nothing worse than infidelity, and although she loved her husband less as time passed, her husband seemed to love her more, and she came to regard this steady and deep affection as another of her burdens because she knew that no one would understand her dissatisfactions, or have patience with them.

Her husband was the kind of man most women dream of having, but Ellen Pine was no longer in love with him, and when she opened her eyes in the morning and saw another brilliant blue sky, she could find no good reason to get up. Her husband's love formed the bars of her very attractive cage. She had to go through the motions—for his sake. She knew what she owed her husband. It was how she had been brought up. She hadn't known there was anything more to wish for than a good husband and children and a nice house. No one told you the passion could die out. No one told you the man you loved when you were young would not be the one you loved when you were older. No one told you that your husband's body could fail and that you would sleep beside him night after night wishing you had a room of your own, that all you wanted was to be left in peace.

She told each of her daughters in turn that she wasn't afraid to die. She did not, as her daughters said, draw them a picture, not precisely, but they knew exactly why their mother was unhappy, and her complaints shadowed their lives.

All of the children worried incessantly about their mother. Was she unhappy? How unhappy was she? Was she crying or was she angry? When she was unhappy—and it seemed to them that she was unhappy almost all of the time—she had a way of scolding them so that they felt as if her misery was their fault. They hadn't made their beds. They hadn't swept the sand out of the kitchen. They had no regard for her, none at all. Why didn't they simply say they thought she was worthless, a terrible mother? Why didn't they say they hated her?

Except, of course, when she *was* happy. Then she was a different person. And then she was happy in such a dizzy, intoxicating way that they thought it would never end. The whole world turned golden. She praised them to the skies and they knew they were perfect.

And whenever Warren, her husband, came home he was not surprised to find one or another of the girls weeping in her room, refusing to come out for dinner, but he told himself his wife was strict, a perfectionist, and hadn't his own mother told him that daughters were harder to raise than sons? His daughters said, "He can't see anything wrong with her, what's the use?"

When Jack was born, Ellen, who all her life rushed up to cribs and cradles exclaiming, "I *love* little boys!" was not only happy but for years afterward seemed in a trance of ecstasy, a trance her husband, Warren, did not enter into because, unlike most men, he openly admitted that he preferred girls.

His wife believed that whatever troubles they had came from their different backgrounds. Her family were lawyers and architects. Her husband's family were plumbers and carpenters. Boys ran in her family, girls in his. Money ran in her family but not in his.

Although he was not poor, he was simply not rich. He was, he thought, well-off. They lived near a resort town where pipes always froze in the winter and toilets backed up in the summer and after a few years in business he was known as trustworthy and reliable and on the back door were rows and rows of little hooks. A key to a vacation house dangled from each.

"WE NEVER HAD those problems," Dennis said, interrupting me. "My parents didn't care about money."

"Why should every family suffer with the same symptoms?" I asked him. "We didn't have those problems, either, and my mother had no money and my father's family was wealthy."

"Either people love one another or they don't," Dennis said, thinking it over. And I thought, That's true. Either they do or they don't. Explanations are like Band-Aids over abysses. What good could they possibly do?

"So did the father become rich and in the end did everyone live happily ever after?" Dennis asked me, and I asked him if he really wanted to hear this story, and he said, "Go *on,* Doris, go on. I'm teasing."

"Well, don't," I said.

AS TIME PASSED, Jack's father began to build houses, at first only a few, but more and more, people asked him to build for them.

He would have been entirely happy with his life were it not for his wife, who had a habit of walking out into the lake when life displeased her, walking slowly, not looking back, making no pretense of wanting to swim, simply walking, slowly, until she came to the place where the ledge dropped away and the water was suddenly over her head, and if she knew her children were watching her from the screened-in porch that ran the length of the house, she would step off the ledge, let herself sink down, and hold her breath as long as possible before surfacing.

Her children knew what she was up to. Her husband knew, but each time she walked out into the lake without looking back, each time the set of her shoulders said, I've had enough, I won't stand for more, the girls began crying and ran down the path and flung themselves into the water, crying and choking, Mother! Mother! Her husband stood on the porch, watching, thinking, She's done this before, so many times, I'm not falling for it again. A man can be made a fool of once too often—but if he didn't see her break the surface of the water in ten seconds by his watch, he'd be down the path after her, thinking, One of these days she's going to do it. She's a proud woman. She can't stand to think we see through her. She'll do it just to show us how wrong we were, to show she's a finer class of woman, someone who means what she says.

In the end, he always gave in.

It would be hard to say who Jack Pine hated more for these theatricals, his mother for performing them or his father for tolerating them—although Jack didn't believe he hated them. No, he was certain he not only loved but cherished them both, especially his mother, who had had six children and five miscarriages, and it didn't seem odd that he worshiped his sister, Jane, twelve years older than he was, Jane who asked him, "Which one is weaker? You tell me! Or maybe they're not weak, maybe they're crazy." His sister said, "She doesn't like men, can't you see it? The way she goes on about his arthritis! Isn't it *pathetic* the way his hands are! Isn't it *too bad* he can't turn his head! Isn't it *too bad* he can't bend his knees! She doesn't want him! He makes her stomach turn!"

What did his sister mean? His mother didn't want his father? What did she mean when she said they were terrible people, his father as well as his mother. Yes, their father was terrible. But *why* was he terrible?

His sister said, "Because he puts up with her! Let her walk into the lake, for God's sake! Let her drown if that's what she wants! She's not going to drown! She's been walking into that lake for years! Years! When she doesn't get her way, she walks into the lake. She doesn't fool me! Don't let her fool you! Blame, blame, blame! That's all she knows! She's not going to die. She's going to be killed! By us!"

Jack said, "He should tell her not to walk into the lake."

"Oh! Yes! *Then* she'd drown herself. Just to show him! He should leave her! Walk out! Not keep saying, 'I'm Ellen's man.' As if that were something! To be Ellen's man when Ellen's completely crazy and doesn't care! I hate them! I'm never going to get married," she said, and Jack said he wouldn't marry, either, but his sister said, "Oh, she'll marry you when Daddy dies. That's what's wrong with her, that she can't marry you." And his sister said she was going to get away, she had planned it. And *he* could get away. He was smart. "She wants you to stay here," she said. "She thinks, I'll get sick, he'll stay and take care of me; he'll want to be like his father.

She's setting traps. Don't let her get you. She won't get me! I'm going far away! To Chicago."

So the house was full of noise, of children fighting, of radios blaring different songs. It was a beautiful house, a porch running the length of it, a two-story porch on which everyone sat, even in winter. The aspens quivering on shore and the water were so lovely, the sky trembling in the water, the clouds moving over the surface of the water, the sun splintering and quivering and trembly in the water, so much more interesting and animate than the unchanging sun in the sky.

The canoes bobbing gently, tied to the shore until lunch is over, the wind that ruffles the aspen leaves, lifting them slowly, dropping them slowly, as if they floated in water, the familiar green taste of a pine needle crushed between teeth, the soft warmth of pine needles on the path down to the lake, the sun-warmed pebbles that press into the soles of the feet, the shade-cooled pebbles where the pines hang down over the edge of the lake where the canoes are. The sound of rain on the windows, the long lines of silver striking the lake's surface, the silver drops of water flying up from the lakeskin where the rain struck them, a completely beautiful place where his mother whispered to him, letting him know that his father displeased her, telling him how his father's powers failed him, what remedies he tried and how they disgusted her, criticizing the girls who followed her son home, saying each time, You can do better, telling him not to make the mistake she'd made, not to settle down too early, if she had only known. Better not to marry at all.

And meanwhile his father told him how lucky he was to have married his mother, what a perfect wife she was. Of course she resented him, but wouldn't any woman who felt she'd married beneath her? If he had to do it all over again, he'd marry Ellen. He wouldn't think twice. He was Ellen's man. In the mornings, when his hips hurt so badly that he didn't think he could stand up, he'd remind himself. He was Ellen's man. Ellen needed him. He'd stand up, walk slowly, holding on to the windowsill, wait for the rust to settle in his joints, and go to work. He supposed Ellen admired him, the way he kept on going. Didn't she stand there in the kitchen and watch him grip a hammer in his twisted, swollen hands and say, "It's amazing that you can do *anything* with those hands!"

OUTSIDE THE CAFÉ, thunder and then lightning. My right wrist ached, the one I broke when my brother kicked me, and I rubbed it, and as I did, I wondered what coming generations would think of us when they finally solved the problems of aging, when they had altered and realtered the genes, when every mortal garment was made to last, when nothing human decayed under the sun. What would they think of us with our little life spans, with our lives spent dreading death. Would they laugh at us, would they think us pathetic, and I thought, No, we will be their tragic ones, the ones who possessed the secret of tragedy, the mayflies, the birds who flew so fast through the sky we burned up. We will be like music, like chants in the chapel. They will pick up our things and turn them over. They will think, What was it like for them?

They will turn us over slowly. Some of them will long for us, long for the lives we lived, so vivid! Some of them will adore us, will be smitten with us, will think, If I had only lived then, then I would have *really* lived. Some of them will think of suicide, will actually attempt it. They will think, as the drug haze takes over, as the blood slows, This is what they felt, what an exaltation!

But others, others will dismiss us, of course they will, will say pitying things. "What a shame to die so young, before you knew anything, before you had time to make sense of it. What a terrible existence, to look at the sun each time and think, This may be the last, to enter each summer thinking, This may be the last. What a chaos of experience, unworked, unintelligible, like a man starving to death in a beautiful restaurant, like an artist suddenly struck blind in his studio, his paints all around him."

Occasionally they may think, What gallantry in the face of disaster, and then they brush this thought aside as if a fly had settled on their noses, and they think: Artists manqué, all of them, deprived of their artistry by the shortness of their time, but still—were the colors more vivid to them, was each moment worth more? How could there be depressed people who slept and let the time go by? Didn't they know how little was left? How could they bear it when they awakened, got out of bed, began washing their hair?

They will think, We are all artists now. Of course we can't understand them. Piteous, of course they were piteous, but still . . .

This surfacing into my own life, how I hated it!

CHAPTER

TWENTY-FIVE

ALMOST EVERY DAY when I came to the café, the little man came in, propped his crutches against the wall behind him, opened his sketch pad, and began to draw someone in the café. One day I knew he was sketching me, and I didn't like it.

"Who knows what he does with the drawings?" Eva had said, her eyes skittering over the room and so I knew. Either she didn't understand why she was uneasy when he looked at her, or she didn't want to tell me. And there were times when we sat together at our table, and without realizing it, I began drawing one of the women bent over her newspaper across the room, or sketching the people waiting for the bus across the street, drawing automatically, not realizing what I was doing, not caring if the drawing did or didn't turn out well.

But as soon as I did realize, I stopped. I began to crumple the paper place mat I'd drawn on, and soon I had destroyed the evidence. All that was left was something that looked like a fossilized snowball.

Where was Antonio? With Rose? Did she love him? Did he love her? Did he tell her about Florence? About me? Was he headed for trouble? What did he expect from her? Did he expect her to make up for all the things Florence had taken from him when she left? It was a terrible thing to be young. I should call him more often. Regardless of how it had come about, we belonged to one another. Another person who looked like me! A *young man* who looked like me. Who could have been my son. Who was, so to speak, my son. I'd wanted a son and now I had one—more or less. I couldn't think of him without wanting to cry. We were born under a devilish star, Florence and I.

If I had never started to paint . . . How many times had I blamed myself for that? But it was Florence who said to herself, I've been a twin, I've had that, now that's over. She must have said to herself, Now all I have to do is convince my sister.

When I proved impossible to convince, she became more difficult. In the end, she hated being a twin.

She was determined to have the world take note of her and only her.

When we got to Chicago, she was in for a shock.

—⟨⟩—

"I WAS STANDING there by myself," she wrote in her journal, "thinking, What happened? No one's looking at me! I'm invisible! And then I realized I expected everyone to stare at me because everyone always did stare at me, or at us, because we were twins, but now I was one person and wasn't *slightly famous* anymore, and in any case, I told myself, I didn't want to be *slightly famous,* I wanted to be enormously famous, completely in my own right. It was my birthright, wasn't it—to accomplish things in my own right? Even if we were born together, we didn't have to die together. Everyone wants to be recognized for herself. It's more important than love. Everyone can have love, whether they want it or not! Everyone's born *for* something! I was born to be famous! By myself! As myself!"

BUT WE WERE waiting. I didn't know for what. In the end, it was a small thing. It is always the small things.

Florence was looking for the last straw and she found it on the long, boring summer day we drove into Lofton to buy our mother a birthday present. We argued, as usual, over who would drive, and we decided, as usual, that one of us would drive to Lofton and the other would drive back. Florence said she would drive first, and on the way home, it would be my turn.

We were hungry, and I pulled off the main road, stopped the car under a large oak tree. We got out and sat on a rock and ate our lunch, and when we were through, I said, "Where are the keys?" and my sister said, "I have them."

I said, "Well, give them to me if we're going," and Florence said, "No, I'll drive the rest of the way," and I said, "It's not fair! We agreed! You would drive one way and I'd drive back."

"You already drove back," Florence said. She would not look at me.

"I'm driving all the way back!" I said.

"*I'll* drive."

"Give me the keys!"

"No."

"Then I'm not getting in the car."

"You will."

"I won't."

She got in the car and started the engine. "Are you coming?" she asked me.

"Not until you move over."

"I'm not moving over."

"We can stay here all night for all I care," I said. I was standing next to the hot car. I felt the heat of the sun on my face, my bare arms and legs.

"Fine, we'll stay here," Florence said, and from the glove compartment, she took out a small green pad and a ballpoint pen and began writing, and this so infuriated me that I reached in, grabbed the pad, jumped back, and began tearing the pages to pieces.

"Give me that!" Florence said.

"Get out of the car!"

I tore more pages from the notebook and flung them into the air.

"When we get home, I'm slashing your paintings," she said.

"No, you won't!"

"No. I'm not as crazy as you are!"

"I'm not crazy! Get out of the car! You're the one who's crazy! You can't even keep a bargain. I'm supposed to drive."

When Florence refused to answer, but switched on the car radio, I sat down on the grass. The sun was low on the horizon. The serrated outlines of the pines on the hilltops cut into the sky. I said, "It looks like we're staying all night. I don't mind. Mosquitoes don't bite me."

"Because you're so sour!"

The wind began to pick up and rustled the leaves and then blew them sideways so that they shone silver in the dimming light. Florence began singing along with the radio.

"All right, let's go," I said finally, and I got in the car. "We wasted two and a half hours."

"*You* wasted them."

She backed up into the field and then turned back onto the dirt road, and onto the road to Peru.

She had declared war. And of course, life cooperated. Life presented her with the necessary weapons.

The next week, the school was assembled in the auditorium. A girl from Islington was coming to sing opera. Her name had been in the local papers and it was generally thought that a career awaited her. An *agent* had come to see her. She had auditioned in New York. Probably she would leave the valley. We sat next to one another and waited, tapping our fingers on the armrests of our chairs. We looked at one another. *This will be boring,* said our eyes. Then the girl came out onto the stage and began to sing an aria from *Madame Butterfly.* She was small and had long blond hair that curled in tendrils about her face, but her voice was enormous and full and it rose like a sun in the small auditorium. Her hair, the expression, the sound of her voice—she was angelic, and I thought, I hope she goes on forever. But in a few minutes, I was bored.

"How long can this go on?" I whispered, but when I saw Florence's face, I saw that my sister was looking at the girl the way she once had looked at me. She lives in Islington, I thought. Florence won't see her again. But my sister had slipped out of her seat and was running up the steps to the stage and disappearing behind the curtain. She was looking for the girl. *Cecilia Bolton.* That was the name on the program.

After that, whenever I began painting, Florence took the keys to the car and drove to Islington. She took some of the money she'd put aside for college and bought a record player and recordings of opera singers, and then she brought Cecilia to the house, and when Cecilia saw me, she said, "Oh, nice! Two of you!" And Florence said, "We're not the same at all, we don't really look alike," and Cecilia laughed at her and said, "You're exactly the same!"

She asked to see my paintings, and she said, "Yes, well, anyone can sing, really, but I can't draw anything anyone would recognize. Do you mind if I sit and watch?"

In the background, Florence fumed, but finally the three of us were friends, although one day Florence and Cecilia were sitting on the porch's wicker love seat and I was sitting in the wicker armchair, and for no reason at all, Cecilia picked up Florence's hand and kissed it, and I saw this and thought, I wanted that kiss. Tears burned in my eyes, and I got up and went into the kitchen and came back with a pitcher of grape punch.

"Are you going to college?" Cecilia asked us, and we said yes, we were, if we could get scholarships, and Cecilia asked us if we really wanted to go. Wouldn't it be boring, four years taking classes? Florence said she thought she could spend the rest of her life studying, and I thought, I'm going because Florence is going. If Florence wants to go, I must want to go too.

"And will you go to the same school?" Cecilia asked us.

I said our mother would feel better if we were both in the same place, and Florence said to me, "Be honest, Doris, you want to go wherever I go. That's the only reason you want to go to Chicago."

Cecilia looked from one of us to the other and said, "At least in Chicago you won't miss the snow," and Florence said, "But that's not why *she's* going; she could go to school anywhere on the East Coast and she'd have plenty of snow; you could go to Denver and you'd be up to your ears in snow. Anyway, I'm the one who loves the snow. You love the summer and the heat and lying around like a melted candle," and I stared dumbly at my hands in my lap—what a victim I was in those days, what a silent sufferer—and Cecilia looked from one of us to the other and said, "Florence, leave her alone."

And our mother was deceived into thinking all was well—she must have seen three girls sitting on the porch talking in low, languid voices, and occasionally one of us laughing. Our mother didn't know the betrayals had already begun. I didn't know. They were small at first, then not so small. Our mother must have thought that if trouble came, it would come in the shape of a boy with whom both of us would fall in love and there would be no solution to that problem because you couldn't divide up a suitor as if he were a loaf of bread, but since there seemed to be no boys in whom we were interested—there were boys we watched playing ball on the common, there were boys we giggled about, but none we took seriously—she must have thought all of us were safe. She lived in a house above a general store in Peru and felt comfortably invisible when she closed her front door.

"YOU TOLD Cecilia about Mother and Dr. Steiner?" I asked Florence. "How could you do that? It's no one's business. It's not *our* business."

"She won't repeat it," Florence said.

"That's not the point! It's not her business! That's the point."

"Well, Doris, I don't know why I did it. Happy now?"

"I know why you did it! You want her to be interested in you. You're jealous!"

"I shouldn't have done it. All right? I agree with you."

"No, you shouldn't have."

"I'm the bad one, aren't I?"

"Let's not make this into a melodrama."

"Family members keep each other's secrets."

But she *was* keeping a secret.

When she drove alone to Islington, she sat on the back lawn of Cecilia's house and painted Cecilia's portrait. She'd never painted anything before, but she felt as if she'd been painting all her life.

"You know, it is good," Cecilia said. "It looks just like me."

"Do you mind if I paint you as if it were snowing hard and your face was coming through the snow?"

"No, why should I mind?"

"I've always wanted to paint things in the snow," Florence said. "I wrote poems about snow but I like painting it better. You can look at the painting on the hottest day in the summer and it cools you off. Look now."

"I'm buried alive!" Cecilia said, laughing.

"Sing while I paint," Florence asked her, and Cecilia asked, "What should I sing?" and Florence said, "Sing 'The Raggle Taggle Gypsies,' sing 'The Three Ravens,' " and while she sang, Florence painted the snow into the portrait, painted until it was almost dark, until Cecilia's face was misty, vague, but shone out, somehow recognizable, and bright and golden, through the falling snow.

"I think that's a wonderful painting," Cecilia said. "We should show Doris."

"No," Florence said, flushing. "I don't want Doris to see it."

"But why? It's a marvelous painting!"

"She's the one who paints. I'm not supposed to paint."

"What are you talking about? Why shouldn't you paint?"

"It's just that . . . it's just that we agree on things. Some things are hers and some things are mine."

"This isn't a *thing*," Cecilia said. "It's a talent. I wouldn't give up singing for my sister. If I had a sister. If I had a *twin* sister."

"That's the point. You don't have a twin sister. You don't know."

And Florence thought, I am skating on thin ice. I am skating on cracking ice. But Doris won't find out.

She began going into Lofton, where there was a man who restored paintings for museums and who examined old paintings, and if he saw someone had painted on top of an already existing painting, he knew how to expose the original. And Florence told him, "What I want is to paint something on the canvas, let it dry, and paint over it. But I want the first image to come through what's on top, you know, as if you were seeing it through water. Or snow. Can it be done?"

And that was the beginning. She was looking for the technique she perfected for the White Paintings, figures shimmering through snow, things half visible, invisible really, until you sensed their presence and began looking for them, what students of her paintings now call the pentimento technique. And she tried again and again, mixing the top coat with turpentine, with varnish, painting the first layer over with paint thinner, letting it dry, and painting over it, putting the paintings out in the sun to dry, aging the canvases in the sun, leaving them in the barn for months to see if the first images bled through, and gradually she began to find the techniques she needed.

"Temper, tantrums, and fury, that's what it is," she told Cecilia. "I can't stand it."

And meanwhile I had no idea she had picked up a brush. And she didn't want me to know.

But she hadn't counted on Cecilia, Cecilia who thought it was so wonderful to be a twin and who was upset by the discord between us and who thought it was wrong of me to keep Florence from doing something she did so very well, and so one afternoon Cecilia called me and asked me if I would like to come over for the afternoon, and I, who had never before been invited to Islington, said I'd see if I could get the car, and if I could, I'd be right over.

"I have something to show you," Cecilia said, and she took me out to the screened-in gazebo in back of the house and pointed to an easel on which rested a covered painting.

"Oh, do you paint?" I said. "I didn't know you painted. You said you couldn't do it! We could paint together."

And Cecilia lifted the cloth covering the painting and there was Cecilia's portrait emerging out of the thickly falling snow.

I asked her, "Who painted that?"

"You know who painted it!"

I said it looked like my painting, like something I painted—except for the snow. And she said, "The snow makes it mysterious, don't you think?" And then I knew it was Florence, and I said, "She wants to kill me, she won't stop until she kills me," and Cecilia asked herself, What have I done? But it was too late. She had thought I'd go home and Florence and I would paint together. And she looked at me and I was standing in front of the painting, my hands pressed against my eyes, and I said, "Please cover it up. Please don't make me look at it."

It was better than my paintings. It was magical. It shone with imagination. And I said again, "She hates me."

"I'll drive you home," Cecilia said nervously.

"I came in the car."

"I'll bring Florence back and she can drive the car back to Peru."

When we got home, my mother took one look at me and asked Cecilia, "What happened to her? Why can't she walk into the house herself?" and Cecilia said, "She can't seem to stand up," and my mother called, "Albert! Leave the store alone and come out here! Carry your sister up to your room! And don't drop her!"

"What's wrong with her?"

"Take her upstairs and get the doctor."

"SHE'S HAD a shock," Dr. Steiner said. "I gave her a sedative. I want her to come talk to me in the morning."

Our mother bent over me and called my name, but I didn't move. She wouldn't get any answers from me. She found Florence sitting on the porch, staring out over the common to the mountains beyond. "What happened to your sister?" she asked.

"I don't know."

"You do know."

"I didn't mean it! I didn't think she'd find out!"

"Find out what?"

"I didn't mean her to see the painting."

"What painting?"

"The painting I did of Cecilia."

"Oh, Florence! You planned this all along!"

"No! I didn't think she'd see it. I thought Cecilia would keep it and she'd never find out."

"You can lie to me, but you can't lie to yourself. You know what her painting meant to her!"

"It means something to me too."

"Only because your sister had it first!"

"Not only because she had it first. I'm better than she is! You should see the painting! You'd know I'm better."

"Come here, Florence," our mother said, pointing at the ground in front of her. "Right in front of me." And as soon as my sister stood in front of her, she reached up and struck her across the face, and then she turned and walked away from her, and when, later, Florence came to her room and said, "*Please,* Mother," our mother ignored her, wouldn't look up from her book.

"Mother, *please!*" Florence said, and our mother turned a page—as if no one had spoken, as if no one were there.

And after that, was there any hope for us?

It is terrible to think of us as we were then, so young, so brutal, so *unchangeable.* It is terrible to look back and see inevitability and not to be able to warn, to go back into the past like an ineffectual ghost, to see ourselves as we were, so young, so bent on our own ways, so completely determined and absolutely blind.

AFTER THE MEADOW, after the bodies in the meadow, Florence picked up her life as if it were a glass paperweight and held it to the window and the light.

What really was hers?

She'd always thought she'd been the one who had chicken pox and fainted in the bathroom, but our mother said, "No, that was Doris. If you don't believe me, ask Dr. Steiner," and of course our mother never expected her to go, but she did, crossing the common after dinner, asking him to look up his records, and he said, "I don't have to look up my records. I remember it was Doris."

So not even that memory was hers, not even that—lying on the floor, her skin on fire, the tiles cold against her, looking up at the ceiling as if she had fallen into a deep well, Doris kicking her—even that belonged to me and somehow she'd borrowed it.

She tried to remember something that didn't include me, but whatever she thought of, there I was, watching. She remembered something yellow, but what was it? And she remembered how our grandmother used to hold her high over the bed heaped with all the feather comforters and then she'd let her fall. Just before she dropped her, Hilda used to say, "Now fly!" and she would fall down into the comforters as if into a snowdrift. The yellow was the bedspread. Dandelion yellow. She remembered that was what her grandmother called it.

And did she play that game with Doris? Of course she played it with her. So perhaps that was her sister's first memory too. But when she asked me, I said the first thing I remembered was a black candy I put into my mouth and spit out.

"And was I there?" she asked me. "Was I there when you ate the candy?"

"Weren't you always there?" I said.

Florence now loved words like *only, solitary, unaccompanied, single, unique, specific, private,* and she repeated these words over and over, arranging them as if they were a chant, a precious poem, a prayer. She liked to think of them as pearls she held in her hand. She fingered the plastic pearls of her necklace and said to herself, *Only, alone, solitary. Unaccompanied, single, unique. Individual, specific, private.* Let's see if she knows what I'm talking about *now,* she'd say to herself.

I didn't know.

She asked herself, What kind of person am I? Am I nice, am I quiet, am I good? Am I moody, angry, sad, placid, excitable, nervous, intelligent? She could say what we both were. *We* were intelligent, *we* were talented, *we* were pretty. Were we reliable, steady, well balanced? Were we happy, were we satisfied, what did we think of life? She only knew what we were together.

It was enough, really, to drive you crazy, and if she went crazy, could I follow her even there? Into madness?

"TELL US about yourselves," said the psychologist who was interviewing twins all over the country.

"There's not much to tell," Florence said.

"No," I said.

"Would you rather I spoke to you separately?"

"What's the point?" asked Florence.

"It would only waste your time," I said.

"You two are so much alike?"

"Oh, yes," we said together.

But when we went home, we thought about it.

That seemed long ago, in the time Florence thought of now as the happy time, before she turned on me once and for all.

"WHAT NOW?" our mother demanded. "I'm afraid to leave you two alone! You're seventeen going on eighteen and you fight like mad people!"

"She applied to the same colleges!" Florence said.

"I wanted her to do that. You can look after one another."

"Mother, we're not children anymore! We're not walking down a road in the dark or walking back from school in the snow. I don't need anyone to look after me! Maybe she needs someone, but I don't! I *want* to be alone! That's why I want to go away. I want to start over!"

"As if I never existed!"

"All right," our mother said finally. "If you want to be alone, you won't mind spending the rest of the day in my room. You want to be separate, I'll separate you."

But Florence stood motionless, staring at her as if she were pleading with her, speaking without words. "That won't work with me, Florence," our mother said. "I can't read your mind. You'll tell me later. I want to talk to your sister. *Privately.*"

"About me, no doubt," Florence said bitterly.

"The world doesn't revolve around you. Out!"

Our mother asked me, "Why is she so angry?"

"Because we're going to the same college."

"You were both accepted?"

"We both have full scholarships."

"Was anyone going to tell me?"

"We just found out yesterday."

"And that's why she's angry?"

"You heard her, Mother! She's angry because I exist. She said she can't even stand looking at couples because they remind her of twins! Two of anything remind her of twins! She hates salt and pepper shakers that come in pairs. She hates the sound of two women talking—*they* sound like twins. Two of the same books on a bookshelf, she wants to throw them in a wood stove."

Our mother sat down on my cast-iron bed. Her fingers traced the bumps and dips in the thick coat of paint. She said, "Braille must feel like this."

I said, "She's the strong one, isn't she? It's true there's always something wrong with one twin. She always said the first twin was the strong twin and the other one was made up of cast-off cells."

"Is that what she said?"

"I knew what she *thought.* I was there when she thought it."

She said she didn't know what to make of it, but maybe the two of us ought to steer clear of each other for a while. I said I tried, but Florence showed up wherever I was so she could blame me for being there.

She asked, "If I sent one of you to live at Hilda's until the fall?"

"Which one would you send?"

How suspicious I sounded!

In the end, she didn't send either of us.

"I CAN still see," she said wearily, "the two of you sitting at the table, pushing your glasses of milk together so you could be sure neither one had more than the other. You were only two. And it's still going on."

I said I was going to Cecilia's and I'd sleep over, and my mother said I didn't have to, she wouldn't have me driven from my own house, but I said I wanted to go.

"To paint?" she asked me. "I haven't seen any paintings lately," and I told her to look in the attic. Florence hid her paintings there.

"You haven't stopped, have you?" she asked me, and I said, "Not really." But I had stopped. "Just leave and don't let her know where you're going," she said. "I don't want any more arguments."

And she must have wondered, which one *was* the stronger? Was it Florence, who needed to deny there was anything between them, or Doris, who could tolerate the closeness, who didn't run away? Or were they both weak in some unknown way so that soon they wouldn't be able to live either together or apart? Couldn't live at all?

When she closed the store and found Hilda sitting on the back porch, she must have asked her which one was stronger, which was weaker, was either strong enough?

Hilda must have said, "When they were small, you always held Florence, remember? Doris used to sit there watching the two of you, smiling, she was always smiling, as if she believed you were holding her. Remember? I said then, That child gets things through her sister. You give Florence attention and Doris feels as if she has it. You give Florence something to eat, and Doris thinks she shouldn't be hungry. I thought, Isn't that remarkable, the child doesn't mind, but she didn't mind because that was the only way she could get things, through her sister, and she didn't mind because she loved her sister, she had to figure that out at such an early age, and if she did work it out way back then, and I believe she did, she's never going to forget it, that she loves her sister."

And Mother must have said, "But Florence loved Doris. Remember when Doris had scarlet fever, all she wanted to do was stand outside the window and look at her?"

"Florence thinks if her will is strong enough, she can change her nature."

"They had no empty spaces. They were completely full," our mother must have said dreamily.

"They're paying for that now," Hilda must have said.

WHEN I CAME IN unexpectedly, when I closed the screen door quietly behind me, didn't let it slam, although I loved to let it slam, loved to smell the faint dust it let loose, I would see Florence standing over her precious tubes of paint, her lips forming the names of their colors, saying them again and again, or picking up her palette and ecstatically inhaling the odors of oil and turpentine, and I knew she'd fallen in love with paint and painting as I never had. She would not give up until she worked it out, until she had her technique, until she understood the properties of pigments and solutions, until her paintings shimmered with the images she saw just beneath the thin skin of the world we all could see.

How could I have known? How ruthless she could be, how desperate she could be? How she felt about me? It was all in her journals, and she saw to it that I got them, she saw to it that I would go through it all again, saw how I would still go through it—after she disappeared.

This was one journal entry, typical enough:

⌒⌒

EVERY NIGHT, I expect a knock on the door, I expect Doris to drift in and begin moaning about Mother alone in Peru and how hard it must be for her and have I written to her yet? And I will say, Doris, that is your job this month, you sign my name to some of the letters and I'll take over next month. We will divide up the letter writing, won't that be easiest?

The first time I told this to Doris she looked at me as if I were a snake and said, "I thought you wanted to be separate!" Well, she's right. I said I would be cruel and not write letters at all the first month, and she could be the good daughter, and she said again, "I thought you wanted to be separate."

Then someone knocked on my door and I made her hide in the closet until she left—it was Frances, who also paints. When I let Doris come out, she said, "You'd like to drive a stake through my heart, wouldn't you?" and when I didn't answer, she said, "You really are an idiot."

But I refuse to let her cast a shadow on my happiness here. I will not even think about whether or not she is right. I don't think Doris would be here if she weren't following me. She isn't really interested in studying, in taking classes, in sitting in quiet libraries. Then what *is* she interested in? I don't know.

If she'd used her head, she'd have stayed in Peru and continued painting, but no, she had to come here, where she doesn't want to be, just because this is where I am, and now that she's here she won't compete with me. She won't touch a paintbrush. She says vaguely, "I think I'll write a poem, I think I'll write a story." When she never did like writing as much as painting.

I hope she doesn't think we've made a new arrangement. I'm through with dividing things up. She is no longer my responsibility and I am not hers. She could paint as well as I do, I suppose, but she doesn't have the same *visions.* She's content with the world as it is, she likes to take the world as it presents itself. She is *literal-minded.* Why did I never see this before? Whereas *I* have never been made happy by things as they are because things are never as they appear and so I've always conjured up pictures of the world as I see it. I live in a world of metaphor. I paint my metaphors. Doris would not know a metaphor if it knocked her down! I'm sure I'm going to triumph here! And yet I wake up in the middle of the night half frozen with fear, certain I'll fail all my exams and everyone will say, What can you expect from a girl from Peru? A girl with half a brain?

I wake up in the morning in a state of terror and count to ten, and to ten again, looking out the window before I get up and get dressed, and the worst of it is that I know Doris is waking up in her room, doing the same thing, and sometimes at night I dream she is talking to me or that her arm has reached out and pushed me or her hand is on my shoulder or her arm is around my waist, and then I sleep peacefully. It will take time to grow apart.

I WAS pouring myself a glass of cider when there was a scratching noise at the door, and when I opened it, of course it was Doris, her white nightgown trailing out from beneath her raincoat, and I said, "What are you doing here?" and she said, "That's not very friendly," and I said, "I'm tired of these visits in the middle of the night! You'd think we were lovers meeting secretly! It's ridiculous! Why can't you sleep in your own room like a normal person?" And she said, "I just wanted to see you." I said, "Why waste your time? Why not just look in the mirror?" She said, "Why are you so mean to me? What did I ever do to you?" I said, "Well, now you've seen me," and she said in that pitiful voice—how I hate that pitiful voice, when I know how guilty it's meant to make me feel—"I missed you," and I said, "I don't want you to miss me and I don't want to miss you," and she put on her coat and stood up and I knew she would leave without complaint because now she had seen me and she could go back to bed and fall asleep immediately, and she said, "What do you want me to do? Jump out the window? I'm leaving as fast as I can." And I said, "I'm not a sleeping pill! I'm not some kind of tranquilizer!" and she left, shaking her head.

LAST NIGHT we went to a mixer. A thin, tall man came up to me right away, glasses and curly brown hair, and Frances said, "He's from New York," and we nodded at each other, and he went off, and then someone came up to Frances, and I was standing there by myself, thinking, No one's looking at me! Again! I'm invisible! And then I realized I still expected everyone to stare at me because everyone always did stare at me—or at us, because we were always together.

And I thought, Well, this will be a new experience, being a wallflower, when a tall man came up to me, very tall and blond, and I thought, He ought to be dancing with my blond friend, Jill. He looks enough like her to be her brother. And he asked me if I wanted to dance. Everyone was dancing. Strobe lights were flashing through the room, and I said I didn't dance well, and he said no one did, you weren't admitted to college here if you'd taken dancing lessons, and I got up and began dancing with him, and before I knew it I was dancing away, happy as I ever was, dancing with someone I didn't know, someone I'd never seen before.

The music was very loud and it didn't stop and he shouted in my ear, "Someone's staring at you!" and I looked over and said, "I don't see anyone!" and he said, "That girl! Over there!" and a beam of light settled on my sister and I saw she was staring at me, her face wild with jealousy as if she were staring at a lover who had betrayed her, and I said, "Oh, my God, she's here," and he said, "Who is she?"

And I said, "My sister," and he said, "Your twin sister?" and I said, "Yes, my twin sister," and he said, "Don't you want to go talk to her? She looks upset," and I said, "No, I really don't, I'll see her later," and when I looked at her again, tears were streaming down her face and I knew she was thinking, There's Florence, dancing away, having an easy time of it, and I'm here suffering, and I thought, Why can't she realize that's over, it's over, I won't let it go on? and I pressed my body up against the boy I was dancing with, I didn't even know his name, he was surprised but certainly he wasn't unhappy, and I thought, I'm going to sleep with this boy and she'll know it, she already knows I'll do it, now she'll really be sorry. He took me home. He was quite a gentleman. Too bad.

And of course she came scratching like a dog at my door. Crying. "What now?" I said, and she said, "I can't stand it," and I said, "Well, you'll have to stand it," and she said, "What if I can't?"

"Then you'll have to go home and let Mother take care of you. At least then she won't have to be alone," and she said again, "What did I ever do to you?" and I said, "I am sick and tired of hearing that. You hang around my neck like a stone. What have *I* done to *you?* Do you want to drown me?" and she said, "I would never hurt you, you know I would never hurt you," and I said, "Find someone of your own, just find someone of your own," and she said, "And you? You're going to sleep with that blond boy, aren't you?" and I said, "Maybe I will, maybe I won't," and she said, "Don't sleep with him to get even with me, it's not worth it," and I said, "If you don't pull yourself together, you'll end up in the hospital," and she became furious and said, "You want me to pull myself together? I will!"

I thought she was leaving, but she turned to me and said, "Last night I had a dream. Freud"—was she taking a psychology course? I didn't know she was taking a psychology course—"was walking with another man, and they were both tiny, the size of dolls, and Freud said, 'Life is a dreadful business, a long sigh and then waiting to hear the sound of your mother's voice again,' " and in spite of myself, I said, "That's lovely, really. You should write it down," and she said, "Don't talk to me!" and left, banging the door.

AND THIS is another entry, also representative, after she went for a ride on a motorcycle and was thrown over the handlebars.

⌒⌒

I WAS out of the hospital, not seeing double anymore, thank God for that—what a shock it was to look up and see two Dorises at the foot of the bed, to see two of me in the mirror, everything doubling, a world malignantly twinning, it was horrible. And funny. I couldn't stop laughing, all because I wanted to ride on that motorcycle and Doris's boyfriend thought he was taking her, and I thought, What harm could it do? And I found out soon enough when he hit the log and I flew into the tree and ended up with a concussion—very glamorous, isn't it? I thought only people in films had concussions—and when I got out, Doris came to see me.

She knew about the painting of the golden rope, she knew a gallery bought it. She knew they were making posters of it. The whole school was talking about me. "This is the beginning," she said. "I'm so proud of you," she said. Weeping.

It is so pathetic, so enraging, the way she sits there weeping, as if she were in a fight but refused to defend herself, and because I understand that, I weaken and say, "It's been so easy for me," as if I had nothing to do with it—or everything to do with it—as if it were enough to simply *think* what I wanted and the world would hand it over to me. "It worries me, how easy it's been."

"Why?" She looks up. Startled. Concerned.

"Because there's always a price to pay."

"Some people are born under a lucky star. Fortune's favorites. You know the expression."

"*We* were born under the same star."

"Then soon I'll be fortunate too," she says. Weeping.

"Oh, Doris, stop! Get up! Let's go for a walk!"

"Do you want to go for a walk?" (I didn't, not really, but I didn't say so. I didn't have to. She knew.) The smile trembling through the tears, gone.

My paintings on postcards, on posters, talked about at other colleges, on display in the Cabochon Gallery, letters from strangers asking, How did you see into my heart? Saying, You have painted my life. How can I thank you? How I hate them, those people who write saying I have seen into their hearts, painted their lives! My paintings have nothing to do with them, nothing to do with anybody. Emily Dickinson said her poems were her letters to the world. My paintings are my letters to *me!*

But we've been talking long enough and I tell her she has to go.

"You won't come home at all? This summer?"

"Maybe for a weekend," I say. Vaguely. She knows I won't come. She weeps away steadily. What does her boyfriend make of this weeping?

"He says when we're married I'll be happy and then I'll stop."

"I hope he's not counting on *that*," I say.

"It can't go on forever, can it?" she asks. Imploring.

"I certainly hope not, Doris," I say, picking up my books.

"Where are you going? You don't *have* to tell me."

"To the studio and then to the coffee shop and then to the cafeteria for dinner and then to see *The Seventh Seal* and then back to the dorm, where I'll take off my jeans and my sweatshirt and my underpants and my brassiere and my socks and go to bed."

"All right, Florence," she says. "That's enough."

"I am sorry," I say.

"Are you? For what?"

And that is where things stand.

AND OF COURSE it hasn't escaped me—it hadn't escaped me then—that her journal entries read more like letters to someone she knew very well, as if, eventually, they should be mailed to the person for whom they were intended. As, of course, they were.

Even now it was scalding to read these pages, to think how much she hated me or wanted to hate me. Whenever I read them, whenever I thought about them, I felt myself erased, as if I were nothing but a chalk drawing on a blackboard and someone's hand began scouring me off, and the sound, that terrible shriek of the nail scraping against slate.

Even if she had come back to me and said, I made a mistake, I should have known better, even then I would have heard that sound, as I always hear it when I say her name, when anyone says it: Florence.

I WENT ON alone until I came to a house precisely like the house I had drawn in the mud. Even from a distance, I could see the great front door was open. It yawned widely and I walked through. Then I realized there was no door at all. Someone had taken it down from its hinges.

One pair of shutters was open. The light streamed in through that window and then lit the huge room weakly. There was little furniture in the room, only two chairs draped with sheets. In the corner of the room was a pile of sheets, neatly folded. It was dim in the room and I rubbed my eyes. Across the room was a great fireplace and in it someone had set an enormous mirror and the mirror was cut to fit the mouth of the fireplace. In the mirror were the green trees outside, the drying beige grass, the mountains in the distance. I lay down in front of the mirror. I reached out with my real hand until I touched my reflected hand. Then I willed myself to ignore my reflection. I concentrated until there was nothing in the mirror but the dry grass, the rustling trees, their leaves showing their veined silvery sides. Then it was windy, then it was going to rain. The mountains were dimmed by distance, by the dim light in the room. I preferred the reflected world to the real one.

The man who owned this house had ordered the mirror. He disliked walls. He invited the trees in, the grass, the mountains. The owner of this house wanted a cave, always open.

I slept in front of the mirror, and when I awoke, the mirror was empty. Night empties everything out. Beneath their sheets, the two chairs had vanished. Only if I squinted could I make them out. I thought, I will travel at night and sleep during the day.

It was cold in the room, and damp. There was no door. I could not shut myself in. Would anyone come back to the house, would anyone find me here? During the day, I left my passport faceup, open on a windowsill. It baked in the sun. My face was fading. The typed letters of my name were splattered by rain, by dust. It gave me great satisfaction to watch the sun's sharp teeth chew on my small face in the picture. I thought, As it changes, so will I change.

At first there was very little to eat, only apples. And then I found the attic, its boxes of dried fruit, nuts, an enormous fruitcake steeped in wine. I would leave when I finished the fruitcake. It was simple, lately, to make decisions.

There are always empty houses waiting for me, brick houses painted white, the pitch of their roofs steep, two brick chimneys scraping the sky. So many white brick houses, all the same. There will always be an empty house waiting for me.

CHAPTER

TWENTY-SEVEN

I WENT for a walk on the heath. I watched a man and his two daughters flying a kite while his wife sat next to me on a bench. I said to her, "That kite's going to hit me on the head," and she smiled. If she had been Florence, she would have jumped up. She would have understood that the kite *was* going to hit me. We always knew things like that. But she wasn't Florence, and so I went on sitting there, and of course the kite did hit me on the head, not hard.

After she and her family left, I stayed on the bench, looking out over the burnt-orange tiled roofs of Highgate, watching the sky darken behind them, the uppermost line of houses still outlined in gold light, that chain of houses still held by daylight, the houses below immersed in the soft blue-violet light of early evening, and I thought, The people in the houses up above are saying to themselves, "The day's almost over," getting up out of their chairs, getting ready for evening. The people below them are turning on the lights and saying, "Night? Night already?" They are pulling their curtains closed.

We are always given more than we need, more than we think we have. There are always more than one of the important things. There is more than one view of the world. There's the day view and the night view, two distinct things. Their feel is different, the way things look is different, in light or without light. We move differently through a room with light, without light, we think different thoughts, we are happy in a dark room when in the light room we are miserable.

There is more than one of each of us, uncountable versions, the youngest one, the young one, the middle-aged one, the old one, some of them happy, some of them not, some wise, some bent on vengeance. People say, No one ever changes, but what do they mean? Everyone alive changes, that's the pity of it, sometimes from one minute to the next. We are like prisms with something solid in the center. That center never changes, but who knows what it is? It's always there. It makes us say, This has been no life, I'm tired of it. It makes us say, It's a beautiful world, I'm not ready to lie down and die yet.

Mother, father, sister, grandmother, someone we met on the street who impressed us, we are all of those, as shifting as light on the wall, as borderless, as amorphous, all of us—not just my sister and I, because we were twins.

It is comforting to think that there are hordes of Evas, that early in the morning there may be an Eva who gets up, makes herself tea, sings happily to herself as she looks out the window.

It is better to live without journals. Why did Florence keep them? Better to let the mind erase what it will erase, lose what it can lose. Must we all travel like burdened-down camels through a desert? Must we all unpack enormous trunks in whatever small rooms we come to?

Florence kept her journals for eight years. I've had them for more than twenty. They are like hot coals. When I'm home, I change their hiding place frequently. I'm careful where I put them. If I put them in a closet, I avoid going past it. I don't open it. I wouldn't be surprised to see thick smoke snaking out beneath the closet door. I hate them but they are all there is.

In my study at home, we stack the family photograph albums on the floor, an archaeology of them, the newest ones on top, the old ones on the bottom. Those are my journals, those endless pictures, and what an irony it is, only words left of Florence, only pictures left of me.

When I came back to the café, it was night. It was the same café, but then again it wasn't. The streetlamps had gone on. When I sat down at a table and looked out, I didn't see the street clearly. I didn't see people waiting for the bus. I saw the café suspended in the window, everyone reflected in it. And inside, everything had changed. The lights were dimmer; they were soft and glowed pinkly. White candles balanced arrowheads of gold light, the white tablecloths shone. A transformation.

And the people too were transformed. The ones I saw now were better dressed, had more money, sat behind plates filled with beef stew or moussaka or fish, had a different air, less distracted, less floaty, more concentrated, sat next to chairs weighed down with briefcases, leather portfolios, gray shopping bags with twisted cord handles, white paper cones of cut flowers, lilies and roses and dahlias, had an aura of purpose, of prosperity, the redolence of people who went to work, who had spent the day doing the work, and if they had done it well or badly, still they had done it, said to themselves, That's done, another day done, sighed deeply, felt with gratitude the strength of the chair holding them up, if they were very tired, leaned their elbows on the table's edge, sighed the sigh that means, Here I am, this is what I was waiting for, opened the menu, made a choice, told the waitress.

For an hour, the world existed to serve them. There were not many now who chose by price, not many who appeared to have schemed all day, asking, Can I afford this? I can if I skip lunch tomorrow and the next day—not many of those. Everyone watched the other diners, looked out the café window, tried to see the dark street.

Occasionally someone came up to the window, pressed her moth face to it, saw someone she knew and waved and walked on, and inside, people opened their handbags or attaché cases, took out their paperbacks, reached into their shopping bags for their newspapers. Everyone appeared happy or, if not happy, content, the prosperous contentment of the tired who have come to rest and be served.

An extra world, as my sister used to say when it snowed. There are always extra rooms. The world is so big.

And if it was so big, why was I thinking of going to Goult?

It would be like walking *into* my sister's journals, wouldn't it? I wasn't simply curious. Curiosity is never simple. Once, I loved reading the passages about her daily life in Goult, when she was still happy, love-struck and sun-struck. Once, when I read them, I imagined myself there.

"Reading those journals again?" my husband said, his voice sour. As if I were betraying him, as if I were carrying on illicitly right under his nose. "What is it this time, the red dress or happy days in Goult?"

After she had been in France for five years, it was still almost always happy days in Goult, and I liked to say it—*Happy Days in Goult*—as if at least part of my sister's life could be given a title that belonged on a cheerful children's book.

It would not be happy days in Goult when I got there.

I drank my glass of wine. I called up the journals, read them in my mind's eye. I thought about all the times we had talked to one another over the phone and how she had never talked to me about Jack and how they got along together, that's how jealous she was of him. And yet she did send me the journals.

—⟨∘⟩—

THE HOUSE is very beautiful and difficult to describe, three levels, not stories, each level with its own terraces and small gardens. It is a white stone house, the walls well over a foot thick, and the steps are solid blocks of gray stone worn down in the center by hundreds of years of people going up and down. They are extremely steep and very easy to slip on if your shoes are wet or if you've spilled something and haven't mopped up every drop since there is no such thing as a handrail in the place, so I still try to hold on to the wall as I go up and down.

The first floor has a small, circular living room, part of the wall entirely occupied by a great stone fireplace, and a surprisingly modern kitchen. Someone who lived here before us loved to cook.

The wooden beams are ancient and the heavy wooden shutters equally antique. Jack says that in the morning, when it is still cool from the night air, we will run through the rooms slamming the shutters shut and fastening them in place with the great iron bars that spend the night hooked to the walls, and we won't open them again until the sun goes down and the temperature begins to drop. Even then, sharp brilliant blades of sunlight will see their way between the shutters and the walls and pattern themselves like arrowheads on the floor. The one rug left here is faded by these sun-shaped, triangular knife blades.

I never want to think of Doris again, but it seems I can't help it. Odd things recall her: an ad for Coke in a magazine, the question of temper, and she materializes the ways scenes and people used to pop up out of the expensive books Grandma bought us for Christmas and birthdays. *I may never see her again,* I think, and take great satisfaction in the thought. I look at myself in the mirror and find myself saying, *I'll never see you again. Would you mind removing yourself from my mirror?* Then her face grows sad and inside I feel a swelling happiness, and I realize I am looking at my own face after all.

Children. Do I want them?

I am careful of this new happiness. As time goes by, I'll write Doris and my mother less frequently. Meanwhile I write and say how much I miss them and the endlessly falling snow and how I wish I could write more often, but I'm so busy, busier than I ever was at the university, and if I am to be a painter, isn't it better simply to paint? When I have Jack, who is five years older, to teach me? And if I'm eccentric about concealing my whereabouts, aren't all artists eccentric, and who knows? Perhaps I'll grow out of it.

Of course, they will worry, but their lives will get them by the throat and shake them and they'll begin to forget me.

Mother writes and says Doris is engaged to a man who is kind and quiet and very rich. Nevertheless, she cries, cries endlessly, and of course I know what she's crying about.

I cannot give her any comfort. I cannot give her any openings.

It is enough to know that she can't find me, that I am safe from her, that she can speak to me only when I call her.

Are people punished for protecting themselves? Jack doesn't think so. Then I am not using unreasonable force.

Uncle Fritz once took us to a dogfight in Islington. Two dogs had their teeth in one another. Neither would let go. "They'll bleed to death that way," Fritz said. One of us asked if anyone would stop them, and he said no, the men had placed their bets.

I am doing the right thing. Otherwise we would end as those two dogs.

I lie to Jack. I say I'm an orphan. Do I feel guilt for these lies? No. I take pleasure in them. I feel like Mother, making up her endless stories. The trouble with a liar, Grandma used to say, is that she can't remember all her lies and that's when she trips herself up and is caught. But I remember everything and am not tripped up.

I HAVE GONE back to painting snow. In this heat! But it is the perfect antidote. While I paint falling snow I believe I feel it settling on my skin. My eyes grow taut the way they did in Peru, and when I wipe my forehead, beaded, naturally, with sweat, I believe I am wiping away melting snowflakes. Today I began an enormous painting of a tiny thing—I like these confusions of scale—an entire village in a glass globe, snow falling at the same time inside the globe and outside the globe while people crossed the common, rode their cars slowly down steep roads from the hills, everything precisely as it was when I last saw it, Mother (tiny Mother) standing on the porch, and for some reason the funeral home was entirely gilded, a gold building, as if Midas had touched it, and the body visible through the window (you would have to take a magnifying glass to the painting in order to see it) gilded also, turned to solid gold.

Doris and I are not in the painting.

Although there *are* two willow trees reflected in the pond (there are no such trees bending over a pond in the village) and there are two geese sailing on the pond waters and there are two black cars parked one in back of the other. There are two of too many things. I will paint out some of the duplicates.

Six months and I am happier than ever. Can it go on like this the rest of my life? Why not?

I've been trying to puzzle out the riddle of my last few days in Chicago and always I come back to the morning in the Hobby House when Jack asked me to marry him, which is what I so desperately wanted, and I reacted strangely, as if I couldn't make up my mind, as if I didn't know what I wanted.

Why wasn't I overcome with the proverbial transports of joy? Why didn't I jump up and shout for joy? All my dreams settling on the table like motes of light, little gold nuggets, and still I didn't pick them up, I didn't cry out in rapture. I carped, I complained, I watched Jack as if he were an impostor, an annoyance, an intrusion on my familiar world! When he had become my world. When I could no longer imagine a world without him. And what could he have made of it, my phlegmatic, almost indifferent reaction? Today he says he believed me when I said I was in shock. He says I went white, I shivered, he put his coat over me and stood behind me, afraid I would fall from my chair. If I had simply babbled, or worse—if I had grinned in triumph—he wouldn't have been so convinced he'd done the right thing, so it was fortunate I reacted so oddly. Why did I? Everything I did—even my insistence on taking the dog—pleased him deeply. Who had he met before who made decisions so simply? And to tell the truth (and sometimes I wish he wouldn't), he'd never expected to be so happy, not because of me. He didn't believe himself capable of such happiness.

So all is well there.

But not quite well here. At times I seem two people, both of whom cannot exist at the same time, as a radio cannot simultaneously broadcast two channels. I was a different person the morning he proposed. I am not speaking here of split personalities, nothing so dramatic. I mean parts of my personality vanish into mist and then without warning they slide back into place, and the person I was an instant before is gone. Not *gone,* but shoved aside. Watching, listening, but shoved aside. If she has anything to say, she can't say it. If she wants to interrupt and say, *Look here, don't pay attention to her,* she can't make herself heard.

Psychologists must have a word for this. They have a word for everything.

But I don't have a word for it.

It is a kind of disease, a contagion, a minor melody taking over, drowning out the main theme, someone I had once seen whom I now imitate, someone who is me but not me, a dybbuk, a shadow person, a double.

A double!

Who could the double be but Doris? But no one proposed to Doris in the Hobby House. Doris never loved anyone as I love Jack. Doris married the man who saw her crying at the dance and took her home and decided he wanted to keep her—the way Jack and I decided we wanted to keep the dog we found on our camping trip. But when he asked her to marry him, I'm sure she was overcome with emotion, with joy, wept and laughed, flushed, carried on over her ring, held it up to the light, grabbed his hands, kissed them, shook her head as if she couldn't believe what was happening to her. She probably said she couldn't wait to call Mother. Did he mind if they went back to his apartment and called home? Did he mind if she called Grandma? Did he mind if she stopped everyone she knew? Did he mind if she stopped people she didn't know on the street and told them? And by the time she was finished, he must have felt like the most important person in the world.

Doris is good at that, making people feel as if no one could possibly be more important. I remember how she used to look at me. She radiated love and approval. And how infuriated I became by that look, that adoring look I told her belonged only on a dog. I know what she did. It's as if I were there. *She* didn't crab away about why she'd been called out early in the morning in the middle of a blizzard.

And how unreasonable I was, to complain about snow, because when Jack called and asked me to meet him, it hadn't yet begun to snow, and if, in Chicago, we all had waited until the snow stopped before we made our plans, we would all of us have sat alone in our rooms until spring.

It must have been pleasanter to propose to Doris than to propose to me. Why my resistance, my pulling back, my unwillingness? But perhaps all people are this way. People are, Jack says, profoundly mysterious. It is surprising, I think, that people can be both deeply boring and profoundly mysterious at the same time.

I remember—I haven't thought about this for so long!—that after we saw the couple dead in the meadow, Doris said the oddest thing. She said, "If I were going to kill myself, I'd never shoot myself in the head. Anywhere else but in the head." And I said, "Why not the head? Everyone shoots himself in the head." And she said, "Because then I wouldn't look like you anymore."

And I said, "How would you do it?" And she said, "If I had a gun and that's all I had, I'd shoot myself in the chest. But I'd rather use pills or gas," and I said, "I've never thought about killing myself," and she said, "I have. Every time Mother has one of her spells, I think about it."

"But you wouldn't do it?" I said. She scared the life out of me. And she said, "How could I leave you? If you needed me?" And I patted my bed and said, "Come on, get in here with me," and I put my arms around her and I fell asleep breathing into the back of her neck, and as I was going under, she said, "I love that, listening to your heart beat, I can feel it through my back," and I could feel hers too, but I was too sleepy to say so.

I AM pregnant!

I should have known! Doris and I can be on two continents and still we will end up doing the same thing!

Pregnant and not very happy about it. Not happy at all. And who can I talk to about it? Not Jack, who is positively wild with happiness. He says things—he actually *says* these things—like *Another Florence. What could be better than another Florence?* I said, If he is a boy, he will be pretty peculiar looking. And he said, Don't you want another Jack? And I said, I *have* my Jack! And he said, Don't all women want a child who looks like their husband?

And I thought, Be careful. It's gotten so we can almost read one another's thoughts. Don't let him know you're not happy. Don't let him know your first thought was, If we're going to England, I can have an abortion there. Abortion has never entered his mind, that's obvious. And yet we agreed we didn't want children. We wanted always to be the most important people in each other's lives. I *still* want that.

Oh, for once I wish I could talk to Doris, and not on the phone! When she speaks to me on the phone, how do I know if her husband's there? Then what she says to me is directed at him as well as at me. It's not the truth. It's not what she *really* thinks. And now Mother tells me she thinks Doris will have the child after all and the doctor is happy his early suspicions were mistaken.

I *know* Doris would understand that I don't want a child and she wouldn't blame me or disapprove of me. She never blamed me or disapproved of me in her life, not even when I treated her so badly at the university. If I could sit in a room with her, if I could be magically transported there for an hour, I know I could think clearly. I would see the solution swim into view. Like a whale, like the whale I am to become.

Doris, of course, will not mind being pregnant. She will like it. She would say, Florence, look at me. Look at me until you get used to the idea. And if I could, if I could sit there and look at her, I *would* get used to it.

Hopeless. I am on my own.

I can have the baby. I can drive off to a distant town, leave it on church steps, drive home and cry *Kidnap*.

It won't work. They'll find the baby, they'll find me. What nonsense.

And Jack! "Can you hear its heartbeat? Is it kicking? You didn't suspect? Let me listen." And I become irritable, horrible, and push his head away and can't look him in the eye, start to cry, and he says, "Poor Florence. Poor Florence. My mother was crazy as a loon with my little sister. Would you want my sister to come over?"

And I said, "Who? Your sister? I've never seen her before!" And then I really cried. A new baby, a strange sister-in-law who almost certainly would not like me, who would see through me, who would know immediately how unhappy I was about this baby. Because women see through other women. Grandma always said that, and she was always right.

"Will I be enough for you?" he asked in a strange, trembly, humble voice, and then I was sorry, then I sobbed my heart out. I said he would be enough for me and more. And he looked at me sharply and said, "Florence, do you want this baby?" And I said, "Of course I want this baby," and I thought, How fortunate this journal locks, how fortunate I've hidden the key. And *then* I thought, This is terrible. I bought this lock to keep the journal from Doris (who would never have dreamed of touching it, who wasn't even here), and now I'm afraid my own husband will read it!

Would he?

I don't think he would.

We trust each other.

IT'S HAPPENED. I'm not pregnant. I slipped on the stairs and fell all the way to the bottom. The doctor said I would be fine, but I wasn't.

And now we have buried the baby. In its tiny, piteous coffin.

Jack's extravagant grief hurt me most. What could I say to him? The sight of me injured him. Something had happened to me he could not fix. I have come to know how important it is for him to believe he can shield me from everything harmful.

Any attempts I make to comfort him make it worse. He thinks I am brave, noble, long-suffering—wounded more deeply than he is and yet I comfort him.

And perhaps I am wounded. Perhaps if I had had the baby, I would have taken one look at it and fallen in love with it, changed suddenly, as I seem to do, as I did that first moment I saw Jack reflected in the pane of glass facing me, as I did when I fell in love with our dog when it scratched at our tent. How do I know what I would have felt? I don't know. I'm like an old map of Africa, a map with huge white spaces. I know I will recover. But I don't know if he will. Everyone has his illusions. Jack's was that he could shield me from the world. Now he no longer believes it.

What I fear is that he will look for someone else he believes he can protect. The tough exterior he presents to everyone, his lack of sentimentality, his belief he wanted an independent woman who wasn't afraid of bears or possibly rabid dogs—all surface, surface, surface. Deep down he wants a woman to protect—a child. A child who will have children of her own. He might replace me, if he found such a person.

A YEAR has gone by since the miscarriage, if that is what it was. I think of it as a stillbirth. I find it prudent to have dependent attacks. We are as happy as we once were, although we are happy a little differently and I am now watchful, as if I've seen the shadow that pursues me and know I must outrun it. Shadows pursue all manner of things through my paintings. I hate them, these pursuing things.

Perhaps one day I *will* end up an orphan. You tempt fate, don't you, when you tell lies?

Reality wants to be what you say it is.

WHAT WILL HAPPEN when I reread you years from now, when I am old? Will I see meanings I never suspected in what I have written? In the end, will you shock me as all mirrors do?

It seems fitting that I write my last entry in you on my twenty-first birthday, the day on which I am of legal age anywhere in the world. It seems so old! Tomorrow I begin another volume.

Jack says, "You keep me off balance, Florence." And he seems contented. Does it ever occur to him that I do this because I myself am off balance?

And I think he likes it—my being famous. I barely believe it myself. It all takes place in the ether.

Oh, but he is a camera hound! If there is a flashbulb within a mile of him, he will sniff it out and turn toward the camera. A television camera rouses him and he expands before my eyes. Even I am seduced out of rages by the sight of my husband on that little screen. He is not larger-than-life; he *is* life. He cannot take a bad picture, and of course that doesn't hurt his career. Letters from smitten women pour in from every known country. They want to type for him. They want to act for him. They want *him*—though few are bold enough to come out with it. They send pictures too—nudes. I've used some of these pictures as models for my paintings. I strip and ask, How does my body compare to hers?

I am used to someone seeing my naked body.

Doris.

I cannot say her name. It summons her up. An American member of the troupe was named Doris, but she didn't last. She couldn't act, wouldn't cooperate, wasn't pretty enough. Who knows what was wrong with her? They simply didn't like her. I was overjoyed when she left. "Doris, stand farther back. Doris, don't look at the audience when you say those lines." And an electric shock would pass through me. It was the wrong Doris.

I do not think she is happy. My sister.

When I think of her, my thoughts cloud over, as if a storm is coming.

There are days when I would give years of my life to see all of them again. It could be done. It could. But they would ask so many questions. I might let something slip. I would have to lie to Jack. I would tip a delicate balance. Everything must stay as it is.

Someday we should have children even if we give them away, on the chance they would look like him, be like him. Priceless. But if he grew old and a child grew into what he was when I first saw him? Would that be terrible? What does a parent feel when that happens?

I wonder if Doris has changed.

I remember how annoyed I was by how she moved, how she flopped into a chair, how primly she pulled her skirt down over her knees. How often I said, Don't *do* that! And how puzzled she was, saying, What's wrong with what I'm doing? It's exactly what you do. And that was the trouble. In her I saw things I would never have seen in myself—how, from behind, her head always seemed bent slightly forward, as if she were a bird looking for grain. How she walked with her toes turned out, how she blinked rapidly when her feelings were hurt. I'm changing that, I'd think, watching her, and I'd keep my head up when I walked, until our mother said, "What's wrong with you, Florence, walking with your head in the air that way? Why are you pointing your toes in? Do you want to be pigeon-toed?" *Is it you, Florrie?* my sister called out when the door slammed behind me, and I'd think, Who else could it be, calling out for me in my own voice? That moment when my mind was hers, that moment of confusion when we were both in different places, but why? She was me but not me, just different enough to confuse.

I am glad I never saw her when she was pregnant.

I never cooked for her. I refused to cook for her. I never kissed her. I refused to kiss her.

Lately, I try harder to be sociable. I don't imagine I'm terribly successful. People here must think me distant and reserved, perhaps downright unfriendly, whereas Jack chats with everyone as if he'd known them from birth, and there are restaurants we've abandoned because, as he says, he ruins waitresses. He is so friendly and they become so friendly that it's no longer possible to have a private conversation. We gave up our last inn when the waitress who was also the proprietress began to sit down at the table with us. That, of course, was the bad part. The good part was the woman's own cooking, which she served to no one else. She tolerated me the way you might tolerate the child of a very good friend. Whenever I thought of something to say to her, she and Jack were already laughing, deep in conversation. It is his skill. He can change his stripes instantly, whereas I am stuck with what few stripes I have.

Do I mind? I don't think I mind. I think, This is how Doris must have felt all those years together. But it was not the same, not between us. We had worked it out, what one of us could do best, what the other did best, and so, since we divided everything, probably we were only on duty half of each day. No wonder I feel so exhausted now! There is no sitting back in my chair, knowing my sister will take over and I can cease to exist until she calls me back. Knowing that I can float. We called it that—floating.

But there is no floating here. When we take a trip to the canyon—
neither of us tires of it, although it is a very long drive—Jack calls my
attention to every unusual configuration of melting greenish-gray rock,
to every glimpse of the brilliant green river winding its way hundreds of
feet below us. If he sees a bird he's never seen before, he asks me to look
carefully at it and draw it so that when he gets home he can visit the
local ornithologist and discover what they call it here. It is enough for
me to look at the bird and see that its wings are yellow interspersed with
gray and that its beak is bright red, but Jack says it is very important to
know the right names of things.

Lately, I've added a sketch pad and colored pencils to the great plastic bag full of water, bread, and chocolate we always take with us in the
silver car (I wrap the chocolate in a wet towel and this keeps it quite
cool, a trick I thought up myself, remembering my physics lessons at the
university). I'm also expected to learn the names of cars, to recognize
them from a distance. Jack says it will train the eye, and then flushes
when he remembers my eye is as well trained as anyone's. But, he says, it
could always be better. You can't have seen everything you need to see at
your age.

Then there are gatherings, not formal enough to be called parties. I
can't say I like them. The entire troupe is always there, babbling and
acting, and I am never sure. How do I know when they're acting? When
they're themselves? I don't know and Jack says neither do they. Why
don't I talk to the playwrights if the actors confuse me?

There are quite a few of them, these days. Jim Hamilton is the nicest,
so of course Jack doesn't particularly like him. What he particularly
doesn't like is the way Jim leaves who he's speaking to when I come into
a room. Then he gets me a glass of wine, and soon I am leaning against
a wall, listening to him. He is like everyone else in the troupe, full of
ambition, full of desire to begin life again.

Jack and I read to one another. We like things that take a long, long
time to finish, because, as Jack says, they remind you that life should be
long and seamless and eventually reveal intention and form. I rumpled
his hair and said I didn't think he believed in either, and he said, Florence, don't you know by now I'm a conventional man?

Jack, conventional! I protested, but he insisted he was conventional,
he wanted all the conventional things. Success, happiness, a wife he
loved.

THESE WERE the journals seen in the light of the night café, and in the night café's light, I saw what should have been obvious long ago. I was there. On almost every page, I was there.

For the first five years, the journals were a record of almost inconceivable happiness, the sort most of us would sell our souls for, the kind of happiness that brings tears to the eyes of even the most cynical onlooker, who, if he spoke, would say, There is paradise, there, as I once knew it! It was not my imagination after all. It existed. Look at them. They are the evidence.

The entries of the next three years recorded increasing suspicion and resentment, until finally they arrived at that all too familiar stage where resentments are more cherished and passion-soaked than the love that once seemed so important and invulnerable—that once seemed the axis on which the earth spun.

And they were so young. That is the pity of it. She was nineteen when she married him. She was—on the surface, to herself, to others—happy with him for a full five years. She had made him her life. She gave up her family because she was sure there was nothing more she needed. And she was right. For five years she was right. But five years is a long time. People change. She grew more famous. He grew more famous. Finally, their names were known throughout the world. They ought to have been satisfied. For a long time they were. But if it is true that as people grow older their essential natures reassert themselves, then perhaps this is what happened to them.

Was Florence right? Had he seen that he couldn't protect her? Did he need someone he believed he could protect? Or was he simply away from home more and more and found one thing had not changed. He disliked a certain kind of loneliness, he disliked being without the company of women. And perhaps he thought that Florence would never find out what happened in Canada, in Australia, in Delhi. And perhaps she didn't. And perhaps after a while he grew careless and began to carry on at home the way he carried on out of the country. And perhaps he thought—he knew she loved him—that even if she learned of an affair here or there, she would forgive him. She would understand, would say, as his sister used to say, You have to forgive men their tomcatting ways, and if you can't forgive them, then shoot them. I believe this is where he made his mistake. He thought she would forgive him anything.

And perhaps for a while she did try. Perhaps she first tried a kind of selective blindness, a kind of intermittent stupidity. He often worked late.

Women often called him at home, and the phone was on her side of the bed, and when she answered they often hung up without giving their names.

Perhaps they were embarrassed to have called so late and they didn't want to explain and apologize the next day. Perhaps it was only consideration for her that led him to call in an electrician, who rewired the phone so it now rested on the end table at his side of the bed. After all, she needed far more sleep than he did. He could get by on three or four hours a night, whereas if she didn't sleep eight hours, she stumbled about the next day like a patient coming out of anesthesia.

Perhaps when she saw his car parked at night in front of a woman's house, and he came home and said he had been at an emergency rehearsal, she believed him and thought he had merely driven one of the cast members home. Perhaps when she saw the car there again and again and called the woman's house—her name was Tobie; what an idiotic name, Tobie, and what an idiotic way of spelling it (she wrote this in her journal)—and asked to speak to her husband, she put the fear of God into him, and after that he told himself he'd reform, and he did. He behaved admirably. Things seemed just as they were.

If she now went through his pockets while he slept (he slept like a stone) looking for—what?—lipstick? notes? a shred of paper saying, *Meet me at 8 tomorrow in Cavaillon, the usual place*—what of it? She found nothing except for the gold pocket watch she'd never seen before, engraved on the back with initials she'd never seen before, E.Z. He later said the initials stood for Ezekiel Zanderson, Tobie's grandfather. She'd lent him the watch when his own watch stopped one night when they worked late. Didn't she remember he overwound his watch and had to have the spring replaced, and the balance wheel also, and thus Tobie had lent him the watch so he could keep an eye on the time. She knew how Florence worried when he was very late, he said it so often: I don't want Florence pacing up and down all night, worrying—it was so touching the way he worried about her. If she now went through his pockets, burning with shame and embarrassment, did she ever find anything conclusive? If she had her own ideas about what "E.Z." stood for, didn't they sound fantastic? Could she be the first one to acknowledge the decay that had somehow eaten into them? Must she be the first to sound unreasonable? To be called a jealous woman, as if she lived in a bad novel, or a harpy or a shrew or a bitch, because if he called her any of these things (and surely he would call her something, surely he would have something to say if he found her going through his pockets like a woman from the marketplace), wouldn't she know he was guilty of *something,* wouldn't she have to know, and then would there be any going back?

And if she asked herself whether she believed in him, didn't she also ask herself what she believed in most? Didn't she most believe in the value, the importance, of what she had given him? Hadn't she given herself over entirely? She thought she had. Hadn't she handed over her soul and said, Here, it's yours to do with as you please, and if it was his pleasure to take her with him into the bedroom of other women, if he had simply grown bored with her, wasn't he shaking her belief in herself? Wasn't it her own gift—herself—she valued more than she valued anything he gave her? More than she valued him?

She wanted nothing to happen. She wanted life to stay as it was. She didn't want anger, recriminations, to say cruel things that could never be unsaid. And so she hid her anger. She rarely lost her temper. She rarely raised her voice, probably never threw things. She believed in dignity, in dignified behavior. Why? She didn't know, couldn't have explained.

And perhaps he took her calm as an indication of her lack of concern. Perhaps he thought, Anyone so imperturbable can't really care. Anyone who doesn't see the evidence before her eyes doesn't want to see it, doesn't think it's worth her while. Perhaps if she had smashed pitchers, attacked him with a knife, hit him with a rolling pin—he was used to that. He used to describe fights between his oldest sister and her husband. They both drank, but they loved one another and they always would. He said this proudly and with certainty, meaning, I'll never lack people who will take me back, I'll never be the worst person on earth. No matter what I do, I'll be forgiven. Perhaps then he might have given up his women, at least for a while, and in that time she might have grown used to him, to his straying, might have understood her role as one of the Keystone Kops, a violent Keystone Kop, a female one, dedicated to keeping him in line.

If she had been anything but patient and steady and blind—which was what she was, almost until the end, and then it was too late. If she had fought for him, if he had seen she was willing to fight. If she had forgiven him. As he believed he had forgiven her: for being childless.

Once, she had known how to fight. She had fought me off. But otherwise all she had seen was gentle behavior and subterfuge, her mother silently crossing the common at night in a black bearskin coat, almost invisible in the night air. So she knew. She knew even women practiced deception and deceit, grew practiced in duplicity. But they were ordinary mortals acting out their ordinary, inconsequential loves.

If she hadn't believed her love was transcendent, sacred, exempt. If she hadn't been so romantic, so idealistic. But she was. She was all those things, and her husband loved her idealism, her fierceness, her greediness, her passion. And what he saw now was calm, calm, and more calm.

If he had awakened in the middle of the night and seen her digging through his possessions like a wolf digging for a buried piece of meat! Something small might have saved them, small and ordinary. But they believed, he still believed, that they were exceptions, they were extraordinary.

And when she did grow angry—when she thought, If he's not home by ten, I *will* explode—she thought repeatedly of me, who came to her room late at night at the university, and the unforgivable things she had said to me. But she had wanted to drive me off. Did she again feel my hands tighten around her throat? Oh, yes, she could still feel them. And there were times when she thought she saw me smiling, saying, You see? There is justice after all. Now it will be your turn.

So there was a new crop in the garden and new plants flourished—bitterness, jealousy, and anger, and of anger only so much can be allowed into the open, because before both parties have agreed to give up (and do both parties ever give up at the same time? is there ever an agreement to give up?), anger must be suppressed, must be starved, bound with barbed wire, whipped, lashed, kept in check. Anger is the most dangerous emotion there is. It is like fire. It burns everything up.

And after a time (as she knew, as he knew), you become an arsonist of the emotions. You love to watch the fire burn. You throw wood on the fire. Anger scorches the walls. The roof catches fire and lights up the sky like an amazing sunset. Later, you warm your hands over the embers, still orange, still brilliant, still glowing. They should have known what would happen. They did know. And then again, like any two people to whom this happens, they didn't.

And they should have known that anger purifies.

Yet they lived as if they knew none of this. And they began to turn on one another, and the pity of it was that they still loved one another. As long as they lived, they would love one another. Jack would go on loving her for the rest of his life, long after he believed her dead. She would love him as long as she lived, even if her passion took the form of vindictiveness, an appetite—a new appetite—for making him suffer.

But it was far more complicated than that—because he had no idea that I existed. He had no idea of the part I was to play and had always played, and if she had had her way, he would never have discovered how she and I plotted together against him.

I was the trouble. I was the shadow. I was the snake in the garden. Because I existed.

I hoped I was exaggerating my importance—I always needed to believe I was important to her, even when she wouldn't speak to me, even when she called me names, even when her face showed disgust at the sight of me. But I didn't think I was.

When I looked up, everyone in the night café looked touchingly young—like children. When you grow old enough, the world is foreshortened, time compressed. Everyone you see is just lately a child.

CHAPTER

TWENTY-EIGHT

I WAS DRINKING my cold coffee, slowly, sipping it, staring out the window, and so I didn't see him come up, but when his shadow fell across the table, darkening it, I looked up.

"Oh, you," I said. "What are you doing out at night?" and he said, "I'm always out at night; I'm not a child," and I sighed and said, "Of course you're not a child."

"I've written to him," he said.

"Who?"

"To Jack Pine, my possible father."

"He *is* your father. Your *biological* father, as you like to say."

"He doesn't *have* to be my father and I hope he's *not* my father. Maybe my own father lied to me. Maybe I *was* his child and he didn't tell me because he didn't want to ruin my mother's reputation. His generation still believed in reputations. It's not modern, where he came from. Maybe that's why he went back to South Africa and raised me there. He might have thought she'd come back. Nobody would have known who she was there. Maybe he wanted to protect her name."

"Now you're telling yourself fairy tales. She left her husband and in less than eight months she had a child. Whose child could it be?"

"Someone else's. Someone else she knew in Goult."

"Oh, I don't think so," I said.

"The selfish bastard wouldn't want children!"

"We don't know that."

"Someone knocking at his door and saying, 'Hello, Daddy, you don't know me, but I'm your son and I go to school in England. I'm too old to play with electric trains, but there must be something else we could do.' "

"Think about it," I said. "If you are her child, she's taking a wonderful revenge, isn't she? When is the poor man ever going to get some peace? I'm going over there and then you're going to turn up! He'll take up residence in a monastery in Tibet! And he won't be safe even there."

"Oh, well," Antonio said, staring down at the table.

"Think before you send your letter. *He* doesn't know *anything* about you. You can't just run around hurting people."

"Why not?" he said.

"Because you're not a petulant child."

"Didn't *he* want children, either?"

"I suppose he did. When he had a wife. But he never married again."

"No," Antonio said. "I wonder why not."

"Who knows? *You* don't know. *I* don't know. Let me tell you, it comes as a shock to have someone show up and say, You don't know it, but you have a child."

"Did it?"

"Of course."

"Why do you care if I shock him?"

"Antonio!"

"Don't worry," he said. "I'll think it over."

"Please," I said.

"Well, I've got to get going," Antonio said. "You won't take me with you to Provence?"

"No. One thing at a time, that's all I can handle."

"Handle!"

"You know what I mean! Stop pretending to be so angry!"

"I *am* angry."

"At me?"

"Not at you. What did you ever do to me?"

"Then you're going?"

"Call me," he said. "Please."

Other people are just odds and ends, Florence said contemptuously. *Rags in a ragbag! We belong together. How do they know they're sister and brother? How do they know they've got the right mother? How do they know the hospital didn't mix them up? We're the only ones who know. No one else can be certain of anything but us—right, Dorrie?*

Words from long ago. And yet there was something to them. How could anyone be as certain of anyone else as we were? And what was left of that certainty now?

I went to the café the next day and then took the bus and wandered through the West End, looking for a pair of shoes. It was still bright when I got back to the flat. It grew dark so late here. Light poured in through the curtains. The hospital, which I looked at quickly once I came in before pulling the curtains, had yet to turn on its night-lights in the corridors, and few lights gleamed in the hospital rooms. Inside, everything was as I had left it, the sofa, the chairs, waiting for me. I was always surprised when I came back in and found everything as it had been—an orange pleated scarf thrown across the bed reminding me that I had expected rain in spite of a forecast calling for clear weather, and that I'd thought of taking the scarf instead of an umbrella but at the last minute changed my mind.

How long ago that seemed now, as if I'd been gone not for hours but for days. And it was always this way. Those things that rivet your attention and seem so important while you're doing them, you forget instantly as soon as you're distracted, and you never think of them again unless something happens to remind you.

I suppose everyone is like that. I suppose none of us would get from one room to the next if we had to remember everything we thought and did.

But was everyone so surprised to come home and find the furniture where it had always been, the pair of silver and gold earrings still on the living room mantel? Those startled me. Had someone else come in, tried them on, and decided they suited her? Or had someone come in and seen the earrings lying on the mantel and said to herself, Can't she ever put things away? and picked them up and put them back. For a moment, I didn't remember trying them on, deciding they were too long, taking them off, and setting them down. When I came back, I expected to find the earrings replaced in my jewelry box, or gone altogether. I expected to go into the bedroom and find the bedspread rumpled, the indentation of a body that had been lying there.

I always thought that while I was gone, someone had come in and occupied the rooms, and always, when I came back, I went through the apartment looking for her, half expecting her to leap out from behind a door, and I thought, All this has to do with being a twin. And I wondered if I was, as usual, complicating the everyday, explaining something quite ordinary, something that happened to everyone, saying, This happens to me because I'm a twin.

I would have to ask Eva. Eva, the beloved aunt! When she unlocked her door and went into her room, did it surprise her to find a blouse thrown over the back of a chair? Did she hesitate in the doorway and ask herself, Has anyone been in here?

Of course I knew women who left their doors open until they searched through their apartments, until they looked under their beds. They wanted to be sure no one had broken in while they were gone, no one was lying in the dusty, narrow space beneath a bed, waiting to grab them by the ankle as they went by. But this wasn't the same thing. I wasn't afraid someone had been here. I hoped someone had been.

What did I intend to say to Jack Pine? What could I say to him? As far as I knew, he knew nothing about me, whereas I knew a great deal about him. Well, it was inevitable, wasn't it? Women will talk to one another, and sisters will certainly talk, even if one sister is in Goult and the other is in New York, even if the sister in Goult likes to think she's broken from her family, escaped her twin, even if she likes to pretend she's entirely free of her, which she is—when she isn't talking to her on the telephone.

Still, she has a telephone, she can call when she pleases, she knows her sister will never hang up, and she does call—not for the first three years, but after that she called almost every day. But she wouldn't admit there was anything between us. When she hung up, I vanished. *We lead our own lives,* she said again and again. And finally, *I don't think of myself as a twin anymore. Do you?*

So I knew quite a bit about Jack Pine. What do lovers do, really, but feed each other bits of their own lives? If I were still painting, that's how I would paint them. Two bald-headed gray birds in an enormous nest made of mud and twigs, feeding one another bloody bits of their own flesh—while everyone and everything on the ground below marveled at the sweetness of their song. It is a mark of love, isn't it? Wanting to share one's life, one's unique, precious life. What paradoxical creatures we are, really. Everyone insists so on the uniqueness of his life and everyone is so anxious to share that life, to find a lover to whom he can tell his stories, make them so vivid that the beloved will feel as if he led his lover's life as well as his own. And if the lover succeeds, if he shares his life so well that it comes to belong to his lover, what then? Then his life is no longer precious and unique. Then, I suppose, he sees boredom in the eyes of his beloved and this is unforgivable, and the retribution begins.

But when lovers first meet, what astonishing optimists they are! They will share—they insist on sharing—lives that seem so lonely, such burdens to them. Now both of them will carry the burden. They hear a key turn in the great lock. Their lovers are letting them out of those small cramped rooms they call the self. They will have all the rooms of the other's life. And then they grow bored. They begin to compete. Which of them is the more interesting? The more precious? They learn they can be claustrophobic in two places.

We were experts on love, my sister and I, before we ever knew what love was. We loved each other. But I kept on loving her. And she—she was seduced. She wanted to be special, she wanted to be an individual. She was the normal one, wasn't she? She wanted what the whole world wanted, to be valued for herself. And I was not normal. I didn't care. I wanted to love her. That was enough. And later, when I met my husband, I wanted to love him. I thought *that* was enough. Until he said, "If I wanted endless adoration, I'd have gotten a dog." I said he would have been happier with my sister, so insistent on her own ways, but he looked at me as if I'd just said something absolutely preposterous, and said, "Why would I want your sister? Do you think there are only two women in the world?"

There have been many times I've wondered, not if I love other people enough—no, I seem to have a gift for that—but if anyone else seems as real to me as Florence. And then there were times, nightmare times, when I knew that other people were not real at all. My life itself was not real, nothing that happened to me—until I told Florence.

All those phone calls from Goult—the same must have been true of her. "I pay all the bills," she said. "I let Jack think I do it because he's disorganized, but I don't want him to see the phone bills."

"Because they're so high?"

"He doesn't have to know who I'm talking to."

"You could say you were calling your mother."

"I don't like to lie."

But that wasn't true. She lied when it suited her and never felt the slightest remorse. After all, she'd told Jack Pine she was an orphan. *Of course* she couldn't say she was calling her mother. And she couldn't say she was calling me, because he didn't know I existed. And yet she called me almost every day for years and during that time he thought she spoke to no one but him, thought of no one but him, relied on him entirely, was wholly sustained by his presence. How important he must have felt.

She made a mistake there, I think. It would have been better if he'd known there was someone else, if he'd thought, At any minute she may pack up her bags and leave; better if he'd come home to an empty house and heard his echoing footsteps and thought, I've been late once too often, I've made excuses once too often, now she's gone, how will I get her back? He would have been more careful. He was a selfish man. He'd have taken measures to keep what was his.

And if he'd found out—would he have forgiven her the deception? My existence—what a mockery it would have made of everything she made him believe: that he was the only person in the world important to her, that she could never love anyone else, had never loved anyone else, and there I would be, the rival, the first love. And what was I? Nothing but a sister. And he was not a man who trusted easily, especially women. She knew that.

He wouldn't have forgiven her. He wouldn't have understood. He was young. He was puffed up with his own importance. I suppose artists have to be, in order to go on. The more I thought about him, the more I wanted to meet him. If he had suffered, I wanted to know it. I wanted to see it for myself.

IN THE BEGINNING, my sister and Jack shared everything, or seemed to. But they did not, either one, want to speak of their families, and this upset Florence. What seemed like complete trust was not, after all, complete.

And Jack believed what she told him. Why wouldn't he have? Who makes such things up?

According to her, our memories of our mother (who died young) were vague, as were her memories of the aunt she lived with for a few months after her mother died.

She told Jack an elaborate story about a mythical aunt and uncle, who were wealthy and lived in a Back Bay town house and who went to bed every night at eight and were unused to children and who one morning said to her, "Florence, last night one of your little friends called at two-thirty in the morning and you know we can't have that. We thought someone died. Please call her and tell her not to do it again."

And she told Jack she did call. She thought the girl's name was May, and May told her no, she hadn't called her, not at all, her mother would kill her if she made a long-distance call. But the next morning our aunt Estelle said, "Florence, your little friend called again at two-thirty. Why on earth is a small child allowed to make telephone calls at that hour? Do her parents know what she's doing?" and she said, "Aunt, I'm sorry, I'll sleep next to the phone and pick it up right away if it rings." And our aunt looked her over and said, "Florence, I think it best if you stay with your father's sister," and so she was sent off and stayed there until she graduated from high school and came to the university.

She said her rich aunt and uncle didn't like children and she was acceptable to them while they were graciously taking her to stores and dressing her up like a little doll and showing her off to their friends, but when the novelty wore off, that's all she was, a doll they were tired of playing with.

Jack believed all this.

When she told me what stories she was telling him, I said, "Florence, life isn't a game. You'll be sorry later." But she said she wouldn't be sorry. Now that she'd told Jack about her life, he'd tell her about his. She was shrewd and she was ruthless. She understood that one confession begets another. When we were young, she was good with animals; she could tame anything—we both could—and now she began taming Jack. He told her his parents were terrible people who thought they were happy. He said it wasn't an act. It was something worse than that. Inside, there was nothing.

You're uneasy when she tells you your father really is perfect. But it's the arthritis—lately he has trouble in bed, if you know what she means, but she won't complain, they've had so many good years together. Of course things go wrong when a man gets older.

"She talked to you about sex?" Florence asked him incredulously, and he said yes, she did, he was her little confidant. She made him feel important. And a traitor to his father. Florence asked him if his father was a good man. She said he *sounded* like a good man, but Jack said he was nothing of the sort.

If his father had been good, he would have knocked his mother down. He should have thrown her down the stairs! He should have seen what she was up to. He was weak or he was stupid. They were two people driven by nothing they understood. One morning she'd get up and she'd think—but she didn't think, something drove her: it was some kind of body-thinking, if you can call that thinking—today I'll fix him. Today he'll see what he gets for being happy. Today I'll take the canoe and paddle into the middle of the lake and wait until everyone sees me and then I'll start off down the Mushroom River, all black flies and mosquitoes, and he'll think, She's going to drown herself. He'll have to come after me. Look at how he has to hold those paddles in his hands—and what caused it? I brought home a girl. That would do it.

She'd take me aside. What a lovely girl, so much nicer than the last one, and she'd go down to the dock and get in the canoe. But it wasn't obvious. You couldn't put your finger on it, not at the time. You only saw it years later, after you'd left, when you had time to think, when you could think about them as if they didn't belong to you, when you knew what she meant was that she would have liked *you* so much better than the husband she did have, when you knew she would have liked anyone better, anyone whose hands weren't twisted. But meanwhile—meanwhile it was the perfect family. You had to believe that for her sake, because how else could she go on when she wanted everything perfect, when she always thought she deserved everything perfect? And he went right along with her. What an innocent! What a stupid bastard! He believed everything she did.

And now they go on being perfect. He lies on the bed and she chews on him. She has tiny little teeth. You wouldn't believe how tiny her teeth are. The dentist used to say even small children didn't have such little teeth. And her son was something to torment him with. According to her, Jack was a grown man from the time he could walk.

Florence wondered what his mother would have thought of her. He said he wouldn't have let his mother within a mile of her. She'd have taken him aside and said how much nicer *she* was than the last one. *Each one gets better,* the old refrain. Then she'd have taken Florence out for long walks and long drives and drawn her out. She'd have found her weak spot and started chewing, and there'd have been more drives and more walks and more chewing and finally Florence would have looked at him strangely and then one day his mother would have come back with her arms full of groceries and a big smile and Florence would be trailing after her and it would be finished. Pure poison. She'd have done that to Florence.

But Florence told him she thought she'd be safe. After all, she loved him. He didn't agree. Someday she might meet his mother. She shouldn't underestimate her. She *was* a monster. And he told her that goodness didn't have a lot of appeal to him, not after life with them. Honesty did. Cannibalism: if it was honest, if you knew what you were eating, if you didn't tell yourself this was a wonderful roast turkey, then that was all right. He didn't put a premium on good behavior, not on anything but honesty.

He cut his world open for her: like an orange.

And she lied and went on lying.

Jack talked to Florence. Florence talked to me. And I was still bitter, embittered about the way she'd broken from me when we were in college, but not so resentful that I didn't warn her. I said, "He may mean it, Florence. He may value honesty more than anything else, and if he values honesty, he's not going to like dishonesty, is he? Stop making up these crazy stories about being an orphan! Tell him about me! He doesn't have to meet me! I won't go anywhere near him. You don't have to worry. He'll find out, sooner or later he's bound to find out. How can you be so reckless? And even if he *doesn't* find out, don't you think he'll suspect? You talk to me *all the time.* You *can't* seem like someone who talks only to him! He'll sense it, Florence, he will! He'll sense there's someone else!"

She said, "Don't be ridiculous. You're not someone else! You don't count!" And I didn't have enough sense to be insulted. I said, "You know I'm right! You always say 'Don't be ridiculous' when you know I'm right. Why do you want him walking around thinking you're up to something? He had enough of that with his mother! He *told* you about his mother! He's told you what he wants from you! He doesn't want lies, he doesn't want an act, he wants the truth! Tell him the truth!"

And she said, "I'd rather die than tell him about you."

I said, "It may come to that, Florence, it may! You said you'd die if he ever left you. You said you'd die if you had to live without him."

The line went silent. She didn't say anything. I could hear her breathing. Then she said, "I'm going to hang up now," and I said, "Don't hang up. Think about what I said. Tell him! It hasn't been that long! He'll understand! You can explain it to him! He's telling you everything! Tell him now!"

And then she did hang up.

I GOT UP. My phone was ringing, and when I picked it up, I expected to hear Florence's voice. I expected her to say, "I don't want you going near him! He knows about you now, all right, but he doesn't really believe it. He hasn't seen you. And this reporter! Why is he asking about me? Of all the useless, insulting things! Why should anyone think you know the first thing about me, simply because we look alike? That's *your* mistake."

I expected, in short, a diatribe. I expected Florence to come back from the dark place to which she'd gone more than twenty years ago, simply to shout at me.

But it was Dennis, and he wanted to know if I'd decided about Provence, and I said, "I'm standing here in the dark. The window's wide open and the rain's blowing in. What do you think I should do?" And he said, "Oh, you know perfectly well what you should do."

"You mean go see that monster?"

As soon as I said it, I was sorry. All this time, I'd gone along with everyone else, blaming him. Wasn't it his fault my sister was gone? I had warned her. I myself had warned her.

"I'll go," I said.

Dennis said he'd pick me up in a taxi at seven the next morning; he said he wouldn't be home for the rest of the day and might not be back at night. He wasn't going to take a chance on my seeing him and panicking and changing my mind.

And I sat down and thought about my sister and about Jack Pine, whom I had seen but never spoken to, not really, and I thought about the story Florence told me, about how he bought her the red dress and forced her to wear it to a party and humiliated her in front of everyone there. But now the meaning of that story was changing. The events were the same. Oh, no, the events hadn't changed. But why he'd done it, that was a question. Hadn't that always been the question?

He was seeing other women, wasn't he? But he didn't lie to her. No, he forced her to see it. *Anything is all right, even cannibalism, if you don't lie to yourself, if you don't pretend you're eating turkey.* Was he giving her a lesson in honesty? Did he know he was tangled in lies? Did he know it had happened again? Another woman had caught him up, a woman who loved him, who said she loved him? He must have known. Somehow he must have known. I would have. Was he trying to force her to tell the truth? If she'd told the truth then, would he have forgiven her? How had he lived with her paintings, those endless paintings of doubles, without asking questions? *Who* is that other? *Why* such an obsession with that other? Florence, what does it mean? And she wouldn't have told him, no. She would have invented more stories. He would have grown more suspicious. Didn't he say, in one of his plays, we marry the thing we most want to avoid? Did he know that from experience? He was married to my sister. Was the red dress another chance, was it her last chance? Did she not understand?

She understood how terrified she was of me. She understood that.

And when I warned her, she laughed at me.

I sat down in the upholstered armchair, the chintz-covered armchair. In the bluish-white light of the streetlamp that leaked in through the leaves, everything in the room was sinister. Everything cast such enormous shadows. And for the first time I asked myself, what had she done? To me. To Jack. To everyone who knew her.

But still, it *was* his fault. Wasn't it? I was too old for the simple, clean answers of my youth. Still, there *was* such a thing as right and wrong, no matter what anyone said. It was wrong to be unfaithful. I saw her face that day in Goult, red and swollen. I saw that terrible suffering. Someone had to be to blame.

And now there was Antonio, Jack's possible child. What was I going to do about that?

I wanted to tell myself, as I always did, that in the morning, when it was light, everything in this room would look as it always looked, as it's looked for years. But I didn't believe it. In the morning, the sun could rise right outside my window and nothing would ever look the same again.

PART EIGHT

I Dreamed
About Her
Quite Clearly

CHAPTER

TWENTY-NINE

L AST NIGHT I dreamed about her quite clearly. As if she were here, as if she and her husband were standing in the same room I slept in. And it seemed to me the outlines of her house, her rooms, were clear and solid, and the outlines of my house and my rooms were visible in hers, but the angles of my rooms were traceries, the shape of the chairs covered in sheet traceries, hinted at barely.

They were discussing children and I could hear them quite clearly. She was weeping, in floods of tears, and I heard my mother, her voice faint and quavery. She said, *When you cry like that, I know better than to believe you. You and your large tears. Florence cries nice, small tears.*

So I knew my mother was not there, not really, but was dreaming about my sister, as I was. Then she was still alive, my sister—if she was dreaming.

And my sister said, *I want children, you know I want children.* And her husband said, his voice exhausted, *Maybe next time.*

And my sister said, *It's only that if I do have one, it will start all over again. It will bring everything back. The first time she walks, the first time she talks.*

She was crying, almost inaudible.

But I could hear what she did not say.

She did not say, A child will be like a wolf, a wild dog with a sharp nose, digging up the grave, unearthing my sister. Digging up what I have so carefully buried!

An unnatural child, freakish, born singly, born alone, depending on no one but me!

And if there are two? What will I do then? Wait until one turns on the other? Because one *will* turn. Go through it again? All the little things of growing up? I won't do it, not again.

I have a child, I have two, I have them already, I've always had them. My children, named Doris and Florence.

She will not tell him the truth. She doesn't know the truth. I know it. It was always up to me to tell the truth. Wasn't that part of the bargain? Wasn't that my job?

I didn't think she could find me here, in these empty houses, one like another, standing in empty fields, the weeds taking back the cleared and mowed pastures, the saplings standing about like people who have come early to the theater, these white brick houses without addresses. I thought I was perfectly safe here. Where could I go that was far enough away?

In the evening, I will finish the fruitcake, pack my backpack with nuts and dried figs, and start out.

I will wash in the little stream. How kind of the owner to leave a bar of lavender soap in the bathroom, perfectly good soap even if the teeth of rats have gnawed it. I must wash my hair. I must not frighten people. When I come to the next town, I must look ordinary. I must not walk into a new town with twigs and filaments of gray spiderwebs in my hair.

There is red dye in the bathroom, and a bottle of bleach. Once, a woman lived here.

At night, it is colder, and when I cough my chest rattles.

There is loose dirt in my lungs, loose dirt and a shard of white bone.

CHAPTER

THIRTY

I T W A S raining when we left London, a soft, grayish-beige rain that seemed to drift lazily down, falling more like snow than water, but when we drove up to the white stone house in Goult, the sky was clear blue, the sun was a white-hot ball you looked away from, the landscape appeared to be covered with a fine whitish dust that follows heat everywhere. In the summer, the leaves in Peru looked like that.

On the plane, I'd had nothing to say. I felt like a kidnap victim. I looked over at Dennis, and what was he doing? He was reading a copy of *Either Island,* my first book. In it a young girl is shipwrecked and washed up on an island, and when she begins to explore, she finds all the people her own age exactly resemble her. All the older women look as she will when she grows older. And finally she sees the very old women, who look exactly as she will if she lives long enough, and at last, in a panic, she picks up a snail, and when the snail pokes its head out, she sees the snail too has her face, and she picks up a rock and smashes it.

It is not a cheerful book.

I said, "It's only a horror story, that's all I meant it to be," and he said it was more than that. It was very good. And I said, wearily, "It's about us, of course. Everything I write is about us," and he nodded and smiled, slightly impatiently, as if he'd taken a plane and found himself sitting next to an irksomely talkative stranger, and went back to his reading. I thought, This is a fine thing; he persuades me to come, he interrupts my life, which was going along so well, and he can't be bothered talking to me because he's reading my book—again. Didn't he tell me he'd read it already?

It seemed to me we were flying backward, backward in time. Jack would be in Goult, and I would, and we would meet, and everything, as Florence would have said, would be *fraught*. I was tired of emotional upheavals, resentments, recriminations. I was too old for a life like a novel, full of plot and incident and suspense. At my age, I should busy myself studying what had already happened—as I had been doing. I should try to make out patterns, study the smaller designs, the watermarks on pages, everything the young were too frantic to study.

And what would I find in Goult? What *could* I find in Goult? I would find our younger selves, and it seemed to me I was thoroughly sick of them and their melodramatics.

If only I could loosen myself from everything that's gone from me. The expected fullness in my ears. The plane was coming down. Jack Pine. Goult. Whose idea was this? If I tugged at Dennis's sleeve and said, No, I'm not going, I'm taking the next plane back? And for the rest of my life, I'd despise myself. I'd tell myself what a coward I was.

No, we never learned.

THE HEAVY BLACK WOOD DOOR swung back and there was Jack, Jack Pine, and he looked impossibly like himself, and the room behind him looked impossibly like itself. Hadn't he changed anything? White walls, dark furniture, gray, flat-stoned floors, everything as it once was.

We were standing still, staring at one another.

Dennis was standing behind me.

"My God," Jack said. "Then it's true." He raised his hand as if he intended to touch my face, but I took a step back, stepped on Dennis's toes, lost my balance—Florence always said I could trip standing still, I could sprain my ankle trying to move out of someone's way—and Dennis grabbed my upper arm.

Jack and I resumed our staring.

I wanted to say something—I'm the twin sister you heard about, this is what your wife would have looked like—*something*, but I was incapable of opening my mouth.

Jack licked his lips. His mouth must have been dry. "Well," he said. "I suppose you want to look around. Check out the closets and the basement, see if I have a body hidden anywhere."

I felt my eyes open wider. He flushed. "There are people who think I killed her," he said. "I suppose you're one of them."

I continued staring. What else was I to do? Was I supposed to say, I

know about your mother and father, I know all about the red dress and I'd
like your version, please? Was I supposed to say, I know how much she
loved you—what made you do it? Has anyone since loved you as much?
She warned you, didn't she? She said no one else would ever love you as
she did. Should I say, I know what it's like to have Florence turn against
you? But he wouldn't believe that. He wouldn't believe the same thing had
happened to both of us.

Behind me, Dennis whispered, "Say something."

I shifted my weight from one foot to the other. I felt unbearably light.
I felt unbearably young. I had nothing to say.

I continued staring.

Jack's face changed. It softened, it blurred, it grew younger. "Is it you?"
he asked. "Is it?" His voice was hoarse.

"It's Doris James," Dennis said. "Florence's sister."

"Your hair's just the same," Jack said. "It hasn't gone gray. I thought
you'd cut it. Most women cut their hair, don't they?"

I put my hand to my head. I wouldn't have been surprised to find myself bald.

"Why did you go?" he asked me. "Like that? Without saying a word?
It wasn't a human thing to do, was it? You wouldn't do that to a dog."

I looked at him, astonished. I cleared my throat. "Are you speaking to
me?" I asked.

"It is you!"

"I'm Doris. You can see I'm Doris." Of course, he could see nothing of
the kind. He believed the evidence of his own eyes. He was looking at
Florence. And then I found the question I wanted to ask him. "Did you
ever really love her?" I asked.

He turned red, he took a step toward me, and I thought, He's going
to kill me, he did kill Florence, he did. Then he sagged. In front of me he
grew smaller.

"Will you take her downstairs?" he asked Dennis. "To the kitchen? I'll
be right down."

Dennis led me to the steps and as I walked across the room I looked
back over my shoulder at Jack, as if I thought he might disappear if I didn't
keep my eye on him, as if I believed I'd dreamed him up. What was I thinking? This could have been my husband, those could be my paintings on
the wall, this could have been my life? I believed that. Didn't I think,
hadn't I always thought, that if Jack had married *me,* there would have
been no red dress, no disappearance, we would still be married? *I* had the
knack of fidelity, people I loved were faithful to me (except Florence), my

world respected my wishes (yes, because your wishes are so small, *paltry,* Florence says). He would have been happy, I would have been happy.

"Be careful on the stairs," Dennis murmured. "They're slippery." The famous stairs! Great smooth chunks of gray stone, worn down by feet in shoes, my sister's feet, her husband's. Why was Dennis whispering? We weren't in church. We weren't at a funeral. No one had died. "He's in shock," Dennis said. "Aren't you?"

Was I?

I was asking myself, What did I owe Jack Pine? *Was* it my fault that Florence had disappeared as she did? Was it my duty to make it up to him? But then no one could make it up to him, twenty years of persecution at the hands of the world. I might as well have been an amnesiac presented with a husband from her life before the car accident. People ask the woman without memory, "Doesn't he look familiar? Do you recognize the sound of his voice? Does anything come back to you?"

Of course I recognized him. Of course I remembered. All my life I had lived through Florence and Florence had seen to it that I knew what her life was like. I knew what she cooked for him and how she waited for him and at which window she waited. I knew that she called him Beast and he called her Beastie, as in beasts of the field.

I thought, I want him back. *Back.*

And I thought, This is insanity.

"Well," Jack said. "I'm back."

Back.

His eyes were red and his face was still wet. Little drops of water clung to his cheeks. He'd splashed himself with water. Wasn't that supposed to wake up the dreamer? Make the apparitions vanish? And still I was here.

"Florence would hate this. She'd hate it if she knew I was here. She thought of you—"

"As her property? Yes, well, she wasn't alone in that, was she? She was just more so. More so in everything. Intense. Insatiable. She didn't like my friends, she was happy we lived far from my family, she made up those stories about her own family—well, you know all that."

"She didn't see why you needed anyone else." She'd told me that. When she met Jack's friends, she studied them. What did he find in them that he couldn't find in her? If there was nothing new in them, he didn't need them. If there *was* something new, something she didn't have, she was frightened by them. She tried to scare them off. Then she tried to *become* whatever they were, so that Jack would see he didn't need them if he had her. She wanted to be his world. She existed and he existed. The rest of the world was contemptible and unreal.

There was another long silence, which threatened to prolong itself indefinitely.

"So," I said, my voice hoarse. "You see I'm her sister."

"I don't see any such thing."

"Well, then, you *know* I'm her sister."

"If you were Florence, you'd say you were her sister, wouldn't you?"

"Don't make yourself unhappier than you already are. I'm not Florence. I'm not here to play tricks."

"You want her paintings back, don't you? Are you the one behind those rumors that I stole her legacy? That I tore up her will? That I should have given everything back? Even though I didn't know who to give them back to!"

"I don't want her paintings," I said. I thought, She stole the paintings from me. She stole everything from me. Let her have what she wanted so badly.

"I think you should have them. Well, some of them," he said, thinking better of it.

"If she'd wanted me to have them, she'd have arranged it. How could there be a will? If there was no body?"

"People make wills when they're still alive, don't they? That's the idea, isn't it?"

He'd gotten into the British habit of turning his baldest statements into questions.

"I can't believe she'd have made a will," I said uneasily. "We were so frightened of death. We had an agreement—oh, I don't know—when we were eight? Or nine? If one of us decided to kill ourself, we'd take poison or gas, we wouldn't shoot ourselves in the head because that would change our face, then we wouldn't look alike. I don't mean we were suicidal, I don't think we were, but we saw so many bodies, in Darlington's Funeral Home—she must have told you about that. She didn't? We did see them.

"And the couple we saw in the meadow, she told you about them, that's where the trouble really began, I still think so. Death-haunted, both of us, the whole family, really, how could we not be?"

I stopped, astonished. He didn't *deserve* to know us better. If he had been faithful to her, eventually Florence would have told him everything. Why should he know what we once were?

I wanted to be angry.

We were sitting at the kitchen table, a black refectory table, and I stared down at it, at its long cracked planks, at the tiny holes bored here and there in the surface—woodworm. This must have been her table. I intended to go on staring at it forever.

"You must have hated her," he said. He said it with great venom and it startled me awake.

"You were the one who killed her!"

"I was the one who killed . . ."

He stared at me, then struck the table with his fist. Now we stared at each another with open hatred, and I had the odd feeling that I'd seen this before. I knew exactly what the two of us looked like. And then I remembered. Florence had a dog, I had a cat, and the two of them used to lie on the living room rug, facing each other, staring each other down. "I was the one who was killed!" he said.

"Doesn't Princess Di have a house around here somewhere?" Dennis asked. We both turned to him, staring. "She does, somewhere," he said. "Someone told me. If it's not her house, it belongs to a relative. Maybe that's it."

"Princess Di!" Jack said.

"Do all betrayed women end up here?" I asked. "Is it something in the air?"

"She knew what she was getting into when she married him," Jack said sullenly. Now *he* was staring down at the tabletop.

I said, "She expected a faithful husband."

"Then she was a fool."

"I suppose that's what such people are to you. People with ideals."

"She's not an American," Jack said. "Europeans have a different attitude toward marriage."

"Oh! It's not your fault! Nothing's your fault! If only my sister had been a sophisticated European."

"If only your sister had been fucking *sane!*" he shouted.

"She *must* have been mad. To fall in love with you!"

"She never loved anyone in her life!"

"Then why did she marry you? Why did she shut herself up here in a country where she couldn't speak the language? And she *hated* the heat."

"You're the one who did it, aren't you? You got hold of her journals and you turned them over to the newspapers. You're the one who wrote me the letters!"

"What letters?"

"You know what letters!"

"I don't know what you're talking about."

"You do!"

"Where is Princess Di's house?" Dennis asked. "Is it nearby?"

"Will you shut up?" I shouted at him. "What do I care about Princess Di?"

And Jack shouted, "That's enough about Princess Di!" And for an instant, we were united in our fury at Dennis, sitting across from me with the hurt, slightly mischievous look of a child caught in the middle of his parents' argument.

"I thought," Jack said to Dennis, "*this* one didn't have a temper."

"I wouldn't count on that if I were you," I said.

"Unlike your sister, who threw things. Very expensive glass things."

"First of all, she never threw things, but if she did, she must have had a reason."

"And I didn't? I didn't have good reason for the things I did?"

"Was I here? Do I know why you did anything? She told me about the red dress. She told me everything about that."

"Not everything," he said. "Not everything. She didn't tell *me* everything. She didn't tell me how you got the journals."

"Well, that must have been a blow, when you looked for them and couldn't find them and realized you couldn't sell them to the highest bidder!"

"You're as bad as she was," he said slowly.

I said I would take that as a compliment.

"Why don't we all go for a walk?" Dennis suggested brightly. Evidently he hadn't learned his lesson.

"A walk?" we both said together.

I wasn't going for a walk with Jack Pine. What made me think I would be safe near him? Perhaps he was in the habit of murdering people who looked like me.

"I'll come along," Dennis said, his eyes on me.

"In that case," I said, "yes."

"Afraid they'll be looking for you at the bottom of canyons?" Jack asked me.

"Of course that's what I'm afraid of. I'm in my right mind," I said.

"Yes, but whose mind are you in?"

"And what do you mean by that?"

"How do I know you're who you're supposed to be?"

"Here!" I said, opening my pocketbook and digging into it. "Here are pictures! Two of us! Exactly alike! What an idiot you are! I have birth certificates! Do you want to see those?"

"What will that prove? How will they prove you're not her?"

"Oh, I give up—he's an idiot. Let's go!" I said to Dennis.

"Let's go? Without threats? Without gloating? Maybe you *aren't* Florence," Jack said.

"Come on," I said to Dennis. "Don't forget your sunglasses. They're upstairs on the table."

"Let's take a walk," Jack said. I said I hated walking. "See if you can't bear up for an hour or so," Jack said. "See if you can survive without Dennis. I'm not likely to murder you while he's waiting for you to come back."

"Let's all go for a walk," Dennis said. "Please."

"All right," I said. "Dennis, would you mind? Staying here? I won't be gone for long."

"You want me to wait for you here?" Dennis asked.

"Yes," I said. "Let's get it over with," I said. I looked at Jack, who was watching me as if I were a new and fascinating kind of mechanical toy.

"Fine," he said. "Would you like a hat with a veil? I have one."

"Was it Florence's?"

"It was my sister's," he said.

"Give me the hat," I said, and when he did, I put it on.

WE GOT UP, went upstairs and out the front door, and started down the cobbled road toward the village. The smell of lavender was thick in the air. Enormous black and yellow bees buzzed at the screens over the windows.

"Did you always have screens here?" I asked Jack. "I don't remember them."

"Because you were never here before."

"I was."

"You weren't."

"I was here after the party with the red dress. *You* were in Sweden."

"You were here? In this house?"

"After that party. She called me and asked me to come."

"Before I knew you existed, you were here," he said, turning it over. "What a fool she made of me."

"Of you!"

We walked along the main road until we came to a field full of sunflowers. "Let's go sit in the clump of trees over there," Jack said, pointing to a stand of oak trees.

"Fine," I said, wearily.

I kept my eyes on the ground. I didn't want to trip, twist my ankle, find myself carried back to the house by Jack.

"Is this all right?" Jack asked, pointing to a rock in the thick, slate-gray shade. "Don't sit down yet. Don't *sit down!* It's not safe."

"What exactly is dangerous about this rock?"

"Scorpions."

"I'm sorry?"

"There are very large scorpions around here. They can hurt you."

"I'm sure there are no scorpions."

"Then go ahead," he said, bowing deeply, making a sweeping gesture. "Sit."

"If you're going to check, check!"

I didn't look at him. I knew he was smiling. I took off the hat and held it in my hand.

"So," he said when we sat down, "are we going to sit here in silence or are we going to fight?" I was too furious to answer. "You can't stay mad long, can you?" he said. "So maybe you aren't Florence." I sighed deeply. "Although you sigh exactly like her." I said I thought that everyone who sighed sighed the same way. "Actually," he said, "people sigh quite distinctly."

"Doesn't the sun ever go down here?" I asked.

"Never," Jack said.

We sat quietly, staring at our feet. Leaf mold, a hole a few feet from us—a mole's home. We were both caught in the same story. Florence bound us together.

"If this were a novel," Jack said, "you and I would get together and walk off into the sunset and live happily ever after."

"This isn't a novel. This isn't a play. When one of the characters goes, there's no understudy."

"You could have fooled me," Jack said.

"I'm not trying to fool anyone."

"Unlike your sister."

"She wasn't trying to fool you. She was frightened."

"Of me?"

"Of *me*. She wanted so badly to be free of me."

"She should have trusted me. She *could* have trusted me."

"You weren't trustworthy. Remember Tobie."

"I never married Tobie. I never loved Tobie. You'll notice I never married again."

"It's no wonder. You did such a bad job the first time."

"We're together for—what?—twenty minutes? And we're fighting as if it were old times."

"You're confusing us again."

"Well, you know, *Doris,* she never loved me."

"Why do you keep saying that! It's infuriating!"

"She *worshiped* me. She thought I was perfect. She didn't love me.

When you love someone, you manage to admit he has his faults, don't you? I didn't have *any* faults. How could I? I was entirely her creation. Is that love? In your book?"

"I know she loved you," I said stubbornly, thinking, She loved you far more than she ever loved me.

"Oh, well, if you're going to stick to the party line."

"She was my sister! I *knew* her!"

"Then stop parroting this nonsense! You *did* know her! You didn't read about her in the papers."

"All right, she idealized you. Are you happy now?"

"There's not much in this to make anyone happy, is there? There aren't any heroes in this story."

"The people who stay alive," I said finally. "They're the heroes. If she'd had children—"

"Don't kid yourself there. She didn't want children. She was happy after the miscarriage. She didn't want anyone depending on her. She didn't want to share me with anyone. You were talking about the party. After the party, I heard her shouting at the dog. 'It's because of this damn dog I have to stay alive!' She talked to herself a lot."

"I still talk to her. I still ask her what to do. If I'm alone and I'm combing my hair, I ask her what to do."

"I hope you don't take her advice."

"What about you? Do you dream about her?"

"Oh, let's not go into that."

"She's legally dead now, isn't she? Dennis said so."

"I thought it would settle something; you know how it is."

"Did it?"

"No."

"I never should have come here," I said. "I can hear her right here"— I tapped the space between my eyebrows—"and she's saying, 'Doris, will you get out of here! Go home!' "

"She wasn't a very welcoming creature."

"Your play? *Three Raven Wood.* Was that about her?"

"Probably. Although I didn't think so, not at the time. All the actors in the same masks, the ones who lay on the stage through the whole thing, trying to grab the ankles of the ones moving around—well, it was about how the whole world metastasized around you until you were the only one left, and then where were you? Where were you supposed to find anything new? Dennis said you wrote a book that had the same idea."

"Why do you think I hated her?" I asked him. "I didn't hate her. She could do anything to me and I didn't mind. I started painting first and she took it over and I didn't mind. I liked living through her."

"For an egomaniac like me," he said, "that's hard to believe. Altogether impossible."

"I had a lot of practice. I didn't know there was another way. Princess Di," I said, apropos of nothing.

"What?"

"Princess Di."

We both started to laugh.

"Well, that's better, isn't it?" Jack said. "You're married, aren't you? Dennis said so."

"Oh, yes. Forever and ever."

"What's that like?"

"It's very nice."

"Yes, I'd think so."

"You'd be right."

"Can we be of any help? To one another?"

"I'm not going to give interviews saying you really were a wonderful husband to my sister, if that's what you mean."

"No, why should you? You think I did her in."

"Did *both* of us in."

"Well, she wasn't exactly a vitamin pill for *my* family," he said.

"Don't tell me she ruined your life and you're really the victim. You're still alive. People still know where you are."

"Wonderful, isn't it?" he said sardonically.

"You're a very attractive man; you know that. Marry again."

"Once was more than enough."

"Let's go back," I said.

"We could write," Jack said to me.

"Why not?"

"Who else knew her?"

"Yes, well, we have that in common."

"It's something. We *should* help each other." He started to laugh. "You know, if she knew you'd come here to see me, she'd still be here."

I sighed again. I asked him if he thought she was *somewhere*.

"Oh, *somewhere*, yes," he said.

"And will she come back?" I asked.

"How can she come back? It would be like coming back to a city you'd bombed."

"Oh, it wouldn't be that bad."

"Wouldn't it? If she came back . . ."

"You'd want to kill her? Who could blame you?"

"I might. The more she tried to explain . . ."

"Oh, yes," I said. "I know. But I'd want her back. All the same."

"So you think, but it's all sentimentality, isn't it? You left her behind. You had to, to survive. Be honest."

He was quite a lovable monster.

He stood up and took my hand and pulled me up after him, and I thought, From a distance, anyone would think we were an old married couple. On the whole, I wasn't angry that my sister had married me to him—a shadow marriage, a shadow husband. A shadow adulteress . . . that was another matter.

We walked back, past the field of staring sunflowers, now gazing after us, past a field that looked black from a distance, but now that we passed it, I saw it was a buzzing field of lavender, thick with enormous bees, the sun now small and white, floating just over the horizon, and then we were at the foot of the road, looking up at the town. It was very hot. My blouse was damp and clung to me. I plucked at the neck and pulled the fabric and for an instant I felt cooler and then I let it drop back against me and I looked up and saw Jack smiling as if he had just seen something marvelous, and I thought, Oh, yes, Florence used to do the same thing in the heat. She used to sweep her hair up with her hand and hold it to the back of her head, just as I was doing now. She couldn't pin her hair up—that gave her headaches, just as it gave me headaches. She wore only platinum or gold, just as I did, because we were both allergic to other metals. My husband used to say, "That's a convenient allergy you two have."

I wondered if Jack had said the same thing to Florence. I lost my balance. I felt my hand on his arm.

"You have to look where you're going here," he said. "Watch out for loose stones. They don't pave things here the way they do in America. You always tripped over your own feet," and then he said, "I'm sorry; you can't imagine how confusing it is," and I said, "Yes, I can," but the village was above us, and Dennis was waiting outside the house. Soon we'd be driving back to the airport. I stopped and turned to face him.

I asked him, "What do you think happened to her?" and he said, "These days people just disappear, don't they? That's the modern world. People go across a border and they're never heard from again."

"Across a border?"

"Well," he said.

He pushed his hair back out of his eyes.

How many times had he done that? I wonder. How many millions of times had he pushed his hair back? How much energy went into little things like that: brushing your hair, pushing it back, pinning it up, taking it down. And she was back, I could see her sitting in the kitchen in the house at Goult, and he was cooking, sausages and lentils, I could smell them, I could hear the pot simmering, and their happiness was lovely in the air, and what was it made of? The incomparable joy of watching him push his hair back, the amazing, blazing happiness as he watched her sitting at the table, sketching him at the stove, sketching him picking up a wooden spoon glazed with tomato sauce, both knowing that as long as they lived they would remember this insignificant instant in the kitchen. So insignificant, so small, lit up by so much energy: perhaps that was the secret—when something so small ignited like that, like embers that couldn't burn up.

I asked him, What did he mean? Across a border?

"Well, she was furious, wasn't she? She didn't take the car, she didn't take much, the drawers were full. Anyway, they looked full to me. So I didn't know if she'd really gone or if she was out for a walk or if she was somewhere in the village. She could have been next door watching me, couldn't she? Watching me come in and out of the house, more and more frantic. Well, she would have liked all that, wouldn't she? And how would I know what to do? Call the police? But if she hadn't really gone? If we only *thought* she was gone? It would have been all over the papers. Everyone would have been talking, you know how a small town is. So for a while I didn't do anything like go to the police. When friends called me in Sweden, they said they *thought* she was gone. They didn't know. I went up and down ringing doorbells. How many ways can you think of to ask if anyone's seen your wife? Well, no one saw her, did they?

"Then the baker in the next town said he thought he'd seen her walking along the side of the road and she had a blue denim backpack, and you know, Florence did have a blue denim knapsack. So I asked him if he thought she was hitchhiking and he said he couldn't know the answer to that, but on hot days you started walking and it was so hot, if someone stopped for you, then you were hitchhiking, *n'est-ce pas?* So I think that's what happened.

"She was furious, she didn't want anything of mine, anything I'd ever touched, you know how it is, she decided she'd walk away with whatever she could carry, she'd start all over, she started walking, someone stopped for her, and she was gone."

"Gone?" I said. "You mean dead."

"Gone. Only gone. Well, dead, that might be better, mightn't it? We'd know, one way or the other."

"Someone could have taken her? But then she'd have come back. We'd *know*."

"People disappear, Doris. They dye their hair, they go to Marseilles, they fake passports and birth certificates, they vanish."

"But *why?*"

"She was washing her hands of us. Washing her hands of everything she'd ever done. She didn't have much stamina, did she? She used to say that. 'I have a lot of energy but no stamina.' "

"She liked the sound of the words, that's all it was!"

"It's what we have to accept, isn't it? Unless she comes back, we're never going to know. She could be a blonde living on La Costa del Sol. We don't know."

"She could be at the bottom of a canyon. She could be bones!"

"You knew that, didn't you?"

I looked up at the houses of the town. I started walking and he walked along next to me. He said to go slowly, it was a long climb. And when we stopped outside the post office to catch our breath, he said, "You could stay here for a while. We could bait the house—like a trap. If she's somewhere watching, if she's buying newspapers, if she's got a clipping service, she'd come back."

"That's the playwright speaking," I said. "You like being outrageous."

"I *am* outrageous."

"You're unhappy," I said. I was out of breath.

"Well, it's what she wanted, isn't it? I think she'd be well pleased, don't you?"

"Oh, yes," I said, sighing. "She would be."

"Did I marry the wrong sister?"

"More silliness."

"Why?"

"I would have bored you to death. Faithful Doris. I bored Florence to death."

"Oh, I think you were right the first time. You frightened her. Think about it. You'll see I'm right."

We were almost at the house. Dennis was standing on the terrace, watching us. I waved and he waved back. "I am tired of thinking about Florence," I said.

"We get a day off every now and then, don't we? Sometimes a whole night."

I said I didn't often dream about her, not anymore, and Jack said, "Well, you don't have to, do you? All you have to do is look in the mirror." There was something new in his voice, a tightness in his face. Of course. Jealousy. As if he was thinking that I was the lucky one.

Dennis came down the steps toward us. "Are you ready?" he asked me. Jack told us to come in and take two or three bottles of cold water to drink in the car. It was so hot, and if anything happened to the car and we were stuck in this heat, we'd be in trouble. A few minutes later, we were backing out of the narrow space behind the house, and when I looked up, Jack was standing on the highest terrace, watching us. I waved, settled my sunglasses on my nose, and watched him.

He didn't wave back. It seemed to me his eyes were on me as the car rolled slowly backward, as I pulled down the car's sun visor. He turned abruptly and disappeared into the black doorway, and when the car at last turned into the road leading back down through the village, I realized I'd been holding my breath, that I hadn't been breathing at all, and I breathed in as deeply as I could, so deeply that my lungs hurt and I seemed to feel my ribs pressing down hard against them.

I Came into
the Town

CHAPTER

THIRTY-TWO

I CAME into the town and my hair was red and the sky was red also. Best to arrive at a plausible hour. I thought, I will go to an inn, but in the end I hesitated. In the end, I turned around. Up a steep road was the churchyard on the edge of town, and in it a mausoleum, a small house. The moon was full. I would sleep in the mausoleum's angular shadow. Down below, the lights of the town went off, one by one, and abruptly there were none, as if someone had thrown a switch and the town was a room plunged into darkness.

In the morning, I went into the church, as if I wanted to pray.

I expected quiet, the soft sound of wings overhead, the bats disturbed and chittering, the sudden loud riffling of pages—the wings of a pigeon flying up into the eaves—the usual noises. But people came in, speaking loudly of miracles. The priest stopped in the aisle.

"Have you come because of the miracle?" he asked me.

I arranged my face. I shook my head no.

An old woman said, "We are here because of the miracle."

A woman in the graveyard was to be moved from her husband's body, next to the body of her mother. When they dug down, the shovel struck the coffin lid, which splintered. Beneath the coffin lid, the woman lay untouched, as if she had been buried that morning. The lid of the coffin had decayed and rotted, but the woman slept as if nothing had touched her. *You see, there are some of us who time cannot touch.*

I was taken to see the woman. She lay on her back, as if sleeping. Her hands clasped a blackened flower to her chest.

An old woman said, "Do you want to touch her? If she is a saint, she will bless and protect you."

I said, No, no, and walked down the hillside, into the town and through it. I kept on walking until the light died. I was in a field. The only sound was the howl of a wolf in the hills above me. I sat beneath a tree and leaned my back into the bark. I took out three figs and ate them. I ate a handful of walnuts. I drank a small bottle of wine. In the morning, I would look for a stream.

My cough would frighten the wolf, keep him away.

There were moments when I thought quite clearly—terrible moments.

I thought, Once, I believed I had a husband. He was unreal. There was no such person. How quickly he faded. How fast he disappeared, without a trace! There was only one other who was real. She knew it. She knew it first.

What had I done to her, what might I still do to her? If I died, wouldn't she die also? Would she have a choice?

If I were dead, if she had seen the body, that would have been better. She might have thought, Yes, it is really finished: she has ceased to exist. She could have taken a picture of me as I lay in my coffin. They did that once, took pictures of the dead. Sometimes they painted over the closed eyes so that they appeared to be open. She could have cut strands of my hair, had them woven into a wreath around my picture. They did that once, wove wreaths for the funeral picture out of the dead one's hair.

But if I were dead and there was no body? When someone dies, a body is required. If they could not find mine, they would come for hers, of course they would; inevitable, really. Then her body would have died but not died, if I were alive. Then she would be buried somewhere, somewhere she would be beneath the earth, it would be her body that the grubs ate, that the blind moles dug down for. Then she would be alive but not alive, unholy. Then when she looked into mirrors, she would see my face, the face of a dead woman. When her reflection wavered in the hood of her car, she would see a dead woman's body.

Where was I, if not in her mirror? There was a logic to this, our logic.

Once, we believed everyone had a twin, oh, yes. Once, we believed everyone's twin hid in his mirror. "But then," she asked, "shouldn't there be four of us?"

Four of us!

I said, "It's different for us. We are both *here.* We're the exceptions. We don't need to hide in mirrors."

"Oh," she said. "I see."

Whatever I said, she believed.

Her mind would give way. Surely it would.

In the end, I would win. I always insisted on winning.

And yet there is loose dirt in my lungs, loose dirt and splinters of sharp white bone. Twigs in my hair, and bits of grass. And in my lungs, small stones, small but heavy, small but they will suffice.

CHAPTER

THIRTY-THREE

WE WERE on our way to the airport in Marignane, and as we drove I remembered a few lines from a poem Florence had written as a child (unless, of course, I wrote it—it's so impossible to remember who did what). The poem was called "Jonah," and the first lines were

> Clouds streak the sky,
> Giant rib cage of the whale

and I remembered how taken we were with the idea that the world, which looked so enormous to us, might actually be very, very small, no larger than a fish swallowed by an enormous whale, and when I looked at Dennis, driving, smiling to himself, the countryside taking on a coppery tinge as the sun set, I asked myself what he had to be so happy about. I wasn't happy. Had anyone asked me if I was ready to go back? Might I not have wanted to stay on in Goult or a nearby town and see the sights, whatever those might be? Hadn't my sister described a wonderful canyon? Hadn't she said it was worth the heatstroke? Mightn't I have wanted to talk to the baker, the last man who saw her? If he was still alive, of course. But no one had asked me, and I was packed up in the car like a dog in a carrier, and in a few hours I'd be put on a plane. With Dennis Cage, who had his own motives, whatever they were. His pure love of Florence and her paintings. His patient quest for the truths of her life.

It occurred to me that one reason I loved Dennis was my knowledge that one day he would bring me to Jack Pine.

I had nothing to say to him while we were in the car. I stared out the window at high-arched stone aqueducts left behind by the Romans, at oak-lined avenues whose leaves met overhead, at the dappled black road disappearing under the shadow of the car. He concentrated on driving and left me alone and after a while I fell asleep.

I was settled in my seat on the plane, in the back, in a cloud of smoke in the smoking section, because it was my theory that survivors always staggered from airplane wrecks only if they had been sitting in the tail.

"How *did* you get the journals?" Dennis asked.

"She shipped them to me," I said.

Which is what she did. But I didn't tell him that she sent them one at a time, each double-wrapped in heavy paper, sent a volume every two weeks for many months. I didn't say that I knew she was sending them one at a time so that Jack wouldn't notice they were missing, so that he wouldn't suspect she intended to leave. I didn't say that if she shipped the journals to me, if she wanted them kept safe, she must have intended to come back. She must have intended to begin again, without him.

But she may have changed her mind. Or I may have misunderstood. She might already have decided to disappear and wanted me to have something of hers. She might have thought, I'll give Doris the books. They hold eight years of my life. Surely that's enough for her.

Or she might have thought, When Doris reads the journals, she'll come to Goult for me.

But I didn't think she wanted me to read them. I didn't read them until after she disappeared.

"Really," I said, "I don't want to talk about Florence."

"You're in a strange mood," Dennis said, and he opened the *Evening Standard* and began to read, and I began to float—not sleep exactly, but float—into that state somewhere between waking and dreaming, staring at the cabin wall, and I remembered we once had an enormous book of fairy tales and we were sure that the book contained the people my mother spoke about when she read stories aloud, and at night, after she put the book down, all the people from all the stories fell through the pages, talking to one another as they fell, stopping when they wanted to by treading water—it made perfect sense; anything can happen in a book—and sometimes they decided they liked someone else's story better than their own and refused to go back and that was why, when Mother next read from the book, the story had changed from the time she read it before. And probably all that had happened was that we were getting older and we still wanted the same stories, and at various times she decided she could read us certain portions she had skipped over before.

When our mother first read us "Bluebeard," the wives died the moment they opened the forbidden door because they fainted dead away, but later, when the story changed, the wives opened the door and they saw bodies hanging on walls and they themselves ended up on meat hooks. So naturally we thought the characters in the book had changed things for their own reasons, and at night I'd fall asleep watching the characters in the book go from one story to another. Bluebeard came to Cinderella's ball and coaxed her into his carriage and she ended up on his meat hook. Beauty came to Bluebeard's castle, and when he saw her he was a reformed man and everyone praised his generosity and his gentle nature.

I still thought of my life as a story in that book. My life had always been like that book, and I was forever falling through the lives of my mother and my sister, and I was doing that now, staring at the cabin wall, drifting into my mother's story, her life as it was after her first husband died, before we were born, the time I loved to hear about always, before she managed to persuade herself that she loved her second husband. I was accustomed to this drifting from one story to another. Always it seemed to me a condition of my life, inescapable, determined by the peculiar nature of my mind.

She used to lie on her bed, our mother, and stare at the wall in Hilda's house, as I was staring at the cabin wall, and she thought, The wall might not be real. All the things I thought were real may not be. There were times she believed she could see through a tree if she stared at it hard enough. Harmless fancies, Hilda said, but our mother knew they were not harmless. She believed she could bring her mother back to her, and her father.

These houses, these mountains—if you could peel the horizon back, underneath might be city streets. She thought of how she and Lotte, her foster sister, had stripped wallpaper from the Hewitts' smallest bedroom and how the first layer, white roses on a grayish-green background, gave way to a design of cherry blossoms on black branches, and in turn that layer gave way to blue and gray stripes, and beneath that were little girls in yellow sunbonnets, with black and white dogs at their feet, until finally they reached the original plaster, threaded with horsehair to give it body, and when they pulled the last sheet of wallpaper from the wall, some of the plaster pulled loose with it, and behind it was the skeleton of a cat and a child's white shoe. Only one white shoe. And she thought, These are real things, the skeleton of the cat and the child's shoe, and she dreamed about them for years, the cat who must have gone through the lathing when the house was being built, after a mouse or a rat or a squirrel, and the wall was plastered up and the cat scratched and scratched and never realized she was trapped. She only grew hungry and cold and tired and lay down, intending to scratch again when she awakened, but she never did.

And the shoe. Who had put the shoe in the wall? Was a child playing in the room and did she take off her shoe and throw it so it flew through the strips of lathing and came to rest on the wrong side of the wall, and before anyone noticed it was missing, the wall had been plastered over, and did the cat when she grew weak lay her head on the shoe? They were so close together, the skeleton of the cat and the white shoe. And she thought, My life will come to this, I will end up behind that wall.

On days like those, she told herself, Really, I am not normal, something is wrong, I wonder if anyone suspects. Can anyone walk a high wire forever? And she thought, No, I am not as I should be. But I am well made and will last.

My mother was well made and she did last. She lasted out two husbands. She lasted out the disappearance of one daughter. She retired to Florida, where she is now. A good woman, so everyone said, very good. Of course, there were times when she could not make herself get up, answer the telephone. She kept candy bars in the night table next to the bed. If she decided to get up, she would need the energy. That was her great fear, that one day she would decide to get up and her body would not obey her.

After a while, she said, "You see what your life is and then you stop struggling. It's a relief to bend your head to fate. You're at that age, almost at that age, aren't you, Doris?"

My mother. Mad as a hatter.

But good. As people said I was good. And evidently because I was good, people took me for someone much older than I was. Even my mother did. She spoke to me as she would speak to someone her own age. And yet I looked young. People who didn't know me always said, "Oh, you're too young to remember that." When often I was older than they were.

It occurred to me that I no longer felt old, as I had felt every day in the café, talking occasionally to Eva. No, once again I felt young—as if something or someone had picked me up and thrown me back into life.

I was not sure I liked it.

"Is your seat belt fastened?" Dennis asked.

My ears swelled and popped. Outside the window I could see land, a patchwork of fields, dun-colored, brilliant green. Soon we would be on the ground, I would fall back into my old familiar story, in which I was good, never disappeared, never terrified my friends and relations, was a faithful wife, always ate my chicken sandwich, rarely complained, listened happily to others, went along with whatever was suggested to me (such uninter-esting suggestions), was *tractable*.

And I realized I had absolutely no desire to leave Goult.

"Is it fastened?" Dennis asked again.

I'd fastened the seat belt when we took off. Beneath the thin red blan-ket it was still fastened. I felt for the buckle and snapped it open.

"I'll call you," Dennis said. "After you've had time to think things over. You know I'm going back to the States for a few weeks? Pretty soon; I don't know just when."

"Think things over?"

"It must have been a shock, to finally meet him."

"Oh, yes, a shock, yes."

What on earth am I going to tell Antonio? What should he do? No, Antonio shouldn't be hurt. But what was the right thing to tell him? What should he do? I had no idea.

At home in the rented flat, I sat on the bed, holding the television's re-mote control, staring out the window at the thick green leaves motionless in the cool bluish air.

The phone rang. It was my husband, telling me something about the weather in Prague or a committee meeting or how much he missed me. "I'm fine," I said, "I'm fine, really I'm fine."

"Call me," he said, and I said I would. Then the phone rang again.

"Well," Antonio said, "what's he like?"

"Don't you ever say hello?" I asked him.

"What happened?"

"Nothing *happened*. We talked about her. It was strange, being there."

"Was he surprised to see you?"

"Very."

"Did you tell him about me?"

"No."

"Why not?"

"I didn't think it was my place. Anyway, that's not why I went to see him. I wanted to see what he was like these days. I wanted to see if your mother punished him enough when she left, and she did, believe me, she did."

"I'm going to see him," Antonio said.

"When?"

"Not for a while, but I'm going."

"Really? You're sure? I don't think you want to go, not really."

"Do you think it's easy," he asked me, "just barging into other people's lives?"

"I think you should wait until he answers your letter," I said. "He's a little touchy. Well, worse than that. Don't make strange phone calls, don't call and hang up, don't just walk up to the house. He has three vicious dogs. People should be prepared."

"You make me sound like some kind of walking disaster!"

"Well, *that's* exaggerating. But people don't walk up to you every day and announce that they think they're your child. You wouldn't like it if he said, 'Oh, really?' and closed the door. Would you?"

"No." He sounded sulky.

"I'll see you tomorrow," I said. "You can ask me whatever questions you want."

"He doesn't know anything about what happened to her?"

"Nothing. He thinks she may have been picked up by a hitchhiker. He thinks she may be dead."

"Dennis thinks she's alive. He thinks she's gone back to Peru."

"What!"

"He had a dream or something. On the plane. Didn't he tell you? Probably he doesn't want to upset you."

"Dennis is slightly unhinged," I said. "I'm sorry to hear it, but Antonio, it happens to everyone who looks for my sister."

"I'm not looking for your sister. I'm looking for my mother."

"Oh, well, then you're protected," I said wearily. "Tomorrow?" I asked him, and he said yes.

I would, I thought, have to decide what to do about Antonio. I was growing accustomed to his voice on the telephone, and when he didn't call I grew restless and then worried. And he was so impressionable. All Dennis had to do was tell him he had a dream about my sister going home to Peru, and Antonio might be on the next plane to the States. He didn't understand what chaos surrounded everything to do with my sister, what lunacy, what horror—and what comedy. He had just stepped into a perpetual game of hide-and-seek. He couldn't spend the rest of his life chasing after every rumor. I wanted to be sure he understood that. He was still only a boy. My sister's boy. Mine.

Dennis, however, was another matter. To go home because someone had seen Florence—or thought he'd seen her—was one thing. To go home because he'd dreamed about her—well, that was the kind of thing my husband would find very worrying. "I think we'll just keep him in a locked room," my husband would say. Lately, I was sure, we were all dreaming about one another. There is such a thing as dream logic, I know, but it's disastrous to import it into waking life.

I would have to speak to Dennis—if he wasn't already in Peru. But I didn't think he would leave without seeing me. I was still his anchor, the person closest to Florence, the one who knew most about her. He wouldn't let go of me so easily. Meanwhile I had other decisions to make, and quickly.

I had a sense that soon life would have emptied out its bag of tricks, would stand before me as the poor thing it was, while in the house next door, life would just be arriving, its bags full, a sparkling over everything, like snow on the branches outside the chapel, the sun high and white, the sky luminous and blue and thin, stretched tight, a brilliant blue film, the thinnest possible film, anything could tear it, stretched tight over the black night sky and the sharp spikes of stars. How permanent it looks when you first see it. My parents must have seen it: my mother, embroidering a bird amid flowers, my father, sitting in his chair, reading his paper.

I am, I thought, a very careful person. I read labels on food packages. I read the inserts in bottles of medicine. If I had my way, there would be warning signs attached to streetlights, little illustrated books describing the kinds of accidents that could happen, warnings to stand back from the curb because cars went out of control, jumped onto the sidewalk, knocked down young mothers standing next to mailboxes, holding their children's hands. There would be so many warnings and so many notices that no one would dare cross the street.

I was tired of being careful.

CHAPTER

THIRTY-FOUR

THE SUNLIGHT came slanting in through the leaves, splashing the walls green and golden, and the air was cool and the sky was bright blue, but not deep-hued, thin, as if diluted with water, and I thought, Yes, I'll go to the café, I'll have my chicken sandwich, I'll talk to Eva, I'll settle into my rut, that's best. It's best to be careful and cautious and predictable. There's nothing like habit to cure restlessness, to reconcile you to your own life.

And when I got to the café, early, the first one to sit down, I picked up a newspaper and began reading. Some society had carried toads from one side of the MI to the other. Too many were being run down by cars and couldn't get to the other side to mate. But now the society had discovered that they had been carrying the toads the wrong way. The toads they picked up and transported had already crossed the road, and so the society members were catching the toads and taking them back.

Life was preposterous, even for a toad.

"Oh, you're here, are you?" Eva said. "I saw you yesterday, you know, through the window, but I couldn't come in, you see. I had to go to the shops. The baker never showed up. I was up and down the aisles in Sainsbury's. I see you're reading about the toads. What a country!"

"I wasn't here yesterday," I said.

"Oh, if you don't want anyone to know, I won't tell anyone. Believe me, no one's likely to ask *me,* but if there's somewhere you want me to say you were, I'd be happy to say it. Friends should stick together, don't you think?"

"I was in Provence yesterday. I didn't get back until evening. It couldn't have been me. It must have been someone who looked like me, another tall, thin person with wild black hair."

"It was you or your double!" Eva said.

I opened my pocketbook and pulled out my plane ticket. "You see?" I said. "I was on that plane. Look at the date."

Eva looked at it. "Impossible," she said. "I saw you."

"Who was I talking to?"

"A red-haired woman."

"I don't know any redheads."

"*Everyone* knows a redhead."

"I mean I don't know any redheads in London."

"Well, you were talking to her."

"Eva, I wasn't here!"

She looked at the ticket, at me, and at the ticket again. "One of life's mysteries," she said, handing the ticket back to me, regarding me suspiciously. "But why would you want to lie to me?"

"I'm not lying!"

"A hallucination," Eva said, sighing. "Of course, it was a hallucination."

"I couldn't have been in two places at once!"

"Of course you couldn't. It's not important. Well, they say everyone everywhere has a double. I met mine once, at a party a Pakistani friend had over in Maida Vale, and I wasn't the same for weeks. She was my friend's mother, five years older than I was and very fat, but there was no mistaking the resemblance. She was wearing a sari and her hair was oiled and flat against her head, but the face was the same, and her air, the way she carried herself. I couldn't stop staring, I was fascinated. I must have been a dreadful guest. So *that* was what I looked like when I laughed, when I frowned. Oh, it was quite remarkable, quite fascinating. You never do know what you look like to others, do you? I wanted to know all about her, I wanted her to tell me the story of my other life! I thought I was behaving quite oddly, but no one noticed, and she didn't seem to mind my staring, but she was quite vain, I knew that immediately. She was my double, you see. It was wonderful. I knew what I looked like, for the first time."

"Yes, you know what you look like from the back, for example," I said. "If you have a double."

"But no one else thought we resembled one another in the slightest. Isn't it strange?"

"It's strange we exist at all," I said.

"Well, I have to get back to the kitchen."

A little later, I got up and paid my bill, and as Eva was counting out my change, I said, "Eva, are you sure about my coming in yesterday?" and Eva said, "I only saw you for a moment, but I was at shops and the dentist's, so I wasn't here until late in the day," and I said it was funny, but really, I was in France. I only came back last night, and Eva said, "Well, sometimes my imagination runs away with me, perhaps that's what it was," and I said, "Yes, I'm sure that's what it was."

I was *sure* that was it, but all the same, would she mind asking people who had been here yesterday? If they had seen someone who looked very much like me?

"I should ask them if they saw you?" Eva said doubtfully. "Or if they saw someone who *looked* like you?"

"You know," I said, "I have an idea. I'll go out and buy some bottled water—well, you know the papers say there are little fish or something swimming in the tap water—and while I'm gone, you could ask someone if I was in here yesterday, because I've lost something and I'm trying to find it, and I think I lost it here yesterday, but I'm not sure. . . ."

"Yes, yes," Eva said. By now she looked uneasy and her cheeks were flushed and probably she'd decided I was a lunatic. "I'll ask them if you were here or if they saw someone who looked like you, how is that?" I said that was fine. "But if you were here," Eva asked me, "then you don't remember it?" I said I didn't *think* I was here, but really, I'd been wandering all over the city, so no, I wasn't sure. "I see, yes," said Eva, who was examining the deep-green cover of her café's menu as if she had never before seen it.

"Well, I will go off and get some water," I said, "and you will ask them."

"Anyone who was here yesterday, I will ask him," Eva said.

When I came back, Eva motioned to me and said she had spoken to three people, none of whom had seen me or anyone who looked like me, but I should sit down, because the café artist was about to come in, and as I'd probably noticed, he sketched almost everyone in the café but Eva. She didn't like it if he sketched her. Once, she shouted at him, saying she wasn't an artist's model, she was too old for that, but he didn't speak much English in those days. He wanted to say he would never ask her to take off her clothes.

"I can ask him if he saw anyone who looked like you and I can ask him if you can look at his sketchbook," Eva said.

A few minutes later, the artist came in, a little man who sometimes leaned heavily on a stick when he walked, and Eva immediately went over to him, and he looked up at her, alarmed. Was she going to object to how long he stayed here? Had she finally begun requiring a minimum order?

"Madame Doris, come over," Eva called, and I went over to the table.

"He says he doesn't remember seeing you yesterday but you're welcome to look at his sketchbook. He wants to know if you mean this woman," Eva said, and the artist smiled and nodded and opened the book to an ink drawing of a woman holding a cup of coffee in one hand, her head bent over a newspaper. She was tall and thin and her long black hair was wild and curly.

"It looks just like me!" I said.

And then he turned the page, and the woman was looking straight ahead, full face, and all resemblance was gone.

"So you see it is not you," the artist said. "You are so much prettier. Here you are," he said, turning back to the beginning of the book. "You see you do not look like her to my pencil."

"Oh, yes, that is me," I said.

"You identify yourself?" he asked happily.

"Oh, yes, but I can't say I recognize the dress."

"Sometimes I draw the dress in later. It is such work to get the face in fast, before the person grows long nerves."

"And is that what you did? With my picture?"

"If you don't remember the dress, it's what I did. I think so, don't you think so?" I said I didn't know what to think. "You lost something?" he asked me, and I said, Oh, yes, I'd lost something, something large, and he said what a pity that was, and I said it *was* a pity, and I went back to the counter with Eva and asked her if she would offer the artist ten pounds for any one of his sketches, but not to do this if she thought he'd be insulted because the amount was too small, and she said he wouldn't be insulted, not at all. No one ever bought his pictures. I asked her to wait until I'd left the café and if he agreed, to please hold the sketch for me.

I went outside, waved to a taxi, asked to be taken to the Air France terminal at Heathrow, told the clerk behind the desk I wanted to be put on standby for the next flight to Marseilles, got on the plane, rented a car when I got off, and drove straight to Goult.

CHAPTER

THIRTY-FIVE

A S I D R O V E through the immense heat with the windows wide open and the brilliant day dimming through the windshield, I looked over at my handbag on the seat next to me and realized I had nothing with me, not a change of clothes, nothing. What if he wasn't there? I could sleep in the car, couldn't I? It was possible someone had seen my sister in London. It *was* possible. But in that very café? Wasn't that too great a coincidence? And there had been someone there who looked like me—if you didn't see her face. That must have been who Eva meant.

Was it possible my sister was following me, just out of sight? What an idea!

Or was she close by, watching Jack? He felt watched by her. He used to say that. In her journals, Florence said so.

"I hope she likes what she sees now," he'd said yesterday when I came with Dennis.

There was smoke on the horizon, trees burning in the hot, dry, acrid air.

It would serve me right, I thought, if he's gone somewhere—like Sweden. I would be lucky if he had gone off.

And sooner than I thought, I was turning onto the road into Goult, driving my little blue car between two houses up toward his house, the highest house in the village, scraping my side-view mirror against a house wall, that's how narrow the street was. It was terrifying, driving through the small gap between the houses. And then I pulled into the space behind Jack's house and stopped the car. I took off my sunglasses and was letting my eyes adjust to the light, when I saw Jack looking down at me from the topmost terrace, and he nodded, as if to say, Well, I see you got here. I opened the car door and got out. My legs were wobbly and my head hurt.

"Come in," Jack said. "Have some cold water. Or some wine. Which would you like?"

Was he out of his mind, or did nothing women did strike him as strange? "Don't you want to know why I'm here?" I asked him. "What I'd like is a very large glass of water with lots of ice."

"That is exactly what I thought you'd want," he said. And I thought, My sister was right. This is a man who's been spoiled by women in more ways than one.

"But you like me anyway," Jack said. "I should tell you: I read minds as well as your sister did."

"That's comforting."

"Isn't it?"

"You knew I'd come back?"

"I didn't know that."

"You understand, I hope, that I don't know what I'm doing here."

"You do know. You're here in the interests of symmetry."

"Symmetry! You're being coy! I'm here because I was interested in *you*. I was curious about *you*. I wanted to know what you were like."

"You mean in bed."

"Yes, in bed! Among other things."

"I know what *you'd* be like."

"Well, that's a delusion. You know what I'd *look* like. You don't know what I'd *be* like."

"You're funny," he said. "You're cute."

"I'm too old to be cute."

"You are. All the same."

"I suppose Florence was cute."

"Florence was rarely cute."

"Was she funny?"

"No. She was sarcastic, she was witty, but not funny. She had no sense of humor at all."

"Oh, I don't know. She disappears, spends about twenty years doing what she wants to do, and the rest of us live about twenty years in varying degrees of agony. That's pretty funny."

"We aren't laughing."

"No, but we're smiling. Because we're happy."

"And what are we happy about?"

"You're happy because you have her back. Well, that's the simple truth.

You look at me and you see her. You think, That's what she would have been like if she'd stuck around. And I'm happy because I have her back. While I'm here with you, who am I? I'm Florence. It's true, isn't it true? We get together, we both get Florence back."

"You don't mind?"

"No, I don't mind. Because we both know I'm not really Florence."

"What happened to you when Florence left?"

"Nothing electroshock couldn't take care of."

"Really?"

"Really."

"Are you hungry?"

"I'm always hungry."

"We could go out—if you put on a blond wig—or I could cook us something."

"Sausages and lentils?"

"That's still the extent of my expertise."

"Well, then," I said, "I'll set the table."

I was very happy. We were going to be very happy.

I knew what the days here would be like. Florence had described them in her journals and over the phone. For whatever time I was here, I would be young again. He would be young again. Nothing could touch us—unless my sister came back. And perhaps even that was part of my happiness. If anything could cause my sister to materialize, it would be my presence in her husband's bed.

From the kitchen, I could hear Jack talking to someone on the telephone. I knew immediately he was talking to a woman. He was making excuses, and for less than a second I felt sorry for her. Interesting, the way my sister came back to take her revenge. Interesting, the way she came back to make amends to her husband. Interesting to feel my sister taking up residence in me. I intended to keep her there indefinitely.

IN THE MORNING, the room was dark, and sharp stilettos of white light sliced in through the shutters. I lay on my side and watched him sleeping. His face hadn't changed in over twenty years. Time had deepened the lines so familiar from the old photographs, but the face was the same. I supposed the same was true of me. We were lucky in our bones.

And I thought, I love him, I've always loved him, how could I not have? Florence loved him. What choice did I have? She never hated him, not really. If she had, I would have known. I wouldn't be lying here so happily. I wouldn't be propping myself up on my elbow so I could watch him sleeping. And he sleeps so beautifully, I could lie here forever, watching him.

And then he stirred, opened his eyes, smiled, reached out lazily, took hold of a curl of my hair, stretched it out, and let it snap back. "I used to love the way that hair snapped back," he said.

"Our mother always said she couldn't leave us alone because of our hair. People came up and said how pretty we were and the next thing she knew, they'd be pulling our hair so they could watch the curls snap back. We had the curliest hair of anyone in Peru."

"Peru," he said, stroking my hair. "I thought she meant the country."

"Peru, Vermont. Blue mountains and blue shadows on the snow. She didn't make it up."

"She loved snow."

"Our whole family did. Our grandmother—we called her Hilda— used to take us out on a sled for an airing, round and round the common. She was wonderful, our grandmother. She wasn't really our grandmother, she was my mother's foster mother. Did Florence tell you about that? Well, she wouldn't have, would she? Hilda was very sick the first year we were at college, over Christmas. That's why we went home. I don't think you'd met Florence yet. Had you met her yet? I don't think you had. I don't think you met her until August.

"We went home to see her, and Hilda was delirious and she thought I was my mother, and my mother, you know, always called Hilda by name. She never called her Mother. And we all looked so much alike, so when she saw me, she thought I was my mother, and she asked me if I wouldn't call her Mother, and I said of course I would, and I said there never was a better mother. Whatever she wanted me to say, I said it, and when we went out, Florence was furious!

" 'Why do you have to be the good one? You're not happy unless you make me look bad!' I didn't know what she was talking about. What did she want me to do? Hilda was an old woman. We didn't even know if she'd live."

"What did you say? To Florence?"

"I was too tired to argue with her."

"You couldn't *not* argue with her. You couldn't walk out on an argument. She'd follow you right onto the street in her nightgown."

"Florence," I said. And sighed.

"What will you tell your husband?"

"My husband doesn't have anything to do with this. I won't tell him anything."

"Oh, yes, of course. What made me ask? Women are the ruthless ones, we all know that. Not men. People get that one backward. When a woman decides she wants to get married and have children, *then* she suddenly develops scruples and a conscience and morals. She starts sounding like the Pope, she never heard the word *affair,* she starts reading the lives of the saints—she particularly likes the saint who flew up to the ceiling when a man touched the hem of her garment. Well, you're laughing, but isn't it true?"

I said I supposed it was.

"And no one," he said, "was more ruthless than Florence."

"Oh, I don't know about that."

"We lived together for seven years and she lied to me every day. Doesn't that qualify as ruthless? In your book?"

"She must have thought she had a reason."

"Oh, come on. If a criminal said that, they'd lock him up and throw away the key."

"*I* don't know why she lied. I told *my* husband. He knew *all* about her. Of course, when he met me, I was at a dance and so was she, and she was dancing and I was crying, so I couldn't have kept it a secret even if I'd wanted to. He suffered through *all* the photograph albums and the yearbooks and the crying jags after she disappeared, but I don't know why she didn't tell you. My husband doesn't think he'd like her, and I used to say, How could you not like her? She's just like me, we're the same."

"That's not true."

"No?"

"No."

"I don't know how we're different. I don't suppose I ever will."

"You're not so brittle."

"She wasn't brittle. She wasn't fragile."

"She was. You had to watch what you said to her. The least thing set her off. She'd start to cry, she'd go to bed and you couldn't get her up. You don't make up a whole phony life story if you're not fragile."

"Why did you do it, then? The red dress? The party?"

"I thought I'd force her. There was so much wrong, she had to face it. I couldn't be the only one who faced things. I couldn't come to conclusions on my own. She was supposed to be in on it somewhere. If I had to come to make decisions without her help, well, she had to know what decisions I'd made, didn't she? Of course you blame me. How could you not?"

I didn't answer.

"We have to get you something to wear," he said. "Cavaillon is closer, but we could go to Aix."

"And buy me a red dress?"

"If I'd known . . ."

"Then you wouldn't have done it?"

"Then I wouldn't have done it. But I'd have had to do *something*, you can see that."

"Let's go to Aix," I said. "I've never been to Aix."

"Then we'd better go now," he said. "We don't want to be in a car after noon, not in this heat."

"But if people see me? You know what they'll think!"

"I can fix that. I have a blond wig in here somewhere."

"You just happen to have a blond wig?"

"I just happen to have it."

"Well, I'll wear it. Why not? Somewhere on the Costa del Sol, Florence may be wearing hers."

"Oh, I think she's dyed her hair. By now."

"You don't have any work to do? I'm not keeping you from anything?"

"Well, a writer like me, you know—it occurred to me last year—I've been retired all my life. I'm free. And you? What have you been doing in London?"

"Learning to live alone. Looking over my shoulder for my sister, your wife. Talking to a woman named Eva who runs a café. I'm going to miss her when I go back."

"When you go back—you mean to America?"

"Yes, well, you know I'll go back. You'd be in a perfect panic if you thought I'd stay here forever."

"Let's go," he said. "We'll stop at a café for some breakfast. Come on. You need money?"

"Not if I can trade you pounds for francs."

And so I got dressed in yesterday's limp clothes and put on the short blond wig. Jack came into the bathroom and tugged it hard over my ears, pulled it to make sure it wasn't likely to slide off, and we walked out onto the terrace, stood in the shadow on the still-wet flagstones, and then walked to the car. I was back where I belonged, where I was intended to be, and Jack took my hand and he bent down and kissed me and I stood up on tiptoe and kissed him back, and he put his hand up to my cheek and said, "People all dream of this, don't they? Getting their first love back?"

"Yes, getting them back just as they were," I said, "not covered with wrinkles, not hobbling on an arthritic knee. I have an arthritic knee, I'm always swallowing aspirin, I bruise easily. When the cat kneads me, I have little cat-paw-shaped black-and-blue marks. You didn't bargain for that," and he said, "No. I used to look in the mirror and think, If she's dead, think what she missed, all the cancer scares, the debates over face-lifts, the children who drive you crazy."

I said, "Please, she's my sister," and he said, "*Was* your sister," and I said, "*Is* my sister," and he looked at me and said, "Well, we don't know, do we? It's better if we don't know."

Twenty-six forever. No, I didn't think of her that way. She aged as I aged. Wherever she was, she grew older day by day in my mirror.

"All right," he said, pulling up in front of a store. "You go buy something to wear and I'll go to the hardware store. We'll meet back at the café near the railway station. O.K.?"

"Fine," I said.

A couple of pairs of slacks and three or four blouses—what else did I need?

It wouldn't take me long. One pair of gray slacks, one pair of black. It was cool in the store, elegant and strange, with headless mannequins painted silver or black in various postures. Some loosely knit cotton tops, fine, wonderful. And then I saw the pile of silk shirts, such beautiful colors, jade greens, scarlets, deep burgundies, purples, oranges, yellows. I picked out four and on an impulse asked the saleswoman if they made these shirts for men and she said, *Regardez, madame,* and I looked at the pile of men's shirts, grays and crimsons, blues and yellows, and I said, And this one, and I picked up a crimson shirt and added it to the others and handed the shirts to her.

When I left, I'd leave this shirt on his pillow.

I paid for everything and then went back out into the heat that grew heavier and thicker with each step I took and walked slowly toward the train station and the café. Jack was already there, sitting at a table beneath a red and white awning, and when he saw me he picked up a straw hat with an enormous brim and half waved it at me, half fanned himself with it. "You needed a hat," he said as I walked up to the table. It was the kind of hat I liked best. "I knew you'd like it," he said. "Guess how?"

"I have something for you too," I said. "But it's a surprise—for later."

"A going-away present?"

"Something like that," I said.

"HOW DO YOU feel about adventure?" Jack asked me the next day, and I said I was being adventurous enough, wasn't I? Simply coming here.

Jack said he hadn't done any canyon climbing in two years, maybe three, and I had no idea how beautiful it was to climb into a ravine and sit there watching the green river way below. "But you'll be afraid, won't you?" he said. "After everyone wrote about how she might have fallen into a canyon."

"Or been pushed," I said.

"Don't come," he said, "if you're frightened of me."

I said I'd never climbed a mountain in my life. I tripped over my own feet. And he said he knew an easy path. We wouldn't go all the way to the bottom, just far enough to be out of sight of the road, just far enough to be surrounded by those ancient rocks. "You'll like it," he said. "Once I found a hawk's skeleton and once a skeleton of a fox." I said I didn't know why he'd want to climb down into a boneyard, and he looked at me and shook his head. "It's the pure world there, Doris," he said. "Everything stripped to essentials. It's amazing how beautiful the essentials can be."

"All right," I said. "Let's go."

"Early tomorrow morning," he said. "I'll buy some bread in Lumière and we'll take cheese sandwiches and chocolate. You won't be sorry."

The next day, before the sun came up, we were driving to the canyon, and when the sun rose, the sky went rose-colored and pale yellow, and then it was another brilliant blue day, and hot. I asked Jack, "Doesn't it ever rain here? Doesn't the sky ever go gray? How can you live in a place like this? If you're gray and gloomy and the sky's always blue? How can you be depressed in peace here?"

"You close all the shutters and you keep them closed," Jack said.

When we got to the canyon, Jack said, "This is where we climb down," and I looked down to the river below and it was so far away it might have been in another world.

"I don't know if I can do it," I said, and Jack said, "The first step's the hard one. Because you think you're going to fall, but after that, it's as easy as going down steps. I'll go first. You come after."

"Someone's going to come here and go home and say, 'I saw the most lovely human skeleton,' " I said, and then I stepped over the edge, and the ground, which had seemed to slope away so sharply, was not very steep.

"You see?" Jack said. "Would I lie to you?"

"Probably."

"We're not going very far. Ten more feet and then there's a flat place. We'll stay there."

It was beautiful. All around us gray rocks veined with black reared and plunged as if they were still alive. Gnarled trees grew out of what appeared to be solid rock. Bright blue wildflowers grew out of rocks and between rocks, and brilliant pink flowers also.

"Look at those red flowers," I said. "I'm going to get them," and I started to stand up, but Jack stopped me.

"Stay here," he said. "It's not safe farther down. Farther down you have to know what you're doing."

We sat in silence, looking across the ravine and down to the river. Every so often, I felt Jack's eyes on me and I looked up and smiled, and when he saw something that interested him, I found myself staring at him. How familiar that face seemed, as if I'd always known it, as if I'd lived with him every day of my adult life, as if I'd watched him age day by day.

He looked over at me and said, "You're watching me," and I said, "I suppose I am."

"Florence used to watch me. It was amazing, how long she could stare without blinking. Like a cat."

"We both do it," I said. "Once, I had dry eyes, and when I went to the doctor, he examined me and said, 'You don't blink often enough. Tell your sister you should both blink more.' My mother said she didn't know why we had to pay such quacks. All the same, he was right."

"I've never been sick. Ever. I'm doomed to a long life."

"Doomed?"

"Doomed."

Just then the shadow of a hawk passed over my lap and then over Jack's shirt.

"Did you ever really love her?" I asked him.

"I knew we'd get around to her sooner or later."

"Tell me what she was like."

"She was greedy, your sister, about everything—food, sex; a great devourer, that was what she called herself. She was greedy about *me*. She used to look at me as if I were her next meal. I used to wake up in the middle of the night and she'd tell me how beautiful I was. She'd been lying there, propped up, watching me. She said she adored me. She said she worshiped me."

"Did you like it?"

"I liked it. How often do you find someone who looks at you and thinks you're perfect? You don't know you're doing it, but you're always waiting for someone like that. Everyone is. In the beginning, I was embarrassed, but I got over it. No one can ever be praised enough.

"She said she wanted to be faithful to someone forever but had never thought she could be. She thought she could be faithful to me. You know, Doris, I didn't like that word: *faithful*. Not then. I said I wasn't ready to be faithful, and she said, 'You are, you are,' and she laughed at me and said, '*Struggle!* You're not getting away from me.' Well, I didn't, did I?"

I knew all this. I'd read what he'd written soon after he met her.

"I knew what I had there," he said. "I knew she'd die to protect me, not that I needed protecting. I knew she would study me like a text. I knew she'd learn me like a language. I knew there was nothing I couldn't ask her for. It was like living in a folk tale. She'd grant whatever wishes I made. So I should have been happy. I shouldn't have been what I was—claustrophobic. But I *was* claustrophobic. You know, Doris, I don't like talking about this, not to you."

"Why? Because I'm her sister?"

"I don't know why."

"You said you were claustrophobic?"

"You're not going to let me off the hook on this, are you?"

"No."

"Look, right from the beginning, I knew how it would turn out. We had arguments about the way we slept in bed. I never could breathe when someone else's face was close to mine, but that didn't stop her. I'd end up with her nose pressed into my cheek. And your sister! She didn't move when she slept! In the morning, she'd wake up in the same position she was in when she fell asleep. But I'd move during the night, and she took it as a betrayal. So I knew what was coming. She'd want to know why I moved away from her. I'd get up and I'd spend half an hour reassuring her before breakfast.

"I *knew*. One day she'd say, 'But when we first met, you were so wonderful. You always had such patience. You bought me little gifts.' She'd go on like that until I'd be jealous of the person I used to be! One day I'd lose my temper and tell her, 'If you like him so much, what are you doing with me?'

"Well, it would be ridiculous, wouldn't it? You're laughing. I *knew* it was coming. It always happened. One morning she'd wake up and look at me differently and I'd be my own rival."

"You can't know these things in advance," I said.

"But I did. Everything happened the way I knew it would happen. My sister used to call the girls who followed after me the Enraptured. They'd all take one look at me and say they wanted children. Florence said she didn't want them, and I thought, Terrific, wonderful, someone who wants to wander the world with me. But I *knew* in the end she'd be like all the others. One day she'd be sitting there slowly twirling her spaghetti on her fork, and she'd look up at me and say, 'I want a child who looks just like you.' They all did. She'd say, 'Let's have a child. A child wouldn't be so bad. One who looked like you.' But I *never* looked at one of *them* and thought, I want a child who looks just like *you*. Well, not then, not right away."

"But you asked her to marry you."

"I did, didn't I?"

"Why? If you were so sure it wouldn't work out."

"Oh, I asked myself that. I wasn't even sure I loved her. I used to ask myself, 'Do you love her?' Someone said if I had to ask, the answer was no. I was going to tell her I had to leave for Europe. I could have told her I had a fatal illness. I could have left and not come back. I *should* have. I should have left her alone. Well, I knew the end at the beginning, that was the worst thing. But then who was to say I *did* know what was coming? Maybe I only thought I knew.

"It was *possible* I loved her. I didn't know. I didn't know if I'd ever loved anyone. And I was obsessed. She wasn't the only one who was obsessed. I wanted her. It was as simple as that. The passion she had! It's irresistible, that kind of thing. And I proposed to her and I didn't say I loved her and she didn't ask me if I did. She took it for granted. That was the most remarkable thing. She was so certain.

"I *never* thought it would last. Was it such a sin? What I did? Asking her to marry me if I didn't believe it would last? Well, you know you can talk yourself into anything. I told myself it was better to marry knowing what was coming. I could prepare myself. I could prepare her. It was *better* she couldn't see the future. It was enough that one of us could. So I took what I wanted. *I* was what she wanted. I thought she'd be happy now, and later she'd think it was worth it, you know, to have married the man she loved. We'd have happy memories. It made sense to me."

"It makes a kind of sense," I said. "Especially since no one really knows what's coming."

"Well, I didn't know," he said. "I never thought I'd fall in love with her. I never thought *I'd* want to have children. The miscarriage nearly killed *me*. You never do know, do you? Love. The one truly unknowable subject. Along with marriage, of course, but it's all part of the same thing."

"Isn't that hawk coming down awfully close?" I asked him.

"No; they're curious birds. Don't worry."

"We could stay here," I said, "until we were piles of white bones."

"Not a bad idea," he said.

The hawk was flying in smaller and smaller circles, coming lower, his eye on us. Jack picked up a large stick and settled it on his lap. "Sometimes they're so hungry they lose their minds," he said. "I'll get him if he comes too close."

"You said not to worry," I said.

"You don't have to worry. I'll take care of the hawk. If he needs taking care of."

We sat still, watching the great bird. I could see the colors of its feathers—gray and brown. And I could see its talons.

"What would I have to do to keep you here?" Jack asked suddenly.

I watched the circling bird. "Oh," I said. "Nothing much. Just erase this world and start the whole thing over again."

"Erase this world. What a good idea," he said.

"If we were in a painting, we could wave our arms and get the artist's attention and he'd fix things for us."

"Or paint over us."

"With thick black paint."

"So it's not possible?"

"You tell me," I said.

"It's not possible," he said. "But it's too bad, isn't it?"

"Is it my imagination, or is that bird going back up?"

"A hawk deserves to be called a hawk, not a bird."

"Is the *hawk* going back up?"

"It is. It knows we've already been eaten," Jack said.

"We are not eaten," I said.

"Are you ready to go back?" Jack asked me, and I said I was.

It was a short climb to the rim of the canyon and when we got there Jack took my hand and pulled me up and we got into the car.

"We are white bones lying there," Jack said. "It's a nice thought, isn't it? The two of us together. Visited by other mad people, inspected by mad hawks."

He turned the key in the ignition, reversed, turned the car around, and we were on our way back to Goult.

Was it the hawk above us, circling? Was it the white pile of bones Jack said we could become? Whatever it was, we were not the same that night, in Jack's bed. In the bed that used to be his bed and my sister's, I grabbed him by the hair on both sides of his head and licked his lips and eyebrows. I nibbled at his lips. I bit into his chin. I lay down on top of him and pushed into him until I knew he felt my pelvic bones, and he said, "You must stay up at night filing those, they're so sharp," and I said I wanted to push against him so hard that my rib cage went through his skin and our ribs intermeshed. Yes, that was what I wanted, and he laughed, he sounded gleeful, he grabbed me by my hair and slid me off and pushed me down and lay on top of me, and he was beautiful, he was the most beautiful thing I'd ever seen, and I said, again and again, *Bodies, bodies,* and it was a chant, it was a kind of music, it was as if we were in water, were weightless, had done this hundreds of times before, knew what to do, and yet it was new, it was surprising, it was as if it were the first time, it was as if it would always be like this, as if it would never stop, as if we would spend the rest of our lives in this bed. *Bodies, bodies,* I said, laughing softly, and Jack said, *Bodies, bodies, oh, yes, bodies,* and he laughed and I laughed, and the moonlight streamed in the window and I knew we would fall asleep in the moonlight and the moonlight would fall on us like a blessing.

"You are so perfect," he said.

"No, you are so perfect," I said. "You are. Absolutely perfect." And he said, "Don't argue," and we began again and then we lay next to each other, our faces close together, breathing in each other's breaths, and he said, "You're violent, you're wonderful, you are, Doris, don't go. Stay. I'll learn your body, inch by inch," and I pretended to be asleep. I pretended to sleep and I reveled in my body, I knew every cell, I knew every nerve, and I heard him whisper, "Doris, what a wonderful name: Doris." But I was not Doris, I was not Florence, I was some new person, some third person, I should rename myself, I should have a new name, and finally I heard him breathing deeply and regularly and I stayed awake, I shook my head to stay awake.

I belonged to myself and my body. I was going to stay awake and enjoy it. But of course I fell asleep.

And so it went on and it was marvelous and I belonged to myself and I knew I was changed and every day I called my answering machine and checked for messages, and if the Impostor called, I ignored the messages, although his voice was becoming more and more forlorn, and if my husband called, I called him in Prague when I knew he wouldn't be there and left a message for him, and I never said I was in France. I never mentioned Goult. I didn't want to lie. I said the weather was impossible, and it was, it was so hot.

CHAPTER

THIRTY-SIX

JACK," I said in the morning. The blinds held back the thickening sunlight, the buzzing, lavender-scented heat.

"You're going home. Aren't you? When?"

"Tomorrow."

"I'll drive you to the airport. We don't want another Meek getting lost on the road in Provence."

"You don't have to. I've got the rental car. I'm a good driver."

"We'll turn the car in today in Apt, and I'll drive you tomorrow. No arguments, right?"

"Right," I said.

"Can you imagine if something happened to you? What people would do to me? I'd have to cut my throat."

"We'll write. As they say at the end of summer camp."

"Of course we'll write."

"What will you do now?"

"All the usual things. And you'll go back to your café and talk to Eva and Dennis."

"What else?"

"Let's go take the car back. Bring your hat, bring your sunglasses. I'll bring the water."

"You really don't have to bother."

"I want to. I want to see you get on that plane."

"No more mysterious disappearances?"

"No."

"All right," I said. "That's fair enough."

He asked me later that night, Why are you going? I said, Because life isn't infinitely revisable, like a story, and because I am not my own work of art. And he said maybe life was revisable, maybe it was only middle-class blinders that made me think I had to finish my life as I began it, the way some people believed they had to finish every book they began. "Do you finish every book you begin?" he asked me.

I said, "As a matter of fact, I do." He said Florence never worried about finishing a book. No, if she didn't like the book she was reading, she'd throw it across a room, and if no one picked it up, there it stayed until she found a use for it as a paperweight.

I said Florence hadn't set an example the rest of us wanted to follow, had she? Once, Florence and I both believed in responsibility and duty. I still believed in them although no one would guess that, watching how I was behaving now. No doubt I'd feel guilty enough later.

"You're tired," he said. "Aren't you tired?" and I said he could see what would happen. We couldn't talk very long without blaming one another. Really, it was inevitable, and then I started to laugh and he asked me what I was laughing at and I said I was remembering Dennis and the way he looked when we started fighting at the kitchen table, and Jack said, "I liked him, I read that book of his three times. He reminded me of someone, one of my cousins, probably, but he'd be like the rest of them in the end, wouldn't he? A hyena in a graveyard, pawing at the earth under a head-stone. He wanted the two of us together. Well, it was the closest he'd get to seeing me with Florence. That's what they all want, isn't it, a ringside seat, raised voices, tears, maybe a little blood on the tablecloth, maybe a plate smashed on the floor, maybe her black eye or my scratched cheek—you know, the real thing. He got a glimpse of it."

"He's not so bad. His motives are good. He loves her paintings."

"He loves *her.* It doesn't disturb him that he's never met her. No, why should it? He thinks, If she'd married *me,* she'd be here today. It's what they all think. It's what you think—if she married someone else, she'd be walking around. I'm the only man on the planet who doesn't think, If she married me, she'd be here today. Because I'm the one she *did* marry."

"Do you honestly think," I asked slowly, "do you really believe the same thing would have happened no matter who she married?"

"She picked me. I was what she wanted."

"And you only gave her what she wanted?"

"Didn't you? When she wanted you out of her life, didn't you go? As long as she lived, did anyone *ever* resist her?"

THEY ARE SITTING in the window seat, my mother and Florence, Florence on her lap, and my mother holds a glass to Florence's mouth and Florence drinks. Her mouth tightens and her eyes open wide and I know the lemonade is sour. I taste the lemonade as if I were drinking it. I would believe I was drinking it if my mouth weren't still dry. Don't drink it all, leave some for Doris, my mother says, and Florence looks over at me, her eyes narrowed. She puts her hands up to the glass and my mother says, No, save some for Doris. Doris, come here. And I am happy to have what's left in the glass.

Florence comes first, Florence is the oldest, Florence has the first turn, Florence is the first to hear the stories. She goes into my mother's room at night when the thunder rattles the windowpanes. She says, I'll be quiet, I won't make any noise. My mother moves over to let her in, she pulls the covers up over Florence's shoulder, she puts her arm around her. The lightning turns the sky grayish violet in the window downstairs. In a few minutes I will creep onto the foot of my mother's bed. It has to be done this way. We've never discussed it, but we know. If I came in first, my mother would say, Doris, it's only a rainstorm, go back to bed.

"SHE WAS the favorite," I said to him.

"Aren't you tired?" he asked me again, and I said, Yes, I am tired, and I began reciting:

> The Rices are priceless,
> They are, they are,
> Wherever one is,
> The other's not far.
>
> Today one's the shadow,
> The next day the sun,
> And if they are two,
> Yet still they are one.
>
> But I am not she
> And she is not me
> And though years go by
> We still will not be—
>
> Although God has lashed us
> Two birds to one tree.

"I wrote that," I said, "when I was ten."

"Lashed to one tree," he said, looking at me.

"Lashed to one tree," I said.

"Of course you have to go home," he said.

IT WAS still dark in the morning when the alarm went off, and the air was still cool, almost cold. When I came down to the kitchen, I found a tray of rolls, a small platter of bitter chocolate, and a saucepan filled with instant coffee.

"Don't try to pour that," Jack said. "There's a trick to it. Here."

I picked up a piece of chocolate, and when I next looked, I'd eaten my way through most of the platter.

"Well, that should keep you going," he said. "There's enough caffeine in there to keep you sparkling."

I didn't know what to say and so I said nothing.

"Whenever you're ready," he said, and when I got up, he nodded and we went upstairs. He took my suitcase and we went out to the car. Water drops like crystal beads glittered on its hood. I said again that I'd never seen anything as beautiful as this car, and Jack looked at me thoughtfully, opened the door for me, and I got in. "Fasten the seat belt," he said.

Was I going to spend the rest of my life listening to people telling me to fasten my seat belt?

"Oh!" I said, unfastening the belt. "I forgot something! Is the house locked?"

"It's not locked. Tell me what you want and I'll get it."

"No, no!" I said. "It's a surprise."

I ran back up the stone steps, back into the living room, past the White Paintings, which I hadn't looked at since I'd come—it's amazing what you can block out—up a flight of steps to the bedroom and opened the bottom drawer of what had been my dresser. In it was the silk shirt I had bought for Jack in Cavaillon. I took the red shirt and laid it on his pillow.

The brilliant scarlet silk was beautiful and festive against the cream-colored pillowcase.

"Everything taken care of?" Jack asked me, starting the car.

"All done," I said, fastening my seat belt.

CHAPTER

THIRTY-SEVEN

THE TROUBLE WAS, as Jack had a character say in one of his plays, a woman cannot go to her grave with a secret. I had to tell someone before I went home. So the time in Goult would be real. So it would not seem so strange to have gone. So completely mad.

People need a mirror when they feel uncertain, do something odd, something they didn't expect. They say to themselves, This isn't like me. What's happening to me? Why did I do that? Am I a little mad, am I losing my mind? If they look down at their hands and find them unfamiliar, if a picture crooked on a wall makes them dizzy, makes the room tip and tilt, then they go to the mirror and there they are, familiar and substantial as always, the eyes the color they've always been (blue), the face the same shape (triangular); the wild, curling hair (black), the cheekbones (high), the eyebrows, the mouth, the lines from each side of the nose to the corner of the mouth (faint)—all the same; the eyelashes, the eye sockets (deep), the shape of the eyes (enormous and round, a baby's eyes, a baby's startled eyes) . . . what an inventory they take, and how quickly.

And how quickly they're reassured, talking to their faces in the mirror, the beings they *feel* themselves to be, there in the mirror, saying, Why the fuss? I'm here, you see I'm here, I don't change. Don't think about it, that momentary rippling, a disturbance of the surface of the pool, everyone suffers it—a slight tear in the fabric of life. Here I am, looking back at you, nothing's changed, you see nothing's changed. Go back to work. Go back to what you were doing. Make a phone call. You can always come back to me.

When I was in college, I worked as an attendant in a ladies' lounge. I

348

had a talent for making myself invisible (people like me do); I saw women come in, sit down on the upholstered stools in front of gilt mirrors, and stare at themselves, eyes wide, drinking themselves in. When they first came and sank onto the bench or the stool, they often trembled, shook. They were pale. Not only their cheeks but their faces sagged, as if they'd just witnessed an accident, just *been* in an accident, and they had. They'd collided with the stony knowledge that they didn't know who they were. But as they sat on that stool, unaware of me—or perhaps they were aware, but I was so unimportant compared to the face they saw in the mirror, compared to what the face in the mirror was saying to them—they were as important as they'd always known themselves to be, as beautiful as they needed to be, solid, substantial. It was *this* face, looking out of the mirror, that mattered, *this* face that knew their value, this face that gave blessing and benediction, this face that said, You are the one who matters, the only one who matters.

I watched them reconstruct their faces. I watched them gaze into their own mirrory eyes, and their eyes began to sparkle; I watched them apply lipstick, leaning forward, appearing bent on kissing themselves in the mirror. I watched them thrust their heads forward. I watched them bring their chins forward, lift them slightly, as if they were looking up at their beloved. In the mirror, the outline of the chin grew firmer, the skin of the neck stretched tighter. They looked younger, they grew younger before my eyes.

I saw them nod at themselves in the mirror, as if listening to the face saying something important: *Everything will be fine, look how beautiful you are. If anything goes wrong, come back here. I'll make it right. I'm always here.*

And when they had enough of this, when their vanity was once more smooth and fat and unpunctured, when they sat up straight, serene and confident and beautiful, then they would notice me in the corner, in my black uniform and white apron. Then their eyes would narrow. Then their vanity would pierce them. Then they would get up and stalk past me as if to say, What is *she* doing here? What business does *she* have here? Doesn't anyone understand that a woman in front of a mirror wants privacy?

And the most fragile of them, the ones barely held together by the mirror's shiny glue, they would not put a quarter on my little tray. After all, it was my fault I'd seen how their hands trembled, how they shook their heads when they first looked in the mirror. It was my fault I saw how they talked to themselves, how they argued themselves back into confidence and beauty—in those moments when the mirror was more important than their vanity.

But now they were once again themselves and vain and now they were angry. And the more arrogant ones, the more confident ones, they would drop a quarter onto my tray—without looking at me, as if they didn't know I was there but assumed I was there, as if I were a piece of newspaper on the street they stepped over in their shining sharp high heels.

Once, I had a mirror who spoke to me. Once, I did not need to look at a mirror on the wall.

"W E L L, there you are," Eva said, sitting down. "I've looked for you every day, but no Doris bent over a newspaper. I said to myself, The country is impoverished, isn't it, if she's gone, but surely she'll be back, she has to come back.

"Well, I took an afternoon off. I've been feeding the pigeons on the heath and watching the herons. I think I even saw a fox, a beautiful brown fox—they come all the way down from the heath at night. Sometimes we see them on the stone wall at the back of the garden. It is getting colder, isn't it? The days aren't lasting as long, are they? Early darkness, Doris. It means more the older you get, I can tell you. You're very brown!"

"I went to Provence," I said, and I began to tell her what had happened, and then I realized I was leaving something out.

"I'm a twin," I said suddenly.

"You're not a twin, you're an only child," Eva said. "I decided that the first day I saw you: She's an only child. Of course you are, so sure of yourself, so self-contained. They're always recognizable, only children. I know you spoke of a sister, but I dismiss her. I don't believe in her!"

"But I am a twin, and my sister's name is Florence. Florence Meek."

Eva stared at me, her mouth open, and then her hand flew to her lips. "My God!" she said. "You look like her! She's your sister? That painter? The one who disappeared?"

"She's my sister."

"Then that man you went to see is that playwright? Jack Pine? Don't they say he murdered your sister?"

"He didn't murder her."

"Well, they never arrested him, they would have done if he'd committed murder, even here they arrest men who murder their wives. Good Lord! Florence Meek! Your sister! You do look like her! I knew your face was familiar, but I thought it was only that I liked you. When you like someone, they seem familiar to you, beautiful! I suppose you don't want to talk about her. People never want to talk about famous family members, do they?"

"I always thought we were just the same, but I suppose it wasn't true, it never has been true," I said.

"And her husband?" Eva asked me. "Did you like him?"

"Oh," I said. "I liked him altogether too much."

"Altogether too much. I see."

"A disgrace to my sex."

"We're all disgraces to our sex, we just don't admit it."

I smiled happily at her. "I've always been so good," I said.

"What a terrible burden it is, being good. But now! Look how pleased with yourself you are! Aren't you? But let me tell you something: when you go home, don't breathe a word of this, don't decide to confess; it won't do you any good, it won't do anyone any good. Don't act like a Catholic going into confession. No one forgives you for confessions. Let some time pass. It will all become a dream; my childhood in Serbia seems like a dream—well, it is a dream, I only remember it properly when I'm asleep. Tell yourself it's a dream. We don't have to feel guilty about our dreams. We don't sin in our hearts—what nonsense that all is. You're not Catholic, are you? No? Thank goodness for that! You just keep quiet about it."

"That man you've seen me talking to in here? He's a reporter."

"A reporter! For God's sake don't tell him! I know you think he's your friend, I could see that when you talked to him, but you must never, never tell a reporter the truth! They must take some kind of terrible oath as babies. Look what they've done to the royal family. No, don't tell him anything!"

"I won't tell him about running amok. It's probably overrated, anyway."

"Oh, you don't believe that for a minute, you know you don't," Eva said. "Most of the time we can't run amok, but every now and then! Certainly every now and then!"

I said I felt as if I didn't recognize myself, as if I'd left my sanity somewhere. *Unfaithful*. What a word.

"It's a terrible shock to find yourself doing what you want to do, isn't it?" Eva said. "I've always envied the way cats can rip off a mouse's head without the least sign of guilt. You'll feel less mad tomorrow and even less mad the day after."

"We'll see," I said. "I hope so."

"I *know* so," Eva said. "I'm older than you are. I've had more experience, especially in running amok. Would you like a chicken sandwich? I would. I'll be right back." She got up and came back with two plates.

She patted me happily on the arm. I was wearing the red silk shirt I'd bought in Cavaillon. Eva looked at me sadly and said, "Now that we know each other so well, you'll probably be going home, won't you? London is a wonderful city for temporary émigrés, not so wonderful if you have to stay on forever, but you'll be coming back, won't you?"

"I certainly will be coming back," I said. "You and this café, it really does become the center of the universe, doesn't it?"

"When you're in Provence, calling on in-laws, yes," Eva said. "Really, I'm proud of you. I didn't do better myself when I was young."

"Look at the light," I said, pointing at the café window. "Look at all that leaf shade and shadow. It really is the most wonderful place," and Eva said this café was like a fever thermometer. If you thought it was beautiful, you were in fine fettle, but if you were sour and cold, you saw every crack in the paint, you noticed every patch of rust on the water pipes going up the wall and across the ceiling. You saw the scuff marks on the linoleum. You paid attention to the gloomy conferences in corners after the Serbian papers came in. You noticed who was holding a paper up against his nose so no one would see him. You opened the paper to diatribes about the falling economy. You went on and on about a class society. Yes, when you were unhappy, you noticed all these things. "I notice them far too often myself," Eva said.

"You decide to be happy: someone told me that once," I said. "Do you believe it?" I was thinking about Antonio and what I was going to do about him.

"Some people can. Of course they can. They decide to be happy and they spend all their energy seeing to it that no gloomy thought passes through their heads, but do they ever think an interesting thought? I don't know. Can you think, 'Everything I'm doing now can be wiped out tomorrow, all my heart has to do is skip a few beats and that's the end of me,' and be happy? Show me a person who can do that and I'll show you a very happy and very boring person. But of course, you should try. You should try everything. As our mothers used to say to us when we turned up our noses at the pickled beets and the horseradish."

"It is," I said, "the most beautiful café."

Eva looked from table to table. A bright-red bus was stopping across the street.

She said, "It's not bad."

I WAS PULLING my suitcase down and starting to pack when the doorbell rang. It was Antonio, and I went to the window and threw down the keys. It was almost midnight. When he opened the door, he strode past me and walked over to the window and stood still, staring out at the hospital.

"What's wrong?" I asked him.

"Nothing. Absolutely *nothing!* It's what I should have expected."

I said I didn't have any idea of what he was talking about.

"I went to Provence," he said. "To see *him*. Well, when you were gone, I thought, Who's left? He was the only one left. So I went. He wasn't happy to see me."

"Just how did he show his unhappiness?"

"Well, he heard me out. I told him I thought I was his son and he went all red and he picked me up—he *picked me up*—and threw me across the garden. *Then* he said, 'Now get out of here before I turn the dogs loose on you.'"

"He didn't hurt you, did he? I warned you about the dogs."

"It wasn't much help, that warning," he said gloomily.

I couldn't help smiling. "I tried to tell you. I didn't think he'd believe you. I didn't think he could face up to something that enormous."

"Enormous?"

"Well, it *is* an enormous thing to have a child."

"I don't think I'm his," Antonio said, and started to cry.

"Well, of course you could be someone else's," I said. "We don't really know what my sister was up to in those days." I was trying to be helpful.

"You mean, if she was a whore, I might have the good luck to be someone's bastard?"

"I think you should calm down."

"I thought," he said, "I thought he'd look at me and . . ."

"And what? And what?"

"At least he'd *listen* to me. I thought if he cared about her, he'd want to know what became of her. Even if he didn't care about me!"

"Really, if you want to talk to Jack Pine, you should go with Dennis. He's very fond of Dennis. He trusts him. I shouldn't have let you go alone. I should have *known* you'd go. I really hoped you'd talk to me before you tried to see him."

"And what could you have done?"

"I don't know, really."

"But he didn't throw *you* out."

"Of course not! All he had to do was look at me and he knew I was who I said I was."

"I don't look like him," Antonio said. *"At all."*

"You look more like me," I said. "I think." His eyes were closing. His hand seemed to be twitching, and I placed my hand over it. He sighed and shook his head. "Go to sleep," I said. I was thankful no one was here to see him. God knew what someone else would make of it. And if I told the truth and said he was my nephew who was *almost* my son, everyone would be certain we were up to no good.

I watched him sleep, and I decided, I'll keep him. As if he were a pair of shoes I'd just bought but thought about returning, or a puppy, and then I realized that I meant it and that I fully intended to keep him. I thought, This will be interesting, explaining him to my husband.

Better late than never.

When he opened his eyes, I said, "I want you to come to America with me," I said. "I'm leaving in a week."

"I can't come right away," he said. "I have papers to finish up at university, but I'll come as soon as I'm done."

"Plan on spending a long time," I said. "Bring Rose. We have an unbelievable number of family albums. At least," I said, "I won't have to declare you when I go through customs."

"Your sense of humor," he said, "it takes getting used to," and I said, "We have years and years." Really, I had never felt so fortunate.

LATE AT NIGHT, something woke me—as if someone had called my name—and I was awake immediately, listening, but the house was quiet. Naturally it was quiet; my landlady and her husband must have gone to bed long ago. I got up and went to the window. The oak tree in the garden next door was illuminated by the bright light that went on automatically every night, and there the leaves were, floating in the neony glow, their veins traced black on the air. And then I saw the couple, in the corner where two garden walls met, the woman pressed against the man, her arms around his neck, his arms around her, clasped together over the small of her back. Would they move? It didn't seem as if they would ever move. Did they sense me, there at the window, watching?

Wonderful, a couple in the silent garden, in the middle of the night. Wonderful how you know immediately that they're young, very young.

From the street came the sound of high heels striking against the concrete, astonishingly loud, the sound a horse would make clop-clopping down the road. Why didn't these walkers in the night wake up the entire neighborhood? And then I thought, Every night at all hours people have been walking by, their heels striking hard against stone, another lover going home, afraid of the dark and walking fast, another character in a sad story that might take a turn for the better, why not, but I was sound asleep and didn't hear them, so much life going on all around and you're asleep or busy or too preoccupied to take notice.

I saw that the couple had heard the person walking in the street. They moved slightly apart, tilted their heads and listened, and when the sound of footsteps died away, became a faint *click, click,* they moved together again.

Was there anything we did, no matter how small, that didn't affect someone else?

I went to the closet and began to take out clothes. I threw down on the bed anything I didn't expect to wear in the next few days, and then I began folding sweaters and blouses and skirts until I was sitting on the edge of an orderly pyramid of clothes, and I was tired and I thought, I'll lie down for a minute, just for a minute, and then I'll finish this and I won't have to face it in daylight—the evidence that I'm leaving.

The foxes that came down from the heath, the eight peacocks I'd once seen in England's Lane, looking for their front door, the enormous window of the café, embroidered with trembling silver beads . . . it was an enchanted world here, Florrie, wasn't it? The smell of lavender outside your windows in Goult, the bees fatter than my thumb, the scorpion who lived beneath the trash can, the rose-colored castles clinging to the edge of gray and rose-colored cliffs, the hawk floating on the air currents beneath us . . . it's beautiful, Florrie, isn't it? We could decide to be happy.

And there is Antonio. I've decided to keep him.

And Mrs. Mudd said, I'll collect fireflies for you but not for your sister, she's too sour, she *had* said that to Florence, after all, not to me. No, what she had said to me was, You're too quiet. Right, Florrie? And I heard her answering. I heard her quite distinctly. *Right, Doris. Who's been sleeping in my bed?* she said. *Who's been sleeping in my bed?* And I said, *Not you,* and she said sadly, *Not me,* and my eyes opened and for I moment I didn't know where I was. Was I in Goult? Was I back in my Manhattan apartment? Where was I? And of course Florence wasn't there.

The ringing phone awakened me. I was asleep flat on my back, tangled in streamers of sunlight. It was Dennis, just back from the United States. "Can I come talk to you?" Dennis asked. "It's important." And I thought, this is where I came in, he is how it all began, he is how I found Antonio. He is how I found Jack, how I found more than I ever expected to have, this is how I started finding things and stopped losing them. And yet, even now, thinking of him, I was enormously impatient.

"When do you want to come over?" I asked him, and he said right away.

"Give me an hour," I said. "I'm still half asleep. Bring some coffee. You hate the way I make coffee."

And then the phone rang again and this time it was my husband.

"Should I come to get you?" he asked. "We could spend a few days together, instead of your going home next week."

"Going home next week? Yes, I'm going home next week. Is this ESP?"

"You left a message on the answering machine," he said. "Don't you remember?"

"Actually, I don't."

"Well, someone did, and she had your voice."

"No, no, I'll just go home and we'll go somewhere once you're back. Is that all right?"

"That's fine." His silver-framed picture watched me from the mantel. I'd just put it up there last night. He'd become real again—last night. So you wake, from one dream into another.

"I'll call again in the morning," he said. "Or call me before you leave. You can give me all the details then."

All the details.

"Is it very hot there?" I asked.

"Very."

"I'll see you in a few days, then."

It was a long conversation, really, although no one listening to us would have thought so. What a terrible waste of time it must be, bugging the phones of people long married, when all the important exchanges go on in silence, in the pauses between words.

After I hung up, I thought back to when I first came to London, a childless woman, a woman who had trouble staying awake, and I remembered how I had felt then, as if my life were painted on glass, so fragile, trying to remember that once I had seemed so substantial to myself, my wrist as solid as a thick bough of wood, the pulse beneath the skin inevitable and strong, but that was so long ago, so far away, I thought I could never feel that again.

And still, even then, I knew I had reached that place, not a place, but a point, really, toward which I had been heading always, and it was like sailing at night under a full moon, as if I had been doing that for years, the journey going on beneath everything, and I always unaware of it, knowing, somehow, the destination, knowing it better than I knew the daily landscape of my familiar life. As if I had two minds: one buzzing with husband and family and daily events, the other without content, about water and the direction of water, colorless too, like black water, constantly moving, but moving where?

And it seems to me that I have always been like this—until now. I was always listening for something. A note? A high sound? Something that means the curtain is going up, finally going up.

These last few months had been like snowy days in Peru when you set out and you're not sure you see a flake of snow but you think you do, and then you see a flake drifting lazily down, and after you've walked for a while, the snow begins to fall, still slowly, and you walk farther and the wind picks up and blows the snow at you in slanting lines and you begin to notice the sidewalk and the road sparkling with snow, and now the snow is blowing horizontally, coming straight at you, directly into your face and eyes. And when the wind blows like that, the snow intends to keep falling.

And you keep walking and soon you can't make out the houses across the road or the trees. They don't seem important, the world is so different. What's important is the snow, how it falls, how it transforms everything, how the world looks in that instant, a way it will never look again. And you reach the general store and go inside and the window is white, huge clots of snow forming on the glass, then sliding down slowly in eccentric paths, and it's warm inside, and dry, but you want to be out in the falling snow and you're not out five minutes before your scarf is covered with snow, and your hair, but you keep going because everything is transformed, the snow has transformed everything. It has transformed you along with everything else.

Well, I have been happy, here in my rented flat, in the café, in Goult. What a name for a town—so like the word *guilt*. I wonder if Florence thought of it. I'm sure she did. She must have loved the countryside, great hills like dripping gray clay, gray-skinned olive trees, tortured by the wind, leaning over the edges of cliffs, those rose-colored towns, the lavender and yellow sunsets. I have been happy and I have been changed and I don't know why.

My bell rang. "It's me—Dennis," he said, and I went to the window and threw my keys out to him, and he came up.

"All right, tell me," I said. "What are you so excited about?" He squirmed in his chair, he crossed his legs, he uncrossed them, he pushed invisible hair back from his eyes. "It can't be that complicated, can it? Just get started. Say anything." A cold wind was blowing in through the window, and he jumped up and closed it. "Good," I said. "Well?" I said. When he still didn't speak, I said, "Has anything happened to Jack? Has anything happened to Antonio?"

"As far as I know, they're both fine," he said gloomily.

"Then what! You said you had to talk to me. About what?"

"I think I know where she is. I think I've seen her."

"Florence?"

"Yes."

"You saw her? You spoke to her?"

"Yes."

"When?"

"Last week."

"And it took you this long to tell me?"

"Well, it's not as simple as it seems, Doris. I'm not *sure* I saw her, well, not while I was awake, not the first time, but when I went back, I was awake."

"Antonio said you had a dream," I said impatiently. And there it was again, the smell of my dreams, wet leaves buried all winter under snow, and now the snow was melting, and the smell of wet leaves filled the room. As if, by telling me he believed he had found her, he was calling her up, causing her to hover in the corner of my room.

"It's not *just* a dream, Doris. The next day I went to look for the house I dreamed about, and there it was. I *saw* it in the dream and then I went to look for it and it was *there*. Just like Jack and Florence and the tame raven."

"Dennis," I said, "mysticism doesn't suit you. You've spent a lot of time driving around Peru. You saw some house or other and then you put it in a dream and you got up and went out and found what you knew was already there. That's all it was, that's all the raven business ever was."

But Three Raven Wood. How did he know about Three Raven Wood? I didn't think I'd told him the name of that place. Had I told him about the bloodhound, the dead couple? I couldn't remember. Why did I sense her, as if she were behind me and might at any instant lightly touch the nape of my neck? Why was I so afraid?

"I'll tell you the dream," he said. "This happened in the dream and then it *really* happened. I went up to the top of a hill. I came out into a clearing, and there was a wooden sign nailed to a tree, saying *Three Raven Wood,* and I saw her. She was higher up. She was older than I was, I could see that right away, thicker in the figure than she used to be. She was wearing a faded cotton dress, grayish purple. Her hair wasn't brushed. From the minute I saw her, I recognized her!"

"And what did she do when she saw *you?* A woman alone on a hilltop, and a perfect stranger starts marching up to her? Calling her, I presume, by her magical name! Florence! I hope it wasn't hunting season, Dennis!"

"She didn't *do* anything, Doris! She said hello and I said hello and I said I was looking for someone and *she* asked *me,* 'Did you find her?' and I said I didn't know."

"Well, that must have reassured her," I said. "What did you say next?"

"I said my mother used to tell me, 'Learn to love the snow,' and she repeated it after me and said that was lovely. And I said it was, because if you learned to love the snow, then you could paint it."

"And she went into the house and called the asylum and said she had a certifiable lunatic on her property."

"Doris!"

"Well, I'm sorry, Dennis. Go on."

"She *did* ask me why I thought she'd want to paint the snow."

"Good," I said, interrupting.

"And I said, 'Because you're Florence Meek.' "

"Tell me, Dennis, *when* does this poor woman call the Sheriff? Or turn her dogs loose?"

"She didn't think I was crazy, Doris! She said, 'Florence Meek? Florence Meek is dead.' "

"And what did *you* say to such a preposterous statement?"

"I said, 'Then you're her double.' "

"I hope she laughed at you."

"She did. She said, 'Her double! All right, come in. There's bean soup and coffee and apple pie.'"

"Bean soup," I said. "And apples taken up from the cellar, no doubt. You must have felt right at home."

"Doris," he said, "I don't like your tone."

"Well, I'm sorry, Dennis. You expected me to jump up and down and say, 'Let's all get in the car and go see Florence'? I don't know if this is a dream you're talking about or if it really happened!"

"Let me finish."

"I'm not stopping you. Be my guest," I said.

"Well, after she cleared the table, she said, 'Look, I know who you think you've found but I don't know why you're looking or how you recognized me.' Then she didn't say anything for a while. Then she said, 'Her double,' and then she said, 'All right,' you know, the way you do when you've made up your mind. Then she asked me, 'How *did* you recognize me?' So I told her I'd aged a photograph of her taken just before she died because I wanted to see what she'd look like now—well, I *did* do that, Doris, before I met you—because I wanted to see what she'd look like if she'd lived to be forty-seven . . . of course, she *did* live to be forty-seven."

"Oh, for heaven's sake," I said. "And did she look just like me?"

"No, not really. But people can change terribly in twenty years' time—you said so yourself."

"Dennis! Florence was my twin! My identical twin! We would still be identical!"

"Not necessarily. Not necessarily at all. If she'd been ill, if she'd spent a lot of time out in the sun, if she'd had surgery."

"If she weren't Florence," I put in.

"Well, she *did* ask me about Jack."

"Doesn't everyone ask you about Jack?"

"Do you want to hear this story or don't you?"

"Go *on*, Dennis." I would have to tell my husband about this, how it felt to see a mind loosing from its moorings as you watched.

"We sat in her parlor—you know, velvet chairs, carved claws on the feet, and there were large pictures of men in tight collars and women with tight, oiled curls. 'Ancestors?' I asked her. She said she had an agent buy them for her at an auction and they came from her grandmother's house. So I asked her if anyone knew where she was, and she said she had a great talent for invisibility."

I sighed. Even Eva wanted to know about Jack Pine, Eva who didn't watch the news because her customers kept her posted, and enough tragedy was enough. "What did you tell her?" I asked him. Not much, I hoped, or we would soon be reading this woman's accounts in the *National Enquirer*. And if he had found a madwoman up there in the hills? Isolated for months on end? Dr. Steiner used to say that nine out of ten of the hill people were completely out of their minds. Probably the woman, whoever she was, didn't *know* who she was, and was only too happy to have Dennis climb up the hill to tell her. She'd have been just as happy if he'd thought she was Cinderella.

It was fading, the smell of wet leaves. My hands weren't shaking. It was no longer necessary for me to keep them, fingers tightly laced, in my lap.

"She knew about you, Doris! She said, 'I left her alone and disappeared. I never read her letters. I did give her up.' And she said, 'I'm sorry, I can't drink hot things. I never could. She couldn't, either.' "

"Meaning me? Doris?"

"She said, 'Sometimes I think, if she hadn't come to Goult, if she hadn't found me, if she hadn't given me a way out, would I have ever left? I might still be there, in prison, feeding crumbs to mice—we had such an interesting collection of white, heavy stones all over the dining room, one day I was sure to pick one up and hurl it at his head and today I'd be wearing stripes."

"Do prisoners wear stripes in France?"

"I don't have the slightest idea. *She* said Jack deserved to be lashed to a cliff while buzzards ate out his liver."

"*That* sounds like Florence," I said. But still—it was true neither one of us could drink hot things or swallow anything very hot. How would Dennis have known that? Or this woman? If she was a woman, and not a figment of his imagination? And then I thought, My mother! She's always had a private nurse! Her mind wandered and she talked to her nurses. Young women, middle-aged women! She might have spoken to this woman—if she was a woman and not a creature in a dream.

"She said he wanted to kill her little by little, with doses of Tobies and Ariadnes and Françoises, but people who take in small doses of poison sometimes become immune."

"Dennis," I said, interrupting him, "did you *tell* her Florence Meek had a twin sister? Did she know that or did you tell her? It's important."

"I don't think I told her I knew she had a twin, no, I don't think I told her that." He flushed. He sounded defensive. "She did go on about the rights of twins, though. She wanted to know why husbands should have any rights to their wives' bodies if their wives were twins. The husband and the wife aren't twins. They aren't related by blood. She thought there ought to be special rights for identical twins. And I told her I saw a picture of Doris's at Dr. Steiner's, a portrait of a young blond girl, and she said, 'Cecilia. The opera singer. I wondered what became of her. I think someone told me she had a hemorrhage of the vocal cords and took up some instrument or other and joined a quartet somewhere in Germany. She looked very German. I might have dreamed it.' "

"People who live in small towns know everything, Dennis, you know that. Probably other people asked Dr. Steiner about that painting. Probably my mother has been busy talking. Dennis, you want to believe you found her! Believe me, I know!"

"She said, 'Vengeance is a thin, rich soup. It doesn't take much to keep you going, but you tire of it all the same. That's why I've hidden myself away here.' "

"She's an eloquent madwoman, anyway."

"I asked her if she still painted."

"And?"

"And she showed me the paintings! There was a barn full of them, white canvases, White Paintings, one after another of *The Golden Rope,* variation after variation, Doris, you should have seen them! And she showed me the others, paintings of winged people, people with reptile skin, dead people lying on granite stones in a bluish light, angels, and they were all signed 'Florence Meek.' "

"Dennis, they could be forgeries," I said wearily. "The forgers get better and better. Either that or she's an intelligent madwoman. A lonely woman who'll pretend to be anyone you want her to be."

"I don't think so, Doris. We went for a walk and there was a dead robin on the path and I said, 'Florence, hornets are eating it. Can't you hear them?' And she looked at it and said, 'I wonder what ripped it open?' and she asked me if I'd ever noticed how the predator imitates the habits of its prey. The rat scurries along walls and the cat walks in the shadows of walls."

"So you think you've found your true love? Well, if she's not Lizzie Borden, I suppose there's no harm in it."

"I never thought you could be so cynical. You don't sound like yourself!"

"I am myself! Finally! This is what I'm like! I'm worn out! I don't believe she's alive! Not anymore! No one does! And you! You don't know whether this is a dream or not. Did it happen? Did you see real paintings?"

"I saw real paintings. I brought one home with me."

"And can I see it?"

"I promised her I'd never show it to anyone," he said. His cheeks burned red.

"And can I meet her? Or did you promise her you'd never bring anyone to see her?"

"I did promise."

"Oh, I see. You intend to go back there and live with her?"

"I *hope* to."

"But you'll let me know how you are? You won't just vanish the way my sister did?"

"Oh, no, I'm not the type to vanish."

"I'm not going to let you vanish," I said.

He wasn't the type to suffer from visions. He wasn't the type to mistake dreams for reality. He was Dennis, solid, reliable Dennis, who looked so beautiful when he slept. And after he left, after I lay down on my bed and looked out the window, I wasn't sure he had really been there, I wasn't sure he'd come to say he thought he'd found Florence, who after all didn't look like me. I wasn't sure I hadn't dreamed everything myself, but I was sure I wouldn't look for her again. Oh, sooner or later, I'd cross-examine him. I'd follow him to the house on the hill. I'd go into the barn, but not now. Not for quite some time. When I was old. Very old. I had so much to do. I had Antonio. I had *Dennis's* sanity to worry about. There were so many other people in the world.

ᘒᐤ

A N D I C A M E to the edge of a road, and beyond it was a field, burned and blackened. Someone had burned the field to clear it, and I walked through the ashy field to its far edge, where the field dropped off into nothingness, and below me was a kind of ravine, and I climbed down onto a wide shale shelf and I lay down there and I slept there and I felt the heat of the sun and the cool light of the moon and as time passed I grew lighter and began to dry, and as more time passed I became a husk and turned to seed, all of me became as seeds, and I waited for the wind to pick me up and scatter me back through the fields, and I knew that next year the fields would bloom with me, with hundreds and hundreds of me, and who would say which one I was then, who would say what were my names, and I closed my eyes and thought, I have done well.

A F T E R   D E N N I S   L E F T, I thought I would go to the heath and watch the kite fliers, but when I got there, it was cold and very windy and no one was there. I sat on a bench and the orange tiled roofs of Highgate looked more than ever like the roofs of a toy village. I was sorry the kite fliers were not there. I admired their kites, which floated and sailed on currents of air strong enough to hold them. Invisible, but still the currents were there. I thought about our lives when I had first come here and how they had seemed to be part of a tapestry eaten at by moths, so that all of us seemed separated from one another, as if by patches of uncrossable water. And then it was as if a weaver's benevolent hand had taken up the tapestry and re-woven it and now we were all together on the same shore, Antonio, Eva, Dennis, Jack, and I. It was as if the world that had been so empty had suddenly been peopled, and all were people I wanted to see.

The silver-quilted seas, my shattery face reflected in them, the ponds quivering with tree leaves, my face reflected in their surfaces. Beautiful world, I said, alone and not alone.

I was sorry Dennis was still looking for my sister, but he would have to wear himself out, as I had. I was sorry that Jack would never again live easily in the world, but it was beyond my power to cure that. I was sorry I didn't have another life, to live with Jack. You can grow greedy when you think there are two of you, you can come to think that you're entitled to two lives. I was happy that Antonio would come to New York and that at my age I would suddenly have a son and that son would have a mother, and I found myself smiling. I knew I would always seem like a mosaic to myself. I would always find it hard to believe in the preciousness of what little self I had. I am a twin, after all. Is the golden rope woven of love or is it woven of uniqueness, or are uniqueness and love the two indistin-guishable, compatible strands that make the rope so strong? I don't know.

My husband and I were happy, not as my sister had been happy, but then I didn't expect her sort of happiness. I didn't want it. I wanted a hus-band who would let me love him all his life, and I had found him. I wasn't suited to it, all that blazing up, all that fear. I knew how much I owed to others, how much of me *was* someone else. I didn't object. It seemed natural. I don't think others know how little of themselves they own. But I knew. I had a twin sister.

So many people spent their lives trying to become what we were from the moment of our birth, the soul mates, the doubles, the ones who are never alone, never lonely. It didn't last, not for us, but at least we had it.

I was not as like Florence as I thought, or as unlike her as she thought I was. From the moment we left home, her main business was forgetting her family. She wanted a new life, to be reborn, as if by magic, from pollen and air, as much her own creation as her journals and her paintings. She may have succeeded. I don't know.

I miss her. I miss Peru, sunk in mists in the early mornings, the white houses and churches and spires rising up out of those swirling ghostly clouds, the autumn leaves beginning to burn behind the houses as the mists clear and the sun rises. I miss the winter, when the little town draws everyone with a camera and an easel, the white fields of snow, the purple and lavender and blue shadows of the steeples, the gazebo, the huge elm trees, each branch and twig outlined in its sleeve of snow, or, if the snow has melted and then frozen, the trees standing encased in ice, and when the light hits them, the glass trees sparkle and shine against the pale-blue sky. In autumn, the trees of the hills around the town burn with every conceivable color—reds and oranges, lavenders and pinks, yellows and golds, and the town is the one restful place, the white buildings always freshly painted, white and shining and startling, as the birches will be when the leaves fall from the trees. Even in the rain the town is beautiful.

I miss the stories my mother used to tell. When we were small, she made up a story about the people who lived on either side of the West River where Vermont and New Hampshire come together in their southern corners. She told us that winters separated families on either side of the river, and when the first snow fell, they would come down to the shore and wave to those on the other side, and in time this became a tradition, and many people came and waved after the first snow fell, and gradually people came from miles around to watch. Of course it wasn't true.

It wasn't untrue, either. My mother understood that each person had to make up his own world out of the bits and pieces he was given. She had fewer bits and pieces and so she made up more. I was the one who made do with what was given—at least until recently, when I discovered you could take what you wanted, if you wanted it enough. It's about time I learned that lesson.

I miss everything and everyone.

But I have stopped looking for her. Sooner or later, you have to decide what it is you most want to find. I am no longer trying to find her. I want to keep what I have. I have grabbed onto the golden rope, and I find that it will hold me.

It seems to me as if I am beginning again, or beginning—for the first time.

I think often of two women dressed in black, kneeling down on the splintering ice, swept over the falls, their arms around one another. When I sit still and look out a window and see only blankness, they are what I see.

And It Was
Very Early
in the Morning

CHAPTER

THIRTY-NINE

A ND IT WAS very early in the morning when I began to walk, and I saw her far ahead of me. These days, I see her frequently, and always she is walking. She is walking along a narrow path, a dirt road through gray and stony mountains, and every so often, like a child, she kicks at a stone, and when the road grows dusty, she kicks clouds of dust into the air. When I began to see her, the dust swirled beige, but now it is red. It settles on her clothes and reddens them, and on her skin, the reddish color of clay.

At times she vanishes, and then, in her place, I see colors, and sooner or later some of the colors form into shapes. There is a blue archway, recessed into a green wall, an alcove meant to hold a statue of a saint, but the saint is gone. There are two orange rectangles set in an indigo-blue wall, and, in a rotting green gate, a tiled painting of angels. There is a deep-green wall covered with framed photographs. There are marble columns the color of toadskin, patterned green and black. There are striped awnings, yellow and red, so bright they hurt the eye. There are striped hammocks, blue and orange, hanging from clotheslines in front of deep purple houses. There is a child whose apron is shockingly white. She is running quickly past a violet wall. Some nights, the child reappears at a scarlet window set in a peach-colored wall, and this is a good sign. She is in the attic, at a round window like a porthole, just beneath the gray roof of the house, and above her there are pigeons, and occasionally they fly up in a storm of feathers, and then the child leans out to look at them. The sun is always shining, and it is very hot. This landscape has grown familiar. Places are always very familiar as you are about to leave them.

There is always a house at the edge of each village, deserted, empty, except for the birds who nest in the rafters, waiting for me. I hesitate before the houses I choose, entering in.

Yesterday everything changed. I was walking along the road, and when I grew tired I looked for a large tree and lay down beneath it. In the dream, the sun was still shining, so I shaded my eyes with my hand. My hand grew translucent and seemed to shimmer, and I saw my hand had become glassy and in fact was a mirror.

I closed my eyes. I would not look in it.

And then I heard her voice, whispering in the trees, and I still would not open my eyes. I thought, I will not let her in. And I remembered what people used to say of us, that we were one spirit that for some reason lived in two bodies, and how we hated to hear that, as if we had less than others, as if inside we were empty, as a house is when the children grow up and there are more rooms empty than full. And I understood how empty I felt, and that I had always been empty, and I understood also how I had resisted her, how carefully I had chosen my weapons. I understood what I had done.

And I thought, I will let her in, what harm can come to me after all this time? And I opened my eyes slowly, and there was her face, reflected in my palm. And she said, Is there room? And I said, I'll move over. She said, But the wall is cold. And I said I always liked the feel of cool plaster against my skin; the wood stove kept the house so hot and our flannel nightgowns were so thick and heavy.

I moved over and she slid in beside me.

She said, Oh, this is better.

I went to the window and looked out and the drifts were high and heavy on the ground and their shadows were ice blue and there was pale bluish-gray smoke rising from both the chimneys, and across the fields, Darlington's Funeral Home had gone dark and its outline was only a vague hull, like a gray ship on a white sea, and I knew that everyone was in the house, and the house was full.

I should have taken you in, I said.

Oh, well.

I'll take in the boy. If he's yours, he's mine; whatever he says, it's absolutely true.

Oh, well.

At least I have a place to stay, she said.

You don't mind? she asked. The crowding?

I smiled and didn't answer.

And then I was out in the snowy field, looking back at the house, and in every window of every room a light shone, the light spilled golden onto the blue drifts of snow. And there was a kind of music that rose from the house, a sort of humming, like bees. Finally, we were like everyone else. And I said, Things are just as they should be, and I was happy, I had never been so happy. And she stirred in her sleep, as if to answer me, but she slept too deeply. And still I knew I could wake her— if it was important. But she slept so soundly and so wonderfully. I knew, if I turned on my side, I could take her hand and she would ferry me down deep into sleep.

It was hard to wake up from that dream. I had to struggle, I had to swim past our old house, past the house in Goult, up through the blues and the burnt oranges and the lime-colored walls, through the crimsons and the reds, the coughing, the earth in the lungs and the small stones, up to the circle of light on the surface of the water, but when my head broke through into the air, I heard myself gasp, drawing the air into my lungs, and I heard her gasp also. I waited until I heard her gasp—I waited until she took the air in—before I opened my eyes. And someone was saying, Explain this, and I thought, No, I'll never have to explain anything else again, not as long as I live.

AUTHOR'S NOTE: The account of the couple swept over the falls is based on the description of that event given by Ernest Jones in his article "On Dying Together."

A NOTE ABOUT THE AUTHOR

Susan Fromberg Schaeffer was born in Brooklyn and educated at the University of Chicago, where she received her Ph.D. in 1966. In addition to *The Golden Rope,* she is the author of nine other novels, among them *Anya, The Madness of a Seduced Woman,* and *Buffalo Afternoon,* and five volumes of poetry, one of which, *Granite Lady,* was nominated for a National Book Award. She lives in New York.

A NOTE ON THE TYPE

The text of this book was set in Monotype Columbus, a contemporary face designed specifically for digital typesetting by Patricia Saunders. Named for Christopher Columbus and released on the quincentenary of his 1492 voyage from Spain to the Americas, Monotype Columbus has a distinctly Spanish flavor to its letter forms. Saunders did, in fact, draw inspiration from fonts created by Jorge Coci in sixteenth-century Spain, as well as from italic fonts by the brilliant typographer Robert Granjon, to create this lively and highly readable new face.

Composed by ComCom,
Allentown, Pennsylvania
Printed and bound by the Haddon Craftsmen,
an R. R. Donnelley & Sons Company,
Scranton, Pennsylvania
Designed by Cassandra J. Pappas